The Fraud of Moldova Square

Jill Wells-Wane

In loving memory of Bobert,

whose love, faith, and inspiration made this possible.

Our journey may have ended, but our love will go on forever.

Chapter One

I don't know how I got here. It's not something that I wanted, planned, or even sought. Yet here I am, living in the home of Lady Mary McKenzie, formerly the Dowager Countess of Orkney, on Moldova Square in the affluent area of Mayfair in London. It's one of the city's most expensive and sought-after areas, just across from Rotten Row, where the best of London's aristocracy goes to see and be seen, among other areas of the great city. Unlike me, my life is now a mixture of lies, deception, visits to the modiste and balls.

How did I get here? Now, that is the big question. I was born in 1830 to Martin and Sophia Beddoes and brought up in Cornwall, not far from Newquay, in the small fishing village of Porth on the north-west coast of the county. There, the sun would shine bright one minute and the sea would be as calm as a mill pool, then within a short space of time, clouds would gather like dark avenging angels across the land, the sea would broil and the wind would blow with such a force that the trees would have no choice but to bow down in homage to the might of nature. If you don't believe me, let the trees bear witness. Even when the wind isn't blowing, the trees look like they have had all their leaves and branches blown off from one side and bent over one way. When the wind blew, and the trees bent, it would whip up the waves so they would crash against the rocks, flinging great plumes of sea and foam into the air, only to slap back down on the rocks again. I used to love watching the sea on days like this, but usually, it was too windy and cold. The wind, in all its might, would blow people nearly off their feet as they would scurry about, trying to get out of the storm as fast as they could, so I used to sit on my bedroom windowsill with a massive log fire burning in the grate and look out.

On days when the weather was good, and the sea used to creep onto the beach like hundreds and thousands of tiny opaque crabs pitter-pattering onto the sand, I would find myself a rock to perch on and sit and watch for hours. I would be mesmerised by the waves to-ing and fro-ing on the beach. I would lose myself completely, letting thoughts trip into my mind and just as quickly trip out again. Only when I heard Mrs Watson's voice calling my name would I rouse myself and walk back home.

My home was called The Lodge. It was situated in Porth Bay, overlooking Porth Beach. It had six bedrooms, all on the first floor. Because my grandfather, Doctor Edgar Trelawney, was the local doctor, some bedrooms were used as rooms for patients who were too ill to go home. On either side of the front door were large bay windows overlooking the beach. These bay windows were taken up to the first floor as well. My father slept in one of the upstairs bedrooms at the front of the house, with the bay window, and my bedroom was on the opposite side. My bay window had a window seat, which, on wet days, I could sit on and still enjoy the sea view. At night I would fall fast asleep with the sound of the whoosh and shush of the sea in my ears. I loved my bedroom with its view over the beach, but it also had a large, comfortable bed and a massive fireplace that, on cold days, held a roaring fire to keep me toasty warm.

Gramps (my grandfather, as I called him) had another bedroom at the back of the house, next to the large room with six single beds, which he called the 'hospital room'. He also had another room off this, which he used for his surgery and where he occasionally conducted operations which contained a large wooden table to operate on, and Mrs Watson would assist him. Because the hospital room and his surgery were on the upper floor, Mrs Watson's son-in-law, Jethro, with his massive frame and arms like tree trunks, would help Gramps carry his patients up the wide staircase so that Gramps could treat them or operate on them and Jethro would again carry them into the hospital room. Gramps's bedroom was next to this so that he could check on any patients in the hospital room during the night. Mrs Watson, who was the housekeeper, Gramps's assistant, and also my nanny, had one of the bedrooms at the back of the house.

Downstairs was our lounge, with one of the bay windows overlooking the beach. Mrs Watson used to tell me that the lounge was one of my mother's favourite rooms. She would sit in one of the armchairs, looking out of the window over the beach, watching the sea in all its guises; that was when she wasn't helping Gramps on his rounds. It was my mother who decided on the décor of the room. It was filled with paintings of seascapes, and she would keep seashells that she had found on the beach on the mantle shelf over the fireplace. She had been collecting them since she was a child.

The room with the other large bay window was on the opposite side of the big entrance hall. Dominating this room was another large fireplace, and there was always a roaring fire for nine months of the year. Gramps had this room as his 'waiting room' for his patients, which was rarely empty. Leading from this room was Gramps's office, where he kept his patient's records and drugs locked up in a cabinet. The ground floor also had a dining room, and next to that was the kitchen, which was Mrs Watson's domain.

Mrs Watson was short and dumpy, all bustle and efficiency, a no-nonsense sort of person, who, when the need arose, could be gentle and caring one minute, or if someone offended her or 'hers', she would turn in a blink and rail at them as if she was a woman twice her size. I have even seen her chase someone down the main street, brandishing a rolling pin! Woe and betide anyone on the receiving end of Mrs Watson's temper. She had been married at one time but lost her husband, who was a fisherman, many years before to the cruelty of the sea. Occasionally, Mrs Watson's daughter, Elsie, would help her with things like spring cleaning, or if the hospital room were busy, she would also help there, if only cleaning and emptying chamber pots. I used to help Mrs Watson as often as possible, but my Gramps and my father insisted on me learning reading, writing, arithmetic, geography, history, Latin and French. It was no hardship for me to learn. My father and Gramps would say I was greedy and would soak up knowledge like a sponge.

My father, Martin Beddoes, was the manager of the Trevelgue tin mines. He was tall and slim, and I have seen one or two local women set their caps at him, but he always said there would never be another woman for him after my mother died.

The Trevelgue family owned six mines all over Cornwall, so my father was kept very busy overseeing all six and ensuring their smooth running.

Where in all this narrative is my mother, Sophia? Unfortunately, I killed my mother on the day I was born. Of course, I didn't mean to, but I gave her such a hard time giving birth to me. She laboured long and hard, with my father and Mrs Watson at her side, holding her hands, while Gramps was at the 'business end,' as he called it. Gramps did everything that he could to save his daughter, his only child, but in the end, he had shaken his head, tears in his eyes, and wiped his bloodied hands on a towel. Everyone was devastated, not just my family and Mrs Watson, but the whole of the district. My mother used to help her father, acting as his receptionist and nurse, so obviously, the people of the village and surrounding districts knew her, as she had often travelled with Gramps. According to my father, Gramps and Mrs Watson, my mother was beautiful, with long, thick, curly, mahogany-coloured hair that reached down well past her waist and brilliant emerald-green eyes, which were fanned by thick dark lashes. She was also slightly built, only just reaching my father's shoulder. She had dainty hands and feet. She took after her mother, and I took after my mother, but of course, I only had their word for it, as our family was devoid of females, apart from me, and there were no pictures of my mother.

With Mama gone and a new baby in the family, Gramps had to look for someone to feed me. He managed to get a wet nurse from the village, whose baby had died at birth, poor thing. Maisy Jago suckled me from her ample breasts until I was six months old, and even when she began to wean me from her breast, she still came and looked after me until I was three, potty trained and shuffling around, getting into all sorts of trouble, mainly in Mrs Watson's kitchen. Unfortunately, Maisy caught diphtheria and died. This left Mrs Watson, my father and Gramps to look after me. That year, many people died of diphtheria. Gramps couldn't work miracles as hard as he worked to save them. Luckily, neither my father, Mrs Watson, Gramps, or I caught it, so we had to witness the devastation of the people of the villages and the effect it had on the remaining members of their families.

Mrs Watson would teach me cooking and ironing, among other household chores, as well as sewing and embroidery. Mrs Watson was a dab hand with a needle and thread, as she made all my clothes, and she had a ready smile that she would turn on whenever I fell and hurt myself, kissing it better with her 'magical medicine' as she called it. She didn't suffer fools gladly, and when needed, she could use her tongue like a whip and give a verbal lashing to those she thought deserved it. She also used to help Gramps with patients who came to the house and waited in the downstairs room, which we used as a Waiting Room. People from the surrounding districts would go and sit in the waiting room if they were able to get there; if not, Gramps would saddle up old Miser, his horse of many years, fling his medical bag over his saddle and trot off. For all his running around tending the sick and needy, Gramps was of a portly build, bald, apart from a grey pelmet of fine hair growing around his shiny pate. He had twinkling brown eyes with deep laughter lines that creased together when he smiled. I very rarely saw him frown; that only happened once, as far as anyone knew, and that was the day I was born and my mother died. I never saw him lose his temper, although Mrs Watson used to say I would try a saint's patience. As I got older, I improved and became quite helpful around the Lodge, learning to cook, iron and sew as little as I was.

My father, Martin Beddoes, was a good-looking man, tall with dark blonde hair and blue eyes and fine chiselled features, high cheekbones and a slight cleft in his chin. He had broad shoulders, a trim waist, and long muscular legs. When he returned from the mines at night, often exhausted, he would sit and eat dinner, which Mrs Watson and I would prepare for us all. Mrs Watson would somehow keep his meal warm so that, more-or-less, his dinner would be waiting for him as soon as he got home. After he had eaten, no matter how tired he was, he would have me climb on his lap and read stories to me, or when I was older, I would read to him; after that, he would kiss me, saying, "Goodnight, my little love," and I would go to bed and sleep. I never had trouble sleeping, and I suppose that was because I was happy and contented. I lived in a lovely home, I had plenty of food, and I was warm on cold days and cool on warm days. I had three people who loved me and plenty of friends around my age in the village that I could play with whenever I wanted. These friends were never dressed as well as me as they were sons and daughters of fishermen or miners, but this never bothered us as we ran and played around the village or ran barefoot on the beach.

My father was a clever man who had attended university to study engineering. He spent some time in France, so he learned French and, in turn, taught it to me. Because he was a doctor, Gramps had learned Latin, which he also taught me. Between them, I had quite a rounded education at home and enjoyed learning.

I had a good childhood filled with love and happiness, even though I had no mother. When I was old enough, I was allowed to walk into the village on my own and play with the children there (I didn't need any brothers and sisters when I had all the playmates I needed with the village children), or I would go and sit on the wall overlooking the beach and watch the sea. Most of the people in the village, luckily, had jobs. Many were employed at the mines at the behest of the Trevelgue family; the rest were fishermen, who would take their boats from where they rested, bottom up, on the beach, and the men would go out to sea to catch fish they would sell in the village.

The village consisted of rows of single-storeyed, two-roomed cottages leading down to the beach. Within a few miles, we had a blacksmith, and weekly, one of the farmers from outside the village would come down and sell his wares of rabbit, chicken, and occasionally beef, pork, or lamb products, which he would slaughter at the farm, prepare them and sell them at the village. They always had eggs and milk to sell, so, with all this, the village never starved. We never saw a case of rickets in the village, which Gramps said was caused by the lack of calcium in the diet and would cripple people. These pearls of knowledge I drank in greedily and constantly asked Gramps questions on medicine.

There was always food available if you could afford it. If the mines closed, then there would be problems. Many villagers relied on the bounty from the Trevelgues and their mines. Those who were fishermen depended on the weather, and many died in the rough seas and strong undercurrents Cornwall was known for.

When I was ten, disaster struck me again. One of the mines that my father was inspecting collapsed, killing him and three others. They said that it could have been a lot worse, as many more could have been killed, but with his death, I was made an orphan. I was still luckier than some but not as fortunate as others. At least I still had Gramps and Mrs Watson. Once more, I went to my special place on the beach and just sat watching the sea ebbing and flowing, much as my thoughts were doing, entering my mind for me to try and make sense of them, and when I couldn't, I would let them flow away again. The weather had been bad for three days before the mining accident. It was discovered that it was due to the weather that water from the heavy rains had seeped into the workings, causing the roof and the walls to collapse. Now the weather was apologising for killing my father, by the sun shining down from a beautiful cornflower blue sky. I didn't know Gramps had been called to the 'Big House' in Newquay before receiving notice about the mine disaster.

The Big House was perched on the headland and looking to the sea, as the locals called it. Guess what the 'Big House' was called? Very unimaginatively, 'Seaward Manor'. It was owned by the Trevelgue family, well, part of the Trevelgue family, as Mr Trevelgue, the father, had died, as my father had, only several years before. The Trevelgue family consisted of Mrs Trevelgue, Mark, the oldest son, Richard, the younger son, and then came the daughter Edwina, who was just a few months older than me. From the headland bordering Porth Cove, you could look across the beautiful golden sandy beaches when the tide was out and see Seaward Manor perched on the far headland to the left of Porth Bay. From where I sat, Seaward Manor looked magical when the sun shone on the windows, turning them all to diamonds glittering in the sunlight. It looked like something from a fairy tale—a castle. I always imagined Sleeping Beauty asleep there, waiting for Prince Charming to kiss and wake her from her slumbers. But I was wrong. I soon discovered that Sleeping Beauty could not have described Miss Edwina Trevelgue. I always thought that when Sleeping Beauty had been awakened from her long sleep, she would be happy, smiling and kind to all, but none of that could ever be used to relate to Miss Edwina Trevelgue.

Although Master Mark Trevelgue, the older son, was now classed as the owner of the mine, according to Gramps, little was seen of the heir to the family fortune. Master Richard Trevelgue was in Oxford at university, hoping to do well, then return to Seaward Manor to manage the mines in place of my father. Still, Master Richard was recently sent down from Oxford, caught in an embarrassing situation. Nobody knew what it was, but plenty of speculation and guesswork existed.

On the day my father died, Gramps was up at the big house patching up Richard Trevelgue, who had fallen from his horse, recklessly jumping over a wall. The horse had to be shot, and Master Richard had a dislocated shoulder. When the message came to the big house about the mine collapsing, Gramps rapidly strapped Richard up after pulling his arm back in line and got on his horse, riding hell for leather to the mine. Of the twenty miners that had initially gone down there, sixteen had made it out and were back down again, pulling the bodies out and laying them on the ground for Gramps to work on. My father was among the bodies pulled from the mine.

After the funerals of the dead miners and my father, Gramps came to me and said that Mrs Trevelgue had asked if I would like to go to visit them at Seaward Manor and play with the daughter of the house, Miss Edwina. This was indeed a treat, and I was longing to meet who I imagined was Sleeping Beauty, so dressed in my best frock, given a reminder of the good manners taught me by Mrs Watson, my father and Gramps, Gramps attached old Miser to the cart, helped me up to sit beside him and off we trotted to visit the Trevelgues at Seaward Manor.

I was both nervous and excited to go there and see, close-up, the 'fairy tale castle' of my visions. On the journey there, Gramps kept up constant chatter, telling me about the family. As we got close to Seaward Manor, I sat in stunned silence, gawping at the sight before me. A large, broad driveway led up to the house. Carefully clipped and manicured lawns surrounded it, and various colourful flowers bordered on either side of the driveway. A handful of gardeners were milling around, keeping the lawn and borders pristine. Seaward Manor, the house, stood four stories high with masses of tall chimneys and towers overlooking the cliffs, rocks, land, and, of course, the beach. Gramps pulled the little cart up to the front door on the landward side of the headland. He helped me down and held my hand as we walked up to the massive, heavy wooden front door. Gramps lifted the huge brass knocker and banged twice.

Almost immediately, the great door was opened by a butler, Mr Masters, so Gramps told me later. Mr Masters wore grey striped trousers, a grey waistcoat and a black frock coat. Underneath, he wore a brilliantly white shirt and dark grey cravat. He was tall and skinny and had an arrogant demeanour, looking down his beak of a nose as he stepped aside, allowing us to enter. Before I could look about myself in the magnificent hallway, Mr Masters said we were expected and took us to meet Mrs Trevelgue in the 'orangery'. I'd never seen an 'orangery' before. Gramps gave my hand a comforting squeeze as we followed behind Mr Masters.

The 'orangery' looked more like a massive greenhouse, which I had seen pictures of in books.; all glass and metal but filled with beautiful flowers giving off a heady perfume. Mrs Trevelgue was sitting very regally in a rattan chair with a rattan table in front of her on which was a beautiful fine bone-china tea service, with matching teapot, milk jug, sugar bowl, and four cups and saucers as well as a plate of biscuits.

Mrs Trevelgue must have been very beautiful in her youth with honey blonde hair and blue eyes, but of late, the biscuits must have taken their toll on her figure as what once might have been trim had turned slightly to fat. She was not grossly fat but a little overweight. Next to Mrs Trevelgue sat the prettiest girl I had ever seen. Like her mother, she had beautiful blonde hair and stunning blue eyes. Her hair had been styled into masses of ringlets and finished off with a big blue hair ribbon to match her blue dress and eyes. I presumed this was Miss Edwina Trevelgue, who looked every inch of the young Sleeping Beauty I had imagined. Like her mother, Edwina was not slim. I smiled at her as I was asked to sit down, and she stuck her pretty little tongue out at me! She was placed so her mother could not see what she had done, and neither had Gramps. I was so surprised. She was not at all as I had expected. All the children from the village were kind and friendly towards me, like many brothers and sisters. The main things that struck me were the beautiful gowns the mother and daughter wore made of such beautiful material. I had never seen any materials so beautiful in my life. From that moment on, I wished that I would be able to wear such lovely gowns.

"So, you are Julia, Doctor Trelawney's granddaughter? I am sorry about your father, my dear. He was a good man." She smiled at me. "Would you like a glass of milk, Julia?" Her voice seemed to tinkle like a little bell. She spoke very precisely.

"Yes, please," I replied, being on my best behaviour and manners.

Mrs Trevelgue took a little glass bell from the table and rang it. Immediately, a maid appeared, dressed in a black dress with a starched white collar and cuffs, a brilliant white apron and a starched white cap perched on her head. Mrs Trevelgue didn't even look at the maid but gave her instructions to the air above the maid's head. "Bring Miss Edwina and Miss Julia a glass of milk each." I noticed no 'please' or 'thank you' as I had been taught good manners, but I presumed this was how the rich treated their servants.

The maid bobbed a curtsey and swiftly left, returning shortly with a silver tray carrying two tall glasses with ice-cold milk. She handed one to Edwina and one to me. I thanked the maid, but Edwina snatched the glass from her and didn't even thank her. Then Mrs Trevelgue handed Gramps a cup of tea after asking him if he took milk and sugar. Gramps replied, giving his preference. She then offered the plate of biscuits around. I took one and thanked her, and then she handed the plate to Edwina, who took three and began gobbling them down. So, this was my imaginary Sleeping Beauty I had thought about for many years? It was such a disappointment. After Edwina and I had finished, Mrs Trevelgue told Edwina to take me and show me her room and toys.

Edwina approached me, pinched my arm slyly, and said, "Come on then." I looked to Gramps, who nodded his approval.

I followed Edwina as she skipped out before me. We went back the way Gramps and I had come. I stood in the large hallway with a floor of black and white tiles, like the tiles on a chessboard. Scattered here and there were beautifully coloured rugs of oriental design. The bottom of the walls was covered in a dark-coloured wood to match the stairs and bannister. The wood, I later discovered, was mahogany, but at the time, it was just dark wood to me. At the bottom of the stairs, on either side of the first step, were two tall, imposing suits of armour, complete with helmet, visor, and sword. They looked scary to me, as if someone was inside watching us. The stairs swept around elegantly, leading to a landing on the first floor covered in several oriental carpets. The carpets were so thick that I felt my feet sink into them. On the walls, going up the stairs, hung large gilt-framed paintings of men and women. Edwina looked at me. "Oh, they are all dead," she said dismissively. "Come on. Stop dawdling, girl."

I think it was dislike at first sight, especially for me. For Edwina, it was 'hate' at first sight. She acted like a spoilt brat right from the very start. Oh, she showed me her bedroom, fit for a princess, with a beautiful four-poster bed with pink curtains, and, as she told me, I was the orphan from the village, and she was the princess. Of course, I knew she wasn't a princess, but I already knew better than to contradict her. She had already pinched me once. I wasn't going to tempt another.

"Your father worked for us. He was just a lackey," she sneered at me. Had she no heart to talk about my recently deceased father this way? What I had thought was a pretty face turned out to be ugly, the way she sneered and cajoled me.

I kept quiet and let her prattle on about her being the Princess of the Big House. When I didn't rise to the bait, she got bored and told me to go away and leave her alone. I would have done so, but I didn't know how to return to Gramps in the massive house. When I told her I didn't know the way back, she stuck her tongue out and said she didn't care if I got lost. She pushed me from her room and into the hallway again, then slammed the door behind me, and I heard her turn the key in her door to lock me out.

I knew we had turned right down the hallway to her bedroom, so that was how I went. I saw a maid coming from one of the rooms and asked her how to return to the 'orangery'.

The maid smiled kindly at me, "Have you been with Miss Edwina?" she asked me, smiling knowingly.

I nodded; she tutted and then smiled at me again. "Bless you. She is up to her old tricks again, is she?" not expecting me to reply.

I didn't say anything, but the maid kindly took me by the hand and led me to the top of the staircase, then down the stairs and to the door to the orangery. "There you are, Miss, just through that door," she said, smiling at me.

I thanked her and returned to Gramps, sitting quietly by his side until Mrs Trevelgue spoke to me.

"Did Edwina show you her room, Julia?"

I nodded, "Yes, Ma'am."

"Well, your grandfather and I have been talking, and I thought it might benefit you and Edwina to have lessons together. I have hired a governess, Miss Frazer, to teach Edwina, and as I said to your grandfather, I thought you might benefit from the governess as well."

Gramps looked at me, "It is a very kind gesture on Mrs Trevelgue's part, and I am sure you would benefit from having a governess. Your father and I have taught you as much as we can, as has Mrs Watson, but I feel this would benefit you, so I have accepted on your behalf."

"Thank you, Ma'am. I would like that very much."

The thought of a proper education made me realise I would put up with any amount of pinching and nastiness from Miss Edwina Trevelgue. Her pretty looks had deceived me initially, but it didn't take long to realise how deceptive looks could be. She had the face of an angel and the heart of a demon, but I was willing to risk all of that for an education, the education of a young lady. Miss Frazer was arriving at the weekend, and lessons would start Monday after she had settled in. Gramps was to bring me to the big house at eight-thirty on the Monday morning. Mrs Trevelgue would supply me with whatever I needed once I was there and would provide me with lunch with Edwina in the nursery where Miss Frazer would give us our lessons.

When Gramps and I arrived back at the Lodge, he took old Miser back to the stables, and I went straight to the kitchen where I knew Mrs Watson would be baking cakes and biscuits and preparing our evening meal. I sat on one of the hard-backed chairs and waited for her to ask me how the visit went. When she pulled the last cakes from the range and wiped her hands on her pinny, she sat opposite me.

"Well, how did your visit go?"

"Edwina pinched me and called my father a 'lackey,'" I told her honestly.

"Oh dear!" came her reply.

"What is a 'lackey' Mrs Watson?" I asked her.

Gramps then walked through the kitchen door and answered, "It is someone who serves, but it is not a nice name to call someone. Why?"

"Edwina called my father a lackey."

Gramps's face never changed as he said, "Your father might have worked for the Trevelgues, but he was probably better educated than most of them, and he was certainly no lackey." He sat at the kitchen table and sipped his tea, which Mrs Watson had placed before him. "So, how did you get on with Edwina? I gather it didn't go well with your early arrival back to the orangery?"

"She stuck her tongue out to me when we first got to the orangery, then pinched me and pushed me from her room and locked me out," I told him.

"Oh dear, not a very good start then?" he said sympathetically.

"But I am going to have a governess teach me, and I am so looking forward to that," I excitedly told him and Mrs Watson.

"You will just have to make sure you don't stand too close to Miss Edwina, the little madam!" exclaimed Mrs Watson.

"After all we have taught you, you will probably be head and shoulders above Miss Edwina Trevelgue in education," my Gramps added. "With a governess, you will be trained to be a young lady, not that you are not one already, and by the sounds of it, probably better mannered than Miss Edwina. Take it all in, Julia. Education is never wasted. It will stand you in good stead for when you are older," he continued.

Chapter Two

Early on the Monday morning, I rose early, excited about the day to come, but that excitement was marred with some trepidation at meeting Edwina Trevelgue again. I dressed and took special care with my hair. I ate my breakfast with Gramps and Mrs Watson, then Gramps hooked old Miser to the cart, and we were off. The weather was beautiful outside. As I looked at the sea, I saw the sun twinkling, turning it into sparkling diamonds. It boded well for my first day, or so I thought, but there was no telling what Edwina had in store for me.

Gramps stopped the cart outside the front door of Seaward Manor, got down and helped me down. Standing together outside the massive door, Gramps lifted the large brass door knocker, which was too high for me to reach at that time. After he knocked on the door, Gramps bent down, kissed me goodbye, and asked if I would be all right. I nodded yes. Shortly after, when Masters, the butler, came to open the front door, Gramps got back into the cart, waved to me, flicked the reins, and old Miser trotted back down the driveway.

"Welcome, Miss Julia; I have been instructed to take you straight upstairs to the nursery. Miss Frazer is already waiting for you."

We went up the long sweep of the staircase to the third floor, along a corridor and turned left into the nursery. Miss Frazer was standing by a large blackboard, writing something on it with chalk. Miss Frazer was tall and wiry, with brown hair scraped back into a bun. Her kindly brown eyes slanted upwards, but I thought it might be because she had pulled her hair back so tightly.

When I entered the room, she turned and looked at me through brown-rimmed spectacles. "Ah, you must be Miss Edwina?" she said, smiling welcomingly at me. Her voice had a clipped Scottish accent that I found rather comforting. I didn't know why, but she had a ready smile for me.

I did a little curtsey to her, "Er... no, Miss. I am Julia."

I looked around the nursery, but there was no sign of Miss Edwina Trevelgue, who Miss Frazer had originally been employed to teach.

"Take a seat, dear. We are still waiting on Miss Edwina," Miss Frazer said, then continued to write on the blackboard. I sat at one of the desks she indicated in front of the blackboard.

"Well," she chirped once she had finished writing on the blackboard, "While we are waiting, Julia, why don't you tell me what you have been learning."

I told her about Gramps and my father teaching me maths, how to read and write, and how they had taught me French and Latin.

"That is very good, Julia. Well, we will do some little tests today so that I can find out what levels you and Edwina are at in different subjects."

Miss Frazer stood round while I sat, both of us waiting for Edwina to arrive. The large grandfather clock downstairs struck nine, then ten, then eleven o'clock before Edwina skipped into the nursery, as Mrs Watson would say, 'looking like butter wouldn't melt in her mouth'. She wore another beautiful dress, which I am sure the price that had been paid for the material alone would have fed a family in the village for a week, maybe even a month. It certainly made my dress look dull in comparison.

"Good morning, Miss Frazer, Julia. I hope I didn't miss anything," she said, sitting at the desk beside me.

Miss Frazer didn't look pleased. "Edwina, I explained to your mother that lessons started promptly at half past eight. It is nearly lunchtime. Tomorrow, I expect you here on time."

"I can't possibly be here at that time!" Edwina declared in horror at the thought. "I don't wake until ten, and then I have breakfast. Then my maid comes in, puts my hair in ringlets, and helps me dress. No, I can't possibly get here any earlier."

Miss Frazer took a deep breath, "Then you must wake up earlier because I will start the lessons at half past eight, with or without you, and you must stay behind to make up the time you have lost. Am I understood, Miss Edwina?"

"Yes, Miss Frazer." Edwina cocked her head to one side and gave Miss Frazer a dazzling smile.

"Right," said Miss Frazer, thinking she had succeeded in getting through to Edwina. "No more shilly shallying, ladies. Let us get down to work. I need to see what level of education you have reached so that I can tailor your lessons accordingly."

While we were waiting for Edwina, Miss Frazer had been writing maths questions on the blackboard. "You may start, young ladies. You have thirty minutes," she said, consulting the fob watch she had attached to her blouse.

I looked across to Edwina, who was doodling on her slate. I shrugged and settled down to answer the maths questions. I won't say that I found them easy, but I completed them all in the required time. I put down my slate and folded my arms, resting them on the desk to indicate that I had finished.

Miss Frazer smiled at me. "Have you finished Julia?"

I nodded.

She told me to bring my slate out to her, and then I could go and take a walk out in the gardens and enjoy the sunshine. I thanked her and left the room, but not before Edwina pulled a face at me and stuck her tongue out. I was just thankful that I was not closer to her so that she could pinch me.

I found my way back to the main staircase and started to descend when I saw Mrs Trevelgue coming out of one of the rooms on the first floor.

"Julia, my dear, have you finished your lessons already?"

"I had finished the work Miss Frazer had set me, so she said I could go outside and walk in the gardens."

Mrs Trevelgue raised her carefully pencilled eyebrows, "And Edwina?"

How could I tell her that, judging by the stubborn look on her daughter's face, she had no intention of doing the schoolwork? "Edwina hadn't quite finished, Ma'am," I told her, lying as best I could.

"Oh, I see. I was just about to have a light lunch in the orangery. Would you care to join me, or would you rather go out in the sunshine?"

I told her that I would like to revisit the orangery again. She smiled at me, "Well, I shall have the doors to the outside open so you can get some fresh air." She walked over to the high glass doors and opened them, which surprised me as I thought she might ring to get a footman to do it for her, then came back, sat in the rattan chair and rang the little crystal bell. Almost immediately, a maid appeared and gave a little bob, "Yes, Ma'am?"

"A plate of sandwiches, a pot of tea and a glass of milk for Miss Julia. Miss Edwina will be joining us later." Mrs Trevelgue said, again speaking to the air above the maid's head.

The maid did another curtsey and hurried off to do her mistress's bidding. I sat in the chair with my back straight and ankles crossed, patiently waiting for our sandwiches to arrive. The food arrived, and I was given my glass of milk, which I placed on another little side table next to me. I took my plate, which Mrs Trevelgue handed me before offering the plate of daintily cut sandwiches. I helped myself to two, picked up a serviette and placed it, opened it onto my lap, and began to nibble at one of my sandwiches.

As we ate, Mrs Trevelgue asked how I liked Miss Frazer. I told her that I thought she was lovely. "And what was your first lesson, Julia?" she asked me.

"Miss Frazer wanted to know how far we had got with our education and put a test on the blackboard of some sums she wanted us to answer," I explained.

"And you completed the test?"

I nodded as I had a mouth full of sandwiches.

"Who taught you, Julia?"

I gulped down what food was in my mouth and answered her question: "My father when he was alive, then Gramps, and Mrs Watson, our housekeeper. She has taught me needlework, cookery, and other household skills."

"It seems that you have had quite a rounded education, Julia. What was your favourite lesson?" Mrs Trevelgue asked me.

I told her that I enjoyed reading.

"Oh, we have a very large library here. Although I am not sure you can read all the books yet, but, you may look. Would you like to look now and see if there is anything?"

I nearly jumped up and ran off to the library, but I didn't know where it was, and I needed Mrs Trevelgue's permission to leave. I finished my milk and used my serviette to wipe my mouth before Mrs Trevelgue rang the little bell again, and Masters, the butler, arrived. I think she must have had different rings for different staff.

"Masters, would you show Miss Julia the library and help her find the section for children, the books that Master Mark and Master Richard used to enjoy reading?" Masters bowed and asked me to follow him.

We returned to the large hall and followed a corridor to the right, past a door on the left and one on the right. The next door on the right, Mr Masters, opened, and we walked into a massive room with shelves full of books lining the walls from floor to ceiling. "I believe the children's section is on this wall, Miss." Mr Masters said as he led me to a wall beside the colossal marble fireplace.

"Which shelf, Mr Masters?" I asked, my eyes unable to take in all the titles printed on the leather spines.

"Oh, all of them, Miss. Masters Mark and Richard loved to read; I can't say the same about Miss Edwina. If you see any titles you can't reach, pull the bell sash by the fire," he indicated, "and I or one of the footmen will help you up."

I looked at the rows of books, running my fingers along the spines as I read the titles. I picked up one book called 'The Swiss Family Robinson.' I showed it to Masters, "Oh, I think you will enjoy that one, Miss Julia," he said, "Would you like to sit in this big armchair and read it?"

I looked at the big and comfy chair. I nodded my head, "Yes, please, Mr. Masters. Do you think I could also take it home with me to read, Mr. Masters?"

He smiled at me, he seemed a lot nicer to me now that I would be visiting the Trevelgue family practically on a daily basis. "I am sure you could, but make sure you return it before you take another one," he warned me.

I told him I would and sat in the large, winged armchair. I started to read until I heard Edwina come storming down the stairs, screaming and crying that Miss Frazer was cruel to her and that I was Miss Frazer's favourite. I didn't know what to do, whether to go out and face Edwina in her tantrum or stay where I was. Ultimately, I decided it was best to stay where I was and continue reading rather than risk Edwina's tantrums. I think I heard Mrs Trevelgue trying to reason quietly with her daughter. I also heard Miss Frazer come down and try to explain herself and her actions to Mrs Trevelgue. I couldn't read with all that was going on, so I sat in the chair, eavesdropping. I heard Edwina tell her mother that she couldn't see why she would need to know maths when she had a house full of servants to do all that sort of thing, so she stormed. Mrs Trevelgue tried to explain to her daughter the benefits of an education, but Edwina seemed to be railing against her, Miss Frazer, education and me! What I had got to do with it, I didn't know, but for the time being, I would try and stay well out of Edwina's way for fear of a pinch again.

I gathered that Mrs Trevelgue had taken Edwina into the 'orangery' for lunch while Miss Frazer searched for me. She found me in the library and asked what book I was reading. When I told her, she said that was also her favourite book. "Perhaps you would like to read aloud to Edwina and me this afternoon. I think that maybe if she hears the start of a good story, it might encourage her to want to start to read," ghe grimaced at me. "We can but hope." She sighed. "I may need your help, Julia, with Miss Edwina. She seems rather reluctant to want to learn anything."

"I can try Miss Frazer, but I don't think she likes me," I told her honestly.

"Oh, what makes you say that dear?" Above the rim of her glasses, Miss Frazer's eyebrows creased together in concern.

"She pinched me and stuck her tongue out at me when we first met."

Miss Frazer shook her head in despair. "Oh dear, it looks like we might have our work cut out for us," she told me.

That afternoon, I did as Miss Frazer suggested and read aloud from the book I had picked from the library. Just as Miss Frazer had predicted, Edwina began to get engrossed in the story. When it came time for me to leave because Gramps had come to collect me, Edwina wanted me to leave the book so she could continue reading the story. Miss Frazer said that I had picked the book from the library to read it.

Edwina stamped her foot like the petulant child she was. "Well, she can choose another book to read. It's my library and my book, and I want this one."

My reading of the book had the desired effect on Edwina, so I supposed it was a small price to pay. I returned to the library and chose another book, 'The Three Musketeers'. Miss Frazer walked past me and mouthed, 'Thank you.'

On the journey back to the Lodge, Gramps asked me about my day, and I told him about it, omitting the parts of Edwina's misbehaviour. I said that I liked Miss Frazer. In time, we would become co-conspirators in Miss Edwina Trevelgue's education.

Every day when I returned to the Lodge, Mrs Watson asked what news about the big house. So, I would relate everything to her, including Edwina's tantrums and Miss Frazer's ways of getting her interested in our lessons.

In the weeks and months that followed, it was obvious, even to me, that I was head and shoulders above Edwina regarding our education, if not in stature. Where I sailed through lessons, Edwina struggled. Then, I would receive Edwina's sly pinches and punches when Miss Frazer's back was turned. Then, Miss Frazer and I would conspire together to get Edwina to learn. Sometimes, we succeeded; sometimes, we failed. The months passed, and the winter weather was closing in. Mrs Trevelgue invited Gramps to talk with her in her drawing room.

"Doctor Trelawney, the weather is getting bad now. The nights are drawing in, and you and Julia would go home in the dark. I know you say dropping Julia off here daily is no trouble, but I have a proposition for you. Julia seems to be settling down here, and between Miss Frazer and Julia, they are encouraging Edwina in her lessons. I would like to have Julia live here with us. She could have the bedroom next to Edwina's with an adjoining door between them. I would feed and clothe her as a form of repayment for her being Edwina's... companion, shall we say. What Julia learns here will help stand her in good stead when she is older. I could give her references to become a lady's companion or even a children's governess and make her way in life. She could earn a good living and even make an acceptable marriage. Isn't that what you would want for your granddaughter, Doctor Trelawney? Isn't that what her father would want for his daughter?" she said, obviously using emotional blackmail on Gramps, but he could see the sense in it, as I could, so it was agreed.

As young as I was, I knew that Mrs Trevelgue was doing it for Edwina and not for me, but to live at Seaward Manor in the lap of luxury was like a dream come true. It might also bring Edwina and me closer together and maybe, in time, become friends. I could but hope!

Mrs Trevelgue knew how to get what she wanted. Gramps agreed, so I left the Lodge in Porth and moved into Seaward Manor in the room next door to Edwina's with the adjoining door.

Mrs Watson's parting words to me were, "Just because you will be living in the big house, don't you go thinking that you are better than any of us. I hope to see you visiting us here regularly."

I kissed her cheek, "As if. You know that isn't me," I said as I picked up my small bag of things.

I didn't expect a big welcome from Edwina, but Miss Frazer and Mrs Trevelgue were glad I had arrived to stay permanently. I think they hoped that I would be able to help keep Edwina in line.

As I was putting my meagre bag of clothes away in the massive wardrobe in my room, Edwina barged into my room through the adjoining door without even the courtesy of knocking and plonked herself down on my bed. "Just because you have moved into the bedroom next to mine, don't go thinking that you are any better than one of the servants. You have been brought here as my lackey. My companion. So don't go getting ideas above your station. You are my slave, and you will do as I say."

She might be a few months older than me and was taller than me, but I certainly wasn't going to have her order me around. I would help Miss Frazer to get Edwina interested in her lessons, as I had done with her reading. But I didn't want Edwina to think that I thought I was better than her because I was better at my lessons. It just meant they were more important to me because I knew I would have to go into the world and earn a living when I was old enough.

"I might be here as your companion, but I am not your slave or your lackey or anything else derogatory you may wish to call me. So don't come barging into my bedroom. I am entitled, like you, to have my privacy." I doubted that Edwina knew what 'derogatory' meant, which angered her even more because she knew I was cleverer than her.

I suppose I did overstep the mark a little, but I certainly wasn't prepared for what happened next. I was delivered such a stinging slap across my face that briefly made me see stars. What had I let myself in for? Edwina called me a cruel name and stormed off back through the adjoining door. I heard the key turn in the lock as she locked the door between us.

For the duration of my stay at Seaward Manor, the door between Edwina's and my bedroom remained locked.

At Christmas, I went back to Porth to spend a few days with Gramps and Mrs Watson and to sleep in my old bedroom, which I had missed when I was staying at 'the big house', and then in the New Year, I would return to Seaward Manor, Miss Frazer and Edwina. Christmas, with all her presents, hadn't mellowed Edwina and continued to be the bane of Miss Frazer's and my life.

Over the coming years, I was used to coerce Edwina into learning. Miss Frazer and I became partners in crime, trying to entice Edwina to learn. Sometimes, Miss Frazer and I succeeded; other times, we failed miserably, but I was still allowed to continue my education. When the good weather was upon us, I would walk the three miles over to Porth and see Gramps and Mrs Watson. Mrs Watson would cluck around me like a mother hen, asking if I was eating enough and always brought out a plate of biscuits or cake and insisted that I eat, then would send me back to the 'big house' with some wrapped up in a cloth and put in my pocket.

Whenever I arrived back at the Lodge in Porth, Mrs Watson always looked at me and said, "Well, what news from the 'big house'?" and we would sit down and have a 'chin wag', as she called it, going over all that had occurred since we had last met. Sometimes Gramps was around and he would join in the conversation; other times, he was away dealing with the sick in the district, and it was just Mrs Watson and myself. She seemed to enjoy our 'chin wags', which she would relay to her daughter Elsie the next time they met, and then it would be around the rest of the village in next to no time. Because Porth was a small village, any gossip would get around the village in minutes.

It was a reasonable distance from Seaward Manor to Porth, but if I gauged it right, I could walk across the sands at low tide to cut down some of the distance, although it was not always easy. If I managed to walk to Porth, Gramps would saddle old Miser and take me back to Seaward Manor after our visit. Usually, I was armed with some homemade biscuits from Mrs Watson. I never offered Edwina any as, knowing her, she would snatch the whole lot, leaving me with nothing (and Mrs Watson made biscuits on a par with the cook at the manor).

I was relieved when it was Edwina's thirteenth birthday, and she was given her horse. As I was the 'hired help' as she often reminded me, I was allowed to 'borrow' a horse from the stables called Copper, and we would have riding lessons, given by the head groom Arthur, learning to ride side saddle, as all young ladies of quality. Edwina seemed to excel in something for once, but I also became accomplished. Riding a horse would reduce the time it would take to get to Porth. It would give me some form of independence and a chance to get away from Edwina, as she would sometimes follow me around, goading me into saying something I knew that I would regret later by getting a slap, a pinch or even a punch. I always ensured that I would saddle up Copper as I didn't trust Edwina not to loosen the straps on the saddle, with me ending up on my bottom on the floor of the stables. She caught me out once when she stood over me, hands on her hips, laughing and calling me names, but I made sure that it didn't happen again.

Sometimes, she would do something she told her mother I had done, but she wasn't clever enough to cover her trail, such as taking me into Mrs Trevelgue's bedroom to smell her various perfume bottles. She had picked up one of her mother's favourite, expensive perfumes, which had come all the way from France, then tipped it all over Mrs Trevelgue's bedroom floor. Edwina told her mother that I was the culprit, but she was the one who reeked of her mother's perfume, whereas I had no tell-tale perfume on me. Mrs Trevelgue quickly noticed that, but Edwina was not chastised for it. It seemed that her mother overlooked all of Edwina's misdemeanours.

Miss Frazer, as we grew older, started teaching us other things that would stand us in good stead as ladies. She taught us French, Latin, and embroidery, all of which I had learnt from Gramps, Mrs Watson and my father. Mrs Watson had already taught me embroidery, so I excelled over Edwina again. My favourite lessons were playing the piano. I loved to play the piano, and I picked it up very quickly, and once I had mastered the keys and could read music, I could close my eyes and let the music flow from my fingertips, whereas Edwina could only plonk on the piano. According to Miss Frazer, I played with feeling. This again irritated Edwina, so there were more sly pinches and slaps or slamming the piano lid on my fingers.

By now, I had made another friend in the big house. A maid called Jane. She had been relatively new, nearer to my and Edwina's age than the other maids, maybe a couple of years older, and always stood and chatted to me about the house gossip, so we quickly became friends. Jane was taller than me, with sandy-coloured hair and a dusting of freckles across her nose and cheeks. Jane had also been on the other end of Edwina's temper several times and received slaps or kicks. So, Jane also tried to keep out of Edwina's way. I think that Edwina dished out kicks and slaps for no reason other than the fact that she just fancied it. I think she also believed that it was the method to keep staff behaving as she wanted them to, slapping them into submission or some other form of bullying. The housekeeper, Mrs Jessop, had noticed Jane's red face from one of Edwina's slaps one day and had made sure that Jane had nothing more to do with taking care of her; so she was assigned to me instead, not that I needed her to do much for me.

Jane told me, during one of our talks, she wanted to become a real lady's maid, so I allowed her to make my dresses out of fabric Edwina didn't like or alter some of Edwina's old dresses that she no longer wanted. I also let her practice arranging my hair in different styles. Jane would run my baths, wash my hair, and help me dress; it was not that I needed her to help me. It was all a learning curve for her, so I obliged. When we were together, we often used to say that we would catch the coach to London when Mrs Trevelgue had decided that I had outgrown my usefulness as far as Edwina was concerned, where I would go to be a lady's companion or a children's governess. I would give Jane a glowing reference so that she could be employed as a lady's maid.

The only members of staff that Edwina couldn't get away with bullying were Miss Frazer, Mrs Jessop, the housekeeper, and Mr Masters, the butler.

Also, Jane had whispered to me that Mark Trevelgue, the oldest brother, had tried to grab her breasts one day when he was home and pull her into one of the empty rooms. Still, she had managed to push him away and escape to my room, where she stayed out of his and Richard's way until the Trevelgue brothers returned to wherever they lived away from home.

One time, when my body had started developing curves. Edwina had unexpectedly invited me to her bedroom. I never used the adjoining door to our bedrooms, but I always went out into the hallway and knocked on Edwina's door, as she had always told me.

Her bedroom door opened, and Edwina grabbed my arm and dragged me into her room. I knew Richard Trevelgue was home but didn't realise he was in Edwina's bedroom. Richard was nearer to Edwina's age than their older brother, Mark. Edwina slammed the door behind me and, as soon as I was in her bedroom, encouraged her brother to place his hands on my budding breasts.

"Go on, Richard, you've got her now. I won't tell. Go on, make the most of it; she won't squeal; she is too scared that Mama might send her back to her hovel. Go on, feel her breasts." Edwina cajoled her brother. "She's nothing more than a lackey; you can do what you want to her." As Richard began to try to place his hands on me, Edwina excitedly jumped up and down, urging her brother on.

I tried to block Richard's eagerly roaming hands by folding my arms across my chest, "What about under her skirt? See if she is wearing any panties, Richard? Girls like her don't wear any, so I've been told."

Edwina kept laughing, egging him on, and loving every minute. He tried lifting my skirts, none too gently. Again, I tried any way I could to stop his hands, but Edwina shouted encouragements to her older brother until there was a knock on her bedroom door and without asking or waiting for permission to come in, Mrs Jessop entered. She didn't speak but just grabbed my hand and pulled me away from Richard's groping hands and Edwina's room. She pulled me into my bedroom, handed the master key to the adjoining door between Edwina's bedroom and mine and told me to lock both doors. "If you leave the keys in the doors on this side, Edwina can't unlock it from her side. The same applies to the door into the hallway.

"I thought something was going on when one of the maids heard Miss Edwina call Master Richard into her bedroom and reported it to me, so I was looking to see what they were up to." She sat me down on my bed and sat next to me. "He didn't ...invade your body, did he, Julia?" she asked, gently taking my hands in hers.

I shook my head, unable to speak, as I was shaking so hard from the encounter with Richard Trevelgue.

"Now you stay here," Mrs Jessop said, "and I will get Jane to bring up your meals and give you three knocks on the door like this," she said, tapping out the 'special' knock on my bedside chest of drawers. "Now, as soon as you let Jane in, lock your door and keep her with you until you have finished your meal, and she can take your tray back down to the kitchen. If you are here, always keep your door locked, Julia."

Of course, that didn't go down well with Edwina, who began banging and kicking the adjoining door while her brother was busy trying the door from the hallway to my bedroom. Thankfully, both doors were made of heavy, sturdy oak. I don't know what happened, but after a few minutes, the assault on the doors ended, and peace reigned again. I never knew what happened until Jane knocked on my bedroom door to bring me my evening meal. When I heard her knock, I gingerly opened the door, and she slipped into my room carrying a tray.

"One of the other maids saw Master Richard slip into Edwina's bedroom, which was unusual, so she alerted Mrs Jessop and Mr Masters. Mrs Jessop said that when either of the young Masters are at home, you are to stay in your room."

The housekeeper, Mrs Jessop, knew what Edwina was like regarding her treatment of staff, so Jane was assigned to me on a permanent basis. We often talked about our hopes and dreams in London, and I often said to her that when a young, handsome doctor called the home where I would be working, he would see me as the caring companion for the lady of the house or the kind and diligent governess. He would fall in love with me, and after a while, we would walk out together, and then he would eventually ask me to be his wife. We would marry, and I would help him in his profession.

It was between Mrs Jessop and Mr Masters that managed to scupper Edwina's and her brother's cruel and licentious activities.

When I was fifteen, Mrs Trevelgue took Edwina into Truro for the day in the carriage to shop for more dresses as Edwina was growing out of her old ones quickly, leaving me alone with our governess. Miss Frazer suggested that we took a picnic down on the beach, then when our feast was laid out on the blanket, spoke openly to me, knowing that we would not be overheard. She told me I had been a joy and a pleasure to teach over the years and thanked me for my help. "I had hoped that Edwina and you would become good friends, but I can see now that that would never have been. I am so sorry my dear for all you have had to endure. It is a shame that Edwina will become a lady and go to London for a season to try and catch a husband, whereas you will be employed by, hopefully, a great family, but all your acquired gentle skills would be wasted. It would be such a shame."

"They won't be wasted, Miss Frazer, when I can pass on my knowledge to young children. I don't think education is ever wasted," I told her enthusiastically.

"Well, I hope not, my dear. In the meantime, we must try to educate Edwina on the life she will be married into to the best of our ability."

As we grew older and began developing feminine curves, we had our monthly bleeds, as Miss Frazer explained to us. Edwina was the first to start her monthly bleed, and once she had got over her shock of the pain, she would goad me about her being a woman, and I was still a little girl. It was nearly six months later that I started my monthly bleeds. If it hadn't been for Jane supplying me with the rags which I put inside my nickers, I would have been embarrassed, as I had first asked Edwina if she had any I could use. She refused, and I could feel the blood trickling down my legs; thankfully, Jane was in my room when I ran in, crying about Edwina's treatment of me and the embarrassing situation.

"Don't you worry about that little madam, Miss Julia? Now that I know you have started your monthly bleeds, I will make sure that you have plenty of rags ready each month." I thanked her, and she cuddled me, shocked at seeing me cry. I very rarely cried, but after the humiliation that Edwina hoped to put me through and the pain, I could no longer hold my tears back.

Of course, Edwina's curves were more developed than mine; she was beginning to lose her 'puppy fat,' as Gramps would call it, and turn into a very voluptuous female, and she knew it. She flaunted it to any male inside or outside of the house. She had been caught in a rather 'embarrassing position' with one of the stable boys who had been immediately dismissed when Mrs Trevelgue heard about it. I heard her screaming and crying in her bedroom, pounding her pillows in anger at being caught out and the stable boy being dismissed. According to Jane, who could still receive gossip below stairs, Edwina thought that because the weather was bad, no one would go to the stables, but she was wrong. I don't know who found her out, but the gossip was around the house within a matter of minutes. Jane was my informant on this and other juicy titbits of gossip.

Over the years I was at Seaward Manor, Mark and Richard returned home a few times, but Jane and I stayed well out of their way after our first encounter. I didn't like the way either of the brothers looked at me. Once, when I first started my monthly bleed, Mark tried to corner me and touch me in a very embarrassing way; I guessed that Edwina had told him (it would have been the sort of thing she would do.) Mark and Richard thought that any female was 'good sport,' so whenever they were at home, I would stay locked in my room with Jane bringing me my meals, as she also wanted to stay out of the clutches of the Trevelgue brothers.

When the brothers were in residence, Jane would spend most of her time with me, as we both were staying well out of their way. We would talk about our daydreams, where we would both be employed by the same family, and we could take our days off together to explore the big city, as, of course, we would stay in London.

During my time at Seaward Manor, I always treated the staff with kindness and politeness, so they often talked to me and reciprocated. They all knew that apart from my lessons, I lived a solitary existence, with only Jane spending time with me. However, during my time alone, I would enjoy the pleasures of the vast library and read various books.

The year when Edwina and I were due to turn seventeen, the weather had turned bad over the last few days. Autumn had come in with a storm, turning the trees to golds, russets, and browns. The wind had whipped the fallen leaves around in little mini tornadoes while it turned the waves into white tips, and they crashed against the rocks below Seaward Manor, flinging great plumes of water and foam into the air, like they always did.

Because the house was on the headland, the wind up there was so much stronger. Strong enough to nearly blow you off your feet. Everyone wanted to stay inside in the warm and out of the wind and rain, so I hadn't visited the Lodge, Gramps and Mrs Watson for a few weeks, and I felt terrible about it.

One day, after Mrs Trevelgue had decided that Edwina would make her debut the following season, she hired a dancing teacher for Edwina. Sometimes, I just sat watching the dance instructor try to teach Edwina to dance; sometimes, I would sit at the piano and play for them to dance to, so I could watch the steps to the various dances. Edwina was not happy with Mr Lefleur, her dance instructor. He was old, had silver grey hair, and often wore a monocle, but he was very nimble on his feet as he danced with Edwina. "He speaks to me in French, and I can't understand him," Edwina scorned at her mother.

"That is why Miss Frazer is teaching you French, Edwina," her mother said in exasperation.

"But he smells. His breath stinks of onions. He makes me cringe. I won't have him teach me anymore," she said, stamping her feet.

"That behaviour, Miss, is not acceptable in a lady, especially one of your age, Edwina. You will be coming out in a few months and must be able to dance. There is no time for me to find another dance instructor, Edwina, so you must put up with Mr Lefleur, like it or not," Mrs Trevelgue said, stress telling in her voice.

In the meantime, while I had been playing the piano for Mr Lefleur, he would come over and compliment me on my playing. For a couple of minutes, we would converse in French, for which I was pleased to practice with someone other than Miss Frazer.

I had decided that while Edwina was having her dancing lesson, one day, and the weather was fair, I would get a horse from the stables and visit Gramps and Mrs Watson. I felt very guilty for not visiting for a few weeks, but I shouldn't have travelled even on the short journey to Porth with the inclement weather. Even on this day, it was very cold, so I wrapped up warm with a knitted hat, scarf and gloves that Mrs Watson had made for me one Christmas. I told Jane where I was going before I left so that if asked, she knew where I was.

When I went into the stables at the side of the house, I felt tempted to take Edwina's horse while she was dancing. Then, I thought better of it and took Copper, my 'borrowed' horse.

Although the sun shone, the wind was still strong and bitterly cold. There had been a frost on the ground overnight, so I made sure that I steered Copper to the ground where the frost had melted, although it was muddy.

I was looking forward to my visit. Because I hadn't been for a while, I had so much to tell Gramps and Mrs Watson. Although, among the many things I did tell them over the years about the happenings at Seaward Manor, I never mentioned Richard Trevelgue's actions towards me, as I was scared that Gramps would take me away from Seaward Manor. I would lose out on my education, which, although I had a few scrapes with the family's children, was not bad enough to make me want to leave. I liked Miss Frazer, and I enjoyed learning.

When I arrived at the Lodge, the house was locked. I thought Gramps might be out seeing a patient, which would explain why the front door was locked. I tied up Copper and walked around to the back of The Lodge to try the kitchen door, where I felt sure I would find Mrs Watson. I tried the door handle but was surprised to find that locked, too.

It was unusual for Mrs Watson not to be there when Gramps wasn't. If any emergencies needed Gramps, Mrs Watson would always know where to find him. Ultimately, I decided to go down into the village and try to catch her there, where I felt sure she would be. I received some strange looks from the people I had grown up with, and I usually received a cheery greeting. This time, they just looked at me and turned away and I could hear them whispering behind my back. I couldn't see Mrs Watson as I walked around the village, leading Copper behind me, so I thought I would see if she was at her daughter's, Elsie, who lived in one of the cottages in the village with her husband, Jethro.

I made my way to the cottage where Elsie lived, which was only a matter of a few minutes' walk away from the Lodge. I was continually receiving strange looks as I walked towards Elsie's. I would call them outright hostile, but I didn't know what I had done to deserve such hostility. I knocked on the door of Elsie's cottage and waited. Normally, I would have knocked and gone into the cottage, shouting, "It's only me, Elsie." But after my hostile reception in the village, I thought better of it.

Elsie came to her door. She looked me up and down. "Oh, it's you," she sneered at me. I felt the skin on my arms pucker, even under the warmth of my cape.

"So, you decided to come down from the ivory tower and visit us," she said, her voice harsh and cutting, unlike Elsie. Why was she being so cruel to me when we had always been such good friends? Although Elsie was a bit older than me, I had always looked at her as an older sister.

Elsie turned and shouted into the cottage to her mother. "Mam, Lady Muck has finally decided to visit us."

"Why are you being so nasty to me Elsie? I know that I have not been back for a few weeks, but you know how bad the weather has been," I said, tears welling in my eyes, threatening to spill down my cheeks at her unwarranted harshness.

Mrs Watson came to the door, wiping her hands on her pinny. She looked at me.

"Oh, it's you. I suppose better late than never," she said, placing her hands on her hips.

"I don't understand Mrs Watson. Why is there so much hostility toward me? Why aren't you up at the Lodge? Is Gramps out on his rounds?"

Mrs Watson looked at me, her defensive and angry look quickly changing to one of concern: "Why didn't you come when I sent you the message about Doc Trelawney?"

Confusion began to crease my brows, "What message? Where is Gramps?" I was starting to panic now. The muscles of my stomach began to bunch together with fear. Something was wrong, very wrong.

Mrs Watson's face changed from anger to concern to sympathy. "You really don't know?"

"Know what? What is going on?" I shouted in fear, trying to get a simple answer to my question. "Where is my grandfather?" I cried, and the tears that I had tried to hold back due to the hostility began to fall more freely down my cheeks.

Mrs Watson came and put a comforting arm around my shoulders. "Sweetheart, your grandfather had a heart attack on one of his rounds three weeks ago. He is dead, Julia, and you never knew?"

I shook my head, my tears changing from silent tears to great body-wracking sobs. I felt like my heart was breaking. He was the only family member I had left, and now even he had gone. I loved my Gramps, and he always had time for me.

"How would I know if nobody told me?" I cried.

Mrs Watson pulled me willingly into her arms and started to croon to me as she used to when I was little. "Hush, sweeting, you didn't know."

By this time, people of the village had gathered around me, whispering to each other, "She didn't know about the Doc!"

When my tears had subsided a little, Mrs Watson said, "And you didn't receive my note the day before his funeral informing you about it?"

Sadly, I shook my head.

"I sent you another note, telling you that I was closing the Lodge, and we are waiting for a new doctor to come and move in. I told you to come and sort out what you wanted before I finally closed it up. You didn't receive that one either?"

"Nooo..." I sobbed. "If I had known, do you honestly think I would have stayed away, no matter how bad the weather was?" I cried loudly. By now, it seemed the whole village had come out to see the spectacle of me sobbing loudly and uncontrollably.

Mrs Watson called back into the cottage to her son-in-law, Elsie's husband, Jethro. "You did take my notes up to the big house, didn't you, Jethro?"

"Aye, 'course I did," his big, gruff voice came from the back of the cottage.

I couldn't understand it. How did I not receive any of them?

"Who did you give my notes to then?" Mrs Watson asked.

"The young Miss. I would say that I saw her in the stables with one of the stable lads, doing things she shouldn't have done."

"You gave them to Edwina?" I asked through my tears.

"Yes, all three of them. I told her to give them to you, as they were urgent; she was otherwise occupied with that young stable boy again."

"Why didn't you go to the main entrance and give them to the Butler, Jethro?" I asked him.

"Why? They'd turn the likes of me away before I had a chance to explain myself, Julia."

I thought about his reply briefly and supposed he could be right. If he had given the notes to either the gardeners or stable boys, they would have accepted Jethro. But to give them to Edwina... especially if she knew they were for me.

I felt my sorrow being replaced with anger, red-hot anger. I was so angry at Edwina. How dare she intercept messages meant for me?

"Come on inside for a cup of tea, Julia. I got some cakes out of the oven just before you arrived, so they should be cool enough to eat by now," Mrs Watson said, putting her arm around my shoulder. She ushered me inside the little cottage, leaving the rest of the village outside to continue gossiping about me.

"I really should get back to the big house," I told Mrs Watson. I was just in the mood to slap Edwina for a change. I was so angry with her—actually, I felt murderously angry with her. I felt like tugging her perfect ringlets out of her nasty, vicious, stupid head.

"No, you need to calm down, Julia," Mrs Watson said firmly. "You can't go back there like that. Otherwise, knowing you, you will kill that little madam, although she deserves it, and she is not worth hanging for."

I was shaking with suppressed anger. I could willingly wring her neck, the nasty, vindictive... I had never felt such hate before, but at that moment, I felt hate for Edwina Trevelgue with a vengeance.

I sat down and had a cup of tea and one of Mrs Watson's cakes. At first, my hands were shaking so much with suppressed anger that I sloshed some of my tea into the saucer, but after a couple of soothing sips, my shaking slowly subsided. The tea tasted different—

not Mrs Watson's normal brew, but pleasant enough. "This is not normal tea, is it, Mrs Watson?" I asked.

"It's camomile to calm you down. You've had a shock, dear," she explained.

I spent about half an hour discussing Gramps and the big house with Mrs Watson, Elsie, and Jethro. I couldn't talk about Edwina. I was still too angry with her, and thankfully, Mrs Watson never asked. Now that Gramps had gone, I had no one to keep me in Porth, certainly not Newquay. I told Mrs Watson what Jane and I intended to do: move to London and find positions there.

Mrs Watson shrugged, "Well, I suppose you have nothing left here, Julia, now that your grandfather is no longer with us. The new doctor will soon be moving into the Lodge because it belongs to the Trevelgue estate."

"But if it belongs to the Trevelgues, how come Mrs Trevelgue didn't know about Gramps? Who was it left up to advertise for a new doctor?"

"The vicar, Reverend Pascoe. He deals with such things. Mrs Trevelgue wouldn't want to be bothered with such mundane things."

Mrs Watson disappeared to the back of the cottage and returned with some of my things in a large carpet bag. "There are some things that I thought you might have wanted, like some of your books and your grandfather had some money put aside for a rainy day, he always said. If you go to London, you will need it to support yourself until you find a position."

I don't know if Mrs Watson had counted the money, but I just accepted it. I would count it when I was on my own. It didn't seem right to do so in front of Mrs Watson, as I thought she might think that I didn't trust her, and I trusted her with my life, as I had done for many years before my move to the big house. She had been like a surrogate mother to me in the absence of my own.

I thanked her and said that I had better go. I would let her know when I was leaving for London, which I didn't think would be for a few months yet, as Edwina was not ready to travel to London for her 'coming out'. Jane and I would catch a coach and travel there when or just after Edwina and Mrs Trevelgue left for London. I told Mrs Watson I would see her again when I could, but I would write to her once I was in London and found a position. I kissed her cheek and thanked her for all she had done for me. Before I urged Copper on, I asked if she would be working for the new doctor.

"If he needs me," she answered. "If not, I will stay here with Elsie and Jethro," she said as she waved a teary goodbye to me. As I trotted away from her, I let my tears flow once again. As I rode, I was practicing in my mind what I would say to Edwina and her mother.

Once I had trotted out of the village and out of sight of Mrs Watson, I urged Copper into a gallop. I needed to return to the big house and confront Edwina or tell Mrs Trevelgue what her daughter had done. I had covered Edwina's hateful antics far too many times over the years, but this time, she had done the unforgivable, and I was fed up covering for her.

I took Copper back to the stables. No one was there, so I unsaddled her, brushed her down and gave her a bag of oats. By this time, the edge had been taken off my temper, but I was still angry, just not murderously so.

I purposefully strode up to the big house. I let myself in the door of the orangery, as I didn't want to bother Mr Masters to come and open the main door to me when I was perfectly capable of letting myself into the house by another entrance.

It was strange; the orangery seemed deserted, even by the gardeners. If Mrs Trevelgue weren't there, there would generally be gardeners tending the plants and flowers there. I let myself out of the orangery door into the dining room and the large hallway. The hallway was busy with staff standing around, some in shock, some openly crying into their handkerchiefs. What was going on here?

Surely, they hadn't heard about Gramps, and even if they did, it wouldn't reduce them to tears.

The door to the library was slightly ajar, and inside, I could hear someone crying. I gently pushed the door open and walked in. I thought it might be Miss Frazer crying after Edwina had done something terrible to her. I wasn't prepared for the sight that met my eyes on entering the library. The floor was covered in clumps of mud. Mrs Trevelgue was sitting on one of the armchairs, and Edwina's still body, caked in mud, was laid out on the massive library desk. Her face and hair were just a bloody, muddy mess. Her clothes and boots were caked in mud as well.

"Mrs Trevelgue, what has happened?" I asked, concern on my face. At that time, I hated Edwina, but not enough to wish her dead.

Mrs Trevelgue raised her red-rimmed eyes to me. "Edwina rode her horse too close to the cliff edge. It collapsed and..."

I was shocked. Edwina, who had been the bane of my life for so many years, was dead. The evidence was lying before me. Her beautiful blond hair, always so well-kept, was caked in blood and mud. Her clothes, which she had always worn fresh and clean, were now muddy and creased. There was mud in her mouth and eyes, and I stood frozen, shocked.

"Oh, Mrs Trevelgue, I am so sorry for your loss. Edwina was supposed to be having a dancing lesson with Mr Lefleur. When did this happen?" I had never seen Mrs Trevelgue look anything less than immaculate, but today, she looked haggard, devastated. Her usual sparkle had left her looking deflated, and she looked to have aged ten years in a matter of hours. I knew Edwina tried her mother's patience as she did others, but obviously, she was still her child, and Edwina's mother was grieving for her daughter.

"About an hour ago. As you said, she was supposed to have dancing lessons with Mr Lefleur, but she didn't turn up. That stable boy, the one that I had dismissed, found her and brought her back. She was already dead. Nothing could be done." Her voice shook as she started crying again. "If you would leave me, please, Julia." She sobbed. I nodded, not that Mrs Trevelgue was looking at me, and left.

I left the library, closing the large wooden door quietly behind me. Jane was already waiting for me when I went to my room. By the look on her face, she had something juicy to impart. She didn't even ask after Gramps but waded straight in as soon as I closed my door behind me.

"Have you heard Miss Julia?" she asked. She sounded almost excited.

I told her that I had just come from the library.

"She was eloping with that stable boy," Jane told me. "She had a valise with her, and I found a note on her bedside table with her mother's name written on it. I gave it to Mrs Trevelgue's maid, but by then, they had brought Edwina's body back."

That was just the sort of stupid thing Edwina would do. I looked at Jane. "I think that our days here are numbered, Jane. With Edwina gone, Mrs Trevelgue has no reason to keep me here. Is there any way that you can find out how much it would cost for both of us to catch the carriage to London?"

Jane nodded. "How was your grandfather?"

Tears sprung to my eyes again as I told Jane.

"That nasty, evil little—" she started to say, but I interrupted her.

"I know what you mean, Jane, but we can't speak ill of the dead," I told her, "much as I would like to," muttering under my breath since she was mirroring my sentiments exactly.

Jane hung her head in shame, "No, of course not. You are right, Miss Julia."

"We need to wait and see when Mrs Trevelgue wants me to leave, then we can sort out our journey plans."

I didn't tell her about the money Gramps had left me. That was no one's business but mine. I had hidden the money at the bottom of the carpetbag, which I found to have a false bottom. I had brought the bag slung over my saddle from the village with other personal things Mrs Watson thought I might have wanted to keep. Once I was on my own, I would look to see what the carpet bag contained in more detail without the thought of anyone coming into my bedroom.

Chapter Three

Mark and Richard came home for the funeral, and so far, Mrs Trevelgue had not called for me. With the boys at home, I stayed in my bedroom, reading or formulating plans for Jane and me to go to London. I had counted the money left by Gramps, and I hoped it would be enough to pay for our trip on the coach. It would have to last a little while if we were careful with that money once we were in the big city, I hoped. Gramps must have been putting a 'bit away' for years. Enough to keep us in a modest accommodation until we could find positions, if it weren't for too long, although I didn't know how far our money would stretch in the capital city. I had decided to ask Miss Frazer for a written reference, and I would also ask Mrs Trevelgue. I could write a reference for Jane. After all, she had acted as my lady's maid for a few years, so I wouldn't be lying. Jane was going to ask the other staff about the price of the coach fare to London and say that her brother wanted to go there; not that Jane had a brother, living, that was, but the staff didn't know that.

Of course, there was no need for Miss Frazer to stay at Seaward Manor now, with Edwina's death, but she remained for the funeral, as did Mr Lefleur.

Miss Frazer came to my bedroom later, on the day before Edwina's funeral. "Julia, my dear, I fear my days here are numbered. After the funeral, I am sure Mrs Trevelgue will want me gone, as she won't pay me to sit around idly doing nothing. You and I know that we were both here only for Edwina, not for you, my dear."

I told her she would not be the only one to leave, as I couldn't see Mrs Trevelgue keeping me on either, now that Edwina was dead.

She asked me how my grandfather was. I told her what had happened.

"Oh, my dear, I am so dreadfully sorry. So, you have no family left now. What will you do?"

I told her I would go to London with Jane to find a position there. "I thought I could go as a lady's companion or a governess like you."

"If I can do anything to help you, my dear, I would be pleased to help."

I thanked her, "Would it be possible for you to give me a reference? Do you think, after all, you know what I am capable of, Miss Frazer?"

"Of course, Julia. It would be my pleasure. I mean, if you can cope with Edwina and her... idiosyncrasies, shall we say, then you can cope with any child, I am sure. I will write it this evening to give me time to formulate what I wish to say."

"Thank you, Miss Frazer, that will be a great help to me," I told her, then asked what she intended to do.

"I intend to return to Scotland, to my family, for now. After trying to teach Edwina, I think I need to rest for a while, so I will give you my address. You may wish to keep me informed about what you are doing."

I told her I would be happy to and thanked her for everything she had done for me. She gave me a brief kiss on my cheek and said that teaching me had been a pleasure. "You have a great hunger for learning, Julia. Never lose that."

I told her that my Gramps always said that if women were allowed to become doctors, I would have been one of the first.

"Yes, that is such a pity, as I am sure your Gramps was right. I am so sorry for your loss, Julia. Amid Edwina's death, everyone will have forgotten about your loss."

"I don't think they even know yet. You are so kind, Miss Frazer. I will miss you," I said with tears in my eyes.

"And I, you, my dear. I wish you good luck in all you do."

The day of Edwina's funeral arrived, dull and overcast. Mrs Trevelgue, dressed all in black with a black lace veil covering her tear-worn face, walked behind her daughter's coffin, along with her two sons, who were there to give her moral support. I followed behind with Miss Frazer and the rest of the staff. Those who had a black dress wore it. I didn't have one, but Jane said that she could alter one of hers for me to wear.

Edwina had been the bane of my life for so many years, but I still felt 'something' at her passing, but I didn't know what I felt. No one should die at seventeen, and no parent should have to bury their child.

Reverend Pascoe conducted the service. When he had finished, I went to look for Gramps's grave, which wasn't far away. He was buried next to both of my parents, so he had company in the afterlife, I thought. I silently shed tears, but they were not for Edwina; they were for my Gramps, the man whom Edwina and her selfishness had denied me his funeral, among other things. No matter how many years passed, I would never forgive her for that.

I hadn't noticed Mark, the oldest son, walking beside me as we returned to Seaward Manor.

"I heard that the doc had died; he was a good man and patched up Richard and me a few times." I thanked him, thinking he was trying to be nice to me because I had lost the only member of my family that had been left.

I was totally unprepared for what happened next.

His hand shot out then and grabbed my arm painfully. "Is that why you killed Edwina? You were angry at her for not telling you about the doc's passing?"

I was shocked. I couldn't believe my ears. I stopped and looked at him. "I beg your pardon?"

"You heard. You were angry that she had withheld the doc's death from you, so you killed her," he said quite a matter of fact.

"I did not kill Edwina. I was in the village finding out that my only living relative had died. I did not know of Edwina's death until I returned to the manor."

"So, you killed her," her oldest brother continued as if I had never spoken. His fingers were digging into the flesh of my arm. I was sure that I would have bruises.

"I have told you that I was at the village when the cliff collapsed and killed her." I was angry that he would accuse me so without a shred of evidence. "I had heard that she was eloping with the stable lad who found her."

"Oh yes, typical lackey's prattle, never to be believed," he said, his voice raised above the noise of the wind that had been blowing since the day of Edwina's untimely death, but the rain had stayed away, surprisingly. "I will find evidence that it was not an accident, and you were behind it all."

Yet another Trevelgue trying to cause me trouble. At that moment, I straightened my back and looked at him squarely. "You may try all you like, but I have witnesses of everyone in the village that I was with them, so yes, go ahead, Mark, try your darndest, but you have not a shred of proof, none whatsoever," I said with more bravado than I felt. I roughly pulled my arm from his grip and was about to leave when he gave his parting words,

"You seem to forget Miss Beddoes; most villagers are employed in the Trevelgue mines. What would you say if I threatened to sack anyone that said you were there? Think about that, Julia. Think on." He sneered at me.

I felt sick to my stomach. Could he do that? If people believed him, I could hang! My palms began to sweat, even in the cold weather. What could I do? If I ran away to London, it would look like I was guilty, but what if I stayed? I was like a sitting duck, just waiting to be hauled off to jail on false charges.

I continued to walk behind the rest of the mourners, trying to organise my thoughts into actions. I just wanted to lie down and forget about everything, but this torture the Trevelgue siblings seemed intent on doling out to me was getting too much to bear. I nearly ran back to my bedroom at Seaward Manor to fling myself down on my bed and pummel my pillows in anger, but this time, instead of rage at Edwina, it was anger at her older brother. Would I ever be free of this damned family? Who would believe me and the truth that I had nothing to do with Edwina's death? The Trevelgues always demanded respect and attention, so whether it was false or true, the Trevelgues would be believed over me.

A few minutes after I returned to Seaward Manor and went straight to my bedroom, Jane came and looked at me. I had been pacing the bedroom like a caged tiger, not knowing what to do or who to ask for good counsel. She gave me one look at my face, led me over to the only chair in my bedroom, and made me sit down.

"What on earth has happened, Miss Julia? You look as white as a sheet?"

When I told her what Mark had said, she was dumbfounded. "He can't say that. Everyone knows that she was eloping with the stable lad… not unless he is using you as a scapegoat, because they don't want it known what she was doing. Oh, Miss Julia, what are you going to do, run away tonight?"

"If I did that, it would look like an act of guilt," I said, feeling beaten.

I shook my head. It seemed like I was caught between a rock and a hard place. I suppose the only thing I could do was to bide my time until Mrs Trevelgue called for me. Within a couple of hours, I had heard that Miss Frazer and Mr Lefleur had been told to leave as their services were no longer needed. Miss Frazer was told to leave without saying 'goodbye' to me. I presumed that it was grief that had made Mrs Trevelgue say that. I shed a tear when I saw, from my bedroom window, her and Mr Lefleur leave on the coach from the front door. I waited for it to become my turn, but I waited and waited. Jane brought me a tray of food from the kitchen and sat with me while I ate.

"When I was in the kitchen, I heard that the masters are returning to London and Oxford early tomorrow morning, and there is no sign of Mr Mark getting you arrested," she told me, trying to comfort me.

"There is still the morning before they leave," I told her. I dare not even think that I was out of the woods yet. I wouldn't be able to relax until after they had left, and even then, I would not be sure it was safe to breathe easily again.

I picked at my food and pushed my plate away with my half-eaten meal. I just wanted to sleep, to sleep and forget about everything. Unfortunately, when I finally lay down, sleep wouldn't come. I tossed and turned. In the end, I lit a candle and picked up my book to read, but even with that, when I had usually lost myself in a story, I found that I had read the same page time and time again, and still, my brain would not make sense of the words. Nothing would settle me. I had never had trouble sleeping before, but there again, I had never been accused of murder.

I was still awake as a watery sun tried unsuccessfully to peek through the gathering thunderclouds. I was already washed and dressed when Jane brought me breakfast on a tray. Outside, the weather was turning to be as turbulent as my thoughts.

"You look like you didn't sleep a wink last night, Miss Julia," she said as she laid my breakfast tray on the small table in my room.

I sighed wearily. "I didn't. For once in my life, Jane, I don't know what to do." The tears started in my eyes again, threatening to spill down my cheeks. Usually, I would be able to talk to Gramps, and he would give me good advice, but of course, he wasn't here now, so I had nobody. I was all alone. Jane was my closest friend.

Jane looked at me sympathetically. "Oh, bless you. My Mam always said that if you don't know what to do, then don't do anything until you do."

I smiled at her and touched her hand. "I don't know what I would do without you, Jane. Thank you for being there for me. For being my friend," I said to emphasise our relationship.

She patted my hand. "Oh, by the way, both of the masters left early this morning, and Mrs Trevelgue asked if you would meet her in the morning room when you were ready."

"Oh," I said, "This is it, Jane. I think you had better start packing my things in that carpet bag I brought from the village the other day, and if you still want to come with me, you had best pack your things as well."

Jane brushed my hair and tied it back with a simple black bow in readiness to meet Mrs Trevelgue. I was impatient to get downstairs and get this meeting over and done with.

When I finally went to the morning room, I found Mrs Trevelgue dressed in a black bombazine mourning gown with jet jewellery as befitting someone of her station. The black clothes and jewellery complemented her blond hair, and I briefly saw the woman she used to be. She must have been stunning when she was younger.

"Julia, my dear, come and sit down," she said, looking up as I entered the room. The tone of her voice didn't sound like she was waiting for me to be picked up and taken away to prison, so I sat down, my legs crossed at my ankles, my hands held in my lap, and my back straight, as Miss Frazer had always taught Edwina and me to sit.

"Firstly, I am so sorry to hear about your grandfather. He was a good man, and he tended the people of this district admirably. He will be sadly missed. I understand that Reverend Pascoe has already found another doctor to take his place."

That was a shock, so different from her oldest son's attitude.

"May I ask, Ma'am, how did you know about my Gramps passing?"

"Oh, the usual communications between staff in a big house. Your maid told my maid, and my maid told me. She also told me that the housekeeper at the Lodge had sent you a message about his death, but you didn't receive it or the other subsequent messages. I understand they were all given to my daughter, who never passed them on. I can only apologise for that."

I nodded and thanked her.

"I also believe Mark was accusing you of murdering his sister. Again, I apologise. The hot-headed boy. I love all my children, but I know their faults. I suppose it is partly down to me and my parenting; their father died too early, and it was left up to me to bring up my sons. Whether I did a good job or not," she shrugged her shoulders helplessly, "I don't know." She paused, lost in her thoughts. "I suppose they missed the firm hand of a father. Maybe I should have remarried."

I sat silently, listening to all she had to say, not quite believing my ears.

"You have probably heard that Miss Frazer and the dance teacher have already left. I saw no point in them remaining when I had employed them for ... Edwina. Miss Frazer said that you had both discussed what you wanted to do with your life when you left here. She said you considered becoming a lady's companion or a governess to young children. They are both admirable professions. For that, she left a reference for you to any employer." She handed me a letter and a reference from Miss Frazer.

"I believe she has also written you a letter," she smiled at me. "Miss Frazer told me it was a pleasure to teach you," she smiled weakly. "I am afraid that she couldn't say the same...about Edwina.

She said that you managed to get Edwina to buckle down to some lessons between you. Thank you for trying."

Again, she paused. This meeting was turning out to be much easier than I had anticipated, and I felt myself begin to relax after spending all night tossing and turning, fearing being taken into custody and hung for something I had not done.

I don't think Mrs Trevelgue had spoken so much to me in all the years I had lived under her roof.

She sighed, "Now, to get down, why I wanted to talk to you? I have a proposal for you, Julia."

Now, my ears pricked up. A proposal? What sort of proposal? Did she wish for me to become her companion?

"I came from a very well-to-do family," she explained, "My parents were the Earl and Countess of Orkney. We had homes in Scotland and two other places around the country, including a large house in Moldova Square in Mayfair, London."

That was news to me.

"I had my season in London as all young ladies of quality do, but I fell in love with Mr Trevelgue, and we eloped. Because of our elopement, my parents cut me off without a penny. No dowry, nothing. Luckily, Mr Trevelgue's family owned mines here, so they were well off financially in their own right. My mother was a real harridan, stern and unbending. She made my life a living hell, cutting me off without a penny to my name, so I was relieved when I managed to run away from home with Mr Trevelgue, away from all the rules that my mother imposed on me." She stopped and took a deep breath. "I presume you knew that I was planning to take Edwina to London for a season, but of course, she stupidly decided to run off with the stable lad, but it didn't work out that way, as we all know. As I said, I have a proposition for you. I have no need now to go to London... I propose that you go to London to my mother. I will give you a letter of introduction to her, saying that you are my daughter and asking her to give you a season... You are better behaved than Edwina would have been, so my mother would willingly accept you, give you a season, and if you behave as she expects you to, she will probably make you her heir, and you could probably marry a titled gentleman with money."

I could not believe this. She wanted me to pose as her daughter!

"Why should she believe that I am her granddaughter? I look nothing like you, Edwina or your sons."

"Yes, I have thought of that." She steepled her fingers on the table. "Just looking at you, no, she would doubt who you are, based on looks alone, but she knows her daughter's handwriting... If I wrote and said that you were my daughter, she would have to believe me. Your looks, you could say, come from your father's side of the family, as she knew nothing of the Trevelgue side of the family, apart from they owned mines in Cornwall."

"But what do you want from it, Ma'am?" I said, still confused about the whole thing. Indeed, she wasn't doing this for me out of the goodness of her heart, with nothing in return. Was she?

"Our mines are always in need of money, Julia. When she dies, my mother, that is, and makes you her heir, as she probably will, if you behave yourself. You give half of her fortune to the mines. You can keep the rest."

"What if she didn't make me her heir?"

"Well, you will make a good marriage, a titled man with plenty of money and persuade him to invest in the mines."

"What if he doesn't want to invest?"

"Julia, we women can always make men do what we want," she said, dismissing my question as unimportant.

"How?" I asked her.

"Our womanly wiles, my dear. You will learn them as you go on, trust me." She assured me.

"And if I don't agree to your proposal?"

"Then you make your way to London on your own and try to find a job as a lady's companion or a governess, as you originally planned, but believe me, your life would be so much easier if you do as I propose."

My mind was racing with all possible scenarios based on what Mrs Trevelgue said. The main thing was she didn't believe Mark when he accused me of killing his sister. She spoke again, breaking into my thoughts, "If you agree to my proposal, you will travel to London in a comfortable coach, which I will hire, stopping at good quality coaching inns and staying in the most comfortable bedrooms. When you reach London and my mother's home, you will be dressed in the most beautiful clothes, seen in all the right places by all the right people, and presented to Queen Victoria and Prince Albert. Of course, the clothes you are wearing now won't be good enough for my daughter, so you will have everything in Edwina's wardrobe. Jane can alter them all to fit you. I will give you enough money so that you can pay for the best rooms on the journey there. Of course, Edwina and I would have gone to London in the spring, but I think you should leave with Jane as your maid by the end of this week. I know that you have formed a friendship with each other. It will be much colder for you both, travelling at this time of the year, but I will ensure you are well catered for and put a thick travel blanket or two in the coach to keep you warm. You will have Edwina's jewellery, as that will be expected of you as my daughter."

"Do I need to give you an answer now, Ma'am, or can you give me some time to think about it?"

Mrs Trevelgue looked at me as if I were some ungrateful child turning down all that had been offered me. She took a deep, calming breath. "Very well. I will need your answer by breakfast tomorrow morning. If you decide upon it, I will expect you to be wearing one of Edwina's dresses, so Jane had better get to work."

I stood up, and for some reason, I felt that the meeting I had just had with Mrs Trevelgue warranted a curtsey. I dipped a curtsey, thanked her and left the room to go directly to my bedroom. As usual, Jane was there waiting for me.

"I did as you suggested, Miss Julia, and packed the carpet bag. When are we to leave?"

I sat her down beside me on the bed and told her all that had transpired, leaving nothing out. If she was going with me, I needed her to know everything Mrs Trevelgue said.

"Why do you think she is offering this to you?" she asked.

"I don't know. Maybe she feels bad about Edwina not telling me about Gramps and how she treated me over the years. She knows what Edwina was like, so maybe she is trying to make up for that. Also, my father died in the employ of the Trevelgues, but honestly, I don't really know Jane."

"But if you agree, we can both travel to London in comfort, staying at the best coaching inns and rooms. When we get to London, will the Dowager Countess think that you are her granddaughter and take us in, with me as your maid, and you will be dressed in fine clothes and presented to the Queen and Prince?"

I nodded. Jane's words sounded so reasonable: "I must let her know tomorrow morning at breakfast, wearing one of Edwina's dresses, so you will have to alter them all to fit me if I...we intend to proceed with this. It is not just up to me to decide, but you as well." I paused for a while to let it all sink in. "So, what do you think?" I asked her.

"I think that we would be foolish not to take advantage of her proposal," Jane said, which was what I expected her to say. I suppose it would be foolish to pass up such an opportunity.

I nodded slowly, still unsure. There were so many unknown quantities in this that Mrs Trevelgue had obviously not considered. "What if the Dowager Countess doesn't want to accept me as her granddaughter?" I asked Jane.

"Well, we will still be in London by then, and you will still have that reference from Miss Frazer. You could sell off Edwina's jewellery, and we could stay in a modest hotel until we get positions. I can't see any problems with it all," Jane said. I think she had already decided what she wanted, and it would be unfair of me to dash her hopes and dreams.

"Well, I suppose we had better go into Edwina's bedroom and look at her clothes," I told her. "Could you alter them all to fit me within the allotted time?"

"Oh yes, Miss Julia. As she was bigger than you in every way, it would just be a case of taking them in and shortening them. Don't you worry. You will be wearing one of Edwina's dresses tomorrow at breakfast, and by the end of the week, I will have them all done for you. I might even be able to get one of the other maids who is good with a needle to help me."

"But Jane, you must get your sleep." I insisted.

"Well, if we are travelling in style, I can catch up on my sleep in the coach and when we stop at the coaching inns."

We went into Edwina's room, using the key to the adjoining door that had stayed in the lock on my side since I had practically barricaded myself in after Edwina had dragged me into her room for Richard to molest me, and started looking through her wardrobe. It felt strange to go into Edwina's room and not have her bellowing at me for entering her domain. Edwina certainly had plenty of clothes. I picked one dress and gave it to Jane, and then we went back to my room. I put Edwina's dress on, and Jane began to pin it to my slighter figure. Edwina was quite a bit taller than me, so Jane had to take up her dresses by nearly four inches.

I appeared downstairs in one of Edwina's altered gowns the following day. They were indeed a lot warmer than my own clothes and a lot prettier. Jane had done a good job with my dress and was already working on another two I had tried the night before.

Mrs Trevelgue lifted her head and looked at me with a satisfied grin. She knew she had won. She thought I was grateful for her proposal, but I knew that she had altruistic motives, and that was to save her family's mines. My family had already given their lives for her family and mines, so I wasn't feeling so bad about taking her money at that moment.

"Sit down, Julia," she said with a satisfied smile. "I see you have decided. It is very sensible of you. Jane has done a good job. I presume that she is working on the others?"

I nodded and helped myself to some toast, and Mrs Trevelgue poured me a cup of tea. "Obviously, the staff will notice that you are wearing Edwina's dresses, so I have told Daniels, my maid, that I have suggested that you use her clothes rather than throw them away. It will be around the house in no time. I will instruct the footmen to get a couple of trunks down from the attic and take all Edwina's winter clothes until you get a whole new wardrobe in London. I notice you are not wearing Edwina's shoes?"

"They are too big for me, Ma'am, but my own will do quite well under my dresses. No one will notice."

"Hmm..." she said, considering me. "Miss Frazer said that your playing of the pianoforte is quite remarkable. You will play for me after breakfast so that I can judge for myself, and you will also read aloud to me. Miss Frazer also said you have a good command of French and Latin. It will all stand you in good stead in London. May I remind you that no one must know of our little arrangement? That is just between yourself, Jane and me. Do you understand Julia?"

"Yes, Ma'am. May I have your permission to go and say goodbye to my friends in the village on Thursday before we leave on Friday?"

"Very well but remember what I said?" she said sternly to make her point.

"Yes, Ma'am."

"I will have the money for you to pay for your lodgings on the journey by Thursday evening. I will arrange to get the trunks down from the eaves today so that as soon as Jane has altered Edwina's clothes, she can pack them away ready."

After breakfast, Mrs Trevelgue asked me to follow her into the drawing room and play for her. I enjoyed music, so playing the pianoforte was no hardship for me, and neither was reading aloud to her, as I had done it several times to try and entice Edwina to want to read more. All good skills for a companion or governess, I thought to myself, not daring to believe that the Dowager Countess would accept me.

Throughout the next three days, Mrs Trevelgue instructed me on deportment, what silverware to use at the table, which glasses were used for which drinks; she partnered me as we danced around to all the dances Mr Lefleur had been trying to teach Edwina, so that when Thursday came, I had been taught, albeit rather quickly, in all things a young lady would know.

Jane had been working all day and night to get Edwina's entire wardrobe altered, washed, and packed away in the massive trunks with the help of Mrs Trevelgue's maid, Miss Daniels.

It was my last day at Seaward Manor, well, mine and Jane's. While Jane made the final alterations to Edwina's clothes, I went to the stables and saddled up Copper. I might have taken Edwina's horse, but it had to be put down after the accident. I was quite happy with Copper. We were used to each other by now.

It was another cold, windy day. The strong wind whipped up the clouds as they chased across the sky like the devil was after them. The waves were stormily throwing themselves on the rocks and crashing over them, tossing great plumes of foam into the air. From high on Copper's back, I sat by the sea wall and watched the sea, enjoying its final performance that had been put on, I felt, just for me. How could I leave all of this, the place where I had grown up? The place that had stolen all my family from me, leaving me homeless and nearly friendless? Why should I want to stay here? What would I do if I stayed? No families around the area would need a governess or a lady's companion, so what else would I do but run away? I headed Copper to Mrs Watson's daughter's cottage, where I didn't suppose things had changed over the last week or so.

I knocked on the cottage door and stood waiting. Other villagers walked by, waved and smiled at me, so very different from the day I had found out about Edwina's betrayal, and she had died. Word had always travelled fast around the village; good news, bad news, gossip, the villagers were never short of something to discuss.

Mrs Watson came to the door, wiping her hands on her pinny. "Julia, how nice to see you," she shivered. "Come out of the wind and warm yourself by the fire. I've just pulled a batch of shortbread from the oven."

Her welcome was as warm as it had always been, apart from when she thought I had turned my back on the village.

She returned carrying a plate of shortbread and brought a teapot, cups and saucers. She poured out the tea and settled back in her chair to enjoy a bit of neighbourly conversation.

Her usual opening question was, "So, what's happening at the big house these days?"

I told her about Edwina's death, and then I took a deep breath. "I have no reason to stay there now, so I am leaving for London. Mrs Trevelgue has given me all of Edwina's clothes, as Edwina won't need them, and she is paying for a coach to take me to London and enough money to pay for rooms at coaching inns on the way."

Mrs Watson asked if I was wearing some of Edwina's clothes now. I nodded.

"I thought they looked quality—better than what you normally wear. What are you going to do in London, Julia?"

"Mrs Trevelgue and Miss Frazer, our governess, have given me references so that I can become a lady's companion or a governess. There is nothing here for me now that Gramps has gone. There are no jobs locally suited to my education." I shrugged my shoulders, "It's the logical solution."

"I suppose so dear. When do you leave?" Mrs Watson asked.

"Early tomorrow morning. One of the maids is coming with me because she doesn't want to stay here either."

"Well, I suppose you will have company on the journey at least. It's a long way to London, Julia. It's going to take quite a few days to get there."

"I know," I said, realising that I wouldn't be able to return once I had made the journey as Gramps money wouldn't last that long. This would be the last time I would see the home of my childhood. I felt a lump come in my throat. I didn't expect to, but I choked back a sob. I had known Mrs Watson all my life, and now I was leaving her as well, but she had her own family, her flesh and blood, and that was not me.

"Will you let me know that you have arrived safely and keep me informed about what you are doing?" she asked, giving me one of her warm cuddles.

I nodded, unable to speak for the lump in my throat from unshed tears.

"You have been like a daughter to me. I was there when you were born, a tiny, scrawny little thing that caused your mother so much trouble," she continued.

Tears sprang to my eyes. She had been the one constant in my life, and now I was leaving even her behind.

She said as she cuddled me. "You are doing the right thing, pet. As you said, there is nothing here for you unless you want to become a miner's or fisherman's wife, and I can't see you settling for that. No, you go to London and make a good life for yourself. It would be what your parents and your Gramps would want for you. Your Gramps always said that you would be among the first if they allowed women to be doctors. You are clever enough, so you go, sweetheart and Godspeed."

She asked me if I still had Gramps's money. I nodded. "You be careful with that." She dabbed her eyes with the edge of her pinny. "What am I saying? Of course, you will be careful with it. You aren't stupid—far from it."

I stayed for another half hour chatting about this and that, and then I thought it was time to take my final leave. It was getting darker outside, threatening to rain, so I had to leave to get back dry.

I kissed and hugged Mrs Watson again, got up on Copper's back, and, waving, turned my back and left the village.

I saw the first large spots of rain as I walked through the orangery door. Looking back out over the sea, I saw flashes of lightning and heard the distant rumble of thunder, knowing that we were in for a stormy night.

I saw Mr Masters, who looked at me and said, "Oh, you're back, Miss Julia. The mistress has been looking for you. She is in the library."

I handed him my coat, hat and gloves, then went into the library. Mrs Trevelgue looked up when I entered. It looked like she had been writing.

"Ah Julia, did you have a nice visit in the village?" She smiled at me.

I told her that I had. She indicated the chair on the opposite side of the desk. I sat down and folded my hands in my lap.

"I have been writing your letter of introduction to my mother, saying that, because she had been disappointed with me, not to hold it against her granddaughter, but to accept you and give you the season you deserve." She folded her letter up and sealed it, then handed it to me. She also handed me a roll of banknotes. "This is to pay for accommodation for you and Jane on the journey. I have organised a food hamper for you both; help yourself to as many library books as you wish to keep you occupied on the journey. I suggest a pack of playing cards as well. I will ensure you are both warm enough, and I have supplied a couple of thick travel blankets. Are your trunks packed?"

I nodded. She had done so much for me over the years, and I did have a lot to thank her for. Still, all of this was to her benefit or the benefit of the Trevelgue mines, so I didn't feel guilty about what she was doing for me, especially after what I had to put up with from her daughter over the years and then her son's threats after Edwina's funeral.

She rose elegantly from her chair, so I stood too.

"Well, I think that's about it. Do you have Miss Frazer's letter?" she asked me.

I nodded.

She held her hand out to me, "Well, this is goodbye, my dear. Have a safe journey. I won't be awake when you leave."

"Thank you for everything you have done for me, Mrs Trevelgue. It has been greatly appreciated," I said, wanting to leave on good terms with her.

"You are welcome. I owe your father and grandfather a lot for what they have done for us over the years. They were both good men and a great loss, not just to you but also to the community."

I shook her hand and left, not wanting her to see the tears in my eyes. Seaward Manor had been my home for seven years of my life. It wasn't a loving, happy home, but it did give me a comfortable roof over my head, an education and food. In a way, I would miss it.

Chapter Four

The coach left Seaward Manor just as dawn was breaking the next day. Strapped on top were two trunks full of Edwina's altered clothes, and a couple of Jane's uniforms. Inside, Jane and I sat wrapped up against the cold in thick coats, hats, scarves, gloves, and the two thick travel blankets Mrs Trevelgue had promised me the night before. In my carpet bag, which I kept inside the coach, were the letters from Miss Frazer and Mrs Trevelgue to her mother, the money from Gramps, and the money from Mrs Trevelgue. I thought that if we were careful, there might be some money left at the end of the journey, so if the Dowager Countess of Orkney refused us, we might be able to find a small, comfortable hotel, not expensive but clean and decent, to stay in while we looked for work. Under one of the seats was a food hamper to feed us until we reached the first inn; then, we could get further food from the inns at the start of each day. I had also packed Edwina's jewellery at the bottom of the carpetbag to keep with me. Her jewellery looked good quality, but I would not expect it to be anything else. I could sell it, which would fetch a decent amount of money.

The storm had rolled in the night before Jane and I were due to leave Cornwall. Flashes of lightning split the skies and crept around the edges of my heavy bedroom curtains, lighting my room in a ghostly blue light. The same curtains cut down the thunder's rumble, and this morning, watery sunshine kept trying to peep through the clouds but, throughout the day, didn't succeed much.

Jane and I sat talking for a while, but the gentle rocking of the carriage was rocking Jane off to sleep. I didn't begrudge her sleep, as she had worked diligently to get Edwina's clothes altered for me before we left. While she slept, I reached into the carpet bag and pulled out Miss Frazer's letter and reference to me. I wanted to see what she had said about me, and with all the preparations for the journey, I hadn't had time to sit down and read it.

> *My dear Julia,*
>
> *I am sorry I did not have time to say farewell to you in person. For some reason, Mrs Trevelgue wanted Mr Lefleur and I to leave immediately.*
>
> *It has been a pleasure teaching you, and I wish you well in everything you do. I am confident that you will do well in your life. I would like you to write to me occasionally and keep me updated. As I said, I am returning to Scotland, and my parents live in Perth. My father is the Vicar of St Cuthberts in Perth, so you can reach me there. If I have taken a position elsewhere, my father will forward your mail to me.*
>
> *I have enclosed a glowing reference for you and your future employers.*
>
> *With very best wishes,*
>
> *Agatha Frazer.*

I opened the other sheet of paper.

> *To whom it may concern.*
>
> *I taught Julia from the age of 10 to 17. She has always had a great thirst for knowledge, and teaching her has been a pleasure.*

> *Julia excels in Math, English, History, Geography, French, and Latin. She is also proficient in reading aloud and needlecraft. Julia excels on the pianoforte to the extent that she surpasses my expectations. I am sure she will succeed in all her endeavours, either as a governess or a ladies' companion.*
>
> *Yours sincerely*
>
> *Agatha Frazer.*

If Mrs Trevelgue's mother rejected me, I felt sure Miss Frazer's reference would secure suitable employment. I folded the two letters and put them back into the carpet bag, pulled out one of the books I had helped myself to from the library, and settled down to read.

I didn't feel guilty about taking the books. I had never seen anyone use the library, or at least not the books, so I felt no guilt. I felt guilty that I would be lying and deceiving the Dowager Countess, even though I had never met her, but although lying didn't sit well with me, it didn't seem to be a problem for the Trevelgues over the years. I had not been brought up this way and felt uncomfortable about whether she was the cold-hearted harridan that Mrs Trevelgue had described, or maybe Mrs Trevelgue had been lying. I had the long journey from Cornwall to London to think of any alternatives, if there were any. I tried reading, but like Jane, the rocking of the carriage was making my eyelids heavy, so in the end, I put my book down, leaned against the corner of the coach and slept. We did that on and off throughout the journey on the first day, punctuating the journey by eating from the food hamper. We would play cards for a while and look at the passing scenery; there were the occasional stops for nature, and we would talk about our future. The carriage pulled into our first coaching inn as night drew in. While the coachman attended the horses, Jane and I went to look for accommodation. Jane looked at me askance when I asked for one room for us. Jane questioned me when we were shown a room with a large double bed, table, and two chairs and left alone. "Why one room, Miss Julia? Mrs Trevelgue gave us enough..."

"I know Jane; enough money to have comfortable lodgings as befitting her daughter and maid. If we go for a less comfortable room and share the bed, we can save money, so when we get to London, if necessary, we will have more money left to last us until we find positions. So, you have a choice: we can share a less comfortable room and have money left at the end of the journey, just in case we get turned away, or we can use all the money given to us and have nothing at the end of the journey, and if we get turned out, we will have to sleep on the streets."

"But Miss Julia..." Jane started to say.

"Jane, I am no different to you. My name is Julia," I told her.

"I couldn't call you that, Miss Julia," she insisted.

"My father worked for a living, the same as all the men in the village. I am no better, no different from you," I said, taking her hands in mine to try to imprint my meaning on her.

"But you are, Miss. You are educated. I can hardly read, write, or add up numbers. I would feel dreadful just calling you Jul... well, just your name."

I smiled at her.

"Anyway," she continued, "when we get to London, and Mrs Trevelgue's mother thinks that you are her granddaughter, I will have to call you Miss Julia then," she continued stubbornly.

"And if she doesn't take me in as her granddaughter, I will be like you. I will be in employment, and I will be called Julia or Miss Beddoes, depending on the position I manage to gain."

Jane shook her head, "But I couldn't."

"Then we shall have to agree to disagree, Jane."

Jane nodded and reluctantly agreed. Although the bed was not luxurious, it was comfortable and warm. We were given a hot meal and then retired to bed early, as we would start our journey at dawn again the next day.

The next day, after a simple but filling breakfast and having the hamper replenished, I paid the bill with some of the money Mrs Trevelgue had given me, and we were on our way again. I was glad that I had Jane with me. We had been friends for the last three years, and although she wasn't as well educated as I was, she was excellent with needles and threads, altering Edwina's clothes to fit me. She tried to become a lady's maid to me over those three years, but I always looked at her as on the same footing as myself. I looked at her as a friend.

It was a bitterly cold morning with a heavy frost on the ground, but the sky above looked like we might see some bright autumn sunshine. Wrapped in thick coats, hats, and scarves and covered in travel blankets, we started on the second day of the journey. We were leaving Cornwall, and the trees that had all bent over one way looked like they were bowing to us and bidding us farewell. I started to play a card game and taught Jane how to play, too. That kept us occupied for a while, and then Jane started to yawn again and went to sleep. I couldn't blame her for making the most of her inactivity and taking advantage of sleep because once we reached London and work, wherever that might be, she would be kept busy. I picked up the pack of cards and shuffled them, then began to play Patience until I got bored, then picked up my book to read. I never realised that sitting, doing practically nothing, could be so tiring. Through all the sitting and doing next to nothing, by the time it came to getting out of the coach, I was stiff, and my backside was numb. Once Jane and I got to our room on the second night, we stood by the roaring fire, getting warm. I was rubbing my behind, trying to get the blood flowing to it after all the inactivity. Jane started giggling and followed my example until we were both in fits of giggles at the picture. We must have both looked like a comical sight, standing before the fire, rubbing our backsides.

We shared another double bed, and I reckoned that by the end of the journey, we should still have roughly between a half and a quarter left of the money Mrs Trevelgue had given us, plus what money I had from Gramps, and Edwina's jewellery, we should be comfortable for a short while until we could find positions, if we were turned out on our ears. If we were taken in, I could find a bank and open an account, bringing in some additional interest. I cast my mind back to Edwina and how selfish and greedy she had been, thinking she was entitled to everything she wanted. If she had been in this position, she would use up all the money and not care about tomorrow. Thank heavens, I was more astute than that.

The days seemed to blend into one another until I had no idea how long we had been travelling, but it seemed like an eternity. Although we slept in the coach, we fell fitfully asleep at night. Every night was another inn and another strange bed. I would have loved to have got out of the coach and taken one of the horses for a ride, but it was bitterly cold outside, and my backside was already numb; with all the sitting and riding astride a horse, I doubted the activity would alleviate the numbness; besides I had never ridden astride a horse before, as Edwina and I had both been trained to ride side-saddle by Arthur, the elderly headgroom in the stables, as all young ladies of quality did.

During our inactivity on the journey, my mind swung between thoughts of me becoming a governess or lady's companion and that of a young lady of the ton. In my wildest dreams, I was dressed in beautiful gowns with a string of eligible suitors waiting to take me out and about and finally marrying a well-to-do gentleman, but they were in my wildest dreams. I was more practical than that, and what would probably be reality was so much different. I had Miss Frazer as my role model for a governess and hoped I didn't have pupils like Edwina. When I thought like that, I kept my fingers crossed.

We had been travelling for what seemed like ages when the coach driver informed us that we should reach London in two more days. At one of our stops to 'stretch our legs,' I said that I thought he would be glad to reach the journey's end and get a well-earned rest.

"I'm used to it, Miss, after all the years I've been doing it, and it pays well; better than mining or fishing, anyway, and there is always a need for a coach driver."

That afternoon, the weather turned. The wind had dropped, and a thick fog was rolling in. I looked out the window and saw nothing on either side of the road through the thickening fog. Ultimately, the coach stopped, and the driver knocked on the window and opened the door. "Miss, we can't go any further. I can 'ardly see my 'and in front of my face. If we continue, we could end up in a ditch."

"What do you suggest we do?" I asked, thinking he would say we could all wait the fog out in the carriage and then continue, but I was wrong.

"I saw the gates to an estate not far back. If you walked back to that and threw yourselves on the mercy of the 'ouse, and I will turn the carriage round and walk the 'orses back. We will be just behind you, Miss," he told us.

"Come on then, Jane," I said, welcoming the exercise, "best foot forward." I picked up the carpet bag with the money, jewellery, letters, and other bits and pieces.

After sitting in the coach for so long, I was glad to stretch my legs. I tightened my scarf around my neck, pulled my hat down over my ears, and put on my gloves. The coach driver pointed back the way we had come. "It's about 'alf a mile back that way, Miss." He told us to stick to the track; otherwise, we would get lost in the fog.

Jane and I linked arms and began to walk. I could hear the coachman coaxing the horses to turn, and then I heard a loud splitting of wood, and a horse scream out in pain. Shortly after, I heard a gunshot, then nothing.

I urged Jane to keep walking, trying not to think about what had gone on behind us. It took us about fifteen minutes or more to walk to the large gates to the estate, which were open. By this time, the coachman had caught up with us and had explained what had happened to me.

"I tried to turn the carriage around, Miss, to come back, but it rolled back into a ditch at the side of the road and turned over, pulling one of the 'orses back with it. You probably 'eard its scream. I am afraid I 'ad to shoot it and put it out of its misery, then leave the carriage where it is."

I wondered if we could return to the coach with just one horse once the fog had cleared and continue our way to London. I asked the coachman, but he shook his head. "Until I see it in the daylight, Miss, I 'onestly don't know."

So, the three of us and a horse carrying the trunks of Edwina's altered clothes walked along the long, winding driveway to a large mansion at the end of it. We could see candlelight in some of the windows, which was a welcome sight. Just seeing the candlelight in the windows made me feel warmer, why I don't know.

We stepped up to the large, imposing front door, banged the heavy brass doorknocker twice, and waited.

The door was opened by a short, dumpy, balding butler in livery. He looked at us.

"Yes," he said, looking down his nose at us. I imagined we must have looked a frightful sight standing there after God knows how many days on the road.

"I am sorry to trouble you, but—" I was trying to think of the right words, then Jane stepped forward. "This is the granddaughter of the Dowager Countess of Orkney," she supplied.

"We were on our way to London," I continued, "but the fog got so thick that we could not carry on. Our carriage turned over in a ditch, and the coachman had to put down one of the horses. I am afraid we are throwing ourselves on the mercy of the house to shelter us for the night," I told him.

The butler stood to one side to allow Jane and me in and instructed the coachman to leave the trunks in the hallway, take the horse round to the side, and someone would meet him. He asked Jane and me to wait in the large, grand hallway while he informed the master. After the cold outside, the warmth of the house was welcome. The butler disappeared for a minute or so, then came back. "The Master has instructed me to take you into the drawing room to him, Miss. I will arrange rooms for you and your staff, Miss."

I thanked him and followed him down a long corridor to a large drawing room dominated by a massive roaring fire in a large marble fireplace. A well-dressed gentleman stood up. He was tall and lean, with dark wavy hair, sprinkles of silver touching his forehead and sideburns. He had a longish nose but a kind look that softened his face as he smiled when I entered the room. He wore a red velvet jacket over an open-necked, brilliant white shirt with a burgundy cravat around his neck and dark trousers. "I am sorry to receive you in this state of dress," he apologised, "But I was not expecting visitors this evening in this weather. I am William Lamb, Viscount Melbourne. Welcome to Brocket Hall," he introduced himself to me.

"I am Julia Trevelgue, the Dowager Countess of Orkney's granddaughter." I curtseyed. "I am sorry we have intruded on your privacy."

"Yes, my man has explained. It's most unfortunate, Miss Trevelgue. And you were so near London. Where have you travelled from?"

"Cornwall, my lord," I told him. He raised his well-defined eyebrows in surprise.

"I am forgetting my manners. Please come and take a seat here by the fire and warm yourself. It seems you have had a very long journey at this time of the year."

I sat down and held my hands to the fire, which was most welcome. "I was hoping to spend some time with the Dowager Countess before being presented," I explained to him.

Lord Melbourne sat down opposite me. "I am sure your grandmother will look forward to seeing you."

I felt myself colouring up for lying and having to explain myself to Lord Melbourne, a man I had never met before. "Erm, she doesn't know that I am coming. I have a letter from M...my mother asking if she would take me in and give me a season."

He looked at me, amused. "I see, so you will probably be needing an introduction. If you live in Cornwall, I presume you have not met the Dowager Countess before?"

I shook my head. And so, the lies began.

"If I..." He hesitated, thinking about what I said.

"So, you have never met your grandmother, and she doesn't know you are coming to visit her?" he reiterated. "And you have travelled from Cornwall with just your maid and coachman? May I ask why your mother did not accompany you, Miss Trevelgue?"

"There are problems at the mines, as my father died many years ago, so she has to deal with that." I lied. Lies lead to more lies, and with more lies, my heartbeat increased until I felt that I was struggling to breathe.

Lord Melbourne thought again.

"I intended to travel to London sometime within the next few days. I suppose that I could change my plans and travel tomorrow. So, if we travel in my coach and I introduce you to your grandmother, she might not turn you from the door." He sighed, "It is all very irregular, Miss Trevelgue, so I imagine you will need all the help you can get. I will get my men to rescue what is left of your carriage tomorrow."

He asked if I had eaten, which I said in the negative. "Then I think a hot meal first. I have not dined yet, so I am sure we can dine together. My cook will be a great improvement on the food that you have received at coaching inns. I will get someone to show you to your room. Is there anything that I can offer you to make your stay as comfortable as possible?"

"I would love a hot bath, please, my lord," I told him.

"It will be arranged for you. We eat at seven. One of the maids will bring you down to the dining room." He stood and pulled a bell chord beside the fire, bowed to me and gave his instructions for my welfare.

I curtseyed to him and followed the maid who came to collect me.

I was shown to the 'blue bedroom,' which was massive and lavishly decorated in blues. There were blue curtains at the windows, a blue counterpane on a massive four-poster bed, and blue velvet curtains to pull around if required. I noted that the trunks had been carried to my room, so obviously, the coachman had arranged for the second one to be collected from the coach. I thought that my bedroom at Seaward Manor had been large, but this bedroom was nearly twice its size.

A large bathtub was brought in and positioned in front of the roaring fire, followed by an army of housemaids carrying jugs of hot water for me to soak in. To top it off, they poured in sweet-smelling oils. A vast fluffy towel was hung by the fire, to warm and ready to wrap me in when I had finished my ablutions.

"Do you require any help, Miss?" asked the final housemaid, who had poured the fragrant oils.

"I have a change of clothes in one of the trunks. If you could lay them out for me when I have finished, I would be grateful," I told her.

The maid went to one of the trunks and brought out my change of clothes, tutting at my crumpled dress. "Let me take that downstairs and get it ironed for you Miss."

"Can you tell me if my maid is ..." I started to ask.

"Yes, Miss, she has been put upstairs and is sharing a room with me. Shall I send her down to you?"

I told her that I could manage and to tell Jane to rest this evening after all the travelling.

At least I would arrive at the Dowager Countess's home smelling sweet instead of travel weary and dirty.

When the maid had left, I moved the screen to stand between the door and the bathtub, then quickly undressed and got into the water while it was still nice and hot. I slipped under the water, letting it cover my body in warmth. It was pure heaven after all the travelling and coaching inns, where I just had a jug of lukewarm water and a bowl to wash. I just lay there enjoying the hot water and the warmth of the roaring fire. When the water started to cool, I stepped out and wrapped myself in the thick, fluffy towel. I just sat by the fire for a minute before the maid returned my dress.

"There you are, Miss; your dress looks much more presentable after running an iron over it."

I thanked her and said I could manage to dress if someone could take me down to the dining room when it was time.

While dressing, Jane came down to see I had everything I needed. I told her I had and asked her if she needed anything.

"Oh, Miss Julia, I am sharing a room with another maid, but I have my own bed. I will be joining the rest of the staff to eat. If this is anything like the Dowager Countesses, it will be wonderful. I could be quite happy."

Jane helped me put on a clean dress and underclothes. It felt so good to be properly clean again.

At the allotted time, another maid knocked on my bedroom door to show me down to the dining room, and I told Jane I wouldn't need her anymore that night. She protested, "Miss Julia, you shouldn't be alone with this man when you know nothing about him."

"I think I am a pretty good judge of character. The Viscount looks to be an honourable gentleman. Given the circumstances, I really don't have much of a choice. Go now and make the most of your bed, as we don't really know what to expect tomorrow."

Jane left me, grumbling about my honour and virtue, while the other maid showed me down to the dining room. Before leaving, she turned and told me that her master was an honourable gentleman and that I needed to have no worries. I thanked her and walked into the dining room. Lord Melbourne stood up and walked over to me. "You look much better, Miss Trevelgue."

I thanked him as one of the liveried footmen held out my chair for me to sit at the dining table. Lord Melbourne waited for me to settle comfortably, then sat down. He was a very entertaining host, asking me about my life in Cornwall and talking a little of himself, telling me that he was a member of parliament and a widow. I tried to be as vague as possible, as lying still didn't sit comfortably with me, and I didn't want to lie any more than was absolutely necessary.

"You have a very beautiful home, Lord Melbourne," I said, looking around the room between courses.

He thanked me. "In the morning, I will send some men out to retrieve your carriage, see if it can be salvaged, and arrange for the knackers to collect the horse's corpse."

I thanked him. "I am a little concerned about how the Dowager Countess will receive me, not being invited or warned about my arrival, and also about finding out that I spent the night here alone," I told him honestly.

"Well, the door to the dining room has remained open throughout the meal, and two footmen have been standing in the room while we have been eating, so I cannot see that there is any impropriety." Lord Melbourne's brows creased together as he tried to resolve the problem. "I could arrange for a mattress to be put in your room for your maid if you would like," he said, then hesitated.

"I suppose that to save your honour, we could tell a little white lie and say that I found you at the roadside tomorrow morning, and I picked you up to take you to your grandmother."

I breathed a sigh of relief. "It would be a great help to me if you were prepared to lie."

"To save a young lady's reputation, I am sure a little white lie will benefit your situation. I must admit, Miss Trevelgue, I didn't know that Lady Mary had a granddaughter."

I could feel my cheeks redden, "M... my mother and her mother have been estranged for many years. Lady Mary probably doesn't even know that she has grandchildren... I have two older brothers, Mark, the eldest, Richard, and myself. I don't even know if she will recognise me and accept me. M... my mother has written her a letter, hoping my grandmother will accept me. If she doesn't, I don't know what I will do. I have a little money put aside, so hopefully, I can find a position as a governess or a lady's companion. I have a letter of reference from my governess stating my experience, which I hope will stand me in good stead."

"Let's not worry too much about 'what if', Miss Trevelgue. If I introduce you to your grandmother, she might be more ready to accept you. If she doesn't, I will give you my address in London, so you may call on my assistance if you need it."

Lies led to more lies, and I was now involving Lord Melbourne in this deception, which was unfair. What would be the prison sentence for lying and impersonating someone? I dreaded to think. Whenever I thought about what I intended to do, my heart started beating like I had run from Cornwall. Could I possibly hang for it? If not hanged, was it deportation or a prison sentence? My palms grew clammy, and I could feel sweat breaking out all over my body. So much for my scented bath that night.

"You look pensive Miss Trevelgue?"

"Would it be wrong for you to call me Julia, Lord Melbourne?"

"I shall call you Miss Julia if you call me Mr Lamb. There is no impropriety."

"I would feel more comfortable with that, my lord."

"Mr Lamb," he contradicted me. We carried on eating. The food was exceptional, much better than the coaching inns, although most had been quite acceptable.

In the dining room, over the fireplace, where another fire was roaring, hung a massive painting of a beautiful woman.

"May I ask who the lady is over the fireplace?" I asked Mr Lamb.

A pained look crossed his face briefly, and then he looked back at me. "My late wife Caroline. She died some years ago. Since then, I have not remarried."

Again, I blushed, "I am so sorry, Mr Lamb."

"You weren't to know Miss Julia. I don't suppose gossip reaches down to Cornwall."

"I don't think there is much that reaches down to Cornwall, Mr Lamb, gossip or anything else," I said, trying to bring a smile to his face.

I didn't like to pry as I noticed that talking about his wife was very painful.

At the end of the delicious meal, I found myself struggling to swallow a yawn. As perceptive as he was, Mr Lamb must have noticed and suggested I get an early night to prepare for the next day. I apologised, thanked him, bid him a goodnight, and went upstairs to my bedroom. I found it on my own without asking how to get there.

The bed was so comfortable. While I was downstairs eating, a maid came into my bedroom to stoke the fire, put more coal on it, and heat my bed with a warming pan. Once I had gotten into bed, the warmth and the softness were conducive to a good night's sleep.

I awoke the following day as a maid came in carrying a tray with a cup of tea and a substantial breakfast. "Lord Melbourne said that he would be ready by eleven o'clock. Miss, if you and Jane meet him downstairs in the hallway, I have already ordered your trunks to be loaded."

I thanked her and settled down to breakfast in bed. What luxury! After I had eaten my fill, I pushed my tray to the side, washed and dressed, ready for the final stretch of the long journey from Cornwall. Knowing that I was only a few hours away from meeting

Mrs Trevelgue's mother, the nerves started to grip my stomach and dry my mouth out so that when I tried to talk, my tongue stuck to the roof of my mouth. I had already warned Jane that Mr Lamb would say that he had found us at the side of the road that morning so that no gossip would tarnish my name. Jane nodded, and we settled into Mr Lamb's comfortable carriage for the final part of our journey, in which Jane acted as my chaperone. The seats were thicker padded than the ones we had sat on for the trip from Cornwall, saving pressure on my bottom. It was also warmer than the other carriage, although Mr Lamb insisted we cover our laps with a travel blanket to avoid getting cold. In all, he was a very attentive and interesting travelling companion.

As we approached London, Mr Lamb pointed out places of interest to me. The passing scenery attracted Jane's and my attention as we peeked out the carriage windows, overtaking my nerves about meeting Lady Mary, as Mr Lamb called her.

At last, we pulled into Moldova Square. Surrounding the sizeable lawned square, across the road from the enormous houses, were tall railings and gates open during the daytime but closed and bolted at night to keep the 'unsavoury' out, so Mr Lamb told me. All the houses in the Square were large and imposing as they sat back from the road. They were in the Edwardian style with mullioned windows and large bays. We pulled up outside one of the houses. On either side of the large, green-painted wooden front door stood sturdy white columns framing the entranceway. Mr Lamb pointed out the wooden limbs that branched all over the front of the house and told me that it was wisteria, which had beautiful purple, pink, and white cascading flowers covering the branches in the spring.

"It looks stunning when you see it in the spring," he told me.

"That's if I'm still here, Mr Lamb," I sighed.

He grinned at me encouragingly, "Come now, Miss Julia, positive thinking. Chin up and best foot forward," he told me.

Mr Lamb climbed from the carriage first, stepping onto the step that folded down from the carriage door. He held out his hand to help me alight. We walked up three steps to the front door. Mr Lamb looked down at me. "Are you ready?" he asked before lifting the brass knocker and letting it fall.

I took a deep breath and nodded.

He knocked on the door twice, and we only had to wait a short while before the front door was opened.

"Viscount Melbourne and Miss Julia Trevelgue to see Lady Mary. Is she at home?" Mr Lamb said, with certainly more confidence than I felt.

The butler nodded and held open the front door to allow us to enter a light, large hallway, drawing attention toward a high domed ceiling where cupids and nymphs had been painted and a massive crystal chandelier hung. Large windows allowed the weak autumn sunshine into the hallway. A massive circular table with the largest crystal vase I had ever seen, filled with hothouse flowers, stood in the middle of the hallway. The fragrance was beautiful, even at this time of the year.

The butler returned from announcing our arrival, took our coats, and led us into the drawing room, which was decorated in creams and pale lilac. An elderly lady rose from one of the gold velvet armchairs and came to greet Lord Melbourne, holding her hand out for him to kiss.

"Lady Mary, it is a pleasure to see you again and look who I found at the side of the road on my journey here: your granddaughter, Miss Julia Trevelgue. Wasn't it a fortuitous meeting?" Lord Melbourne said enthusiastically.

Lady Mary was a tall, Amazonian-sized woman. Her stance and looks resembled Mrs Trevelgue. Where Mrs Trevelgue had blonde hair, Lady Mary's was a salt and pepper colour, and she wore it in a simple chignon. She wore glasses perched on the end of her nose and viewed me from over the top.

"So, you are my granddaughter, Julia? You look nothing like your mother. Mind you, we haven't seen each other in many years," said the elderly lady.

And so, the lies began. "I am told that I look more like my father's side of the family, Ma'am," I said, wringing my hands with nerves. I reached into my reticule and pulled Mrs Trevelgue's letter to her mother. Lady Mary took it, then before opening it, thanked Mr Lamb. With this as his dismissal, he bowed over her hand again and kissed it, then bowed over mine. Before kissing it, he put a calling card in my hand, unseen by Lady Mary. "Miss Julia, feel free to call on me if I can be of any assistance," he said, then kissed my hand.

He left the room, and I was alone with Lady Mary, my supposed grandmother. "Well, don't just stand there, girl. Sit down while I read what my daughter has to say."

I had not opened Mrs Trevelgue's letter to her mother, but by the speed at which Lady Mary read it, I didn't think her daughter's letter was very long.

I sat in one of the armchairs in front of the fire, waiting for her to rail at me and ban me from her home, never crossing her threshold again. The clock on the mantle shelf ticked away the time, making my nerves raw. I silently wrung my hands, waiting for her to finish reading the letter from her daughter.

"Hmmm. She says you play the pianoforte very well. I think I will be the judge of that..."

"Ma'am," I said, "I can understand if you do not wish me to stay here. M... m...mother said you didn't part on good terms and have never spoken since."

"Oh, she did, did she? So, did she explain to you why we parted badly?" Lady Mary asked me.

I shook my head, "Not really Ma'am. No."

"Hmm. Let me hear you play then, girl, and I will tell you why we parted 'badly', as she called it. The pianoforte is over there." Lady Mary pointed to the instrument in the corner of the room.

I stood, walked over to the instrument she pointed to, and sat down. "Is there anything you wish me to play Ma'am?"

"Hmm... Something soothing, I think," she said, briefly glancing at Mrs Trevelgue's letter again.

I decided to play Chopin, one of my favourite composers.

Lady Mary sat down. "As you know, my daughter was born into a titled family. She had her season with very eligible gentlemen chasing after her. Her father and I had settled a substantial dowry on her, and she would also have money from my side of the family when I died. She became engaged to a titled gentleman; it would have been the perfect marriage for her, but she ran away, not even leaving a note for her father, me, or her future husband. She broke her engagement when she met her husband. Yes, he was a man of means. His family owned mines in Cornwall, as you know, of course, so she certainly wouldn't be living on the bread line. They eloped and returned only when the marriage had been consummated so it could not be annulled. She tried to play us for fools, so we removed the dowry, and I disinherited her. Since then, we have never spoken. Because of what my daughter did, it caused a great deal of scandal that was linked to our family. She was always headstrong; some would even call her a spoiled brat as a child. So, there you have it, miss."

I stopped playing and stood up. From what Lady Mary had told me about her daughter and from knowing and living with Edwina, I could see, like mother, like daughter.

"Lady Mary, Ma'am, I understand that I would not be welcome here after how my m...mother behaved. I appreciate that. I have some money put aside so that Jane, my maid and I could stay in a rooming house and start to look for positions."

"And what sort of position would you take after the luxury and comfort of where you have been living in Cornwall?" she scorned.

I was tempted to say that I had not always lived in the lap of luxury, but that would have given me away immediately for the fraud that I was.

"I have a reference from my governess which will allow me to get a position. I completely understand, Ma'am."

I was about to leave the room and get my coat when she said. "Sit down, Julia, and let us talk," the Dowager Countess said.

I returned and sat down. "I do not wish to impose on your hospitality Ma'am."

Lady Mary looked at Mrs Trevelgue's letter again, then screwed it up and threw it down. "From what you have said, you seem to be an honourable young lady, unlike my daughter. I wonder where you got that from? You can stay for the time being, but I have some rules you will abide by while under my roof... I need time to consider how we shall proceed with this...arrangement as you have caught me rather unprepared by your arrival."

She rang a little crystal bell on the table beside her chair. Immediately, a footman appeared. "Miss Julia will be staying for the time being. You may put her trunks in the yellow bedroom."

"I also have my maid with me, Ma'am," I told her, thinking of Jane, whom I had left standing in the hall.

"She will room with the rest of the staff," Lady Mary said dismissively.

"Thank you, Ma'am."

"You may call me either Lady Mary or Ma'am while you are here, but not Grandmama or any derivative. I am also not the Dowager Countess of Orkney. That title is reserved for a mother whose son is the Earl and is unmarried. My son married some years ago, and he and his family live in Scotland. I am, 'The Honourable Lady Mary McKenzie. My husband died some years ago."

"Yes, Ma'am."

I don't know why she didn't kick me out immediately in the wind and rain, as the weather had changed and the clouds darkened the sky when I was in Moldova Square, but I was relieved.

"You may go to your room, settle in, then return here." I curtsied and followed the footman, who carried one of my trunks to my new bedroom for however long I needed or was allowed to stay.

Jane came to my room just as the footman left to collect the other trunk from the hallway.

"Well, what did she say, Miss Julia?" Jane asked.

I told her what Lady Mary had said and that we could stay, but there would be rules.

"I can live with rules, Miss Julia; I had plenty at Seaward Manor."

"We don't know what rules Lady Mary will make. We might be glad to live in a small hotel or rooming house and look for positions." I told her.

I asked Jane if she had been given accommodation, and she told me that, again, she was sharing a room with another maid, but she had her own bed, the same as she had at Brocket Hall. I reminded her not to mention Brocket Hall, and she nodded.

After I had tidied myself up from the journey with Lord Melbourne, I looked at myself in the mirror, gauging that I looked acceptable, and went downstairs again to Lady Mary's drawing room. When I entered, I found her staring into the fire.

"Ah, Julia, come and sit down and let us talk. You play the piano very well. How is your reading aloud?"

I told her that I immensely enjoyed reading aloud. I nearly told her I often did that to encourage Edwina to read, but I stopped myself just in time. I thought that I was not cut out to be a liar. Sooner or later, I felt that I would trip myself up, and Lady Mary would know me as the liar and fraud I was.

"Do you ride... side saddle as any lady of breeding would do?"

"Yes, Ma'am."

"Is there anything you are not competent at so I can arrange tutors? Do you speak French?"

I nodded. "Yes, Ma'am."

"Latin?"

Again, I nodded. "M...my mother taught me dancing, but I am not sure that the latest dances have reached Cornwall yet."

"So, a dance instructor then. We must also get you suitably attired. Going by what I have seen of your clothes, they might suit Cornwall, but not London society, so we will need to visit the modiste to arrange for you to wear suitable gowns and shoes. Do you have riding habits?"

"One, Ma'am, but I can't have you spending money on me."

"And why not?"

"Because it wouldn't be fair, Ma'am. I have turned up on your doorstep without any warning."

Lady Mary scowled at me, "Let me decide what is fair and what is not, but I appreciate your concern for my coffers; it is refreshing. Now, I want something from you in repayment for all of this." She paused to see my reaction, "I want you to change your name."

I was shocked, "Change my name Ma'am. May I ask why?"

"As I told you, my daughter's elopement caused a terrible scandal. You must learn one thing about the ton: they have very long memories, and although your parents' elopement happened many years ago, there are still members of the ton that will remember. I wish you to change your name, legally, of course, to my family name, Braemar. Not my daughter's maiden name, of McKenzie, but my maiden name. I do not wish the ton to link anyone staying with me to that scandal."

"So, I will not be your granddaughter?" I asked, sighing inside with relief.

"Is there a problem with that miss?" The Dowager Countess scowled at me again, and I had a brief view of what Mrs Trevelgue called 'the harridan'.

I thought about that for a while…while Lady Mary looked at me to gauge my reaction. I had no family living, no one to link my name to; at least I wouldn't be known as a Trevelgue, so I would no longer be lying. When I married, I would change my name anyway if I were lucky enough. "No, Ma'am," I finally said.

From what I had seen of the large home that Lady Mary lived in, there were many rooms, and I had seen plenty of staff milling around the place, but I believed she lived independently. Could she be lonely? Was that why she was keen to keep me with her?

"Good! Then, I will arrange for my solicitor to call on us in the morning to legalise things. Then we will go shopping and no more nonsense about me spending money on you. It is my money to do with as I wish." She looked at me again over the top of her glasses. "I noticed you had a slight stammer when mentioning your mother. Is that normal?"

"No, Ma'am, I suppose that I was nervous, and knowing that you both parted badly, I was worried about how you would feel about being reminded of her," I explained. I hoped that what I had said made some sense as I felt myself floundering under her questioning. How could I succeed in this fraudulent life?

"That is an excellent point. No, I do not wish to be reminded of my daughter and how she deceived me. I hope that you will not do the same." She cocked her head to one side and looked hard at me. "You seem to be a sensible girl, very astute. You certainly didn't get that from her. You look nothing like her. It is not just her hair colouring but your eyes, a remarkable emerald, green shade. You are not similar in build to your mother's side of the family."

"No, Ma'am, I think again it is a throwback to my father's side," I replied.

I blushed to lie and was scrutinised so thoroughly, but it would have little consequence if Lady Mary were prepared to spend money on me for clothes.

"I suppose my eyes are a throwback to my father's side of the family again, Ma'am." I re-iterated.

"Well, that can be no bad thing." She put her fingers to her forehead and massaged the bridge of her nose as if trying to massage away the stress of the day and how her eyebrows had creased together ever since I had arrived on her doorstep.

"Are you not feeling well, Lady Mary? Can I fetch you anything, Ma'am?" I asked her, concerned.

She waved her hand in dismissal, "No, child. It is just that this day is turning out to be nothing as I had expected when I awoke this morning."

"I'm sorry, Ma'am. Are you sure that you want to go ahead with this? I can understand if you don't." Again, I was trying to find a way out of this ludicrous, fraudulent situation.

"Yes, I am sure. I hope my faith in you is justified, and you won't let me down like... like my daughter." Lady Mary said.

"I won't, Ma'am," I told her, secretly crossing my fingers in my lap.

"Hmm. Well, go and play some more for me. I find your playing quite soothing. Who taught you to play? Certainly not my daughter!"

"No, Ma'am, it was my Governess, Miss Frazer." I sat at the piano and let my fingers glide over the keys. It was no hardship for me to play. I found it soothing as I often lost myself in the music, and I hoped it would soothe Lady Mary's frayed nerves as well.

"Chopin, is it not?" Lady Mary said.

"Yes Ma'am, I find his music very evocative. When I play it I can imagine the sea on a warm, moonlit night, with the silvery path of the moon stretching as far as the eye can see, watching the ebb and flow of the waves as they creep upon the beach. I used to love to watch the sea when I was in Cornwall, and I was mesmerized by it. I suppose that is why I enjoy this piece of music; it reminds me of Cornwall."

"Mmm. Yes, it is very beautiful. You have a good way with words. They are very descriptive. I think you will miss the sea."

"I suppose I will, Ma'am. Although the sea can be still and calm, it can also be rough and dangerous. Yet... even then, I enjoyed watching it and watching as the huge waves crashed over the rocks."

"Will you ever want to return to Cornwall again?"

"No, Ma'am. I don't think so. Our island is surrounded by sea, so I am sure other places are just as beautiful as Cornwall."

Lady Mary nodded, "Yes, the sea in the Orkneys is also beautiful, but of course, the Orkneys are so far away. My son, the present Earl, still lives there with his family and is reluctant to leave. He had to travel down here for some time to find a wife, but once he had married, they moved back, and they now have a family of their own."

"Yet you have stayed here?" I commented.

"I have spent a lot of my life here, and the journey north is not one I would wish to undertake, not at my age; besides, it is so much colder up there than here. Although my son is married, many of the ton still refer to me as the Dowager Countess, which is not politically correct."

"Is Scotland as beautiful as they say?" I asked as I continued to play.

"The Orkneys are as beautiful as Cornwall, I should imagine, with its sandy beaches and rocky coastline. Of course, being so far north, the temperatures are colder. After a long coach journey up to Scotland, you must take the ferry across to the islands, and the sea in the north can be very stormy. I haven't been there since my children were small, but my son is very happy there, so he and his family rarely come south."

"Did you just have the two children, Ma'am?" I asked.

"Didn't my daughter ever tell you?" Lady Mary asked, raising her eyebrows in surprise.

"No, she never spoke of her life before she married," I told her.

Lady Mary nodded sadly, "Yes. God did not see fit to bless us with any more. I did lose another two babies, but they never even came to full term."

"I am so sorry, Ma'am." I thought that it must be heartbreaking to lose a child.

"It's not your fault, child." She cocked her head to one side, "You seem to be so much more caring and thoughtful than my daughter. How did that happen?"

I shrugged my shoulders. "I don't know, Ma'am. I suppose I just like people. Miss Frazer, my governess, was a good and caring teacher, and I suppose some of it must have rubbed off on me."

"Hmm..." was all Lady Mary replied on the subject. "You said that you read aloud. Have you ever read Homer's Iliad?"

I shook my head.

"There is a copy on the table over there." She pointed to another side table. "Would you read me a chapter or two?"

I stopped playing the pianoforte and picked up the green leather-bound book. I opened it to where Lady Mary had placed her bookmarker and began to read. I had never read Homer, but I found it captivating. It was about the Trojan War and talked of Achilles and King Agamemnon. I soon found myself becoming engrossed in it.

"You are enjoying it as much as I am," Lady Mary stated after a while, "yet your Miss Frazer didn't introduce you to Homer?"

"We read Shakespeare, Wordsworth. We also read some Byron."

Lady Mary guffawed at that. "Byron, bah, ineffectual load of romantic claptrap. You will no doubt meet him during the season."

"You still wish to give me a season after all mmm...my mother has done to you?"

"For once, I agree with my daughter; why should I hold a grudge against you when you are innocent? Is that not true?" She looked at me pointedly as if she knew the truth... and knew I was a fraud. But why did she not cast me out if that was the case? "Also, you seem to be a very accomplished young lady that deserves a season."

I nodded and continued to read.

I was beginning to think that Lady Mary was not the cold-hearted harridan Mrs Trevelgue had described her as. Seeing that Mrs Trevelgue had not only broken off her engagement to a titled gentleman but also eloped. Yes, Lady Mary was brusque, but knowing the whole story, I could understand why. Mrs Trevelgue had only told me half the story about her mother. I hated lying and felt so tempted to tell her the whole truth at that very moment. Lady Mary deserved to know, but if I told her, she would probably cast Jane and me out, and in just this short time, I thought I could grow to like her. Also, she was offering me a chance to better myself in a way that her daughter had.

The footman came into the drawing room to light all the candles and stoke the fire. Lady Mary looked up in surprise, "I did not realise the time. Go upstairs and change for dinner, Julia; we will eat in the small dining room at seven."

I placed the book on the side table again, leaving the bookmark where I had left off reading, curtseyed to Lady Mary, and went to my room.

Now that I knew I was staying, for the time being anyway, I had the opportunity to look around my bedroom. It was beautiful in creams, gold velvets, and brocade. Even Edwina's bedroom could not compare to this. I had a huge four-poster bed with golden velvet curtains to match the curtains at the mullioned windows, which overlooked the beautiful manicured rear gardens, with ponds and fountains and ducks swimming merrily in the water. At the far end of the gardens, I could see a massive greenhouse, where I presumed the hot-house flowers that graced the house's main rooms came from. A large cream marble Adam-style fireplace dominated my bedroom, and a roaring fire was crackling away, making my bedroom beautiful and warm on that cold winter day.

Jane came in while I was exploring my room. "What did the Dowager Countess say, Miss Julia?"

I smiled. For the first time since I had left Cornwall, I felt like I could relax for the time being. "We have a stay of execution, Jane."

She looked at me, puzzled, not understanding what I meant.

"We can stay for the foreseeable future, Jane. I am to change my name to Braemar, which is Lady Mary's family name, as she doesn't want the Trevelgue's name linked to hers. And I am to be dressed and presented at court."

Jane clapped her hands in glee. "You've done it, Miss Julia."

"I am not completely happy about all this lying to her. I know what Mrs Trevelgue said about her. Yes, she is abrupt, or she was when I first came to her, but after Lady Mary explained why she had done what she had done to Mrs Trevelgue, I would say that, maybe, it was warranted."

"I was talking to the dowager countess's maid, and she said she would train me properly in everything a good lady's maid needs to know."

I touched her hand and smiled at her excitement. "I am so pleased for you, Jane."

"No, Miss Julia. We are to be together. You could make a good marriage to a titled gent, and I would be able to come with you and be a proper lady's maid."

I asked Jane if she could arrange a bath for me.

As I lay back in the warm, scented water, I began to plan things, mainly my finances, for when Lady Mary decided to ask us to leave. She would likely demand that we leave, as I felt she would eventually do. I knew that I could not rest on my laurels.

I had what money I'd managed to save from the journey to London. I would say roughly a third of what Mrs Trevelgue had initially given me. I had Gramps's money, and there was Edwina's jewellery also. Some of it was rather garish for my taste, although by the looks of it, it looked quality. I thought that I would like simple jewellery, such as pearls. I would sort through Edwina's jewellery and keep what I wanted—the rest I would sell. If I had managed the money carefully and invested it or just put it in a bank, then when Lady Mary eventually turned Jane and me out, I would have had some savings for us to fall back on. It wasn't a fortune, but it was more than I had ever had, and more than Gramps had left me. I had no idea what Edwina's jewellery would bring, but, as I thought, every little helps.

The water was beginning to cool, and I thought it was time to get out and prepare for having dinner with Lady Mary in the small dining room.

I went down to the hallway and had to ask the butler, who I later found out was called Mr Ritson, which door led to the small dining room.

He offered to take me there, but I told him that if he could direct me, that would be quite sufficient.

When I reached the small dining room, Lady Mary was already there and seated. I apologised for being late and explained that I had gotten lost.

Lady Mary waved her hand in dismissal, "No worry. No doubt you will soon find your way around. Come sit down, Julia."

I knew that every move I made during that first dinner would be scrutinised to see if I had been schooled as well as I should have been as Mrs Trevelgue's daughter and Lady Mary's granddaughter.

I walked to the chair a footman held out for me and sat down, allowing him to move my chair nearer the table once I was seated.

Lady Mary then began to ask if I knew which glasses, in the array set before me, were for which drink. She named the drink, and I pointed to the correct glass. When all four had been called, she rang a little crystal bell beside her, and our food was brought out for us. I knew Lady Mary was still watching me, ensuring I ate correctly. The first course was soup. She looked to ensure that I dipped my soup spoon in and scooped up the soup away from me, taking dainty sips from the spoon. Once I had finished, I laid the spoon in the soup bowl, dabbed my lips with my serviette, and then placed that down. The footman came and removed the soup bowls. "Very well done, Miss," Lady Mary commented and did so after every course.

When we had completed our final course, I dabbed my mouth again and laid my serviette beside my plate. The footman came to clear our places. Lady Mary told them that we would have coffee in the drawing room. Another footman helped us to leave the table.

I followed Lady Mary into the drawing room and sat opposite her. When the coffee arrived, Lady Mary asked if I would pour. Yet another test, I thought. I had seen how Mrs Trevelgue did it and remembered, so I picked up a cup and saucer, then lifted the coffee pot and took it to the cup and saucer in my hand. I held both steady and poured, ensuring no spill in the saucer or elsewhere. I asked Lady Mary how she took her coffee. She told me milk and no sugar, so I picked up the milk jug, poured some into her cup, and then handed it to her. She smiled as she took the cup and saucer. I had passed yet another of her tests.

Lady Mary asked me to play the piano again, told me to play more Chopin, and tell her what images each piece invoked in me.

I played another piece, but a bit livelier than the Chopin piece I had played earlier, and told her that that particular piece reminded me of puppies playing, trotting around and gambolling over each other, then running around again; how they would play-fight with each other, then yawning, snuggling up close to each other to sleep.

"You have a vivid imagination, Julia."

"Yes, I have been accused of that before, Ma'am."

"Accused? Surely, having a vivid imagination is not a bad thing. I think that it is an asset. It enables you to play the pianoforte with more feeling. Play something else for me and tell me what you can see in your mind's eye."

I played for the rest of the evening and told Lady Mary what I imagined. Then it was time for bed. Lady Mary wished me a good night and told me to 'sleep well,' as we had a lot to do the next day.

I slept peaceably that night for the first time since I had left Cornwall. I slept well during the journey from Cornwall, but I was always plagued with bad dreams and the fear of being caught in this fraudulent act. Lord Melbourne's house was as comfortable, as was my bed, but I still worried about how I would be received in London. Now, for the time being, this was my bedroom and bed, and they were very comfortable.

Jane woke me the following day and opened my bedroom curtains to a cold and frosty morning. She had placed my breakfast tray on my bedside table.

"It's a bit nippy out there, Miss Julia. You must wrap up warm if you are going out today."

I told her that we would be spending most of the time in shops, and before shopping, I had to meet with Lady Mary's solicitor.

"Are you sure you want to change your name, Miss?"

I shrugged, "At least I won't be known by Trevelgue, and I suppose if I did marry, I would be changing my name anyway. So long as it is legal, then that is one less lie for me to make."

"I suppose so, Miss," Jane said as she began laying out my clothes for the morning.

I asked Jane how she was getting on with the other staff.

"Oh, they are nice overall. Lady Mary's maid, Dorcas, is a bit of a stickler for doing everything perfectly, but I suppose that if I want to learn to be a good lady's maid, then it is all to the good."

After I had eaten, I washed, and Jane helped me dress. Then, I was to meet Lady Mary downstairs in the library with her solicitor.

When I reached the library, Lady Mary was already seated at the large Mahogany desk with an old, rotund, bespectacled gentleman dressed in an immaculate black suit, crisp white shirt, and silver-grey waistcoat. He was leaning over Lady Mary, pointing out what looked like where she was to sign.

Lady Mary and her solicitor looked up as I entered.

"Ah, Julia, there you are. This is Mr Woodbine, my solicitor. Mr Woodbine, this is my ward, Julia." Lady Mary said.

Mr Woodbine straightened up and gave me a curt nod.

"Have I finished signing everything now?" she asked him.

Mr Woodbine nodded, so Lady Mary stood up and indicated that I take the seat.

Once I sat at the desk, Mr Woodbine leaned over me and explained the documents.

"This is to say that you renounce all former surnames and will be called Julia Braemar from this day forward. If that is as you wish, you sign your new name here and here." He pointed out where I should sign in my new name.

The night before, I found paper, quill, and ink in my room and practised my new signature, so my new signature flowed comfortably when I signed the legal paperwork.

"Now I must sign to say that I have witnessed Lady Mary's and your signatures and that you were not coerced into changing your name. I shall retain one copy back at my office along with the rest of Lady Mary's legal paperwork, and you will keep the other as proof of your identity."

I nodded that I understood. Mr Woodbine blotted the two documents and handed one to me.

"Congratulations, Miss. You are now known as Miss Julia Braemar." Then he bowed over Lady Mary's hand first, then mine, and left.

Lady Mary told me to go upstairs, put the document somewhere safe, and present myself in the hallway, ready to go shopping.

I curtseyed, ran upstairs with the paperwork and put it in the top drawer of my bedside table. Jane helped me into my coat and wrapped a scarf around my neck. "That will keep you nice and warm, Miss," Jane said.

I ran downstairs to the Dowager Countess, who wore a fur coat and hat and stood ready.

"Are we ready, Julia?"

"Yes, Ma'am," I replied.

We went down the steps to Lady Mary's waiting carriage, which bore the crest of the Orkneys on its doors. Lady Mary was handed into the carriage first, then me.

Once we were seated, Lady Mary looked at me with disdain as the carriage left the house. "Julia, a young lady does not run up or downstairs. A lady does not run anywhere. Please remember that in the future."

I had been well and truly reprimanded. I nodded and apologised.

"I also note that your ears are not pierced. Earrings are very much part of a lady's jewellery, so you should get your maid to do them. If she can't, then ask Dorcas to do them."

"Yes, Ma'am,"

I looked outside the carriage window, and as we neared the city centre, the pavements and roads got busier but also dirtier. Children ran barefooted and dirty-faced, and men sat leaning against walls in threadbare, shabby old coats that certainly would not keep them warm in the cold weather. They had a cloth cap in front of them, begging for money.

As we neared the city's main centre, the occupation of the pavements changed, with young ladies walking with their maids and other ladies hanging on gentlemen's arms. There was a man with a barrel organ, and a monkey sat on top wearing a colourful little waistcoat and a strange hat, which I later found out was called a fez, holding out a tin cup for collecting money from passers-by. There were nursemaids with their charges either in a perambulator, on leading strings or holding on to their little hands and walking. We drove past banks and offices, then pulled up in front of what I noticed was the Modiste's premises. Two large square bay windows flanked the front door. In the windows were manikins dressed in beautiful gowns. Rolls of fabrics were laid out, enticing ladies to go inside and see what beautiful gowns could be made from them. Inside, I could see further rolls of silks and satin, chiffons, crepes, grosgrains, velvets and bombazines, reels holding lace and a coloured rainbow of ribbon trims.

When we pushed through the front door, a tiny bell tinkled inside the shop, and a woman came out; this, I presumed, was the Modiste. She wore a deep plumb, nearly black-coloured bombazine dress in the latest fashion, devoid of embellishments, apart from a material tape measure hung around her neck. Her dark hair was swept up in a loose knot on her head. When we entered, I noticed a large book on a counter, which showed various clothes and gowns of different styles and designs.

"Lady Mary, this is a surprise. How may I be of service to you today?" Madame Yvonne greeted us warmly.

"Madam Yvonne, I have brought you my ward, Miss Julia Braemar. She will need a new wardrobe, so I hope you can oblige."

"But, of course, Lady Mary," replied Madam Yvonne, only too happy to oblige by making and supplying a whole new wardrobe for the honourable Lady Mary McKenzie's ward.

Madame Yvonne asked me to remove my coat and scarf, took measurements, and noted them in a little book. Once she had completed that, she and Lady Mary began looking through the book displayed on the countertop, discussing styles and fabrics. Madame Yvonne looked over to me. "Miss Braemar is so petite and has such beautiful, coloured hair, rich mahogany, and those eyes... such a distinctive emerald green shade. Whatever colours we choose must accentuate her colouring. I should imagine Miss Braemar could carry any colour."

I had never been discussed in such flattering terms before. I always thought I was small, plain and boring, according to Edwina, with her statuesque body, blonde hair and blue eyes. She had always called me 'mousey; plain and mousey.' But of course, Edwina always wanted to be the centre of attention; she hated anyone who stood to threaten that. Now, I was being called beautiful and petite. Words I had never thought would refer to me, but here I was, hearing with my own ears.

I wasn't even asked my opinion as to styles and materials. I was sure Madam Yvonne and Lady Mary wouldn't choose anything that would reflect poorly on them, so I sat quietly, looking at all the beautiful materials.

Lady Mary had ordered two riding habits, three ball gowns, two evening gowns, and numerous morning and tea gowns, so many items that my head was spinning. How on earth would I be able to repay Lady Mary for all this when she found out that I was a fraud? With that thought, my heartbeat increased with fear again. How could I stand being turned away from all of this?

We finally left the shop with Lady Mary telling Madam Yvonne to send my clothes over as soon as they were completed.

Next, we went to the haberdashers for gloves, stockings, and other lady's wear. I was grateful that a woman served us, as the thought of discussing such intimate items with a man would have been mortifying.

From the haberdashers, we moved on to a milliner to choose hats for going out and riding hats. For the riding hats, Lady Mary had been given a swatch of materials from my two new riding habits to match them.

Our final stop was at the cobblers, where they measured my feet by drawing around their shape and measuring around various parts of my calf so that the shoes and boots would fit perfectly and comfortably. Lady Mary ordered a pair of shiny black riding boots, two pairs of everyday shoes, and three pairs of evening shoes for dancing and wearing under evening gowns.

I was relieved when we were finished. I never realised that shopping could be so tiring. If I was tired, I dreaded thinking how Lady Mary must feel. At a rough guess, I thought that Lady Mary might be sixty or nearing that age, so at such an age, I thought that she must be feeling exhausted.

We climbed back inside Lady Mary's carriage and finally went home. When we entered the hallway, Lady Mary waited for the footman to remove her coat and passed her hat to him. I went upstairs, remembering that ladies did not run, but before I left Lady Mary, she reminded me to get Jane to pierce my ears.

"Yes, Ma'am," I replied.

As I entered my bedroom, I handed my coat and scarf to Jane and told her that Lady Mary wanted me to get my ears pierced. Just mentioning it, Jane blanched white and shook her head,

"Oh, Miss Julia, I can't do that. I...I might hurt you. Oh, please don't ask me." I could see a look of sheer panic in her eyes just at the very thought of it.

"It's got to be done," I told her, "Lady Mary's instructions. I think you had better go and get Dorcas if you can't face the thought of doing it yourself."

I had never met Dorcas, but Jane had from when Dorcas was instructing her to become a good lady's maid.

Jane hurried from my bedroom in search of Dorcas, returning a few minutes later with the said lady in tow.

"Good afternoon, Miss Julia. I understand that you want your ears pierced." Dorcas said. She had a matter-of-fact, no-nonsense Scottish accent. She must have been roughly the same age as Lady Mary, with grey hair scraped back in a severe bun and topped off with a brilliant white cap, but she was small and had a busybody sort of demeanour about her.

Dorcas had come into my bedroom with a towel, a bodkin, a tub of something and a pair of Lady Mary's golden ear studs. She lit the candle on my dressing table and told me she was waiting for a footman to bring up some ice from the icehouse in the garden. Jane just stood on the sidelines with a look of sheer terror. I could see her pale, horror-stricken face through the mirror on my dressing table in front of where I was sitting, waiting for Dorcas to start with the procedure.

When one of the footmen had brought the ice up in a basin, Dorcas put the towel over my shoulder and leaned forward to tell me that the towel was for the melting ice more than the blood.

Bang!

We both looked around and found Jane lying on the floor in a dead faint.

"We'll leave her there, Miss, so that if she does it again, she won't have so far to fall," Dorcas said, very matter-of-factly.

Dorcas pulled the bodkin through the candle flame and then put a piece of ice in front and behind my ear lobe. When it was relatively numb, she pushed the bodkin through, then put some cream on my ear lobe from the tub, which she explained was lanolin, then she put in one of the stud earrings and told me that I would need to bathe my ears regularly with salt water for a few weeks and turn the earrings with the lanolin on. "It'll be no good relying on that one." She nodded to Jane as she was coming to.

"Stay down there, lassie," she said, then continued with the ear piercing. "Now comes the difficult bit," Dorcas said to me, "making sure that I make the second hole in the same place in the other lobe."

Bang!

"Och, there she goes again!" Dorcas exclaimed, which brought a grin to my face. "Better get this done before she comes to. Otherwise, she'll go off again." Her face was so deadpan that I couldn't help but laugh. She continued with the second lobe, getting it done as quickly as she could before Jane came to.

"There now. All done, Miss Julia." She leaned down and hooked her hand underneath Jane's shoulder. "Come on, lassie. Ups-a-daisy. It's all done now. No thanks to you, you big wet blanket!" She scolded and cast her eyes heavenwards as she helped Jane stand up. "Go and sit down on the bed," she ordered her. "You should be looking after your mistress, not the other way round, you great daft lummox!" Dorcas scolded.

Jane started in floods of tears. "I'm sorry, Miss Julia. I wanted to be a good maid, and now I've failed you."

I handed her a handkerchief to dry her eyes.

Dorcas looked heavenwards again and tutted as she left the room.

I got Jane to remain sitting on my bed while she got over her tears.

I put my arm around her shoulder to comfort her, "Just because you can't do one thing, it doesn't mean that you won't be a good lady's maid, Jane. Many people can't stand the sight of blood. My Gramps said that he'd seen grown men, big bears of men, pass out at the sight of blood."

"Honestly?" she asked weakly.

"Honestly," I told her, "Now dry your eyes, and I'll go down and see Lady Mary. After today's excursion, I was worn out, so I dread to think how she must be feeling."

When I went downstairs to the drawing room, I found Lady Mary sitting in her usual chair before the fire. I thought she was asleep, but she opened her eyes when she heard me enter.

"Oh, there you are, Julia." She noticed my ears. "How did it go?"

I sat opposite Lady Mary and told her the whole story, and she laughed until she was wiping the tears from her eyes.

"It was the deadpan way that Dorcas said, 'Och, there she goes again,'" I told her.

And both Lady Mary and I ended up laughing till we cried.

"Oh, that has done me good, my dear. I haven't laughed like that for a very long time."

She told me about a musical concert she thought I might like the following week and asked if I would like to go. I asked her who the composer was.

"There are pieces written by two composers, Mendolsohn and Paganini. I don't know if you have heard of them?"

I shook my head.

"It's a bit different from Schubert and Mozart, but you might find it enjoyable. By then, one of your evening gowns should have arrived, so you will have somewhere to wear it."

She asked me if I would read to her, so I picked up Homer again and continued to read from where we had left off the last time.

Chapter Five

It rained solidly for the next few days, so all I could do was read, play the piano, read the newspapers after Lady Mary had finished with them, or embroider. I started working on two antimacassars, pulling thread work and embroidery. I realised that Mrs Watson must have been worrying about me, so I used some of the writing paper in my bedroom to write a brief note saying I had arrived safely. That way, she wouldn't be worried and wouldn't expect anything further for a while.

The following fine day was dry but frosty. I asked Lady Mary if I could go into the town with Jane and look around the shops. She told me it was all right, so long as I kept Jane with me. I curtseyed and thanked her.

I returned to my bedroom and told Jane to wear her coat as we were going to explore the city. While she was getting her coat, I selected some of Edwina's jewellery that I didn't like, as well as the money from Gramps and what was left over from Mrs Trevelgue. I estimated I had about a third of what was initially given to me left over from the journey. I also thought of putting in my proof of identity, in case it was needed, and putting it all in my reticule. I had no idea of the value of Edwina's jewellery, but whatever it was worth, I would add to the rest of the money and bank it all, except just some 'pin' money so that I could treat Jane to a cup of tea in a tea shop and maybe a pastry. I also popped the brief letter to Mrs Watson in my reticule to post once I had opened a bank account.

First, I found a pawnbroker shop. Its window displayed all sorts of things, from jewellery to clothes, household goods, and even false teeth. I opened the door to the shop after telling Jane to wait for me outside. A bell tinkled inside, and the shopkeeper, a man, came out and looked at me, assessing me.

"Yes, Miss?" he asked.

I told him that I had some jewellery that I wanted to sell.

"And who's jewellery, is it?" he asked, as if he didn't believe me. He had a cocky look on his face as if he was used to all sorts of people coming into his shop to sell things and lying to him about where they obtained the goods from. Probably stolen goods.

"My sister's," I lied.

"And how does your sister feel about the fact that you are selling her jewellery?"

"I don't know," I said, "She's dead."

His face changed from disbelief to shame. "I am sorry about that, Miss."

I put the selection of Edwina's jewellery on the countertop and pushed it over to him. I could tell by the look in his eyes, which he quickly disguised, that he liked what he saw.

After he had looked at it all with his monocular, which is the small device jewellers use, he hummed and haa'd, then wrote a figure down on a piece of paper and pushed it over to me. I looked at the figure and went to pick up the jewellery, shaking my head in disappointment. "I don't think we can do business, sir. I will take it elsewhere," I said. I had read in some books back at Seaward Manor about haggling, never expecting to have to put the theory to the test.

His hand shot out to cover mine. "Now, now, Miss, let's not be hasty. Name your price, and I will see if we can reach an agreement."

I looked at the figure he had written down, doubled it, wrote the figure down on the same piece of paper and pushed it back over to him.

"Oh, come now, Miss, I have got to make some profit out of it," he cried.

"I would have thought ten per cent profit for you would be reasonable," I told him, reducing my figure by ten per cent and pushing it back to him.

"I was thinking twenty per cent," came his reply.

"Fifteen per cent, and we have a deal," I told him, holding my hand out for him to shake.

Reluctantly, he shook my hand and said, "Remind me next time I see you come to my shop again to put up the 'closed' sign."

I laughed. He counted out the figure we had agreed to in notes and gave it to me. I immediately pushed it into my reticule. "Nice doing business with you," I said as I left the shop, feeling quite pleased with myself and my negotiating skills.

As we walked along the street, I grinned. Considering I had never 'haggled' before, I was pretty pleased with my efforts and the results.

We passed the organ grinder with the monkey. Jane stood for a while and watched. The monkey scrambled to sit before us and shook the tin cup at her for money, so I took her arm and pulled her away.

Walking to the bank wasn't too far, and I told Jane to wait for me just inside the door. The bank was approached by three steps up to the central part of the building, flanked by two massive columns. Inside the central part of the bank were two large mahogany counters, stretching practically the entire length of the enormous room, placed on opposite walls. There were several positions, and bank clerks stood behind to deal with customers.

It was busy for that time of the day, but I saw an empty position at the counter and walked up to it.

"Yes, Miss?" the bank clerk asked.

"I wish to open a bank account. I am the ward of the Dowager Countess of Orkney," I told him. I thought a bit of name-dropping might help.

He looked impressed. "Could you please wait here a moment, Miss?"

I nodded, and he disappeared briefly before returning with an impressive-looking white-haired gentleman dressed in a black suit, brilliant white shirt, and silver-grey waistcoat with a silver pocket watch attached.

"Miss...?" he asked.

"Braemar, Julia Braemar," I supplied.

"I am Mr Edwards, the manager. Would you like to follow me, Miss Braemar?" He led me to an office at the rear of the building, opened the door for me to enter, and then followed me in, closing the door behind us.

We both sat down, then Mr Edwards rested his elbows on the desk and steepled his fingers, "I trust Lady McKenzie is well?" I nodded and thanked him for asking.

"How may I be of service to you today, Miss Braemar?"

I told him that I wished to open a bank account, opened my reticule and drew out the money, keeping a little back for myself.

Mr Edwards counted the money out and raised an eyebrow. He told me about the various interest rates and asked if I would like to proceed. I nodded my head. He asked if I had any proof of identification, and I showed him the legal papers with my name change; then, he pulled a little book from his desk drawer, wrote my name inside the front cover and entered the amount of money I had given him. "If you need to withdraw any money or pay in any more, bring the book in, and we will update it and add the interest. You are doing the sensible thing, Miss Braemar, putting your money into the bank." He handed me my bank book and stood to shake my hand. I thanked him and left his office.

When I reached Jane, I told her we would find a tea shop and treat ourselves. I felt relieved that I wasn't carrying so much money around with me. The amount of money I had from the sale of Edwina's jewellery was quite substantial; added to the funds from Gramps and what was left from Mrs Trevelgue, it was a tidy amount that I had opened my bank account with. It was a relief to have it gone because I feared pickpockets, as plenty of urchins were running around.

We found a little tea shop with ladies with their maids, mothers with their daughters and gentlemen with their ladies, seated at various tables. I found us an empty one, and once we were seated, a waitress came over and took our order. She returned later with a teapot, cups, saucers, milk and sugar and two plates and forks. When she had done that, she went away and wheeled a trolley over to us to choose a cake each. I could tell by the look on her face that Jane was enjoying herself and my little treat.

We called at the post office after leaving the tea shop and posted the letter to Mrs Watson. Afterwards, we decided to return home. Jane and I had enjoyed our little outing. I hoped that it would be one of many for us. Although in the eyes of the public, Jane was my maid and I was her mistress, in my eyes, we were equals. I hadn't been brought up in a life of privilege any more than she was.

All in all, it had been a good day out. When we got back to Moldova Square, the footman told me that I had had some boxes delivered from the Modiste, and they were in my room. I tried not to run upstairs, but I was so excited to see what had been delivered.

Two large boxes lay on my bed, and a smaller, round one. A riding habit in deep purple wool was in one of the large boxes, with black velvet on the collar, cuffs and buttons. Another smaller circular box was also on my bed. I opened the smaller box to see my riding hat. In the other large box was an evening gown in a buttermilk-coloured velvet, cut low over my breasts and draped in the front to gather into a waterfall-style bustle at the back. When

Jane saw it, her mouth dropped open. "Oh, Miss Julia, that looks beautiful."

I thought that in the shop, it looked quite a dull colour when I saw the material on the roll, but when I held it up in front of me and looked in the mirror, I thought that it might look quite fetching on me. I handed it to Jane to hang in the wardrobe, then held up the riding habit before me and looked in the mirror. I couldn't wait to go riding in the Row. I enjoyed the freedom and independence that horse riding afforded me. That outfit and Edwina's altered clothes also went into my wardrobe.

When I first wore Edwina's clothes, I thought they looked beautiful compared to what I had been wearing, but compared to the evening gown and riding habit, they all looked plain and outdated. I asked Lady Mary if I could go out riding in the Row in my new habit, but she said it would get dark soon, so I should leave the excursion until morning, weather permitting.

"What was in the other box, Julia?" she asked.

I told her that that was the buttermilk velvet evening gown.

"Madame Yvonne thought that you could carry that colour very well with your colouring, whereas someone with blonde hair would make them look rather bland. You will be able to wear it for the music concert next week. Madam Yvonne predicts that you will be betrothed if you are not married by the end of the season. We shall have to wait and see, I think. Shall we see what is happening in Troy, Julia?"

I knew Lady Mary was referring to Homer, so I picked up the green leather-bound book and continued from where we had left.

The nights were drawing in, the curtains were being closed, and candles lit earlier and earlier.

When I went upstairs to change for dinner, Jane came to me and asked what flowers I liked the scent of. I told her I loved the smell of lilacs and asked her why.

"Dorcas said that she would show me how to make perfume for you based on the perfume of the flowers that you liked."

"But lilacs don't flower till the spring, Jane," I told her.

"Dorcas has collected the blossoms from all sorts of flowers, from when they flowered this spring gone."

I raised my eyebrows in surprise and asked her to prepare a bath for me. I lay in hot, scented bath water made from fragrant bath oils. It looked like I may be staying for the season, after all. Further than that, I didn't know. I dare not look too far ahead.

The next morning was misty but dry, so I asked Lady Mary if I could ride in the Row.

"I suppose you want to wear your new riding habit." She smiled indulgently at me over the top of her glasses. "Very well, but make sure you take William, the groom, with you and don't ride without him. Do you understand, Julia?"

"Yes, Ma'am."

I returned to my room to put on my new riding habit: a hat, gloves, and long, shiny black leather boots that had been delivered the previous day.

I stood before my wardrobe mirror and looked at myself with my riding hat veil pulled over my face and tucked under my chin. I could not believe I was the same girl who had left Cornwall. What would Mrs Watson think of me if she saw me? I looked like a sophisticated young lady of the ton.

I walked to the stables and introduced myself to William. He looked nearly as old as Gramps had when I last saw him. He had a warm, friendly smile, a balding head, and was about a head taller than me.

"I heard there was a new Miss at the house," he said. "I am pleased to meet you, Miss Julia. I thought that I would saddle Star for you. Come get to know your mount while I fetch the side saddle from the tack room."

William showed me the stall where Star was kept. She certainly suited her name, a dappled grey and white mare with a snow-white mane and tail. I stroked her nose and petted her. I had picked up an apple from the house on my way out and, holding it out to her in my palm, gave it to her. She munched at it happily until William returned carrying a side saddle for me.

"I think I need to raise the stirrup, Miss Julia. It won't take but a moment, and then we can set off," he told me as he fixed the side saddle on Star and shortened the stirrup.

Once William altered the stirrup, he pulled out a small stool for me to mount Star.

I arranged my skirt to cover my legs, picked up the riding crop, and waited for William to mount his horse; then, we were off. I let William lead the way.

Although the weather was not as good as it had been the previous day, the Row was still dry, but the fog clung to the ground and the trees as if they were covered in a sheet of the finest muslin, and spider webs clung to the bushes like the finest silver filigree. People were already in the Row, but I noticed it was mainly men riding horseback. I don't think the weather was fine enough for the ladies (the damp air might ruin their coiffure). Still, I didn't care. I loved the fog. It made me feel like I was the only person around; all the other figures were just wraiths.

William and I started to ride in the Row. When we passed gentlemen out riding, they would tip their hats to me. I nodded back in acknowledgement. There were one or two open carriages, where the inhabitants were well wrapped up against the cold, with blankets over their laps,

One carriage came up beside us, and I looked inside. "Lord Melbourne?" I said, surprised to see him in the Row.

"Good morning, Miss Trev—" He started calling me by my fraudulent name, so I quickly spoke up, interrupted him, and informed him of my new name.

"It's Braemar now, Mr Lamb. Lady Mary wanted me to change it to her family name," I explained. William, my groom, sat his horse a discreet distance away so that he wasn't eavesdropping.

"Well, it seems you are certainly settling in London, Miss Braemar." In the weak daylight, I had more chance to inspect Lord Melbourne. I knew he was older than me, maybe somewhere between my father and Gramps age, but he was still handsome with dark hair, even if silver touched his temples and sideburns.

"Lady Mary has been very kind to me. I don't know how I will ever repay her for all she has done for me, even in this short time." I told him.

He laughed, "I am sure that she would not do it for repayment but enjoying the company. I had heard that she doesn't go out much these days."

"Oh, I think she will be getting out more in the coming months," I told him.

"Oh, how so?"

"Well, we are going to a musical concert next week, and we went shopping a week or so ago, so I think that maybe I am getting her out more."

"I hope so. Is the concert of one composer, or is it various ones?"

"Paganini, and another, although I can't remember the name. Lady Mary says I have probably not heard of them before, but Lady Mary thinks I might enjoy it."

By now, the carriage had stopped, and I had reined in Star to stand and talk to Lord Melbourne.

"I shall probably see you there then, as I am now in the city for a few weeks before I return to Brocket Hall. I also enjoy various composers, so I think I might enjoy it. At least I shall be in the city until after Christmas, so we will probably bump into each other again over the coming weeks."

"I look forward to that, sir." I told him, "Lady Mary would like to see you again, sir, I am sure. Would you care to call on her one day?"

Mr Lamb nodded, "I certainly shall, Miss Braemar."

"I would also like to thank you for sheltering us in the fog and introducing me to Lady Mary. I am sure that..."

"Miss Julia...Miss Braemar, think nothing of it," he replied, holding his hands up to stop me from saying any more while his coachman could hear.

He lifted his hat to me, and we both went our separate ways.

I was pleased that I had met Lord Melbourne again. I liked him, even though there was a significant age difference. Yet there was no comparison when I thought of Lord Melbourne and my father, although probably similar in age. Lord Melbourne was still a fine figure of a man, whereas my father had always looked his age, and of course, they dressed differently. My father always dressed for comfort and warmth as he did his duties, which I would have thought was physically more strenuous. Lord Melbourne seemed to be dressed to the height of fashion, as befitting a gentleman about town and a member of parliament and the ton. Still, the most strenuous thing he did was attending to his orchids, as he had told me over that first meal at his home.

William and I carried on trotting around the Row, with even more gentlemen lifting their hats to me. Never had I had so much attention before, but I felt that I was a new person, emerging, like a butterfly from a chrysalis, and this was the start of a new life where I was the centre of attention and not Edwina, for once, and it felt good. I didn't want to dwell on what would happen when Lady Mary discovered she had been harbouring a fraud under her roof. Whenever I thought about the possibility, my palms would sweat, my mouth would dry out, and my pulse would increase in fear. I just wanted to enjoy my life as it was at that moment, however temporary it may be.

William and I trotted back to the stables, where I slid from Stars back to the floor and petted Star's nozzle. She sniffed my hand again, I think, hoping for another apple. I laughed, "You are greedy, Miss. You can have another apple another day, but I only brought one."

William started to undo Star's saddle, "Well, Miss Julia, I think you had a rather successful morning in the Row."

My brows creased together in confusion, which he noted as he slid Star's saddle from her back and held it before him.

"You don't think people go to the Row just to exercise their horses, Miss Julia; they do that as well, but they mainly go to see and be seen. You caught the attention of several gentlemen, including Lord Melbourne."

"Lord Melbourne came to my rescue when my coach ended up in a ditch and helped me continue here. I don't think Lord Melbourne would wish to be considered a suitor, William," I explained to the groom.

He cocked his head to one side and, with a twinkle in his eye, said, "Well, you never know. He is a widower and very eligible, and it is obvious that he likes you."

I told William not to read too much into Lord Melbourne's attention and then left him to rub Star down and give her a bag of oats.

When I returned home, the Butler, Mr Ritson, told me that another three boxes had arrived for me. I thanked him and went to my bedroom.

Jane was waiting for me. "I didn't open them, even though I was tempted," she said just as I opened the door to my bedroom. I hadn't even gotten into the room!

I grinned, "Well, I'm here now, so hang up my coat, and we'll open them together." I don't think I had ever seen Jane move so fast. "Anyone would think they were your clothes, Jane," I told her.

"Well, you will be wearing them, and I am dressing you, so they are more or less like my clothes," she said cockily. I grinned at her. She knew that I wouldn't be angry with her. We had a better relationship than that. Jane had already been clothed in Lady Mary's household uniform, a deep lilac dress, white collar and cuffs, and a small white mob cap, but no apron. Lady's maids had no need for aprons, so she told. "It's a lot nicer than the black and white uniform at Seaward Manor," she told me. I think she liked her new uniform.

I thought about our difference in position: I was the young lady of the house, and Jane was just my maid. I sat on my bed and looked at her.

"Jane, don't you wish you were in my position?"

She looked at me, "You mean me being the young miss?"

I nodded, "Yes, I am no better than you, yet I am in a privileged position."

"Oh no, Miss Julia, you have an education. I am not clever enough. Besides, you have still improved my position. I am now properly a lady's maid to you, and I have my own bed and a nice uniform. This is all I ever wanted and more. If you marry well, I will be even better off. I know that you will never be unkind to me. I am happy and content."

I sighed, "Well, as long as you are happy. I just thought that our positions were unfair on you."

"Oh no, Miss Julia, this is all I ever wanted. To live in a big house and be some kind lady's personal maid, where I could dress her in beautiful clothes, with beautiful jewellery and do her hair in lovely styles.

"Now, are you going to open those boxes, or will you make me wait to see what's inside?" she grinned at me.

When I opened the boxes, I found two morning gowns and one tea gown.

"You'll soon be able to get rid of all of your old clothes," Jane said as I lifted the new gowns out of the boxes and held them up against me, going to my wardrobe mirror and looking at how they looked on me.

"I suppose I could donate them to charity," I mused. "It would be no use offering them to you since you have taken them all in and shortened them to fit me."

Jane cocked her head to one side, "I could never be in your position Miss Julia. I am just thankful that you brought me to London with you. We have been out in the city. You have taken me to a tea shop, and I have had fancy cakes, and we haven't been here that long yet. What else might happen the longer we stay here? I know we all have our dreams. When I was a child, we, my family all lived in a two-roomed shack. I always dreamed of living in a posh house and look after a kind young lady, and to have my own bed was a luxury I could only dream of. You see there were eight children plus my parents, so it was very cramped."

"You've never talked about your family before. What happened to your siblings? Did they all go into service like you?"

"I had three older brothers, but they all died young, they worked down the mines."

"For the Trevelgues?"

She nodded sadly. "They died in the mine not long after Mr Trevelgue died. Three of my sisters went to Truro. I don't know what they do there, and then Ma has my little sister who I suppose will go into service when she is old enough. So, you see, I am the lucky one of the family Miss Julia."

I could not imagine what Jane's life must have been like as a child. Ten people crushed together in a two-roomed shack. It must have been dreadful. It made me realise how lucky I had been in my life, living at the Lodge with my own bedroom and no other siblings but plenty of love, food and my own space. If I wanted companionship, I only had to walk a short distance into the village, and I had lots of playmates.

"As long as you are content, Jane."

"Yes, I am content. This was all I ever wanted," Jane said, then shook her head, looking at Edwina's clothes. "I could ask Dorcas what she does with Lady Mary's cast-offs?" Jane said.

"That's a good idea," I said, "Has she stopped teasing you about fainting yet?"

"More or less. Oh, I have this for you, Miss Julia?"

She pulled a small bottle from her dress pocket and unstopped it for me to smell. I caught the beautiful perfume of lilacs. "You made this?" I asked in surprise.

Jane's face lit up with pleasure. "What do you think?"

"It smells of lilacs," I said incredulously. "How did you do it?"

"Dorcas taught me," she said proudly. "She's teaching me many things about being a good lady's maid and making our mistress look beautiful. I never realised all that it involved before, but I am enjoying it, and I want you to be proud of me, Miss Julia."

I took her hand and squeezed it. "I am proud of you, Jane. You are not only my maid but also my best friend. I am glad that you came with me to London."

I was so pleased to see such a proud smile on her face. It made me realise that it doesn't take money or wealth to make a person happy. I realised that with Jane just then, and when I was in Cornwall with Gramps, my father, and Mrs Watson, fate decided to step in, and I ended up with Mrs Trevelgue and, unfortunately, Edwina. However, fate stepped in again. She took Edwina, and here I ended up with Lady Mary. Here, I had been given another chance to improve myself and my status and marry well, but I wasn't going to marry just anyone. A title meant nothing to me without love. I would see what happened during the Season, that is, if Lady Mary still wished to have me under her roof.

I woke up every day and thought about telling Lady Mary the truth. Each day, I seemed to be getting deeper and deeper into this fraudulent life, and the longer I stayed, the deeper I sank. I often looked at the bank account book and the amount of money I had deposited, and I wondered if there was enough money to support Jane and myself, but I had to be honest. I was enjoying myself. I liked my life in Moldova Square and found that contrary to Mrs Travelgue's description, I liked Lady Mary too. I kept telling myself that I would tell her after we had been to the concert. I just wanted to enjoy something of London, something of the life Mrs Trevelgue had tempted me to, then I would tell Lady Mary, or I would leave and leave Lady Mary a note explaining what Mrs Trevelgue had asked me to do.

The following morning, at eleven o'clock, according to the grandfather clock in the hallway, there was a knock at the front door again. I thought it might be more clothes, but shortly after, there was a knock on my bedroom door. One of the footmen told me that Lady Mary requested my presence in the drawing room as Viscount Melbourne had arrived.

"Wear one of your new morning gowns, Miss Julia," Jane prompted me. She didn't ask me which gown I wanted to wear but just went to the wardrobe, which was filling up with my new clothes. She brought out a dress that looked like tweeds in heather and emerald green colours. "That will bring out the colour of your eyes," Jane said. She had already brushed and styled my hair but decided to add an emerald green velvet ribbon. I had put pearl studs in my ears, as the holes had healed with me following Dorcas's instructions, and I wore a simple single string of pearls from Edwina's jewellery.

"There now. I think you are ready," she said proudly.

I stood up, looked in the wardrobe mirror, and smiled my approval. Jane looked at me as an artist would look at a painting they had done and knew it was good. I owed my look to Jane and thanked her.

I knew they were talking about me when I entered the drawing room. I curtseyed to Mr Lamb, who took my hand and kissed it. "Miss Braemar, how are you?"

I told him that I was very well. He smiled appreciatively. "What happened to the young girl that came up from Cornwall? Goodness, how you have changed. I predict you will have a line of suitors queueing all around the Square when you have made your debut," he continued.

I could feel myself blushing.

"I shall escort you and Lady Mary to the musical concert tomorrow evening, as I have neglected you since you arrived. I apologise for that."

"There is no need for apologies, sir; I am sure that you have more important things to do than chaperone us around," I said to him.

"Yes, Melbourne, think nothing of it," Lady Mary told him.

Lady Mary rang the little crystal bell beside her and ordered tea for us all.

When one of the maids brought the tray in, Lady Mary asked me to pour. I knew what she was up to straight away, highlighting my achievements. She watched every move I made pouring the tea and smiled her approval.

"What is happening in the house, Melbourne?" Lady Mary asked.

"There is talk of the abolition of slavery. Prince Albert wants to give a speech in support of the abolition."

"Where do you stand on it, Lord Melbourne?" I asked him.

He smiled at me as I handed him his cup of tea. "What do you think, Miss Braemar?" he asked, turning the question back on me.

I had been reading about the slave trade in the newspapers, so I felt I could give a relatively well-informed answer.

"I don't think any human being should be able to own another human being. How would we feel if the tables were turned on us? I am certain that we would not stand for working for someone and not being paid for it. We stole these slaves from their own country, from their families and shipped them across the oceans to work for us, most likely in terrible conditions, probably treating them little or no better than animals. It is inhumane," I told him quite passionately.

"I think, Miss Braemar, that if women were allowed in the house, then you would be there, shaming all the selfish men that want to retain their slaves. You made an excellent case for abolition. I agree wholeheartedly with your sentiments. Bravo." I felt a warm glow of pride begin to burn inside me. I looked across to Lady Mary, who was smiling proudly at me!

"Julia, I was telling Melbourne about your talent at the pianoforte. I told him that when you play, you talk about what you imagine while playing. What pictures does the music invoke in you? It is fascinating to see how her mind interprets the music, Melbourne. Play something for us, Julia, Schubert or Chopin. I think Mr Lamb would enjoy either."

I sat at the piano and played Chopin and Schubert, describing the scenes I saw within the music. At the end, Lady Mary clasped her hands together in joy, "What did I tell you, Melbourne, a very accomplished pianist?"

Viscount Melbourne agreed. "An accomplished pianist indeed, with a vivid imagination and a good horsewoman." He smiled at me. "Yes, I predict a string of suitors queueing around the Square, Lady Mary."

He sat talking more about various bills being debated in the commons, then said it was time for him to leave. "I shall collect you both at seven o'clock tomorrow evening. Until then." He bowed over our hands and left us.

"Lady Mary, are you matchmaking?" I asked when we were on our own again.

"Melbourne would be a good catch; he has money and a title, and it is obvious that he has taken a great interest in you. He is also widowed."

"Would you tell me about his wife, Ma'am?" I asked her, trying to get her away from the subject of Lord Melbourne being a suitor for me.

"Caroline Ponsonby, as she was. She was a wild one. Her mother was nearly as bad. She had her...amours and Caroline was certainly no better. Even after she married Mr Lamb as he was then, she acted like a mad woman. She had a rather public affair with Byron, the poet, and she wasn't discrete about it either. Not at all. All of London knew about it. Byron toyed with her for a while, then cast her aside when he grew tired of her. There were tears, a suicide bid, oh not quietly behind closed doors, oh no, that wasn't Caro's style, but very publicly at a dinner party. She slit her wrists. Blood was everywhere, according to all the reports. Of course, she didn't succeed. She tried every way she could to get Byron back while Melbourne remained quietly on the sidelines. She then had an affair with the Duke of Wellington. Who would have wanted it to be kept secret if it had carried on? But knowing Caro', as many called her, secret or discreet were not words in her vocabulary, so Wellington ditched her. She wrote a few books (not that I read any of them,) then gradually faded from sight and died. She never became Viscountess, as she died before Lamb got his title. After the affair with Byron was well and truly over, she called him quite publicly, saying that he was mad, bad, and dangerous to know. She got that right, but I would say the same also referred to her. Since her death, Melbourne has never remarried."

"So, is Lord Byron the same age as Mr Lamb if he was having an affair with his wife?"

"No, Caro' was quite a bit younger than Mr Lamb, and although Byron was older than Caro', he was still younger than Mr Lamb.

Despite her affairs, William still stood beside his wife; why, I do not know, he certainly had the grounds to divorce her, but he is an honourable man. You could do worse Julia."

"I don't think Lord Melbourne is interested in me in that way, Ma'am," I finally told her, getting back to the subject of her matchmaking.

"Only time will tell, my dear. Only time will tell," she replied, a grin on her face like a Jewish matchmaker. "You could do worse," she repeated.

I knew that I could do worse, but Lord Melbourne was too old for me, although I enjoyed his company. He was fascinating, but I doubted he was any more attracted to me than I was to him.

Chapter Six

"So, Lord Melbourne is escorting you and Lady Mary to this musical evening, Miss Julia?" Jane said as she dressed me.

"Yes, and I think she is doing a little matchmaking."

"You and Lord Melbourne?" she asked, astonished.

I nodded.

"How do you feel about that?" Jane asked as she was styling my hair. Lady Mary had 'advised' me to wear the cream velvet gown, now hanging on the front of my wardrobe, waiting for me to step into it. For the time being, it was my only evening gown, so I had no choice.

"I don't know. I have met him a few times, and he is very nice. We seem to get on well together, but I suppose that being young, I want to be romantically swept off my feet, which, although very nice, Lord Melbourne does not do that. Lady Mary said that his first wife had a bit of a reputation, and of course, she is dead now, but he has never given me any indication that he is interested in me in that way. Maybe after the way his first wife behaved, because apparently, she wasn't very discrete in her dalliances, maybe he doesn't want to risk it again."

A knock came at my bedroom door, and Dorcas came in with a small, flat box. "These belonged to your...Lady Mary's daughter,

Miss Julia. Lady Mary thought they might go well with your gown this evening."

Dorcas placed the green leather box on my dressing table and left.

When I opened the box, I saw a set of jewellery: a five-row pearl choker with a large emerald clasp, a bracelet, and matching earrings. I couldn't speak. They were beautiful. I never expected to wear such beautiful jewellery or, for that matter, such a gorgeous gown.

"That sorts that out," Jane said with some authority. "I will intertwine cream and emerald velvet ribbons in your hair to pick up the colours from your eyes and jewellery. I think it will tie them all together," Jane said, fixing the choker around my throat so that the emerald clasp faced forward, and threading the ribbons among my curls. I didn't ask her to fit my earrings as she was still squeamish, and I couldn't risk her fainting again.

She looked at me in the mirror with a proud smile. She had done my hair in curls with a single thick ringlet hanging over my shoulder. I fitted the earrings in and put on the bracelet, then stepped into my gown that was off my shoulders and came into a 'v' over my breasts. The front of the gown was quite simple, but it gathered behind into a bustle. "A cream fan to complete the look, I think," Jane said as she went to one of the shelves in my wardrobe and brought out a cream silk and lace fan that Lady Mary had bought me on our initial shopping spree, then handed it to me. Jane stood back to take in the full effect of her 'creation', as she called it.

"Oh, Miss Julia, you look beautiful!" she cried.

I looked at myself in the full-length wardrobe mirror and couldn't believe my eyes. I had always thought Edwina was beautiful, but the person who stared back at me... I felt tears come to my eyes. I wished my father and Gramps could see me.

"Don't you go crying Miss Julia, you don't want to go out on your first outing with red puffy eyes," Jane told me, but I could see that she wasn't far from tears either as she looked at me, her 'creation.'

While we were at Madam Yvonne's, Lady Mary had ordered me a long evening cape in cream velvet trimmed with fur. When I went downstairs, the footman draped my cape around my shoulders. After Lady Mary had given me her final inspection and nodded, she said, "Yes, you will do quite well, Julia."

Just as the grandfather clock in the hall chimed seven o'clock, Lord Melbourne's coachman knocked on the front door.

Lady Mary and I walked down the steps and were handed into the coach, where Lord Melbourne sat.

"Good evening, ladies. I trust you are both well?" he said as we settled onto our seats in his carriage.

Lady Mary and I told him we were and sat facing him for the short journey.

The entrance to the concert hall was bustling, so much so that I couldn't fully appreciate the décor above the crowds. Before entering the auditorium, a footman took Lady Mary's and my cloaks, and Lord Melbourne handed his evening cape over to the footman.

Lady Mary smiled as she caught Mr Lamb looking at me appreciatively.

"Miss Braemar, you look stunning. I am sure plenty of gentlemen here this evening will wish to make your acquaintance."

"And will you be one of them, Melbourne?" Lady Mary asked.

I could have died!

I felt my face colour up and couldn't look Lord Melbourne in the eye.

"It would be a fool who wouldn't, Lady Mary," he replied very diplomatically, I thought. Thankfully, he offered Lady Mary his arm while I followed behind as they walked into the auditorium to our allotted seats. Once he had seen Lady Mary settled in her seat and she had begun talking to her neighbour, I touched Lord Melbourne's arm.

"Lord Melbourne, I can only apologise for Lady Mary's..." I struggled to find the right word without being rude.

He interrupted me. "My dear Miss Braemar, think nothing of it. As a widower, Lady Mary wouldn't be the first sponsor to direct their ward in my direction. Do not worry, my dear, for fear of embarrassing me."

"Embarrassing you?" I said incredulously. "I know she embarrassed me." I laughed, trying to cover up a very uncomfortable moment.

Suddenly, a male voice called his name and moved over to us, "Melbourne, I haven't seen much of you recently."

Lord Melbourne smiled at me, "Rutledge, may I introduce Miss Julia Braemar, Lady Mary McKenzie's ward."

The gentleman standing before me looked at me like a dog, looking at a nice juicy bone. I could feel the skin on my neck crawl. He looked at me the way Mark Trevelgue had looked, and I was uncomfortable.

He lifted my hand and placed a hot kiss on it. "Well, now, things are looking up, Miss Braemar. Are you to be presented next season?"

"Yes, sir," I said, trying to be polite for Lord Melbourne's sake.

"Well, I hope we will see more of you before the start of the season. Are you in the city for the Christmas period?"

"Lady Mary has not said to the contrary, so I presume so," I told him.

"Well, I hope you will attend the ball on Christmas Eve at Lord and Lady Muggeridge's house. I believe there is another ball on Christmas Day and one on New Year's Eve."

"I'm afraid I do not know what Lady Mary has planned, sir," I replied uncomfortably as I noticed he was still holding my hand.

"In that case, I shall have to call on you to insist that she escorts you to them both. You will make the Christmas season even more festive," he said, still holding my hand.

Lord Melbourne touched my arm, "I think they are just about ready to start, Miss Braemar. We should take our seats."

I nodded, made a quick curtsey to Lord Rutledge, who finally let go of my hand, and then thankfully moved back to Lady Mary. Lord Melbourne ensured I was comfortably seated beside Lady Mary and sat beside me.

He leaned closer and whispered, "I hope you enjoy the music. I am sure you will, with your appreciation of music."

I closed my eyes within the first few bars, imagining dancers in colourful costumes dancing around a large campfire. Then, as the tempo changed to something slower, I could imagine dusky maidens carrying large baskets of flowers on their heads, sweeping and dipping to the music. Not all the music made me conjure pictures in my mind, but it was all very melodic and delightful. I was thoroughly enjoying my first concert.

The music ended, and we were at the interval where glasses of punch were offered.

Three gentlemen came over and spoke to Lady Mary, who introduced me to them: Lord Robert Beaumont, Duke of Rochester, was the first gentleman to walk over to us. Although not as tall as Lord Melbourne or Rutledge, he was very broad of shoulder and muscled. I liked him immediately. His open face readily smiled, and he had a cheeky twinkle in his grey eyes.

His dark hair swept from his forehead, and the back was cut so that it just skimmed his evening jacket collar. As soon as he smiled at me with that cheeky twinkle in his eyes, I felt drawn to him. He looked like he didn't take much in life seriously, but I could have been wrong.

"How are you enjoying the concert, Miss Braemar?" he asked.

I told him that I enjoyed it very much.

"I thought that you had," he said. I raised my eyebrows in question, and he laughed. "You had your eyes closed; unless you were asleep?" he teased me.

"Oh no, certainly not, sir; I appreciate the music better with my eyes closed."

He looked at me again, "Have you been riding in the Row?" he questioned, "I am sure I have seen you on a dapple-grey mare. Was that you, Miss Braemar?"

"It was, sir. The mare is called Star, which I think is aptly named," I told him.

"Yes, indeed, she is very aptly named. I breed horses and do believe your Star was one from my stables. Have you been in London long?" he asked.

"I travelled up from Cornwall a few weeks ago; until then, I had never left the county."

"Ah, the county of smugglers and shipwrecks," he teased me. His eyes twinkled, and I noticed a dimple appeared on either side of his mouth when he smiled.

"So, I hear, but I've never witnessed them."

"I should hope not," he said in mock horror, "as you would either be a smuggler, a wrecker, or a witness, in which case you would probably have fled from the county in fear for your life." His eyes twinkled again, and I knew that he was teasing me.

There was a gong banged to signal the beginning of the second half.

"I may see you around the Row again one morning, Miss Braemar?" he said, bowed and kissed my hand. I thought my heart might jump from my breast when he did that. I couldn't understand what was happening to me with the Duke of Rochester. As soon as he looked at me, I felt butterflies. I was unused to talking to men or men of high standing, yet talking to Lord Melbourne or Rutledge never made me feel this way.

"More than likely, sir," I replied. Then I saw another gentleman looking at me, but he acknowledged the start of the second half, so he bowed and left.

The second half was another composer, another I had not heard of. Some of the music I wasn't so keen on. It wasn't as melodic, but then it flowed into another movement. Again, I closed my eyes and imagined a tall, masted ship sailing the seas, with the wind in its sails, billowing out as it gracefully moved through the waves like some stately matron.

I was sad when the concert ended. I had now found two more composers whose music I enjoyed. I began wondering if I could get the sheet music for a pianoforte.

I stood up and was about to move to where Lady Mary was talking to another lady and what looked like her daughter when a gentleman stood before me and bowed. I recognised him from the interval. I bobbed him a curtsey.

"I understand that you are Lady Mary's ward, Miss Braemar, is that right?" He was tall, very slim, and blonde-haired. "Charles Montague, Earl of Rothsay."

"Well, you know my name, sir."

"Indeed," he smiled. "I must admit I was eavesdropping. Did you enjoy the concert, Miss Braemar?"

"I did, sir, very much so."

"Who are your favourite composers, Miss Braemar?" he asked. I was pleased that he wasn't looking at me like Rutledge did. All the time Rutledge talked to me, his eyes roamed over my body as if he were gauging what I wore under my gown, and I felt most uncomfortable. At least when Lord Rothsay spoke, he looked straight into my eyes.

"Schubert, Chopin, I enjoyed certain pieces from this evening, but not all. Some were more melodic than others."

"So, it's the melody that attracts you?" the Earl asked me.

"On the whole, yes. Melodies conjure images in my mind when I play them," I told him.

"So, you play? What instrument do you play?" he asked me.

"The pianoforte."

Lady Mary came towards me then. "Julia, it's time we left, Rothsay," she said, acknowledging him before she turned.

"I hope to see more of you, Miss Braemar." Lord Rothsay said before I left with Lady Mary and Lord Melbourne.

I bobbed a curtsey and thanked him.

Lord Melbourne came to Lady Mary and me with our cloaks and put them around our shoulders. "Well, Miss Braemar, I think you have had quite a successful evening," he said as he laid my cloak around my shoulders.

As we sat in his coach to return to Moldova Square, I told him, "You will need to tell me more about the gentlemen I spoke with this evening, Mr Lamb."

Lady Mary looked at him and scowled, so I presumed that that must be left for another time.

"Maybe I could call by tomorrow to pick up our discussion?" he said as his coach arrived in Moldova Square.

"If it doesn't inconvenience you, Mr Lamb," I said.

"Not at all, Miss Braemar. May I call at eleven tomorrow morning?"

I looked to Lady Mary to see if she agreed to the visit. "That will do fine, Melbourne." She wished him a 'good evening' and thanked him for accompanying us. Then, she allowed him to help us down from his carriage.

We were sitting in the drawing room just after returning from the concert. Lady Mary was drinking a glass of ratafia, and I was drinking a glass of cordial. "Well, my dear, how did you enjoy this evening?"

I was in raptures about it. "It was wonderful, Ma'am. Thank you so much for taking me. Hearing music played by an orchestra gives it much more depth."

"And you had some gentlemen introduce themselves to you. What did you think of them?"

"I didn't like how Lord Rutledge looked at me," I told her.

Lady Mary raised her eyebrows in question.

"He looked like a dog eyeing a juicy bone," I told her. "If I am honest, I felt that he knew what I wore under my gown, and it was most disconcerting, and he didn't let go of my hand all the time he was talking to me."

Lady Mary laughed. "My dear Julia, you do have a way with words. Rutledge has somewhat of a reputation as a rake of the first order. So maybe you should stay away from him as much as possible. What about the others?"

"Lord Rochester seemed nice. He had a mischievous glint in his eye. He said that he had seen me riding in the Row. He told me that he bred horses, and Star was or had been one of his," I explained to her.

"Yes, I brought her from him a couple of years ago. She is a pretty thing and has a penchant for apples."

I laughed, "I know she likes her apples. I brought her one before I took her for a ride, and she was looking for another one after the ride," I told Lady Mary.

"I think it is good that you exercise her; otherwise, she will get quite fat. And Rothsay?" she prompted me. "What did you think of him?"

"He seemed quite pleasant," I told her. "We talked about the music, so I think we have something in common."

"And, of course, Melbourne?"

I hesitated, wondering how to approach the subject of Lady Mary trying matchmaking between Mr Lamb and myself.

"Lady Mary, Lord Melbourne is very kind to us, but I honestly don't think he is interested in me other than that of a friend. I was mortified when you asked him..."

"My dear Julia," Lady Mary said, interrupting me, "Sometimes men need a little nudge."

I took a cleansing breath before I spoke to her, "That wasn't a nudge, Ma'am; that was a definite push," I told her.

"I presume you didn't approve of me interfering, my dear?"

I hated to hurt or criticise her after all she had done for me, but I couldn't have her putting the men in an uncomfortable position, which I felt she had done with Lord Melbourne.

"Lady Mary. I am more grateful to you than I can say, but if anyone is interested in me, they should decide," I told her as kindly as I could.

Lady Mary didn't seem put out by what I had said but grinned at me, "I take it as being well and truly reprimanded," she told me but didn't look sorry for what she had said to Lord Melbourne.

I felt guilty then and blushed. "Lady Mary, I am sorry... You will guide me regarding a marriage, and I promise that I will not cause you any embarrassment by my actions, but I think the final decision should be between me and whatever gentleman offers for me."

She patted my hand, "No, Julia, you are right. I presume you want a love match like my daughter."

"As I said, Ma'am, you will guide me, but in the end, it must be up to the gentleman and myself, but I will not bring scandal to your door."

Lady Mary sighed in resignation, "Yes, my dear, I suppose you are right. Well, it is still the early days. There is plenty of time. You haven't even been presented yet."

I felt bad. Lady Mary owed me nothing when she had given me everything, and I wasn't even a relative. Once again, I felt uncomfortable lying to this kind lady and was tempted to tell her the truth. I told myself I might tell her the truth after Christmas or the New Year.

Lady Mary finished her drink and said that it was time for bed. I followed not long behind her; my mind was still filled with the music from the evening.

The longer I stayed in Moldova Square, the more I wanted to stay. Lady Mary certainly wasn't as Mrs Trevelgue had described her. I thought she was mellowing, certainly towards me, and repeatedly I felt that pang of guilt.

I retired to my bedroom. Again, I felt guilt gnawing at my insides. I caught sight of myself in the wardrobe mirror and wondered where Julia Beddoes had gone. It certainly wasn't the girl that looked back at me. I began to believe the saying that 'clothes maketh the man,' or woman in my case. The cream velvet gown, I thought vainly, made me look nearly beautiful. I wasn't so vain as to think I looked lovely, but I seemed to be attracting the attention of some gentleman.

Jane helped me out of my gown and asked me about my evening. I told her about the gentlemen, the music, Lady Mary, and her remarks to Lord Melbourne.

"Oh goodness, Miss Julia, what did he say?"

"He was the perfect gentleman and sidestepped the comment. I did apologise to him for Lady Mary's question. He told me not to worry about it, as Lady Mary wouldn't be the first to push their unmarried ward in his direction."

"He is such a kind gentleman," Jane replied as she hung my gown in the wardrobe.

I agreed with her as she began brushing my hair. "He will call tomorrow morning to tell me more about the gentlemen that spoke to me this evening."

"Did you like any of the gentlemen, Miss Julia?"

I yawned and told her it was early days. I climbed into bed; Jane wished me 'goodnight' and left me to sleep.

I did sleep well that night with the music from the concert going around in my mind.

The next morning was a dull grey day. The damp hung from the skeletal branches of the trees, and dark grey clouds covered the sun. It was one of those days when all you wanted to do was stay in front of a roaring fire and read or embroider, but certainly not stray far from your hearth.

Jane had dressed me in another of my morning gowns in a rust shade, which, again, she told me, complimented my colouring.

Lord Melbourne arrived promptly at eleven o'clock. He bowed over Lady Mary's hand, then mine. Lady Mary offered him tea, and he thanked her, then sat down. He pulled some paperwork from the inside of his jacket and handed it to me. "I thought you might like the sheet music from last night, Miss Braemar." It was as if he had read my mind from the night before. I thanked him and looked at the music. It was the two movements that I had enjoyed the most from the concert.

I sat down at the piano and began to play the Paginini piece.

"I never realised you could play by sight, Miss Braemar. I thought that you would need to practice for a while." Lord Melbourne's voice was raised in astonishment.

"It is not perfect by any means. It will need refinement, but ..."

"It is very impressive, my dear," he replied to me.

Lady Mary looked on proudly as I continued to play.

"You wanted to know more about the gentlemen from last evening, Lady Mary?"

As I played, my ears pricked up to hear what he had to say.

"So, Viscount Rutledge has had a few rather public affairs and is known as a Rake of the first order. I don't think any lady is safe in his presence. I think he has lost a few maids from his household because of... his nature, shall we say?" said Mr Lamb.

Lady Mary hummed, then asked him about the Duke of Rochester.

"Ah, now Rochester, I have known him for some years. He is a bit of a pugilist. He's quite a bit of a sportsman and very good with his fists. He inherited his Dukedom from an uncle, who was killed in France about eight years ago. The previous Duke was unmarried, so there were no children to inherit. He was married to the army. His younger brother, the present Duke's father, died of a severe case of influenza, so the title passed to Robert. Robert Beaumont, the present Duke is well-liked by his staff. A fair employer. He owns six properties around the country, including one here, although he prefers to stay in Kent. I know he is looking for a marriage this year, or should I say, next year, so he would be a good catch."

"A Duke, Julia," Lady Mary said. "What about the Earl of Rothsay?"

"The Earl has interests similar to Miss Braemar's, such as music. He is also known for his accomplishments on the pianoforte. As you can discern from his title, he is from Scotland. He inherited it from his father, who passed away some years ago. He seems a decent sort of person. I have never heard any scandal linked to him."

"He doesn't have a Scottish accent, Lord Melbourne," I noted.

"Rothsay was educated at Eaton and then went to Cambridge. During his informative years, I imagine he would have had the Scottish accent knocked out of him."

I was shocked, "Surely not literally, Lord Melbourne?" I asked.

He laughed. "No, Miss Braemar. Let me put your mind at rest on that matter. It was purely a turn of phrase, not an actual statement," he assured me.

As 'Ton Protocol' suggested, he finished his tea and stayed a little longer.

"Well, ladies, I have taken up enough of your time. I have things to do."

"Then we must take up no more of your time, Lord Melbourne," Lady Mary said.

Lord Melbourne stood and bowed over our hands, then took his leave.

The weather cleared somewhat when Melbourne left us, and the sun was trying to break through the clouds.

"May I go out for a ride, Lady Mary in the Row? The weather seems to have brightened up a little."

"Take William with you, dear," she said.

"Yes, Ma'am."

After changing into my riding habit, I went to get an apple from the kitchen, then went out to the stables for Star. As soon as she saw me, she snickered and nuzzled my hand. I gave her the apple from my hand and waited for William to saddle her. It was still bitterly cold outside, although plenty of people were out riding. The ladies were mainly riding in the safe confines of their carriages, wrapped in thick travelling blankets, keeping them warm.

Few were riding on their horses. William and I took the horses to a canter. Star loved the canter, but I could tell she wanted to go faster, so I touched my heel to her side, gave her her head and let her go. We raced forward with William following close behind, then Star slowed of her own accord and stopped.

William came to a halt beside me. "It looks like she's cast a shoe, Miss Julia."

I was about to get down and lead her, but I saw Lord Rutledge in his carriage, an attractive young lady with beautiful blonde hair by his side. He pulled up by us. "'Day, Miss Braemar. Is there a problem?'

Sitting with him and the young lady in his carriage certainly did not appeal to me, so I lied. "None whatsoever, my Lord. I'm just giving her a break after a good gallop."

"Oh... very well." I could see that he wasn't happy about my rejection. "In that case, we will take our leave of you." He lifted his hat and wished me a 'good day.' Then his carriage left us.

"Miss Julia, I could have taken the horses back to the stables," William told me as Lord Rutledge's carriage rode away.

"No, William. I am quite happy to walk her back." Once I saw that Lord Rutledge had left us, I slipped down from Star's back and took up her reins to begin the walk back to the stables.

We had been walking for only a few minutes when someone drew their horse to walk beside us. I looked up and saw the Duke of Rochester sitting astride a massive black beast whose coat was so dark and shiny that it had an almost blue tint. Seeing him made me smile. I couldn't help it. He had that devilish glint in his eye.

"Miss Braemar, it looks like your horse has cast a shoe. Do you want to borrow mine? I will walk Star back to the stables for you."

"I am quite content to walk, my Lord," I told him.

"Then may I walk with you?" he asked.

"Certainly, if you don't mind walking?"

"Not at all." He slipped down, took the horse's reins, and walked with me while William kept a respectable distance from us.

"I gather you enjoyed the second half of the concert last evening?" he said

"I did," I confirmed.

"You are wondering how I knew?" he said, grinning at me.

I nodded.

"You were listening with your eyes closed again." He grinned at me, and I noticed that two dimples came just by his mouth when he smiled, making his lips look full and inviting. His eyes crinkled up at the edges in merriment.

I gave myself a mental shake. This was only the second time I had met him, and I was already wondering how soft his lips would be!

"I must admit to doing the same thing. It enables me to let the music flow over me." He grinned, and his grey eyes twinkled with devilment. "It lets me shut out my surroundings and concentrate on the music."

"I tend to imagine scenes that the music invokes when I hear it," I told him.

"Ah, a lady with an imagination and, I think, a true appreciation of music." He smiled.

We walked and talked about music, and he told me more about himself. I never thought I would find a gentleman so open about himself and so easy to talk with.

"Rochester, is that not in Kent?" I asked him.

"The county is often called the 'Garden of England.' It is known for growing hops used to make beer."

"So, do you grow hops on your land?" I asked.

He nodded, "My main interest is breeding horses. As I told you last evening, your mare was one of mine. Lady Mary bought her from me two years ago."

"She likes apples," I told him.

"Are we talking about Lady Mary or the mare?" he teased me.

I laughed, "I cannot speak for Lady Mary, sir, but Star does."

He stroked Star and let her nuzzle his hand. "She is a beautiful piece of horse flesh. A pretty little filly."

"I presume that you are referring to Star?" I grinned back at him.

"Miss Braemar, you are a tease, I think."

"As are you, I think, your grace?" I couldn't help but smile at him and tease him in return.

We continued walking with William, following at a discrete distance behind us.

"So, how long ago did you leave Cornwall?"

"Only a couple of months ago."

"What do you think of London? Is this your first time in the big city?"

I told him that it was, and I found it fascinating.

"Was the concert your first outing?"

"Lady Mary didn't want me to go out until I was properly attired," I told him honestly.

"Well, you were certainly well-attired last evening. Am I to assume your 'attire' when you arrived from Cornwall was substandard?" he commented.

"What attire might be acceptable in Cornwall is far from acceptable here in the city." I could feel my cheeks flame at his compliment.

He could see my discomfort and changed the subject.

"Are you going to any of the balls over Christmas, Miss Braemar?"

I told him that Lady Mary had arranged for us to attend a Christmas and New Year's Eve ball.

"Then I hope I may claim a dance with you, Miss Braemar, as I will be certain to attend both."

We continued to walk. "May I ask you something personal?" he asked, his face turning serious.

I nodded, wondering what his personal question would be.

"Is there an understanding between Melbourne and yourself?" he asked, stopping and looking directly at me.

I wasn't sure what he meant by 'understanding,'. So, I remained silent.

"Has he offered for you?" he asked, clarifying his question.

I think I knew what he meant. "Has he proposed to me?" I tried to clarify his meaning.

He nodded.

"Heavens, no. Mr Lamb came to my rescue when my carriage ended in a ditch the day I arrived in London, and he offered to take me to Lady Mary. I suppose he is just a friend that has taken me under his wing."

"Only I noticed that you and the Dowager Countess were his guests at the concert."

I told him honestly that Lady Mary had embarrassed me by asking the Viscount if he intended himself for me. "I was mortified. I felt I had to apologise to him for her lack of tact."

"He would be a good match," Rochester told me.

"He is quite a bit older than me!"

"Does that preclude him from your idea of a suitor?"

"I have no preconceived ideas of a suitor, indeed, if I would be lucky enough to secure a proposal. Lord Melbourne has been very kind to me, but I don't think of him as anything more than a friend. I think he is at least old enough to be my father."

"I should imagine that you want the excitement of a season," the duke said. "No decent man would take that from you; well, none worth his salt," the Duke of Rochester continued.

"If you are in the city yet live in Kent, may I ask your reason for being here, your grace?"

He shrugged his broad shoulders, "I suppose, like any man here for the season, I am looking for a wife, but I thought I would come to the city early for the Christmas activities."

"Can I ask you, sir, do all men look to marry a lady with a dowry?" I asked him, thinking about my circumstances.

"I like your directness and honesty, Miss Braemar. I suppose some men who need the money from a lady's dowry would, but what would have happened to his own money if that was the case? Had he lost it? If so, how?"

"How could he have lost it?" I asked, finding his conversation intriguing.

"Gambling is the main one, poor investments, or supporting another lady."

"Do you mean a mistress?"

"I wouldn't have put it that bluntly," he grinned, "but yes."

"I apologise for my bluntness, your grace, but having only recently arrived from the country, I do not have the refined conversation of some of the other young ladies of the ton."

"It is refreshing, Miss Braemar. Please, there is no need for an apology."

By this time, we had reached the stables of Lady Mary's.

I thanked him for his company and his candidness. "It has been my pleasure, and I hope to see you again."

"I usually ride in the Row most mornings," I told him.

"Then I look forward to bumping into you again, Miss Braemar."

He bowed over my hand, and I bobbed a curtsey to him before I led Star into the stables. Handing Star to William to take, I turned to watch Rochester leave. He had mounted his horse and left, tipping his hat to me and grinning.

Chapter Seven

When the weather was good enough, I always rode in the Row. Some mornings, I saw Rutledge in his carriage with a different lady each time. I nodded to him but never engaged him in conversation, whereas with Rochester, we often 'bumped' into each other and walked our horses side by side, while William always walked a discreet few paces behind us. We talked and laughed. He teased me, and in return, I did the same. On the mornings that I didn't meet him, I felt sorry. I enjoyed our conversations, and I don't think he took me seriously or I, him. I enjoyed how comfortable our friendship was, similar to that of Mr Lamb and me.

One rainy morning, the Earl of Rothsay turned up on Lady Mary's doorstep with a bouquet. We enjoyed talking about music, but I found him too serious. His only topic of conversation was music, which I enjoyed, but he had no other topic. I discovered that after he had found a suitable match and married, he would return to Scotland with his new wife.

The Saturday evening before Christmas, Mr Lamb had booked a box at the theatre for us to attend a ballet.

Mr Lamb leaned across to me before the opening notes started from the orchestra pit. "I don't know whether you have heard of the composer. If you haven't, I thought this might be a good introduction and get you in the festive mood for Christmas," he told me. Lady Mary and I hadn't been out much in the evenings apart from the one concert. We had been waiting for more of my evening and ball gowns from the Modiste. The ballet was most enjoyable. It was colourful and entertaining, and of course, I enjoyed the music, but I had no need to close my eyes this time and imagine as the story was being danced in front of me. It was the perfect start to the Christmas period.

Christmas Eve arrived amidst clear skies and the possibility of snow, and we were going to my first ball. True to her word, Lady Mary had engaged a dance instructor, Monsieur Balzac, who taught me the latest dances, including the waltz, cotillion, quadrille and other dances that would occur at any ball. I was told the waltz was rather improper because of the close hold. This brought partners very close together with the man's arm around the woman's waist, but it was very much 'en vogue', as he put it, so I was taught the waltz. I wondered who, if anyone, would ask me to dance the waltz. Once again, I was conversing in French with Monsieur Balzac. I enjoyed my dance lessons, but I also enjoyed practising my French on a 'native'. I had found minimal opportunity to practice my French in Cornwall or London, so I made the most of this by asking him about France. Monsieur Balzac complimented me on speaking his 'native tongue' as he put it. Lady Mary also complimented me on my command of French. I nearly let slip that my father had taught me, as he had studied Engineering in France. I kept thinking that one of these days, I would let the truth slip out and be banished from Moldova Square and Lady Mary's home. Each time I thought of it, I kept telling myself that after Christmas, I would tell Lady Mary the truth, but just let me have the enjoyment of going to some balls over Christmas and New Year.

I had decided to wear my emerald, green satin ball gown and Mrs Trevelgue's pearl and emerald jewellery that Christmas Eve.

When I walked downstairs that evening, Lady Mary nodded her approval. "You look very nice, Julia."

I thanked her.

The night was dark, and the air was crisp. Everywhere I looked the frost had cast a silvery sheen on everything. I looked up at the sky before I entered Lady Mary's carriage. The stars sparkled like diamonds against the black velvet of the night sky. Once inside her carriage, blankets were placed over our knees to keep us warm on the short journey across the city. We had passed groups of singers, standing in the bitterly cold night air, wrapped in hats, scarves and gloves against the cold, singing Christmas Carols, on our way to the Muggeridge's ball. This Christmas would be so much more exciting than any other Christmas I had ever known, and my heart swelled with expectation.

The ball was the epitome of Christmas for me. Lord and Lady Muggeridge's house was decorated with holly, Ivy, and greenery, and a giant Christmas tree dominated the magnificent hallway, lit with hundreds of tiny candles and fragile, very colourful glass baubles. It was magical. I stared at it in awe until Lady Mary touched my arm. "Come along, Julia. The ballroom is this way. Don't forget to pick up your dance card from the hall table."

I looked at the hall table where many little cards were laid out with 'Muggeridge Christmas Eve Ball' printed on them and a little pencil attached by a green ribbon. I picked one up and followed Lady Mary to the ballroom. She had been here before. "The Muggeridges hold a ball every Christmas Eve; anyone left in the city makes a point to attend the ball. The Torrington's always hold one on New Year's Eve," she told me as we walked towards the ballroom.

"Where do the other ton members go over the winter then, Lady Mary?" I asked her.

"Oh, back to their home estates," she told me. "Many people here will go home after the New Year and return about a month or so before the start of the Season."

"So, it's like a mass exodus after the new year?"

"I'm afraid so, my dear."

We entered the ballroom, where music was playing, couples danced, and there was much laughter and merry-making. The colours of the women's gowns were like a rainbow whirling around the ballroom before me. Even the gentlemen, although they wore the typical black evening attire, wore a rainbow of colours in their waistcoats; much like the ladies, they strutted about the ballroom like peacocks. The sight of it was breathtaking. There were large crystal chandeliers and massive mirrors around the ballroom. The light from the chandeliers reflected in the mirrors as if the reflection was brought to life, twinkling and flittering and moving as if of a will of their own. Many young ladies turned their heads as they passed the mirrors to check their appearance in their reflections.

I followed Lady Mary to a seat, and almost immediately, I had gentlemen coming up to us and putting their names down on my dance card, including Lord Melbourne, the Earl of Rothsay, Lord Rutledge and the Duke of Rochester. A new face to me was Lord Byron, the poet who seemed permanently poised to show himself off to the ladies, to swoon over as they would an idol. I admit that he was handsome in a contrived way. I noticed he had darkened his eyes to look mysterious, so Lady Mary whispered to me.

"He has been to Asia; apparently, men darken their eyes over there. I told you that Lord Melbourne's wife had a rather public affair with him, among others." She whispered to me behind her fan.

There were so many gentleman's names on my dance card that I struggled to put a face to all of them. I mentioned this to Lady Mary, and she replied, saying, "If you cannot remember their names, just call them 'my lord,' or 'sir,' That will suffice."

Just after she finished speaking, Lord Melbourne approached us and claimed his dance with me.

"You are looking very festive this evening, Miss Braemar."

I thanked him. "Lady Mary says that many of the ton disappear after New Year. Will you be leaving, as well, Mr Lamb?"

"I must show my face at Brocket Hall sometime, Miss Braemar. I have stayed longer than intended and have orchids in my greenhouse that need my attention."

"Of course, but don't you have gardeners to attend them while you are away?"

"Certainly, but it is supposed to be a hobby of mine, so I like to take over whenever I am home," he explained to me. "I noticed that Byron has claimed a dance on your card?"

I nodded, not knowing what to say, whether to let on that Lady Mary had told me about his late wife or not.

"Has Lady Mary told you about him and my...."

I could see the pain on his face when he was about to talk about it.

"I am so sorry, Mr Lamb," I sympathised with him.

"It's a well-known fact amongst the ton. It happened many years ago."

"It must hurt you to see Lord Byron though," I said to Mr Lamb.

"We are on polite, nodding terms now," he said, then changed the subject. "You never saw my orangery when you were at Brocket Hall, Miss Braemar, did you?"

"No, sir, I never did," I replied.

"It is quite something to behold, so I shall return to Brocket Hall after New Year to tend to my exotic orchids but shall be back to see you make your debut."

"I am glad of that," I told him.

We talked about what I would do until the start of the season. I told him I intended to take advantage of good weather days and take Star in the Row.

"If you want to give her her head, I can recommend the downs. It's a bit further out, but I guarantee they are well worth it. Your groom will be able to show you the way."

I told him that I would certainly do that.

When the dance ended, he returned me to Lady Mary and bowed.

Next to stand up for me was Lord Rutledge.

"Miss Braemar, you look particularly attractive this evening," he said with a wolfish grin.

I thanked him.

"I was wondering if we could ride in my carriage one day?"

Did he really think that a few words of flattery would entice me into his carriage? I might be an ignorant girl from Cornwall, but I wasn't stupid enough to fall for his flattery.

"Will one of your ladies be there then as a chaperone?" I asked him innocently.

"Which ladies?"

"The ladies I have seen you driving around the Row with, sir."

"No, of course not; why do you ask?"

"I would have thought safety in numbers, sir. I would need a chaperone."

"You would have my full attention, Miss Braemar, I assure you. There is no need for a chaperone."

I was quiet for a moment, thinking of a retort. "And what if I don't want your full attention, sir?"

He was stunned by my reply, "I...I don't understand Miss Braemar."

"Oh well, my Lord, every time I have seen you, you have had a different young lady with you, unchaperoned. I don't want my name included in your string of ladies. I heard a rumour that you were a rake, but I thought I would give you the benefit of the doubt until confirmation. Now I have, and I wouldn't wish to have my name linked with yours in any way, shape or form. Do you think that because I have come from the country, I am ignorant of the ways of men such as you?" I told him as his hand touched my back in an overfamiliar gesture.

He stopped dancing and looked at me, "Why, you uppity little miss. You think that you can stand in judgment of me when you know nothing of the world. You are nothing more than a frigid little virgin."

"I would rather be known as the latter than the alternative. I think our dance has ended, sir," I said and walked off the dance floor, leaving Rutledge standing alone in the middle of the dancers.

I hoped that I would see the last of Lord Rutledge after that. I was returning to Lady Mary, across the busy dancefloor, when someone approached me and spoke. "You don't want to make an enemy of him, Miss Braemar,"

I looked up to see Rochester standing beside me. "I would rather that than have my name linked to his."

He took my arm and led me onto the dance floor.

"My Lord, this is not your dance," I pointed out to him.

"It's a waltz. Didn't I put my name down for a waltz?" he grinned, knowing full well that he hadn't.

"No. It was a country dance." I pointed out to him.

"Oh well, I am here now." He put his arm around my waist, and I could feel the heat of his hand burning through my gown. I could feel his warm breath on my face; it felt like an expensive wine that went straight to my head. My heart started doing funny things in my breast again.

"I notice your gown matches your eyes," he whispered in my ear.

"It's good that I didn't wear my red gown then, right?" I joked.

Rochester threw his head back and laughed, bringing the two dimples on either side of his mouth, which made me smile. I couldn't help but tease him. I enjoyed our banter; it was so easygoing. I had never known anyone I felt comfortable with like I did with the duke, only Jane, Lord Melbourne, or, of course, Lady Mary.

"In all seriousness, Miss Braemar, beware of Rutledge. From the looks he is giving us; you have certainly ruffled his feathers by leaving him standing alone in the middle of the dance floor."

"Do I seem gullible because I have come from the country? Do other men think as he?" I asked the duke.

"No, my dear, no man would think you gullible. Just men like him."

"Just what can he do to me?" I asked him.

"Maybe get you in a compromising position, tarnish your name... I don't know, but never be alone with him," Rochester warned me.

"I have no intention of doing so. I don't want my name linked with his," I told him as we danced around the floor.

"Tell Lady Mary as well," he told me.

"What can Lady Mary do?" I asked him.

"Oh, knowing Lady Mary, she has a few tricks up her sleeve." We twirled around the floor. "Talking of Lady Mary..." he said.

"Were we talking about her?" I asked, feeling so close to him in the hold of the waltz that my heartbeat began to hammer in my chest at the intimacy of the dance.

"You were my dear. Please continue," he encouraged me.

"She said that everyone leaves London in the New Year."

"Most of the ton do, yes."

"What is there to do until before the Season starts?"

"Erm, well, there is riding in the Row, shopping, reading, backgammon, chess, and playing the piano. There are still some art galleries and museums to widen your knowledge," he said.

"So not much then?" I grinned at him.

"I am sure you found something to keep yourself occupied in Cornwall."

"We had the sea in Cornwall?"

"And what did you do in the sea? Swim in it?" he teased me.

"Heavens, no! It's way too cold."

"Then what did you do?" Rochester asked me.

"When I was not smuggling or looting? I would sit and watch it," I joked.

The dance ended, and he took my arm to return me to Lady Mary's side.

"Rochester," Lady Mary said, acknowledging him.

"Lady Mary. I am returning your ward to you. Please keep her away from Rutledge."

Lady Mary's eyebrows rose in question.

"She's ruffled his feathers," he explained.

"Oh dear. Is that why you left him standing in the middle of the floor? Some of the young ladies around the room snickered. He won't take kindly to being made a laughingstock, Julia."

"What could I do, Ma'am? I don't want to be ..."

"I think we will continue this discussion at home, Julia," Lady Mary said, silencing me. "I see Mr Davenport is here to claim his dance." She looked at a tall, gangly man who walked as if his limbs didn't co-ordinate with each other, but he was handsome in a way. He bent over my hand and offered his arm to lead me onto the floor. A couple of times, as we danced, he trod on my feet and apologised profusely. I hardly dared talk with him to enable him to concentrate on where he put his feet. I was relieved when the dance ended, and he walked me back to Lady Mary.

Next, an elderly gentleman came to claim his dance with me. It was Mr Muggeridge who was hosting the ball with his wife. "Ah, I see a new face in the city, and you are Lady Mary's ward. Welcome to London, Miss Braemar. Are you enjoying yourself so far?"

I told him that I was.

"And you are here for the Season to catch a husband?"

"I am here for the season, sir, but as for catching myself a husband, I am not sure of that," I told him.

"Going by your full dance card, I would predict a successful season for you."

With all these people believing that I was Lady Mary's ward, with probably a dowry attached to me, I once again hated lying. I tried to change the subject away from me.

"You have a lovely home here, sir. Lady Mary says that you hold a ball here every Christmas Eve."

"We enjoy hosting the ball. It is the start of Christmas for us, and many stay, especially for this ball and the ones leading to the new year."

"Do you leave the city after the New Year as well? Lady Mary says that many of the ton do."

"Yes, I have an estate in Doncaster, so my family and I go back home in the new year and deal with my affairs there. We tend to neglect our duties to our country seats during the spring and summer to enjoy the season's festivities, especially if we have daughters due to be presented."

I told him, "I think it will be very quiet here until the start of the season."

He smiled at me kindly. "It will soon be the season, my dear, and you will be far from bored then."

The dance ended, and Mr Muggeridge thanked me and then took me back to Lady Mary.

The Duke of Rochester approached me to claim his country dance. "But you claimed me in the waltz," I told him.

"So, you don't wish to dance with me?" he teased.

"Yes... no... yes," I said, confused.

"I take that you will dance with me then?" he said, taking my arm. "I saw you dancing with Davenport earlier. What do you think of him?" he asked as we came together after parting for a few steps in the dance.

"Ask my toes," I told him, grinning.

"You will have to move your feet faster, Miss Braemar." He teased me.

"Either that or wear hobnailed boots when I dance with him." I laughed. "Will you return to Kent after the New Year, Lord Rochester?"

"Who told you?"

"Lady Mary told me that most of the ton return to their estates in the new year, so I presumed you would be doing the same."

"Unfortunately, I have some mares due to foal in the new year, so yes, I must be there," he told me.

"How many horses do you have?"

He looked to the heavens as if counting, "Oh, I should say roughly about one hundred."

"As many as that?" I asked, shocked by the numbers.

"Well, they will keep procreating. What am I to do?" he grinned. "I supply the army as well as the ton, which is why I have so many," he told me.

"I never know when you are teasing me and when you are being serious."

He looked at me a certain way, and my heart began to beat wildly in my breast.

"Oh, life is too short to be serious, Miss Braemar," he told me. "Tell me what you look for in a husband."

That took me by surprise. The mention of a husband set me stammering. "I...I have not thought about it. I suppose one that doesn't cripple me when we dance." I grinned.

The duke laughed. "Oh, come now, Miss Braemar. You are having a season and have not thought about marriage and a husband?"

"I never thought that anyone would offer for me, so I have not given it much thought. I was just hoping to enjoy the season and all it holds," I told him.

"You mean that you expected to be in that dreadful state known as 'spinsterhood'?" he said dramatically.

I laughed. "I suppose that I have thought of a husband, but I would never have expected a titled gentleman. I have no dowry, you see, so I always thought that no man of the gentry would want someone without a dowry."

"I like your honesty." That was all he said, so I thought I had put him off me.

Once again, I was returned to Lady Mary.

"You look like you are enjoying yourself, Julia," she said after the duke had bowed over my hand and left me.

"Oh, I am indeed, Ma'am. Will it be as enjoyable as this once the season starts?"

"Even more so, although you will have more competition then. There will be many more young ladies vying for gentleman's attention. About two hundred young ladies are presented each season, so you will have your work cut out to secure yourself a husband with a title," she told me, looking at me as a mother would at her daughter, with pride and reservations about what the future held for me.

"I am not bothered about competition or securing a titled gentleman as a husband. I am just enjoying the moment, Ma'am. Thank you, Lady Mary, for all you have done for me. I don't deserve it." Once again, that gnawing feeling in my stomach arose, knowing I was deceiving this kind woman who owed me nothing. I felt truly blessed to have a fairy godmother like Lady Mary and this opportunity, however long it lasted.

The Earl of Waterford was next to claim his dance with me. The Earl of Waterford was a striking-looking tall gentleman with a mass of wavy blond hair and blue eyes. His skin was like the golden brown of someone who spent much of his time in the sun. He flattered me as we danced, asking me how I enjoyed the Christmas festivities. He was a few years older than me but was fascinating to talk to. He told me that Waterford was well known for its crystal, which probably made many of the chandeliers which hung in the great houses around the country.

"So, all of the beautiful crystals that cast rainbows around rooms when they catch the sun are Waterford?" I asked.

"That is correct, Miss Braemar. Any crystals that aren't Waterford are a poor imitation," he said, smiling at me. His voice had a slight lilt, which I later discovered was an Irish accent.

Lord Waterford said he hoped to see more of me shortly after our dance ended. I told him I would look forward to that. He returned me to Lady Mary and bowed.

I don't think I sat out one dance with so many different gentlemen's names on my dance card. We discussed several topics: the season, music, and personal interests. I left the ball with Lady Mary, feeling tired but elated. I had a wonderful time. I felt like I had come from the desert, thirsty and dying for water, and with the balls and entertainment, I was drinking my fill.

We reached home. Lady Mary looked weary as we walked up the steps; she held on to my arm for support. Luckily, as soon as we reached the front door, Ritson opened it for us, who I think must have been looking out for the carriage's arrival.

"Do you want to go into the drawing room, Ma'am?" I asked her.

The grandfather clock in the hallway chimed one o'clock on Christmas morning. I smothered a yawn. I was tired, but my feet were suffering. I had had my toes stood on a couple of times, and now they were screaming out in agony, so even walking up the steps was painful.

Lady Mary did go into the drawing room and sat down wearily in front of the fire.

"Are you limping, Julia?" she asked as I followed her into the drawing room.

I told her I was a little, but it was a small price for such an enjoyable evening. "I just didn't move my feet fast enough," I told her, explaining that the Duke of Rochester had recommended that.

"He danced with you twice, I remember," she said as she yawned. "I also noticed that the two of you were laughing a lot."

"I find him amusing, Ma'am. He teases me and makes me laugh."

"You like him, I think, Julia?" Lady Mary said.

I dare not say too much; otherwise, Lady Mary might start her matchmaking tactics with the Duke as she had with Lord Melbourne.

"I enjoy his company. He never seems serious," I told her.

"And, of course, there was Waterford and Davenport?" she said, trying to gauge my reactions to them.

I nodded, not wanting to be drawn into that conversation, then told her that I thought it was time for bed for me and offered to help her upstairs to her bedroom. Although tiredly, Lady Mary smiled at me, saying she was not used to being up so late. Once, she wearily extracted herself from the armchair and held on to my arm tightly as we made our weary way up the staircase. Lady Mary said goodnight to me and said we would discuss the ball more in the morning.

Jane was waiting for me in my bedroom and helped me out of my gown, asking me how the evening went. I told her I would tell her in the morning; in the meantime, I only wanted my bed and sleep. Although I was tired, I didn't fall straight to sleep. I kept thinking about all my dancing partners. Lord Waterford looked like a Greek Adonis, tall and muscular and golden. He was interesting to talk to and a good dancer. I got to thinking about where Waterford was. Based on my geography lessons with Miss Frazer, I thought it was in Ireland. He did have a slight Irish lilt to his voice. Would he take his wife back to Ireland if he sought a bride?

I thought of the Duke of Rochester, who some would say wasn't as handsome as Waterford. I had to admit that I enjoyed his company, but I think I had put him off by telling him I had no dowry. I was sad about that. I liked the fact that he made me laugh and teased me. I felt comfortable with him, and there had been something there that... Still, he dismissed me when I told him I had no dowry.

Rutledge, he made my skin crawl. I did not even wish to dwell on him, Davenport had big feet, and I would never survive dancing with him for more than one dance at a ball, although he was good looking, in his way. Rothsay, another good looking gentleman, who enjoyed music and played the pianoforte, which was a point in his favour, but he was very serious. I thought those were the only gentlemen who had shown any interest in me and were eligible bachelors. Oh, and of course, there was Lord Melbourne, but I didn't think he was interested in me. He had just wanted to take me under his wing, for which I felt such gratitude. Maybe he felt sorry for me, the poor country mouse. Still, it wasn't even the start of the season yet. With that last thought, I finally fell asleep.

Christmas day, the weather was miserable. When Jane opened the window's curtains, I looked out and groaned in despair. The weather was gloomy for such a festive day. Gunmetal grey skies covered the city. It was not quite raining. It was not quite snowing, but it was bitterly cold, and you only had to be outside for a matter of a couple of minutes, and you would be drenched through. It was one of those days when you all wanted to sit and read and dream of better days in the sun. For Christmas, Lady Mary gave me more of her daughter's jewellery. I had brought her a book of sonnets. I had to review the library's catalogue over the weeks leading up to

Christmas to ensure she didn't have that particular book. I brought Jane a thick scarf so that when we went out on one of our excursions during the winter, it would keep her warm. Lady Mary hadn't taken up the fashion of the Christmas Tree, which Prince Albert had introduced We played a couple of games of Backgammon, then a couple of hands of cards and then I played the pianoforte for Lady Mary. We were to dine out with the Hiddleston's that evening, so I went upstairs to take a leisurely bath and wash my hair in preparation for the evening. Mrs Hiddleston was a friend of Lady Mary, and had a daughter, Philomena, who would be presented at the same time as myself. It would be my first time, meeting Philomena. I felt some trepidation about the meeting, fearing that she would be the reincarnation of Edwina. I couldn't imagine her pinching me or sticking her tongue out, but I did wonder if we would get on together, although this time, I wasn't the underdog or the 'lackey' as Edwina had called me so many times. I was now Julia Braemar, the Dowager Countess of Orkney's ward, on a more equal footing with Philomena.

I wore my purple velvet gown and my pearl jewellery. I asked Jane to do my hair the same way she had done the night before. I liked how she did the large ringlet over my shoulder. Since coming to Moldova Square and Lady Mary's, I had noted that my hair seemed thicker and shinier due to Jane's care and ministrations, probably instigated by Dorcas, who was the epitome of the perfect lady's maid. From what Jane had told me, Dorcas knew practically everything that would enhance a lady's person, right down to ear piercing, but I never mentioned that to Jane. I knew that she was still mortified by the fact that she had fainted during that procedure, and I don't think Dorcas let it lay, although I do believe that the teasing below stairs was all in good fun.

Jane placed little purple flowers in my hair, which we had purchased on one of our outings, to complete my ensemble.

I was getting used to seeing myself in the mirror now in all my finery and often wondered how I had ever looked different.

The carriage arrived at half past six; the weather had turned to snow by now. It carried Lady Mary and me to Belgrave Square, to the Hiddleston's home.

When we arrived at Belgrave Square, all the windows were lit with candles. The path from where the carriages pulled up before the house had been swept of snow so that no one slipped over. Lady Mary and I went to the large wooden front door, which was opened without even having to knock. Lady Mary handed the invitation to the butler, who, after taking our capes, went to the drawing room to announce our arrival. Lady Hiddleston came and greeted us, followed closely by her daughter. "Lady Mary, Miss Braemar, welcome and happy Christmas to you both." She put her hand on her daughter's shoulder and steered her forward to us. "May I introduce my daughter Philomena?"

Philomena had a particular look about her that reminded me of Edwina with her blond hair and blue eyes, but Philomena had a ready smile, and we bobbed a curtsey to each other. Like most people, Philomena was taller than me by a few inches, which again reminded me of Edwina, but I was soon to find out that Philomena was nothing like Edwina in character. She was a bright bubbly character, and the devilish twinkle in her eye reminded me of someone, but I couldn't think who. Immediately after we had curtseyed, she put her arm through mine and walked me around the room, introducing me to people. "And I gather you know this tall, good-looking devil, my Uncle Robert, Duke of Rochester."

Ah, that's who she reminded me of.

I stood, shocked, before him; whatever I wanted to say was stuck in my throat. This was the man who only last evening, as soon as he found out that I had no dowry, returned me to Lady Mary without another word. I curtseyed to him, then stood and looked at him. It didn't matter what had happened between us; my heartbeat still became rapid, and my breath seemed to catch in my throat. What did it all mean? Philomena was not sensing or, maybe, just ignoring the uncomfortable silence between us. "Uncle Robert says we will both be presented in the new year. Won't it be exciting to see all those handsome men queueing up to dance with us, bringing us gifts and taking us on outings? I am looking forward to it, Julia, aren't you?"

I saw the Duke of Rochester look at me, awaiting my response. "It will certainly be interesting. I'm definitely looking forward to it," I told her.

As Philomena and I circled the room, I could feel the Duke of Rochester's eyes burning into my back. Philomena was outwardly flirting with some of the unattached gentlemen invited to dine with the Hiddleston's.

A lady was introduced to me as the Dowager Duchess of Rochester. Philomena whispered loudly in my ear that she was the Duke's Mother, Lady Virginia Beaumont. I curtseyed to her. She had the same cheeky twinkle in her eyes that her son had. "Miss Braemar, I have heard about you from my son, but obviously, I like to meet people and form my own opinions. Goodness, how dainty you are, my dear. I understand that you have come all the way from Cornwall. That must have been a dreadfully long journey. What on earth did you do to occupy your time?"

That journey seemed so long ago. That girl seemed to have all but disappeared and been replaced by Julia Braemar. But who was Julia Braemar? A fraud, an imposter, a liar, and a cheat. Again, fear gripped my stomach. I feared being found out by Lady Mary and all the people I now had as acquaintances; I feared being branded a fraud. I still expected someone to come along and call me out and be publicly accused.

"Miss Braemar?" the Dowager Duchess said, prompting my response.

I didn't realise that I had been standing staring into space. Suddenly, I realised that I had been spoken to. I apologised. "I'm sorry. I just thought it seemed like a lifetime ago. One day seemed to melt into the next. I never realised that spending so much time sitting down could be tiring. I read, played cards, watched the scenery, and slept."

The Dowager Duchess looked at me in sympathy. "I hate travelling from London to Kent, which is long enough for me. Talking of Kent, we are having a house party at Knole Castle over Easter. I would like it very much if you and Lady Mary would join us."

Did that mean I would also spend time with the Duke of Rochester? I told the Dowager Duchess she must speak to Lady Mary about it. I hoped that Lady Mary would have other plans. The last thing I wanted was to spend a weekend with someone who didn't want to be with me. "I am afraid I don't know if Lady Mary already has plans over Easter. You will have to speak with her, Your Grace." I replied.

Philomena hung onto my arm, her head close to mine as she talked to me about her hopes for the season. "You don't know how good it is to finally have someone who will stay in town until the season. We can go shopping, and Uncle Robert says you enjoy riding. He says you ride one of the horses that he bred."

Now, with the talk of horses, we were a few steps away from Philomena's Uncle Robert, and I began to relax. It would be nice to have someone, another female, with whom I could spend time, go shopping, and ride. "Yes, it will be nice," I told her. "We could even go to one of those tea shops without a chaperone, with it being the two of us. I could even show you some of the sights of London, as you lived in Cornwall, you probably don't know much about our fair city," she said. "Oh, this is going to be wonderful, and we can go to the house party at Easter together."

We then talked about clothes and maids, and I told Philomena about the episode with Jane and the ear piercing, which made her laugh.

Finally, the gong rang for dinner; unfortunately, when it came to sitting down at the dining table, I found one of my dinner partners was the Duke of Rochester.

I sat down next to him. "Miss Braemar, I see we are sat next to each other," he said to me. His face and eyes smiled at me, and my heart started to hammer in my breast again. Then, I told myself that he wanted to marry a girl with a dowry.

"So, it seems Your Grace. I didn't realise that you were related to the Hiddleston's?"

"My mother's brother is Sir Geoffrey Hiddleston. You are being presented with my niece, Philomena, next year."

"So, it seems."

I looked at my dinner partner on the other side. He was an elderly gentleman who was another friend of the family—Mr Marston. I managed to keep up a conversation with Mr Marston. I was trying to ignore the duke, but we were sitting so close together that I could feel his thigh so close and warm next to my own, and I struggled to concentrate on what Mr Marston was saying.

The food at the dinner party was delicious. I had never tasted anything like it before. Lady Mary's cook was very good, but this one, whoever they were, was excellent.

Eventually, it was time for the ladies to leave the gentlemen to their port, brandy, and cigars, while Philomena insisted that I go to her room and talk. It was fun to talk to someone of my own age. The cheerful, cheeky demeanour I had liked in the duke seemed to run throughout the family.

"To think, Julia, if you marry Uncle Robert, we would be related. Of course, you know that he is looking for a wife this season. It could be you." She giggled. "You would be my Aunty. His townhouse is on the opposite side of the square, so we could still see each other whenever you were there."

"I don't think the duke has any feelings for me, and besides, I haven't had my season yet. I want the excitement of that," I told her.

I did not want to even think about the duke's offering for me when I thought he was not interested, regardless of any romantic dreams I might have had.

"Oh yes, we don't want to accept any marriage offers until we have had the excitement of a season. What man would deny us that if they truly cared about us?" she said enthusiastically.

"Of course." After the duke's reaction to my revelation about not having a dowry, I wondered how many more would be put off by that. I thought about it and realised I hadn't even expected a season when I lived in Cornwall, let alone a marriage proposal.

I didn't know why; whenever I saw the duke or when he was near to me, my heart rate increased and beat in my breast like a caged bird, and my mouth dried out; I couldn't help but give a sigh every time that I saw him, but I did.

Philomena and I spent an enjoyable half an hour in her bedroom getting to know each other. We talked about our gowns and what we enjoyed doing and found that we had things in common, like horse riding and reading. She asked me what I was looking for in a husband. I told her that I had never given it much thought.

"Oh, I have Julia. He must be tall, kind, good-looking, and have a title," she told me. Then we started talking about hobbies. Philomena said she enjoyed painting and sketching but couldn't play a musical instrument. "The notes on the page look like a foreign language to me. Don't get me wrong, Julia, I love to listen to music, but my pianoforte instructor shook his head in distress when he tried to teach me. He would throw up his hands in despair and finally give up. I would love to hear you play Julia. There is a pianoforte downstairs. Would you please play it for me?"

I was about to shake my head, but Philomena was so persuasive, so, arm in arm, we went down to their music room, where I sat down at their pianoforte and began to play the music from when I had attended the concert. Philomena sat next to me on the piano stool and sat listening. We had our backs to the doorway, so I didn't realise I had an audience. I continued playing, closing my eyes and bringing forward the images the music recalled. When I finished, I heard someone behind us clapping. Thankfully, it sounded like only one person, but the applause brought a flush of colour to my cheeks. Philomena stood up and ran over to the doorway. "Uncle Robert, isn't Julia talented at the pianoforte? Oh, I wish I could play like that."

The duke entered the room with his arm around his niece's shoulder. "Then, my dear girl, you should have practised more."

Philomena left us to go back to the rest of the guests while he remained in the music room alone with me. The look on his face made my legs seem to disintegrate so that my bones felt like they had turned to water, and I could not rise from the stool.

"You truly are an exceptional pianist, Miss Braemar," he said as he approached me. "Would you play me some more?" I realised that I was alone in the room with him. Philomena had run off and not returned.

"Your Grace, we are alone in here," I cried, my cheeks flaming.

"You need have no worries, Miss Braemar. I left the door open. Continue to play, please," he implored me.

My hands shook, but I relaxed once I felt the ivory keys beneath them.

He sat down next to me on the stool. I could feel the warmth of his breath on my shoulder and the heat of his body so close to mine. I closed my eyes, trying to ignore him. I jumped when he spoke to me. "I fear that I have upset you, Miss Braemar."

"What makes you think that Your Grace?" My mouth was drying out with nerves, so I could hardly form my words correctly.

"You hardly spoke to me at dinner, yet I thought we had a good rapport before this evening."

"I couldn't ignore Mr Marston," I said in my defence.

"You are supposed to share your conversation with both of your dinner partners," he pointed out. I felt my face flame as he pointed out my failings. If he criticised me, then I could do the same to him.

"Why did you leave so abruptly after I told you I had no dowry? I would have thought horse breeding was a very lucrative business."

"Are you implying that I would only marry a dowry?" he frowned at me.

"Well, that was the impression you gave." He hurt me because I felt a definite attraction to him. I felt that way after our second meeting. Was that how Edwina had felt about her stableboy? But on consideration, no, I didn't think that Edwina had had a romantic bone in her body; lustful, yes, but I doubted that Edwina had ever loved anyone but herself.

I stopped playing, rose, told him I would be missed, and left him sitting on the piano stool.

When he first came into the room, I thought he might be interested, but now he seemed to criticise me, which hurt—not the criticism, but the fact that it was he was criticising me; I could have probably accepted that from someone else, not caring a jot, but not from him. I was beginning to think that he liked me when we danced, but now I was unsure. Was he playing with my emotions?

I was about to leave the room, but Philomena returned, and the rest of the people from the dinner party were behind her. I looked at them.

"Julia, please play some more for us," she asked me. "I have told everyone what a talented pianist you are. Isn't she Uncle Robert?" Philomena looked to her uncle for confirmation.

The duke looked at me and smiled benevolently. "She is indeed. Please play some more, Miss Braemar," he said and smiled at me. My breath caught in my throat at his smile.

I looked to find Lady Mary in the crowd. When I found her, I looked to see if she approved. She nodded, so I sat down again and began to play again.

Philomena had sat down near me and began sketching me. I was unused to so much attention, but when I played, I closed my eyes, cut out the view of the audience and concentrated on the music. I opened my eyes briefly and saw the duke looking down at me. There was a look in his eyes that I could only describe as pride. Pride relating to myself? Yet he didn't want anything to do with me, did he? What did I know of these things? I was just an ignorant girl from the country.

When I had finished the piece, the people were clapping me. I saw his mother looking at him, then look at me. "Miss Braemar, please play something else for us," she asked.

I began to play something more cheerful that had people clapping and dancing in the music room. I thought that if Lady Mary eventually dismissed me and turned me out, I could think of playing in other people's homes and entertaining others. I could earn money by just playing the pianoforte. A concert pianist? I thought of all the possibilities. When I had finished, the people applauded repeatedly, and I blushed.

Philomena came to me and showed me what she had done. I looked at the paper and saw myself at the piano, with her Uncle Robert standing by me with that look on his face that made my insides turn to honey. I was amazed she could complete something so detailed in just a few minutes. My talent was playing the piano, but my new friend, Philomena, definitely had a talent for art. I complimented her profusely. "That is amazing, Philomena. How did you do that in so short a time?"

She just shrugged. "I don't know. I just did."

By then, everyone seemed to be leaving the room. "When we go to the house party over Easter, will you play for us again, Julia?" she asked.

"If I'm asked, I suppose," I told her.

By then, the Duke of Rochester had left the room with the others.

At eleven o'clock, Lady Mary approached Philomena and me and suggested that it was time for us to leave. Philomena had already arranged with me to go horse riding together one morning when the weather was better. From that, I gathered she was a fair-weather rider, but I looked forward to our outing. As Lady Mary lived near the Hiddleston's, Philomena said she would send me a note when the weather was suitable. I said goodbye to her and her family and thanked them for having us, then left with Lady Mary.

That night, I slept poorly, struggling to try to make out the duke and his feelings towards me, but I still couldn't understand him or how I found him looking at me sometimes. Did he like me? Did he even think of me romantically? We had only met a few times, and he seemed to blow hot and cold towards me. Maybe he liked me as a friend, but nothing more. Perhaps he enjoyed playing with a young lady's feelings, and me being an ignorant country girl, I was the perfect target. I would not be used like a mouse being toyed with by a cat. Were all titled gentlemen prone to play with a young woman's feelings?

Before I finally slept, I thought about my savings in the bank and also the rest of Edwina's jewellery. I thought that if I did leave Lady Mary's under a cloud of my lies and decided to start as a pianist, I might be able to afford to buy a little house for Jane and me. With that thought, I finally fell asleep.

Chapter Eight

The next day was foggy but dry. Miraculously, the snow disappeared overnight, so I asked Lady Mary if I could go out riding again. "Are you sure you want to go out in this weather, Julia? It is very cold, and with the fog..."

I told her I didn't mind the cold but felt I had to leave the house to try to clear my head.

"Very well but wrap up warm and take William with you."

"Yes, Ma'am."

I decided that William and I would ride around Hyde Park. The fog seemed to hug each tree, turning them into ghostly beings. I felt completely alone, as William was somewhere behind me in the mist.

I heard a horse come galloping towards me and ignored it. I urged Star into a canter, but the horse's hoofbeats seemed to follow behind me.

I looked around to see who it was, praying that whoever it was would gallop by me. I felt that I wanted to be alone. I wanted to think. Could I hide somewhere in the fog?

The horse seemed to be getting nearer. Maybe if I reined in, the horse would pass me by. I waited and waited.

"Miss Braemar?"

"Lord Rutledge?" I inwardly groaned. Of all the people in London, it had to be him. I remembered our last meeting and wished he would go away.

"What are you doing out here in the fog?"

Of all the people I didn't want to meet, it was Rutledge. He looked me up and down. I looked around for William, realising I shouldn't have gone off alone.

"Why don't we walk for a while? This weather is not conducive to riding in. You can hardly see your hand in front of your face. You could harm yourself riding in this weather."

My heart was hammering in my breast from fear. I felt that this man didn't have an honest or decent bone in his body. I didn't trust him one bit. I stayed where I was, although Rutledge had dismounted. His hands reached to help me down from Star's back, but I shook my head. "I don't think so, sir," I told him, firmly taking Star's reins, ready for flight. I saw the look in his eye, and it made me fearful, fearful that he might take revenge on me for leaving him standing alone on the dance floor on Christmas Eve, fear I might get my name linked to his, and I would bring further disgrace on Lady Mary. She had already had one disgrace in her family, and although I was not her granddaughter, I was still known as her ward in the city. If it was not fear of getting my name linked to his, it was fear that he might try to do something to me in revenge for leaving him standing in the middle of the dancefloor. Would he try to do the things to me that Richard Trevelgue had tried to, but this time, I had no one to come and save me. I had left William somewhere in the mist. I was alone!

"I am expected home. Excuse me." I turned Star around to head back the way I had come.

"Oh, come now, Miss Braemar. The rumours you have heard are all untrue. I just thought we could get to know one another better."

"I don't think so. As for rumours, I take no note of rumours, but I do believe the evidence of my own eyes, and I have never seen you with the same lady more than once."

"You misunderstand the situation. They were ladies in distress."

I laughed, "The only distress was that which you had caused them. They would not be accepted in polite society, and I have no intention of getting my name linked with yours. Just stay away from me, sir."

He went to grab the reins from me, but I yanked them away, which caused Star to rear up and then gallop away. Once we were away from Lord Rutledge, I dug my heels into Star's side, and we galloped off as if the demons of hell were after us. I didn't know where we were going or where we were and didn't care. I had no idea which way was the way home. I just knew that I had to get away from him. The man scared me. I had the same feeling near him as with the Trevelgue brothers. I was not just scared. I was terrified.

I heard hoofbeats following me again, and I would certainly not stop. I pushed Star on, but still, the hoofbeats followed. I was beginning to get scared, thinking Rutledge was following me, not taking 'no' for an answer. I was shaking like a leaf. The horse caught up with me, and someone grabbed Star's reins, and I screamed and screamed. That seemed the only way Rutledge would leave me alone.

"Miss Braemar," a voice said, "Julia, stop. It's me. Julia, it's Rochester. Calm down. What has happened?"

I looked at him. It was Rochester. I tried to swallow, but it got stuck in my throat, and tears came to my eyes. I tried dashing them away with my hand, but they wouldn't stop.

"Julia, what has happened?" he asked me again, his voice full of concern.

I struggled to speak but only managed one word. "Rutledge..."

"Rutledge? Where? Has he hurt you?" Rochester said, looking about us.

I shook my head.

He slipped from his horse and put his arms up for me. Instinctively, I slipped from Star's back and willingly entered his arms, seeking comfort and reassurance.

"Are you sure he didn't hurt you?"

"He just scared me. I was alone in the fog..."

"Where was your groom?" he asked me.

"I lost him...I left him behind. I shouldn't have done it, I know now, but I needed to be alone."

His arms felt safe and warm around me, like I was home. I turned and looked at him. I could feel my lips gravitating towards his like a moth to a flame, and I waited and waited.

"Come on, let's get you back home before you catch pneumonia in this weather." His hands went around my waist as he lifted me back onto Star's back. "I'll come back with you as far as the stables, then I'll leave you. Just don't go doing that again. I won't always be there to help you." He reprimanded me.

I could feel the tears threatening to fall again. I was going to say I was sorry, but I wasn't—not for him being my knight in shining armour, but for getting myself into a situation I couldn't handle.

We rode back to Moldova Square in silence. I couldn't understand this man. One minute, he seemed attracted to me; the next...he seemed distant, and he continually pointed out my failings like I was some wayward child. I just didn't know what to make of him.

Before he left, I called to him. "Your Grace, how did you know where to find me?"

"I saw your groom, William, looking for you; he was worried that something might have happened to you. I told him to return to the stables, wait for you, and not let Lady Mary know; otherwise, he could lose his position." He shrugged his shoulders, "Then I came looking for you."

"I'm sorry I caused you such trouble, Your Grace," I said and meant it.

He grinned at me. "Just don't do it again," he said, winking at me before turning his horse and leaving.

So why did he initially ask me where William was if it had been William who told him where I was? Did he intend to continue to point out my failings, as he had at the dinner party at the Hiddleston's? The man was exasperating!

As soon as he heard the horses' clip-clop, William came out of the stables, a look of relief on his face. "Oh, Miss Julia, where did you get to? I lost you in the fog and couldn't find you until I saw the Duke of Rochester."

"Well, I'm back now. Let's keep this between us, please. I don't want to get you in trouble because of my stupidity."

"Yes, Miss Julia," he said, sounding relieved.

I slid from Stars back and handed him the reins. Then, I walked back into the house via the kitchens, hoping to slip upstairs without Lady Mary knowing. Jane was waiting for me in my room. "I was getting worried about you in this weather. The fog has got worse since you first went out. I thought you might have had an accident, Miss Julia."

I told her not to worry about me and asked if she could prepare me a bath as the damp air had got to me.

By the time I had bathed and dressed in a warm dress, I felt so much better, and the last hour was just like a dream or a nightmare, depending on whichever part I thought about. But Rochester seemed intent on pointing out my shortcomings. I knew that I was an ignorant girl from the country who should have no aspirations of making a match with someone such as him. So, I should stop daydreaming about him. I told myself.

I went down to the drawing room. Lady Mary was asleep in the chair, so I sat down to read.

About fifteen minutes later, she opened her eyes. "Oh Julia, how was your ride?"

"It was a bit too cold, so I went upstairs and soaked in a hot bath."

"Very sensible," she said, then picked up her embroidery. "Will you play for me, Julia?"

I went and sat at the pianoforte. Lady Mary and I had settled into a comfortable relationship.

"You were very popular last evening," she said as I played.

"I didn't mean to attract attention, Ma'am. Philomena asked me to play, and the next thing I knew, the Duke of Rochester was standing there, and Philomena had gathered everyone to listen to my playing. I'm sorry."

Lady Mary said it couldn't be helped and was proud of me. I felt a warm glow light me up from inside. Where was the old harridan that Mrs Trevelgue had told me about? I hated myself. I hated all my lies, including what happened that day. I hated all the money that Lady Mary had already spent on me and never asked for anything in return, apart from me not bringing shame and scandal to her door again. I hated myself for the sheer stupidity of thinking that a man such as the duke would even think of offering for someone as gauche as I.

New Year's Eve came, and another ball. I sincerely hoped that Rutledge wouldn't be there. I had worn my red velvet gown and was going to wear pearls, but Dorcas came in with another small box for me, which I was told was from Lady Mary's daughter's jewellery. I opened the box and saw ruby and diamond jewellery, a necklace, earrings and a bracelet. I told Dorcas I couldn't keep borrowing valuable jewellery from Lady Mary. "Oh, they're no use to Lady Mary; she has plenty of her own. Take them and enjoy, Miss Julia," Dorcas said, then promptly left.

Lady Mary gave me her usual top-to-toe inspection before we left, nodded her approval, and then left to go to the ball.

As soon as we entered the room, Viscount Melbourne approached us. He bowed over Lady Mary's hand and then mine. "Ladies, how have you been? Miss Braemar, I hear you were a huge success on Christmas day at the Hiddleston's."

"Who told you that, Mr Lamb?" I asked, surprised that the news had reached him so quickly.

"You thought I wouldn't find out?" he said, grinning at me. "It was Rochester singing your praises. Now, Miss Braemar, could I have this dance with you before you are inundated with gentlemen wishing to take you on the floor?"

I nodded and thanked him. We took to the floor. Lord Melbourne was a good dancer, and I enjoyed his company. "Have you been busy the last few days, my Lord?" I asked him.

"As a politician, Miss Braemar, I am always busy."

I asked him if he liked it. "It keeps me occupied, which is always a good thing." Then he changed the subject. "As I said, it was the Duke of Rochester who has been singing your praises," he told me again. I was surprised. "I understand that you and his niece have formed a friendship and are both being presented this coming year. Philomena is a very talented artist. He showed me the sketch that she did of you both on Christmas day."

"He has the sketch of us?" I asked him, shocked. My heart leapt in my chest. Rochester had kept the drawing of us, and I felt a warm glow somewhere near my heart.

"Yes. He is very proud of his niece's talent."

"I knew that Philomena had done the sketch. I agree she is very talented, but I thought she had kept it."

"No, it is in Rochester's hands now," Melbourne reiterated.

He kept it. It gave me that same warm glow that I felt when he held me in his arms. Maybe he was not totally against me after all?

"But what does that mean, Mr Lamb?"

He smiled at me, "Why don't you just wait and see, Miss Julia."

When the dance finished, he returned me to Lady Mary. I looked at Lord Melbourne as he moved on, thinking he looked pale. I hoped that he was not sickening for anything.

Lord Waterford was next to claim a dance. "I hope you had a good Christmas, Miss Braemar."

"I did, thank you," I told him.

"I have brought you a small Christmas present, later than it should be, for which I apologise." He reached inside his pocket and pulled out a crystal on a delicate silver chain. "If you hang that up at your bedroom window when the sun catches it, it will cast rainbows around your room."

I looked at the long teardrop-shaped crystal. It was very beautiful on its own. I had seen such crystals in the Waterford Chandeliers at Lady Mary's house.

"It's beautiful. I shall hang it up when I get home," I told him.

"I should imagine it will be too late when you get home. But it is good to know that you are pleased with it." He smiled at me.

I enjoyed talking with Lord Waterford; it was special that he brought me a gift. "Waterford, whereabouts is that?" I asked him.

"Ireland. The Irish scenery is something to behold. I hope that someday I can show it to you." We continued to dance silently for a while, and then he spoke again. "I understand that you have come up from Cornwall?"

"I have," I answered.

"What is that like?" Lord Waterford asked me.

"We have beautiful sandy beaches, which are breathtaking on sunny days, but the sea is rough in the winter, during storms. The waves are gigantic, and as they crash upon the rocks, they cast great plumes of spray in the air."

"It sounds as if you enjoy watching the sea, calm or stormy," he said.

"How did you guess that?" I asked him, surprised.

"By the look on your face when you spoke of it."

"I did enjoy watching the sea in all weather. I found it mesmerising."

"The crossing from Ireland to England and vice versa can be very rough. Many people suffer on the crossing when the waves are so high that the ship pitches in the rough sea."

"Do you go back to Ireland very often?" I asked him.

"When I can, but not as often as I would like. Do you think you will return to Cornwall?"

The dance ended, but as Lord Waterford took me back to Lady Mary, we continued to talk. "I doubt it. It is a long journey to undertake."

"You must tell me more about Cornwall another time," he said as he bowed over my hand.

"And you must tell me more about Ireland," I said before he left. He nodded, then moved away.

"You were having a good talk with Waterford," Lady Mary commented after he had left. "He is a very good-looking young man, Julia."

I showed her the crystal he had given me and said that he told me to hang it in my window, and when the sun shone, it would cast rainbows around the room.

"That was very generous of him, Julia." Lady Mary commented when I showed her the crystal.

Did Lord Waterford consider a proposal at some stage? Would I accept if he did? He was certainly handsome enough, and according to Lord Melbourne, no scandal was attached to him. But what would I look for in a marriage if I did marry and was so lucky to be offered? Title, or love, and who would marry me without a dowry to attract them? Who would marry a fraud and a liar? Obviously, I would have to confess to whoever offered for me, if any man did.

"That is beautiful, Julia," she said. I asked her if she would look after the crystal for me. Lady Mary smiled at me and placed it in her reticule.

Next on my dance card was the Duke of Rochester. I danced with him, but I had mixed feelings just thinking about him, and my heart skipped a beat. Would he point out more of my failings or joke with me? It was another waltz, and I enjoyed being close to him. His smell of Sandalwood and brandy, which seemed synonymous with him, touched my senses. I breathed it in and sighed. No matter where I was or what happened, I would always think of Rochester whenever I smelt Sandalwood.

"What a beautiful gown, Miss Braemar," he said

"Don't tell me it matches my eyes, or I will be highly offended by Your Grace," I joked, deciding that I would still like to remain his friend despite everything.

He laughed. "I was going to say that it matches the rose of your lips."

I flushed at his flattery.

"Now it matches your cheeks," he said, grinning at my embarrassment.

My hand briefly left his shoulder and touched my cheeks. I looked at his hands, and they looked bruised. "What happened to your hands?"

He briefly looked at them, then shrugged, "Boxing," he said.

"Do you still box?"

"It helps me to keep fit. I enjoy pitting myself against another." He admitted.

"Well, if you look like this, what does the other man look like?" I teased him.

Again, he laughed. "Oh, he came the worse off, believe me." We danced for a while in silence. "Have you recovered from your scare with Rutledge?" he asked.

I told him I had and thanked him again for coming to my rescue.

He smiled at me, dimples in his cheeks appeared on either side of his mouth, and his eyes sparkled in merriment.

"I've not seen him here this evening, thankfully," I told him, looking around the ballroom again to ensure I had spoken correctly.

Rochester just raised his eyebrows in surprise and changed the subject. "Who is next on your dance card?"

"Davenport."

"Oh dear, don't forget to move your feet faster," he said, grinning at me again. I was glad we were friends again. I told him I would try, but Davenport had big feet. Rochester said that he needed big feet to balance his height. I laughed. "You mean that he would topple over if he had smaller feet?"

"Oh, undoubtedly." He grinned. "With your tiny feet, I would have thought you could move them faster. Maybe I should give you some lessons on dancing around, as I do when I box."

I didn't want the dance to end. I wanted to continue laughing and joking with him, but sadly, our dance did end, and he returned me to Lady Mary.

I grinned as I expected Lord Davenport to come to claim me, remembering Rochester's words.

I didn't move my feet fast enough as Davenport trod on my feet repeatedly. He apologised profusely, but somehow, my feet seemed to get in his way. When the dance ended, I limped back to Lady Mary. Davenport apologised to me profusely again, but this time, he had injured my feet, so I had to sit out the rest of the dances. Lady Mary asked me if I wished to leave, but I told her I would like to stay and see the New Year.

We did stay, but I had to refuse to dance further, which I was sorry about. Rochester came over to me again, his face full of concern. "Are you feeling unwell, Miss Braemar?" he asked,

"I'm afraid I didn't move my feet fast enough again," I told him, with a grimace, trying to make light of my pain.

"Let me see," he said, ignoring the fact that Lady Mary was sitting beside me.

I poked my feet out from under my gown, and even after so short a time, both feet were swelling.

"Damned oaf," he said when he saw them.

"Please don't make a fuss, sir," I begged him.

He looked at Lady Mary, who nodded.

"Well, when the ball ends, I will carry you to your carriage."

"That is most kind of you, Rochester," Lady Mary said.

He looked at me, then sat down. I had expected him to leave and honour his other dances, but he didn't.

"When do you go back to Kent, Lord Rochester?" I asked him. I wanted to keep him talking to me if I could, but also fill in the time before we saw in the New Year and then returned home.

"I'm afraid I leave tomorrow, but I will return to see Philomena and you presented at court. In the meantime, try to keep out of trouble because I won't be around to help," he said, teasing me again. Maybe we could remain friends if I didn't mention marriage or a dowry again or have thoughts beyond my station. I realised that I was aiming too high with Rochester.

"And there I was, thinking of you as my knight in shining armour," I replied.

He smiled.

Everyone stopped dancing as the clock chimed midnight and wished each other a happy New Year, then the dancing recommenced.

There were another few dances, and then people started leaving to go home.

I stood up and grimaced as the pain in my feet shot up my legs. The next thing I knew, Rochester picked me up and carried me out to Lady Mary's carriage, with Lady Mary following behind. I could feel the strength and power in his arms as he picked me up and carried me, and my whole body seemed to be aware of him and where our bodies touched. I blushed. I didn't want to look around as I knew people were watching us. News would circulate the ton like wildfire, and my name would be linked to his. Would this force his hand into marrying me or offering for me? I didn't want that. If I married any man, I would only want to marry him because he wanted it, not because the ton's rules dictated it.

"I will follow behind your carriage, Lady Mary, and carry Miss Braemar to your front door. They will swell even worse if you put any weight on your feet. You might struggle to get your feet out of your shoes as they are." He was so kind and considerate.

True to his word, his coach followed behind us until we reached Moldova Square. He came round to my side of the coach, picked me up in his arms, and carried me up the steps to the front door. When the footman opened the door, he put me down briefly and told the footman to carry me to my room. Then he wished me good night and left. I wouldn't see him for a few months until the start of the season. My heart plummeted like a stone in my chest.

Dorcas saw the footman carry me upstairs and came bustling up behind us, giving her instructions.

"Dorcas, Jane can see to me," I told her.

"What, that Lummox? Would you trust yourself to her ministrations, Miss Julia? What if she faints again?"

"I think it was only the sight of blood," I told her. Jane was waiting for me when we got to my room.

"Put Miss Julia on her bed, James," Dorcas told the footman. She then told Jane to fetch ice and a towel and took my shoes off. She looked at my feet and tutted, "Heavens, Miss Julia, what happened?"

"Davenport happened," Lady Mary said as she followed me up to my room.

Jane came with a bowl of ice and some towels. "Shouldn't we get a doctor, Ma'am?"

"Och," said Dorcas disdainfully, "Silly lass. If it had been up to you, you would have had a doctor to pierce her ears. Ice and elevating the legs are all she needs. Miss Julia will be right as rain in a couple of days."

Dorcas instructed Jane on what to do. I lay on my bed for two days until I could get my shoes on again. The swelling went down, but it was another few days before the bruising disappeared. In the meantime, the day after the ball, I received a massive bouquet of hothouse flowers from Davenport with an apology for my feet. I felt so sorry for him. He was so uncoordinated as a dancer, but he couldn't help having big feet and being unable to dance. At the end of the week, I received a letter from Rochester asking how my feet were. I was glad he hadn't forgotten me, and I felt that same glow near my heart again. I thought that maybe, even after so short a time, I was falling in love with him. I never intended to, and I couldn't imagine that I could feel that way after so short a time, and I hadn't even started the Season yet.

I sent a brief note thanking him and telling him I fully recovered after a few days of rest. I said I hoped his duty as a midwife to his horses wasn't causing him too much trouble and left it at that. I didn't want him to think I was anything more than a friend for now. He would have to make the first move if he wanted.

A few days later, Waterford called at Lady Mary's with a bouquet and a box of chocolates. I received him in the drawing room, where Lady Mary was working on her embroidery, and I had been reading a book from her library.

"Miss Braemar, I have recently heard that you had to be carried from the New Year's Eve ball," he said, a look of concern on his face. "What happened?"

I explained about Davenport: "He was mortified that he had injured me so. I feel sorry for him."

"Miss Braemar, you are too generous a nature," he said, taking a biscuit offered by one of the maids.

"Mr Davenport was so mortified that he had caused me such damage that he has sworn never to dance again," I told him, saying that it would be a terrible shame, especially if he were also looking for a wife.

Lord Waterford stayed for half an hour, telling me about Ireland and asking me about Cornwall. Then he stood and said he would not like to outstay his welcome, but he asked if he could call on me again sometime before he bowed over my hand and Lady Mary's and left.

Melbourne had called a few times as news had reached him of my injuries. I told him that I was well on the mend. I was concerned about him; he still didn't look like a picture of health, but when I mentioned it, he just swept it aside, saying that it was old age catching up on him.

In the new year, when the weather permitted, Philomena and I spent time together, talking about books and gowns, and we went shopping together as well. It was nice to have a friend. A real friend who I could laugh with and talk about things without a temper tantrum or histrionics. She often talked about how if I married Rochester, we would be family. "And I would be your Aunty," I told her jokingly. I could not see it happening. I had just that one letter from Rochester and replied, but nothing since then. Every time I thought of Rochester, I gave an uncontrollable sigh. I couldn't help it. I missed our banter, laughing and joking. I was disappointed, I must admit, but I knew that I had to move on. Besides, he was a Duke. He wouldn't want a nobody from Cornwall with no pedigree, and sooner or later, the truth would come out; but on a lighter thought, it wouldn't be long before the start of the season.

Waterford had left for Ireland some weeks ago, risking a choppy crossing, and had not returned to London yet, as far as I knew. I had not heard anything from him either. Then I told myself, why should I? These gentlemen had more important issues to deal with than to think of me.

We had been invited to a poetry reading, with Lord Byron reading some of his poems, at the Duchess of Dorchester's home in Berkley Square opposite where Philomena and her family lived. Lady Mary and I met Philomena and her mother. Byron, as usual, had his eyes darkened and wore what I thought could only be classed as a turban in oranges and golds. He had positioned himself beside the vast marble fireplace, topped by a large ornate mirror, in such a way that he could catch a glimpse of his reflection with just the slightest turn of his head. It was evident to anyone with a brain that vanity oozed from his every pore. He thought he was beautiful. His looks might have taken in Caroline Lamb, but he didn't impress me.

Philomena was enamoured with him. She couldn't take her eyes off him. She hung on every word he spoke. At the end of the reading, Philomena applauded enthusiastically. She was one among many of the young ladies who clapped Byron. In my opinion, he was talented, but many were more talented. The young ladies surrounded Lord Byron when he moved away from the fireplace, talking and chattering like a pen full of chickens flapping around in their colourful dresses. Of course, Byron gloried in the adoration. When I got nearer, I thought he also had rouge on his cheeks and something shiny on his lips.

"Did you enjoy my reading, Miss..." he said as he minced towards Philomena and myself.

"Braemar," I said, then pulled Philomena between us. "And this is Miss Philomena Hiddleston." Philomena blushed prettily in his presence and curtseyed to him.

"Did you both enjoy my reading?" he repeated.

"Oh, it was wonderful, Lord Byron. You are so clever," Philomena enthused.

"And you, Miss Braemar?"

"I found it interesting, my Lord," I told him as honestly as possible. I couldn't be enthused about something that I thought was mediocre, and Lord Byron did not agree. "Interesting, you say, Miss Braemar?" he asked, raising his perfectly arched eyebrows.

"At the moment, I am reading Homer's Iliad, which is completely different from your poetry. As I said, it was interesting. Do you not think that prose is subjective? Some people might like one thing, and others might enjoy something else?" I replied.

Lord Byron admitted, "Compared to Homer, my poetry is certainly different."

"Where do you get your inspiration from Lord Byron?" Philomena asked, inducing him to talk to her. I excused myself and went back to Lady Mary.

"Well, what did the great man say for himself?" Lady Mary asked sarcastically.

"He asked me if I enjoyed his reading. I told him that it was interesting and different. I don't think that sat well with him. Then I told him that I was reading Homer. Ma'am, I thought there was no comparison. Philomena is, I think, head over heels in love with him," I told her.

"Oh dear. I hope Lady Hiddleston has prewarned her daughter of Byron's reputation."

"Indeed," I replied.

Shortly afterwards, we went home. Many of the young ladies at the reading would be having their season with Philomena and myself; we had nodded and spoken briefly to them, asking if they were looking forward to being presented to Queen Victoria and Prince Albert. Of course, they all said 'yes'.

Surprisingly, the following morning, I received a package. I found a green leather-bound first edition of Lord Byron's poetry when I opened it. Enclosed was a note saying that he hoped that I would find this more than just interesting.

I put it to one side and continued reading Homer to Lady Mary.

When I had finished reading Homer, Lady Mary asked if Byron had written anything in his book. I had only given it a cursory glance before putting it to one side.

I picked up the green leather-bound volume and looked. *"To Julia of the Emerald eyes. My heart is at your feet. Byron."*

I scoffed at his note's stupid mentality and tore it from the book, casting it into the fire. What with Rutledge and Byron, I felt like swearing off men, but some men showed honour and integrity, like Marlborough, Rochester, Waterford, and even Davenport. These men were decent and upstanding, but Byron and Rutledge were both Rakes of the first order and shouldn't be allowed in the company of decent yet impressionable young ladies. (When did I become so high-handed, I wondered.)

Chapter Nine

Easter was late that year. Philomena talked to me about the weekend house party at her Uncle Robert's home and that of his mother, the Dowager Duchess of Rochester.

"It's a massive castle, Julia. Knole is going back, I think, to Henry VIII's time with acres of land, and Uncle Robert breeds his horses there. I've been a few times, but it will be much more fun with you there this time. There will be a ball, horse riding, archery, and other forms of entertainment. I shall ask Uncle Robert if we can share a room." Full of excitement, she was by the fact that we might be sharing a bedroom. I thought that it would be good fun as well. Although Edwina and I had bedrooms next to each other, I would have dreaded sharing a bedroom with her, but Philomena was much more fun, and we got on so well together, as friends should. We also discovered that some of the young ladies who had attended Byron's poetry reading would also be there.

Lady Mary and I left London on a Thursday morning and travelled to Kent, overnighting in a good coaching inn at Redhill; Lady Mary found the journey tiring, hence the overnight stay, then continued to Knole Castle on Friday morning to arrive Friday lunchtime, where a warm welcome and a good lunch awaited us. The journey from London to Kent wasn't as far as from Cornwall to London, but this time, I travelled inside the carriage with Lady Mary while Dorcas and Jane travelled up top with the coachmen and our trunks. I was just pleased that the weather was mild.

Lady Mary was a good travelling companion. We played cards or read to while away the time.

"You once asked me if I would ever return to Orkney, Julia. I think this is about as far as I would wish to travel these days, and even after this, I shall need a day to recover," she told me.

We passed through Sevenoaks on our way to the castle. Philomena had said that Sevenoaks was not far from Knole Castle, so I knew we were reaching the end of our journey.

Before we reached Knole Castle, we saw herds of deer roaming the parklands and surrounding woods. Further along were fields of horses. I presumed this was all land belonging to Knole Castle and the Rochesters.

We pulled into the large courtyard of the castle. The courtyard was surrounded on four sides by the building, with a great arch leading into it from the long driveway. I expected it to be a prominent, draughty place, but it was warm and inviting. Beautiful Persian carpets on the floors, huge tapestries on the walls, and paintings of landscapes and portraits adorned the walls. Massive chandeliers hung from the ceiling in the hallway, and gold ornate mirrors were hung in alcoves.

It was the Dowager Duchess of Rochester, Lady Virginia that greeted us all. I hoped the duke would be there, but apparently, he was in the stables with a mare about to foal. "Anyone would think he sired them himself, the fuss he makes of them," she said with a laugh, then instructed the claret and gold-liveried footmen to take our trunks to our rooms, and we followed. "Oh, Miss Braemar, Philomena asked if she could share a bedroom with you. I hope that is acceptable to you?"

I told her we had already discussed this, and it would be quite acceptable. Since I was the first to arrive, I had the choice of beds, so I chose the one by the window.

Shortly after arriving at our bedroom I heard a knock on my bedroom door. I opened it to see one of the liveried footmen. "Miss Braemar, this is a message for you from His Grace, the Duke. He asked if you would like to join him in the stables."

Without hesitation, I nodded and followed him down to the stables, where he left me. The duke was in one of the stalls with a beautiful ginger-coloured mare who looked like she was in foal.

He laid his index finger to his lips and whispered, "I thought you might be interested?"

I whispered back, "Oh yes. Thank you for thinking of me. How long has she been in labour?"

"She's nearing the end now. The foal should be born any minute. You will see a tiny pair of hooves peeking out if you look."

I looked at the horse's rear end, and indeed, I saw the tiny hooves. "What is she called?" I asked, referring to the horse.

"Amber, you can stroke her if you wish. I'm sure she would rather have the gentle touch of a lady's hands than my big paws," he whispered.

I sat down in the hay next to him and stroked her head. "You are such a clever girl, Amber," I said. She lifted her head and put it on my lap, where I continued to stroke it and whisper words of encouragement. I felt that her laying her head on my lap was a sign of trust. The look in her eyes was of such love and trust. I rubbed the velvet texture of her nose. She gave one final heave, and her foal slid from her and lay in the hay of the stall. The duke gathered a handful of hay and rubbed the foal down before her mother licked and let her suckle.

I hadn't looked at the duke when I first arrived, as I was more interested in the horse, and realised he was just in his shirt sleeves. His sleeves rolled up above his elbows, and the top two buttons of his shirt were undone, exposing suntanned skin with a sprinkling of dark hairs peeking out just above the 'v' of his open shirt. I could see the bulging muscles in his arms without his jacket on.

"I don't suppose I should have invited you here, Miss Braemar," he said.

"To Knole Castle, Your Grace?" I asked, "I thought I had been invited because your niece and I had become friends."

"No, no," he laughed, "I meant here in the stables. I suppose it is not the sort of thing young ladies of the ton should be a party to the birthing of a foal."

My heart was beating in my breast like a captured bird. It was apparent that he didn't mind rolling up his shirt sleeves and buckling down with the rest of his staff, and that inspired another form of admiration in me.

"Then why did you invite me, Your Grace?" I asked him breathlessly.

He cocked his head to one side and looked at me, "I sense that you are different. I apologise if I have wronged you, Miss Braemar."

"No, I am glad that you invited me. I felt privileged to see the latest addition born to your stables."

I don't know how long we had been in the stables, but it looked like the sun was going down. He shrugged on his jacket, and we left the stables, walking in companionable silence until we reached the front door.

"I hope you won't get into trouble disappearing as you did, but I thought you might be interested. It might not be something that would be acceptable in polite society, a young lady at the birth of an animal, and I should imagine Lady Mary would disapprove, but I thought that you were..."

"Different," I said, using his own words. "Lady Mary will not learn from me. I think she was going to rest once we arrived, as the journey has taken its toll on her, so I probably won't even be missed."

He smiled and nodded as we stood just inside the front hall.

"It was wonderful. Thank you for thinking of me." He stepped closer to me and reached into my hair. Was he going to kiss me?

"A tell-tale piece of straw," he said and threw it to the ground.

I smiled at him. "Thank you, Your Grace."

I went upstairs to my room, and Philomena awaited me. "Julia, where have you been? I've been here ages waiting for your return. I nearly went and asked Lady Mary's maid. Lady Virginia was conducting a tour around the castle and telling the history of it. Did you know that Henry XIII stayed here? I've seen the castle many times before, but I thought you might be interested in its history. You should see his bedroom. It even has a crown above the four-poster bed." I took her hand in mine to calm her down.

"I had a message from the duke to go to the stables shortly after we arrived. I thought that we might be going riding."

"But you're not dressed for riding," Philomena said, looking at me.

I nodded. "When I got there, I found him in one of the stables with a horse about to foal, so I stayed there and petted the horse until the foal was born. Oh, it was the most wonderful thing I have ever seen," I enthused.

"But you were alone with Uncle Robert?"

"Please don't tell anyone, Philomena. I don't suppose I should have been, and Lady Mary would be angry and probably try to force your uncle into marrying me."

By now, we were sitting and talking on one of the beds together.

"Isn't that what you want, Julia?"

I shook my head; it was what I wanted if I was honest with myself, but I didn't want any man to be forced into marrying me.

"Not unless it is what he wants," I told her. "I wouldn't want any man to be forced into marriage with me."

"I could work on him..." she said.

"No. He must be left to make up his own mind. Please, Philomena, don't say a word to anyone. Promise me." I held her hands in mine. This was what friendship was all about sharing secrets and knowing that they would be safe with your confidant.

"But I want you to be my aunty, Julia!" she cried.

"Well, I don't. It makes me sound old. If the Duke wants me, he must ask for me, but I think we are just friends, nothing more."

Jane came into the room. "Miss Julia, I unpacked your trunk. I wondered where you were?"

I lied when I told her that I wanted to stretch my legs after the journey, so I went for a walk.

"Dinner will be in half an hour, Miss Julia, so you must get washed and changed."

Philomena's maid came in with a gown, which she had just ironed out the creases. "Amy, can you show Julia's maid, Jane, where to find everything? Julia and I can help each other dress this evening, and then you may both return and do our hair," Philomena said.

Jane and Amy left the room briefly so that Amy could show Jane where she could iron my dress, and then they returned it to me. Philomena and I helped each other with the fastenings to our gowns. I had chosen a peach satin with thick cream lace on the bustle and hem. Philomena's gown was an aqua blue with white lace on the neck, sleeves, hem, and bustle.

We sat down to dinner in a large dining room. There were about one hundred guests. I knew that Knole Castle was significant, but to accommodate so many people, I could hardly believe it. When I mentioned it to Philomena, she told me that not all of them were staying at the castle. The dining room was all crystal and gold. Once everyone was seated, what seemed like an army of footmen brought out the first course. There was also so much talk in the room that your conversations had to be restricted to your immediate dinner partners on either side of you. I had seen the duke sat at the top of the table and the dowager Duchess at the opposite end. The food was delicious, as to be expected, with toasts to the duke and dowager duchess with thanks for their hospitality. When the meal was over, the ladies left the gentlemen to their port and cigars while we retired to a large blue drawing room with sofas and chairs scattered around tables, where we could rest our teas or other beverages. In one corner stood a pianoforte. The dowager duchess came and stood by me. "Miss Braemar, would you be kind enough to entertain us until the gentlemen join us?"

I smiled at her. I could see the family resemblance between her and the duke. Also, Philomena looked very much like a younger version of her great-aunt.

I sat down and began to play. I thought it would be background music for the ladies talking, but I was wrong. They sat and listened to me and applauded at the end of each piece. The gentleman joined us, and I stopped playing. It was the duke who asked me to continue. "Is there anyone that would like to sing, and I will accompany them?" I asked. Two ladies stood up, then a gentleman. Tables had been brought out so that people could play various games of cards.

At the end of the evening, the Dowager Countess of Rochester came over to thank me. I told her that it was my pleasure. Philomena approached me and asked if I was ready to go to bed. I nodded. Arm in arm, we walked up the large sweeping staircase to our bedroom, where Amy and Jane waited. We stood while our maids unbuttoned our gowns, and then we sat down for them to brush our hair and plat it, ready for bed.

Philomena and I sat up, talking for ages before she started yawning. She wished me good night and then blew out her candle. I lay awake longer, thinking about the duke and how he looked in the stables with his shirt sleeves rolled up. My heart flipped again, and I gave another involuntary sigh. I tossed and turned, then, in the end, gave up. I got out of bed, wrapped a shawl around my shoulders and slipped my feet into my slippers, and then quietly shut the bedroom door behind me. I found a candle and flint on the small table outside our room and lit it. Everywhere in the house was silent. Everyone had gone to bed. I did think of going down to the kitchen for a hot drink, but the castle was such a massive place, and I had no idea where it was; all the staff must have been in bed, so I quietly went down the stairs and out to the stables to see Amber and her foal. I knew my way now and went out across the courtyard to the stables. It was cool outside but much warmer inside with the animals and the lamps' heat. There were lamps lit inside the stables, and I made my way to Amber's stall.

I jumped when I found someone in the stalls with probably the same idea as me.

The duke was leaning over the stall, watching Amber and her foal. Again, he was in his shirt, without a jacket, sleeves rolled up over his elbows, and the top buttons of his shirt undone.

"I thought I was the only one awake," he said when he saw me.

"So did I," I replied. "I came to see how mother and baby were."

"See for yourself," the duke said as he leaned over the stall.

I looked over into the stall to see Amber and her foal. The foal had four white legs, a mane, a tail and a white face; the rest of her was the same colour as her mother. "Do you have a name for her yet?" I asked.

"What do you think?" he asked me.

Amber snickered and moved closer to me. "She remembers me?" I said, surprised.

"Yes, and see, she has brought her daughter to show you," the duke said. I stroked Amber's head first, then her foal, and remembered Copper, whom I rode in Cornwall. I rubbed the foal's head. "Hello, Copper," I said as I stroked Copper's velvety little nose.

"Copper," he said, testing the name on his lips. "Copper it is." He turned to me, taking in my hair in its long plat to my nightdress, and I blushed. "Thank you for entertaining my guests this evening," he said. He stepped closer and tucked a stray hair behind my ear. I shivered. "Are you cold?" he asked me, his voice full of concern. I nodded. "A little, Your Grace."

"I don't have a jacket to put around your shoulders." He grinned devilishly, "I could give you a horse blanket."

I laughed and nodded. He went to one of the other stalls, brought a blanket, placed it around me, and rubbed my arms to generate warmth.

"If you leave it on the floor outside your bedroom, I'll pick it up and return it here."

My mouth went dry with this intimate moment. "I...I should leave. I shouldn't be here," I told him.

"No... do you want me to see you back?" he conceded.

I shook my head, held the horse blanket around my shoulders, gave him a quick curtsy and left.

I felt hurt that he didn't want people to find out about us and force him into marriage, but of course, I had said that he needed to make up his own mind; I was just the fraud of Moldova Square with no dowry, and also the friend of his niece. Why would he want to marry me? I thought that in any marriage I made, I would have to tell the truth about my history, that I was just a girl from a small fishing village in Cornwall whose father was a mine manager and grandfather a doctor, with no links to the aristocracy. I might as well just make the most of what time I had living fraudulently with Lady Mary, then disappear, either with or without Jane.

I dropped the blanket outside the bedroom door, opened the door and climbed back into my bed by the window. Philomena looked like she hadn't moved. When I lay down and closed my eyes, all I could see was the duke in the stables.

I fell fast asleep until Jane woke me with my breakfast tray the following day.

I looked across to Philomena, whose maid had done the same. We chatted about the day ahead while we ate. When Jane opened our bedroom curtains, the beautiful spring sunshine flooded the room. I could see through the window that the sky was a lovely cornflower blue. After breakfast, archery or croquet would be on one of the castle's lawns. Some of the men would go shooting, and some ladies would take their carriages and go into Seven Oaks sightseeing and shopping.

Although I had never done it before, I fancied archery, so Philomena and I decided to try it.

The day was mild. Some ladies had decided to sit on the lawns on blankets with their embroidery, or a book, a cup of tea, and sandwiches while some of us stood before the five targets set up on the lawn. Some gentlemen had gone off shooting, while others stayed behind and offered to teach us archery.

Philomena and I, Christina Carlisle, Melody Prentice and Belinda Carmody were there. We were due to be presented this year, so we all had much in common. There was a lot of giggling while the men tried to show us how to hold the bow and then keep the arrow to the bow and release it. Arrows flew everywhere but to the target, so we all tried again. In the distance we could hear gunshots from the men who had decided to go hunting. I hoped they were having more success with their hunting than we were with the archery.

Due to becoming the next Earl, James Carmody, Belinda's older brother, was tutoring Philomena. It seemed that the Duke of Rochester had decided to tutor me. The other gentlemen took an interest in the other ladies and showed them how to hold the arrow. Rochester was so close to me that I could smell his Sandalwood cologne. I could feel his warmth against my back as he stood so close to me. His lips were so close to my ear as he gave me instructions. I felt a ripple of pleasure run through my whole body.

"Right now, follow your line of sight along the arrow's shaft to the target. When you have it lined up, breathe in and let go of the arrow," he whispered in my ear.

I let the arrow go, and to my surprise, it hit the target. It wasn't the bullseye but one of the outer rings, but at least it hit it. "Right, Miss Braemar, try on your own now, remembering what I said," Rochester said, cheering me on.

My back felt cool as he moved away, and I missed his warmth. I picked another arrow from the quiver and fixed it to the bow. I pulled the string back, lined it to the central ring of the target, took a breath and released it. This time, it hit the target nearer to the bullseye, and I smiled at my achievement.

"Well done, Miss Braemar. You're so near the bullseye. Try again," the duke said to encourage me.

Philomena looked across at me, "Uncle Robert is a much better teacher than Mr Carmody. Can you teach me, Uncle Robert, please?"

The duke nodded and applied himself to teaching his niece while Mr Carmody looked at me and said, "I do believe Miss Braemar that I am surplus to requirements. You seem to have picked it up quite remarkably quickly. If you would excuse me," he bowed to me and returned to the house.

When Philomena hit the target with her uncle's tuition, she jumped up and down, then turned and kissed her uncle's cheek.

The duke turned as he was about to leave us and said, "Keep practising, ladies. We will have a competition this afternoon."

Lunch was laid out on a long table on the patio overlooking the lawn. There were so many dishes that the table seemed to be dipping under the weight of it all.

I saw the men return from hunting with their guns slung over their shoulders and with a stag tied to a wooden pole and carried by two footmen. Also, braces of pheasants were being carried by another four footmen. I had sat down with Lady Mary and Lady Hiddleston when Philomena joined us, chattering excitedly about the archery competition.

Obviously, with so many people at the house party, I didn't see much of the duke, but his mother, Lady Virginia, seemed to take a particular interest in me and spent quite some time talking to me and getting to know me. At least she only knew me as Lady Mary's ward, so I didn't have to worry about more lies.

After lunch, the archery match started with all the ladies who had been learning in the morning. I don't mean to sound big-headed, but Philomena and I were the best, so it came to a final round with just the two of us. She grinned across at me, "Good luck, Julia."

"You too, Philomena. May the best woman win."

We had five arrows each and tossed a coin to see who went first. Based on the toss, Philomena went first, and I followed. We were about even down to the last arrow, and Philomena got dead centre on the target. I lined mine up and let go of the arrow. It landed on the outer edge of the bullseye. Everyone applauded, and Philomena won. I went and hugged her, telling her congratulations. There would be a presentation for the archery winners and the shooting that evening at the ball.

We all dined in the grand dining room that evening, where there were toasts to the host, the duke and his mother during dinner and, of course, toasts to the Queen and the Prince. As before, the meal was excellent.

The ball started with the duke and the dowager duchess opening the dancing together.

Jane had packed a lemon satin ball gown for that evening. She said that it turned my skin a honey colour. After the opening dance, the duke asked Philomena to dance, then me. As soon as one dance ended, he moved on to another lady. His duty was to dance with as many young female guests as possible. I was busy dancing with different gentlemen at the ball. I don't believe I sat out one dance.

One gentleman, Mr Edgington, whose father owned a large shipping line, which he was preparing to take over from his father once he retired, danced with me. He was tall and well-built, with dark brown hair and eyes. He told me he was looking for a wife this season. I asked him what he was looking for in a wife. He looked down at me with his brown eyes. "You, Miss Braemar. Would you marry me?"

I was so shocked at first to learn that, during just one dance, he wanted to marry me that I tripped over his feet. I apologised. I knew nothing about him, and he knew nothing of me. When I mentioned this to him, he replied, "We have the rest of our lives to get to know one another, Miss Braemar," he said as if he could read my thoughts.

"I'm sorry, sir, but I cannot accept your proposal when I know nothing about you. Don't you think it is rather impetuous to ask after so short a time?" I told him.

He looked hurt, "You will not even consider it, Miss Braemar? I don't mind giving you time to think it over."

I shook my head. "I'm sorry, Mr. Edgington. I don't need time to think it over. Thank you for your kind offer, but I must decline," I told him.

"Very well, Miss Braemar," he said and bowed to kiss my hand at the end of the dance.

I heard the next day that he had made five proposals that evening and was accepted by Miss Belinda Carmody, who had told him that he must first ask her brother. If he agreed, then so would she. It was evident that the Edgington family had money, even if it had no title, but the Carmody family was more interested in wealth. The Edgington family were contented with the match.

It wasn't even the start of the season, and there was already a betrothal! I wondered how many more would there be before the season even started.

The awarding of prizes for the archery and shooting came towards the end of the evening. Philomena went up first to receive her trophy for archery, then Mr Dunwoody, the Earl of Carnarvon, had won the trophy for shooting the stag, so smiling, he collected his trophy. Both were applauded as they stood up.

The duke asked me for the final dance, which I accepted. "So, have you enjoyed the weekend, Miss Braemar?" he asked me as he put his hand on my waist. I told him that I had.

"What was the highlight of the weekend for you?"

"Seeing Copper born," I told him honestly.

"So easily pleased?" he teased me.

"You seem to forget Your Grace that I am just an ignorant country girl. I am easily pleased," I told him with a smile.

"Country girl, yes, but ignorant? Far from it," he replied.

I told him about Edgington proposing to me. His eyebrow raised in surprise. "And did you accept him," I noted a look in his eyes but couldn't think what it was.

"I am not in the habit of accepting proposals from strangers, Your Grace. I had never met him before, and then, out of the blue, he proposed. No, I have more discretion than that."

I thanked him for inviting Lady Mary and me to his home for the weekend.

"Think nothing of it," he said. "And have you had any other gentleman show an interest in you?" he asked me.

"Do you mean this weekend?"

"No, since you arrived from Cornwall."

"Lord Waterford gave me a teardrop-shaped crystal to hang in my bedroom. When the sun catches it, it casts rainbows all over the walls of my room."

We continued talking, and I hoped that he might give me a sign that he might be interested in me, but I was to be sorely disappointed.

"I presume that now Miss Carmody is betrothed, she won't be presented at court or have her season?" I spoke.

"No, really, once one is betrothed, there is no need for a season because the object has already been achieved," he told me.

"So, really, the point of the season is like a cattle market."

He laughed, "Don't let the other debutants hear you say that, or they will be highly offended. I suppose that you are right, though. I understand that a young lady's dream is to have a season. I think that any decent man would want her to have the excitement of it all."

"So, do you think any potential suitor would hold back from proposing so that the lady could still enjoy the excitement of having her season?"

"Well, isn't that what you would want, Miss Braemar? Wearing new gowns and having a variety of gentlemen's attentions on you. Isn't that what you dreamed of on your way from Cornwall."

I thought for a moment. I would have been excited if I hadn't been so worried about being discovered as a fraud. "I had never thought about it like that. To be honest, on the journey from Cornwall to London, all I thought about was being in the big city, there are so many places to see, that I had only read about."

"You said that Melbourne will escort you and Lady Mary to the Exhibition of paintings. I should be attending that too, so maybe we could walk around it together?"

I told him that I would like that.

"I haven't thanked you for entertaining our guests last evening. That is one of the concerns when you host a party of any sort, to keep your guests entertained."

I told him that it was my pleasure. "I enjoy playing the pianoforte; if others enjoy it too, that is all good."

"You do play extremely well. That is not just my opinion. Several guests have commented on it," he commented.

I blushed. "Well, maybe if I don't get a proposal by the end of the season and enter into that dreadful state of spinsterhood, I may become a concert pianist." I grinned as I told him.

"Oh dear, that would be a terrible loss to the ton." He grinned back at me.

The dance ended, and people began to make their way to their bedrooms.

I found Philomena, and we went to our room to discuss the weekend. "I have never won anything before, Julia," she told me, looking at the trophy again. It was only a small thing, but it meant everything to Philomena. I genuinely felt pleased for her.

"Did you dance with Mr Edgington?" I asked Philomena sleepily.

Philomena yawned, "Yes, and he proposed to me. I had never met him before, let alone danced with him before. I hear that the family has made money from shipping. Did he propose to you as well, Julia?"

I laughed. "I think he proposed to about half a dozen young ladies, and I understand that Miss Carmody accepted him."

Philomena sat up in bed, "Never! But she doesn't know him, does she?"

"Not that I know of."

"Maybe the family needs the money," I replied.

"And if he marries Miss Carmody, his family will be linked to a titled family," Philomena replied, then yawned again. "Well, if I were Miss Carmody, I don't think I would be able to sleep tonight, wondering what sort of man I had agreed to marry and spend the rest of my life with."

"I think we had a lucky escape, Philomena," I said, yawning and bidding her goodnight.

We fell asleep. It had been another long day, and the next day would be the same, as Lady Mary and I were travelling back to London with one overnight stay at a coaching inn.

Jane and Amy brought our breakfasts in the morning. After we finished eating, we washed and dressed, ready to travel. When we arrived downstairs to the large hallway, it was a hive of activity, with piles of trunks being carried downstairs from guest's bedrooms ready to be loaded onto the coaches. The Dowager Duchess of Rochester, Lady Virginia, approached me and kissed my cheek, then did the same to Lady Mary. "Thank you both for coming and to you, Miss Braemar, for entertaining our guests on the first evening. I hope that we will meet again soon."

She was such a lovely lady, and she seemed so genuine. I thanked her for inviting us.

The carriage was packed. All that was left was for Lady Mary and me to board it for the long journey back to London.

"Well, my dear, I think that was another success. Again, you did very well. I am glad that you never accepted Edgington's marriage proposal. He was working his way around the young ladies, asking the same question, I presume, until one accepted."

"I certainly wouldn't accept a proposal based on one dance. Miss Carmody has no idea what he is like. When he asked me the same question, I told him the same, and he said that we had the rest of our lives to find that out. I think he must have been desperate to do such a thing."

"The young lady must have been desperate as well to accept," Lady Mary said. "I do not enjoy travelling all this distance back to London, Julia. I don't think I can make this journey again."

"I'm sorry, Ma'am." I apologised.

"It's not your fault, dear. I accepted it on your behalf. I think when we get home, we will have a cup of tea and then go to bed for a while so that I can feel certain areas of my body again," she said with a smile.

I knew what she meant. I must have got soft since arriving in London as my behind was beginning to get numb, yet Jane and I had been travelling for nearly two weeks, and the carriage wasn't as lavishly appointed as Lady Mary's. I had been with Lady Mary for six months and was never happier because of all she had done for me and because we got on so well together. Apart from Mrs Watson at the Lodge, I had never had a maternal figure in my life, and Lady Mary seemed to fit in with my idea of that. I know that she enjoyed my company, but I also enjoyed hers. She was kind and warm and funny. I was growing closer to this woman who had taken me in, yet I was still a liar and a fraud. I didn't dare to tell Lady Mary the truth. Not yet, anyway.

Just let me have the excitement of being presented to the Queen and Prince Albert, then I would tell her. I told myself.

Mrs Trevelgue had been good to me over the years I stayed at Seaward Manor. Still, I believed she must have had an ulterior motive: trying to keep Edwina occupied, but Miss Frazer and I had failed miserably. I know that I was reluctant to give Mrs Trevelgue anything financially. Lady Mary had turned out to be nothing like Mrs Trevelgue had described her to me. I would rather tell the truth and shame the devil. Also, if I married a titled, monied gentleman, I would certainly not try to get them to invest in the mines. If the Trevelgue mines failed, then so be it. The mines had certainly taken enough from the district's people and me personally. Mrs Trevelgue had made up her mind and decided the day she married Mr Trevelgue, so why should Lady Mary invest anything in that family?

We stayed overnight at the same coaching inn that we had on the outward journey, and Lady Mary mentioned several times on the trip and at the coaching inn that she would be glad to get home and rest from the journey.

I was relieved when we returned to Moldova Square for Lady Mary's sake. Sitting for long periods was beginning to make my rear ache, even though the seating in Lady Mary's carriage was very comfortably appointed.

The footmen took our trunks upstairs to our rooms. Dorcas brought Lady Mary and me a pot of tea, then went upstairs to unpack for Lady Mary.

I poured for both of us and handed Lady Mary her cup. By now, I had learnt how she took her tea, so I didn't bother to ask. After she had finished, she went upstairs to lie on her bed. I picked up the book that I had been reading on the journey. It was a lovely spring day, so I took my book outside and some stale bread from the kitchens fed the ducks, and then settled down on one of the garden benches to read. I smiled as the ducks waddled up to me. They were such comics, squabbling over who got to eat first. I told them not to be so greedy as I threw pieces at them. When I had finished, they waddled back to the ponds and swam around, quacking merrily with full stomachs. I sat on the bench for a while, but that was harder than the seats in the carriage, so I decided to follow Lady Mary's example and go and lie on my bed for a while.

Sharing a bedroom with Philomena was lovely, but I missed my beautiful, spacious room in Moldova Square and I wondered how or if I could give up this life I had now spent the last six months in.

Jane was in my room unpacking my trunk and putting my things away.

"Are you all right, Miss Julia?"

I told her I was stiff and tired, so I would lie on my bed for half an hour and read.

"I can't believe we have actually stayed at a castle, like the Queen," she said as she put away some of my things.

"We have certainly come a long way from Seaward Manor, Jane," I agreed.

Chapter Ten

As the weather improved, Philomena and I regularly went horse riding in the Row. The better weather brought more people to the Row. Although people still rode in their carriages, they kept the travel blankets over the ladies' knees.

Gentlemen rode past us and lifted their hats to us. We both giggled together and talked as we rode on. We talked about Byron, or Philomena talked about Byron, enthused about how handsome he was. I asked her if she did not think he was too old for her, but she shook her head. As her friend, I thought it was my duty to tell her about Byron.

I reined my horse under a tree, and Philomena joined me. "You know that Lord Melbourne is a regular visitor to Lady Mary's, Philomena?"

"You are not going to tell me that Melbourne has offered for you, Julia. I know that you are often seen in his company."

"With Lady Mary, Philomena. No, he hasn't offered for me, and I wouldn't expect him to. He is just a friend. I wanted to tell you that Melbourne was married some years ago to Lady Caroline Lamb, but he wasn't an Earl then. Anyway, his wife had a rather public affair with Byron until he cast her aside. Lady Mary said that Melbourne's wife called Byron mad, bad and dangerous to know. I am only telling you this as a friend, Philomena. Please don't pin your hopes on Byron." I sincerely hoped my new friend would heed my warning.

She smiled at me, "Mama has already warned me about him and his reputation and told me that if my name ever became linked with his, my reputation would be ruined."

I sighed in relief and grinned at her, "He wears makeup, Philomena!"

"I know Julia. How could I marry a man more beautiful than me?" she laughed. "He might use my makeup! I couldn't have that." Two dimples, very like her uncle's, appeared on either side of her mouth as she laughed. I could imagine Philomena and Byron arguing over whose makeup it was and started to giggle as we turned our horses homewards.

When we returned to Philomena's, we went upstairs to her bedroom and talked about being presented at court, our debut gowns, and the ball later that evening.

It was only a matter of days before we were presented at the court. London's population seemed to have doubled overnight as families returned from their country seats ready for the new season.

Mamas and daughters hurried from one shop to another in haste to have everything ready for the season before the Modistes ran out of beautiful, attractive materials that would show their daughters off to their best advantage and catch a husband.

Philomena and I spent our days visiting the Modiste to get fitted with new ball gowns in the weeks and months leading up to our debut. We also went to the art gallery that her uncle had mentioned, but he did not arrive as he said he would. I was a little disappointed, but I had other things on my mind, like our presentation. We often rode together in the Row or stayed closeted in one another's bedrooms, talking about gowns, gossip, and suitors.

The wedding between Miss Carmody and Mr Edgington had already occurred, with much speculation among the ton about why the hasty proposal and subsequent marriage. I did not participate in the gossip, although Philomena passed on much of the gossip she had heard. The truth was that the Edgington family, although financially well-off, desired the support and backing of a titled family.

Our presentation was in the afternoon of our 'big day'; once we had been presented, we could go home to rest and prepare for the evening ball, the first ball of the season, the theme of which was exotic birds. We would go to the Modiste together and see Madam Yvonne without Philomena's mother and I without Lady Mary. We would discuss fashion, materials, perfumes, men, and everything young ladies discussed. We would visit each other's homes and spend our time in each other's bedrooms looking at our gowns and discussing which ones we would wear for different balls or afternoon teas.

All the gowns of the young ladies to be presented were in white or off-white, signalling our virginity to the gentlemen who were looking for a wife that season.

But the excellent weather had brought people out before Philomena and I were presented. They went to Hyde Park for picnics or to promenade and feed the ducks on the ponds. The good weather was enticing people out of their homes to make the most of it. I went out with Lady Mary and Lord Melbourne one sunny afternoon. We met several people in the park, and I was surprised to see the Duke of Rochester there, walking with his mother, enjoying a stroll in the sun. We stood and talked for a while, and then Lady Virginia, Lady Mary, and Lord Melbourne got into a conversation, leaving the duke and myself standing by.

"Lady Mary," Lord Rochester said, "May I take Miss Braemar around the park while Melbourne escorts you and my mother?"

Lady Mary looked at me and nodded. We thanked her and went our own way. The duke offered me his arm as we walked around the park. It felt so comfortable to hold on to him.

"How are Amber and Copper doing?" I asked him.

"Oh, they are doing very well, and Copper is growing practically daily." He replied, "Philomena is getting excited about being presented at court; in fact, it is all that she talks about. Are you looking forward to it?"

"Yes, very much so."

"She tells me that you have been out shopping together. I am pleased that she has found a friend in you. She does not have any female siblings, so she needs to have a friend. I am glad it is you."

"She told me that her brothers just look at her as an annoying little sister."

"I think all brothers look at their little sisters as annoying," he told me.

"Do you have any sisters, Your Grace?" I asked, realising that although we had met a few times now, I really knew very little about this man.

"No. I have two younger brothers, one in the army and the other at sea. As the oldest, I was groomed to become the next duke, so I stayed home to learn 'duking' from my father. At first, I was envious of my brothers' travelling the world, but since I started breeding horses..."

"As well as 'duking'," I teased him.

"Yes, I find the 'duking' easier. I have good estate managers on all my estates, so I can spend most of my time doing what I enjoy most."

"How long have your brothers been away from home?"

"A couple of years. My mother misses them, of course."

"And you?" I asked him,

"No, I find them annoying little brothers." He grinned at me.

People we met as we walked smiled or nodded to us, and then the females continued to whisper behind their fans; I wondered if they were speculating on a marriage between the duke and myself.

He checked his pocket watch. "We have been away from Lady Mary for an acceptable time, Miss Braemar. Let's try to find her so that she doesn't think I've run off with you," he said.

'Oh, if only,' my heart was saying. I didn't want our walk to end, but I knew it had to.

He never mentioned the proposed visit to the art gallery that he did not attend, and I thought it best not to mention it either.

We returned and finally found Lady Mary and Lord Melbourne in his carriage. "I am sorry if we have kept you waiting, Lady Mary," the duke said, "but we got talking and lost track of the time."

"Well, you're back now, Julia. I think it's time we left. We have taken up more than enough of Lord Melbourne and Lady Virginia's time," she said.

The Duke of Rochester handed me into Melbourne's carriage, bowed and left us.

When we were returning to Moldova Square, I apologised again to Lady Mary and Lord Melbourne. "The weather was so good, and we talked about his family and younger brothers."

"Oh, you mean Anthony and Alexander," added Lord Melbourne.

"The duke didn't tell me their names, just that one was in the army and one in the navy."

"The fate of younger brothers. Either that or the clergy, but I couldn't imagine either of the duke's brothers entering into the clergy."

Lord Melbourne looked tired.

We returned home. Lady Mary invited Lord Melbourne in for tea, but he refused, saying he had other things to do. He left, and Lady Mary and I sat in the drawing room drinking tea.

After he had left, I commented that he looked tired.

Lady Mary shrugged, "Neither of us is getting any younger, Julia," she said. "Maybe after he has rested, he will be as right as rain."

We sat in silence for a while, thinking about Lord Melbourne.

Lady Mary sighed, "Would you play for me for a while Julia? Something soothing as I have something on my mind that I wish to discuss with you dear."

I went over and sat at the piano, letting my fingers drift over the keyboard, thinking about Cornwall and the beaches, with the sun sparkling off the sea and waves.

"That is something new Julia, what is it? Do I know the composer?" she asked, sitting and listening as I continued to play.

"Oh it is just something I thought up which reminded me of the beaches and the sea in Cornwall," I explained.

"You mean you have made it up?"

"Yes, I don't suppose it is any good, but it just reminded me of home when the weather is nice and sunny."

"My dear girl, is there no end to your talents on the pianoforte? That is beautiful. Do continue, please."

I continued playing for a while as pictures of the calm sea and beautiful golden beaches came to mind, and for some reason, tears began to prick at the back of my eyes and threatened to course down my cheeks.

"Julia, my dear, I have been thinking just lately. I know we have legally changed your name, and you are known as my ward, but over the past six months, you have proved yourself to be all I would wish for. You have behaved yourself, certainly with more decorum than my daughter ever did. You have certainly equipped yourself better. I want my solicitor to come tomorrow so that I can settle a dowry on you and also put you in my will as my heir. I wanted to do this before the season started to give you all the benefits other young ladies have."

I stopped playing.

This was a shock. I had not expected this to happen for some time, and I had been dreading this moment as I wanted so much to be presented at court, but I couldn't see this happening if I told Lady Mary the truth. My stomach muscles immediately gripped in the fear of what was about to happen and I felt sad and ashamed to have lied to this kind woman who had given me everything and asked for nothing in return.

I did not want this. I did not want Mrs Trevelgue to be able to claim Lady Mary's money, so I did not want Lady Mary's money.

"No, please don't do that, Lady Mary. I don't deserve this." My heart started banging in my chest with fear. I could feel tears that had been threatening while I played and envisaged Cornwall, come to my eyes and trickle unchecked down my cheeks. I felt deflated; the burden that Mrs Trevelgue had put on me was too much, and I couldn't handle it any longer. I could not lie anymore to this kind old lady. I was a fraud and a liar, and I would not cheat Lady Mary any longer. I could not lie to her anymore.

"Nonsense, child. I can give my money to whomever I want. I have been proud of your achievements. You are the epitome of a young lady of the ton, probably more so than most."

"Lady Mary..." How could I tell her? But tell her I must. Now was the right time. My charade could not continue, and I was crying hard by now.

"Lady Mary...I am not who you think I am." I sobbed.

Lady Mary sat looking at me. There was no shock on her face. No surprise, as I would have expected. "You are not Julia Braemar? You have papers to prove that you are," she reminded me.

"No...I am not your granddaughter." My whole body was shaking with sobs. I was scared, not of being found out not to be Lady Mary's granddaughter, but of losing Lady Mary. I had grown fond of her over the six months I had been with her. I enjoyed our time together, reading, playing the pianoforte, playing cards or chess or backgammon, and laughing with her like when Jane fainted when Dorcas pierced my ears.

"If you are not my granddaughter Julia, then who are you?" Lady Mary asked, handing me a handkerchief.

I sobbed so hard that I struggled to speak and was struggling to catch my breath. "Who are you, Julia?" she pressed me.

"I...I...I was your granddaughter's companion," I told her when I could finally find my voice.

"I think you had better tell me everything, don't you?" she said. She still didn't sound angry, which surprised me.

I took a deep breath and began my story. "My name is Julia Beddoes, or was before we changed it. My father was the manager at the Trevelgue mines in Cornwall. My mother died in childbirth. My maternal grandfather was the district's doctor, which meant he was the Doctor for the Trevelgue Mines and the rest of the district. I used to go to the big house to play with Edwina, your granddaughter. When I was ten, my father was killed in the mine when a roof collapsed, and he died with three others. After my father died, Gramps tried to keep me with him, to bring me up; he and Mrs Watson, who was our housekeeper and had looked after me since I was born, but Mrs Trevelgue suggested that I move up to Seaward Manor and be tutored with Edwina and act as her companion. I hated lying to you, Lady Mary. You deserved better than that...which was why I tried to persuade you to let me look for positions for Jane and myself." I began sobbing again.

"Continue with your story," Lady Mary calmly prompted me.

So, I did. "Mrs Trevelgue had hired a governess for Edwina and then suggested that I take advantage of the governess, Miss Frazer. She tried teaching Edwina, but Edwina was reluctant to learn, so we devised different ways to get Edwina interested in her lessons, but it was difficult. Edwina wasn't the easiest person to live with. Mrs Trevelgue bought Edwina a horse for her thirteenth birthday. I borrowed a horse from the stables, and we were taught horse riding using the side saddle. Edwina started seeing the stable boy, and one day, they got caught in a compromising situation. The stable boy was dismissed. As we got older, Mrs Trevelgue hired a dancing teacher for Edwina, as she planned to give Edwina a London season. Sometimes, I would play for them to dance, but I never participated in those lessons; I just watched and sometimes I played the piano for them to dance to. Anyway, one day when Edwina was supposed to be having dancing lessons, I went to visit Gramps in the village, as I hadn't seen him for quite some time due to the bad weather. When the wind blows, it can nearly knock you off your feet, so it was over three weeks since I had last visited him. When I got to the village, I found the house locked up. I went looking for Gramps and Mrs Watson. All the villagers, people I had grown up with started giving nasty looks, and I couldn't understand why. When I finally found Mrs Watson, she told me that Gramps had died some weeks ago. She and the whole village thought that because I was living in the big house, I thought I was getting 'too big for my boots', as they put it. Mrs Watson said she had sent me a note when Gramps died, which I didn't receive."

"What had happened to the note?"

"It was given to Edwina, who was again in the stables with the stable boy. Mrs Watson also sent me a note informing me the day before Gramps's funeral. Again, I didn't receive it."

"What happened to that one?"

"Edwina again. Mrs Watson sent me a final note saying that she had to close the house, which the Trevelgues owned, and to come and collect my things. Again, I never received it."

"Edwina again?" Lady Mary asked.

I nodded. "When I told Mrs Watson that I didn't receive any of the notes and broke down crying, she told me that she had kept the things for me, for whenever I did show up. There were some personal things and a bit of money belonging to Gramps, which she gave me. I went back to the big house, fuming. I was so angry with

Edwina; this time, I would tell Mrs Trevelgue what her daughter had done. When I got back to the manor house, the place was in turmoil. Edwina had run off with the stable boy she had continued to see, even when he had been dismissed. The horse that Edwina was riding got too near the cliff edge, which collapsed, killing her. The dismissed stable boy found her, bringing her back to the house, or that was what he told everyone. I expected Mrs Trevelgue to dismiss me after Edwina's funeral, so Jane and I were planning to travel to London using some of Gramps's money. I was going to ask Miss Frazer for a reference so that I could look for a position of either a governess or a lady's companion. I was going to write Jane a reference so that she could look for a position as a lady's maid.

"After we were all walking back from Edwina's funeral, Edwina's oldest brother, Mark, accused me of killing her. I told him I was nowhere near Edwina, as I was in the village and had witnesses to prove it. He told me that most of them were employed by the Trevelgue mines, and if they said that I had been in the village with them, they would all lose their jobs."

"Oh, dear me," was all Lady Mary said.

I was still crying, just thinking about it again. "Mrs Trevelgue called for me the day after the funeral and had a proposition for me: pretend to be your granddaughter. I told her I looked nothing like the Trevelgues, and she said I was to say I was a throwback to Mr Trevelgues's family. Mrs Trevelgue said you probably wouldn't believe your eyes, but you would know your daughter's writing, so she wrote you the letter."

"And what did she want in return for what you have done?"

"Mrs Trevelgue said that if I behaved myself and conducted myself like the perfect young lady, then you would make me your heir, settle a dowry on me and leave all your money to me. That is why I don't want you to do it. She made you out to be a terrible woman and a terrible mother, and I have found out that you are none of those things. Please, Lady Mary, don't do it. I understand you will not want me or Jane under your roof, and I don't blame you. I will leave with the things I left Cornwall with and give you back your jewellery…"

"And what would you do?"

"I still have Miss Frazer's letter of reference, what money Gramps left me, and what was left over from the money Mrs Trevelgue gave me for the journey here. I opened a bank account with it and sold some of Edwina's jewellery." I stopped and looked at Lady Mary. She didn't look angry or have any of the emotions I expected her to have after telling the truth. No, she looked sad and resigned but not angry.

"Why are you not angry at me, Ma'am? I would have expected you to throw me out and tell me never to darken your doorstep again?"

"My dear Julia, did my daughter really think that I would not keep appraised of her life with Trevelgue? I knew every part of her life. The birth of the boys, then Edwina. I knew of her husband's death. What I didn't know was how much she hated me and what I and her father had done by casting her out without a penny. We both knew the Trevelgues had plenty of money from the mines, so we knew she wouldn't be on the bread line. Over the years, she has written to me, demanding what she believes I owe her, so yes, I knew that it was her writing in the letter you gave me. I presume she told you that if you did not do as she wished, you would be cast out without a penny and possibly be accused of my granddaughter's death, am I right?"

I nodded.

"Why do you think I insisted you call me Lady Mary or Ma'am rather than Grandmother? You even had trouble referring to my daughter as 'Mother'. I changed your name so she could not take anything from you. I knew you were unhappy with the situation she had put you in, and I believed she would have some hold over you. My daughter is motivated by money. It always has been and always will be. What would happen if I did not make you my heir?"

"Then I would have to persuade my husband to invest in the mines."

"And if he didn't?"

"Mrs Trevelgue said I could use my feminine ways to get him to do what I wanted."

"Did she now? Like she had used hers on Trevelgue. Oh, I don't doubt that it was her idea to consummate the marriage so we couldn't get it annulled," Lady Mary said, with a hint of anger in her voice. Mrs Trevelgue deserved every bit of her mother's ire. I couldn't help that I was complicit in her daughter's deception.

"Lady Mary, I am so sorry. I would quite understand if you turned me out of your house. As I said, I have put some money aside. It would help if you gave me a reference for a lady's companion, but if you don't, I would completely understand. I can pay back Mrs Trevelgue the money that I got for Edwina's jewellery."

Lady Mary nearly jumped out of her seat, "You will do no such thing Julia. If my daughter was stupid enough to think that I wouldn't find out, then she deserves to lose the money; every penny of it." Lady Mary stretched over and took my hand. "My dear Julia, I know that you are not my granddaughter, that you weren't my granddaughter from that first day, and from what you say, I don't think I would have liked my real granddaughter had she been alive. It seems like mother, like daughter. What was Edwina like, honestly?"

"We never got on. I think she hated me on sight. When Gramps and I were first invited to take tea, she stuck her tongue out at me, pinched me, and got me lost in the big house. She often told me I was her 'lacky' because I was employed as her companion."

"Besides the money aspect, why do you think my daughter did this for you?"

I sat and thought, "She knew what Edwina was like, that she was hard work, but also, my father died in the employ of the Trevelgue mines and Gramps death was kept from me by her daughter. I think that she was trying to make up for it all. The Trevelgue family and the mines were responsible for losing the last two remaining members of my family and making me an orphan."

"Oh, she did have some scruples then!" Lady Mary said.

"Are you going to write and tell her, you know?" I asked.

Lady Mary's face was sad. She must have felt deeply hurt knowing that her daughter was trying to dupe her and that Mrs Trevelgue's machinations were all to extract money from her to support the mines. I felt so sorry for her.

"Do you wish me to leave you, Ma'am?" I asked. Even if she didn't want to get rid of me, Lady Mary might still want to be left alone with her thoughts.

"Would you mind, my dear? Although I already knew or suspected what my daughter was up to, it still hurts to have it confirmed."

I stood, went over to her, and took her hand. "I am so, so dreadfully sorry, Ma'am." She kissed my hand and waved hers in dismissal, I think, before I saw her tears.

I walked slowly, sadly, up the stairs to my room, knowing that I had been instrumental in Lady Mary's disappointment and betrayal by her daughter.

When I opened my bedroom door, Jane looked at me. "You look like you've been crying, Miss Julia?"

I nodded and sniffed, then used the handkerchief Lady Mary had handed me to wipe my eyes and nose.

"What's happened?"

I sat on my bed, my shoulders drooping with sadness. "I have told Lady Mary everything." I felt exhausted, but free of the guilt of lying to Lady Mary. Free of this charade I had maintained for the last six months.

"Oh, Lawks, everything?"

Again, I nodded.

"Should I pack our bags to leave?" Jane asked.

"No, not yet. Lady Mary has known right from the start that I wasn't her granddaughter. She has been kept appraised of what has been going on in Cornwall. I think she was waiting for me to show my hand. Now I have. I don't know what will happen."

I lay down on my bed and closed my eyes. I was exhausted—not just physically but emotionally. Jane continued to work silently, and I nodded off to sleep. The weight of the fraud and lies finally lifted an enormous weight from my shoulders, and I was relieved.

I slept for about an hour, then heard knocking on my bedroom door; Jane opened it to find Dorcas standing there.

"Lady Mary wants to see you in the drawing room, Miss Julia."

I told her I would go down. I washed my face, tidied my hair, brushed out the creases in my dress, and went downstairs to the drawing room.

Lady Mary was sitting where I left her. She looked weary. She seemed to have aged ten years in an hour, and I knew that was partly down to me. I felt ashamed that I had left it so long to tell her.

"Are you all right, Lady Mary?" I asked, genuinely concerned for her.

She pinched the bridge of her nose as if she had a headache. "Yes, Julia, I am well. Come and sit down, my dear." This didn't sound like she was going to dismiss me altogether.

I sat.

"I have been thinking about our discussion, and my daughter coerced you into doing what you did. I knew that she was heartless, but I didn't know to what extent."

"I haven't exactly helped things, Ma'am," I said.

"You were stuck between a rock and a hard place, Julia. I don't blame you for any of this. Can I ask you something?" she said.

"Of course, Ma'am. What do you want to know?"

She sighed and sat back in her chair. "I want you to give me an honest answer. Will you do that?"

I nodded.

"What did you think of my family? Honestly?"

"I never met Mr Trevelgue. He died some years before I knew the family. Mark, well, I don't know why he wanted to accuse me of killing his sister. Richard was sent down from one university for being caught with one of the housemaster's wives. Neither came home very often, and when they did, I always stayed in my room, and Jane would bring me my food. I don't think either of the boys, or Edwina were well thought of among the staff. The boys had reputations within the female staff, so when they were at home I would sit in my room and read or embroider but never go downstairs. Jane would stay away from the boys as well. Edwina was a few months older than me; she was taller, developed early, and cruel, especially to me and ill-mannered. As I said before I understood she was caught in a compromising situation with the stable boy, but I don't know what a 'compromising situation' would be. I...I..."

"You promised you would give me an honest answer, Julia."

"Yes, Ma'am. I don't think you would have liked Edwina. She hated to learn anything. It was only with me reading out loud that enticed her to want to read more of the story. She hated maths, history, geography, needlework, music. She thought that because the family had money, she didn't need to do anything to get a rich husband or run a household. 'That was what the lackeys were paid for,' she would say. The only thing she seemed to excel in was horse riding, but on reflection, I think she had an ulterior motive for that."

"The stable boy?" Lady Mary interrupted then motioned me to continue. "She looked very like her mother, blonde-haired, blue eyes."

"My daughter, tell me about my daughter?"

"I think Mrs Trevelgue was kind-hearted in her way. She offered me a place in her home and paid for clothes for me, which were not the quality of Edwina's, but they were still new. I received a good education, and she was never unkind to me. Edwina made up for that. I think maybe if Mr Trevelgue had still been alive, the children might have been different. I have much to thank Mrs Trevelgue for, even for paying for Jane and me to come to London in a comfortable carriage and stay in decent coaching inns. Because I did not expect you to take me in, I tried to save some of the money she gave me so that we could stay in a modest rooming house for a while until we found employment, so Jane and I shared a bed, didn't have the expensive meals that Mrs Trevelgue had allowed for and as you know, what was left from Gramps and the money left from Mrs Trevelgue, plus I sold some of Edwina's jewellery and I opened a bank account."

"You were very astute to do that, Julia. Thank you for being so honest with your answers to my questions."

"That was the least I could do after what I had done, Ma'am."

"My daughter wanted you to send her half of your dowry and what I would leave in my will. Maybe she could have insisted that if you retained the name Trevelgue, or even Beddoes, but as we have changed your name legally, she cannot claim that, especially if she doesn't know it. I have only known you for six months or so, Julia, but I would be proud of you if you were my granddaughter. Very proud indeed. I still want to give you a dowry, and I still want to make you, my heir. Even more so, now that I know what my daughter wanted."

"But what about your grandchildren, your son's children, Ma'am? You could leave them your money and the dowry."

"They will have enough money when their father dies. Do not worry yourself about them. I want you to tell Woodbine what you have told me about my daughter so that if she or my grandsons come asking for money, they won't be able to get it. I want the legal paperwork watertight."

"I feel terrible about taking money away from your family, Lady Mary."

"If it will make you happy, I will write and explain everything to my son." She waited, expecting me to find some other excuse for not taking her money, but she seemed to have an answer to everything. "I will contact Mr Woodbine and get him to draw up the necessary paperwork, including that I am officially going to make you my ward."

I opened my mouth to complain, but she held her hand up to stop me from saying anything more.

The next day, Mr Woodbine and his clerk came to the house again. I was closeted in the library with them and Lady Mary for nearly two hours. At the end of it, I was legally Lady Mary's ward, her heiress, and I also had a dowry. I still didn't want any of it, but at least I was no longer a fraud or liar. After all she had done for me, I wished I could do something for Lady Mary. I felt thanks were not enough, but what else could I give in the way of thanks?

I asked Lady Mary if I could write a letter to Mrs Watson, our housekeeper at the Lodge, explaining what had happened and where I was. I had only sent her a brief note before telling her that I had arrived safely in London and would write more when I had found a position.

"As long as you impress on her, not to mention it to anyone. I don't want it getting back to my daughter."

"Yes, Ma'am."

I decided that I would sell some more of Edwina's jewellery and send the money or some of it back to Mrs Watson.

The next day, I took more of Edwina's jewellery to the pawn brokers to sell, put some in my bank account, and sent some to Mrs Watson. I sent a message to Philomena to see if she wanted to come with me, but she had a dress fitting at the Modiste, so I took Jane with me, along with my bank book.

We went to the same pawnbrokers as before. I left Jane to wait outside again and opened the door. When the pawnbroker saw who it was, I heard him groan.

"If you don't wish to deal with me, I can go elsewhere?" I told him.

"No, no, come on in, Miss. What do you have for me today?"

I opened my reticule, pulled out the jewellery, and placed it on the shop counter. I still had a few things left of Edwina's, but not much. Again, the pawnbroker's eyes lit up.

"Quality Miss. We are not going to haggle again, are we?"

"That depends on what you are offering," I told him. I knew we had dealt with each other before, but I felt more nervous this time. Why, I don't know.

He wrote a sum on a piece of paper and pushed it over to me. I looked at the figure and tutted. "Now we both know that it is quality. You even told me so when you saw it, yet your opening figure does not reflect that." I doubled the figure and passed it over to him.

"Miss, miss, miss, you are one to drive a hard bargain. Do you want to see me and my family thrown out onto the streets?"

"Oh, please. I know you made a good profit even on the last lot. My price, less fifteen per cent. Do you want me to write down the figure, or can you work that out yourself?"

"Oh, Miss, what do you take me for?"

"I am a lady, sir; I would not wish to sully my lips with an answer to that." I wrote my original figure, less the fifteen per cent and pushed the paper back towards him.

He looked at it

"Do we have a deal?" I asked.

He sighed dramatically, got the money and counted it out for me."

I took the money and placed it in my reticule. "If I wish to sell anymore, do you wish me to bring it here or take it elsewhere?"

Again, he gave me another dramatic sigh. "No, let me see what you have, and then we will see."

"Nice doing business with you," I said as I opened the door.

"I can't say the same," I heard him say. Grinning, I ignored what he said and left the shop.

I took Jane's arm when I got outside, and we went to the same little tea shop, where we had tea and pastries. Then I went to the bank, leaving Jane inside by the door. I handed my bank book to the clerk and handed over most of the money from the pawnbroker, holding back some for myself and some for Mrs Watson in Cornwall. The clerk added my money to that which I had already had in my account, then added the interest and passed the book back to me. I looked at the amount and was pleasantly surprised. I thanked the clerk, placed the book back in my reticule, and then we went to the post office so that I could send my letter to Mrs Watson along with some of the money.

When we returned to Moldova Square and went to my bedroom, I took some of the money from my reticule and gave it to Jane.

She stood looking at it, not saying anything or taking it.

"Take it, Jane," I urged her.

"But what's it for, Miss Julia?"

"It's your wages," I told her.

"But Lady Mary already pays my wages, Miss."

"Then do what you like with it."

"Like what?"

"Jane," I said, "You can do whatever you like. You could buy yourself some new shoes or clothes."

"Could I put it in the bank like you?" she asked, surprising me.

"Yes, of course," I told her. "If you want me to come with you to open an account in your name, I will do so."

The next few days were busy with trips to the Modiste for my final fitting for the gown for my presentation to Royalty and ones for the next few balls.

Lady Mary accompanied me again but allowed me more input these days in my gowns. "Miss Braemar, I have some material here that I am sure will suit you for the ball after your presentation. Its theme is exotic birds, is it not?" Madame Yvonne said.

She brought out a bolt of material and unrolled it on the counter for me to see. "It is the colour of peacock feathers. See how it sheens from blue to green. I can have a mask made from the same material with peacock feathers, black lace, and a feather for your hair. What do you think, Lady Mary?"

Lady Mary held up the material and nodded.

That afternoon, the Duke of Rochester called with Philomena, saying they were going to take a walk around Vauxhall Gardens and asked if I would like to accompany them. I looked across to Lady Mary, who nodded.

We travelled in the duke's open carriage as it was another beautiful sunny day. Since my confession to Lady Mary, I felt so much lighter, as if a weight had been lifted from my shoulders. It was not too hot or cold but cool enough for a shawl and to walk around in the beautiful sunlight with my best friend and her uncle. My world seemed so much brighter. What would my father and Gramps think of me if they could see me now?

Vauxhall Gardens was very busy. The good weather had brought people out; families strolled around, 'promenading', and others sat on the grass having picnics. Nannies walked around pushing perambulators containing their precious cargo. There were acrobats and jugglers to entertain us, with caps in front of them to collect money, which they would live on. Already, butterflies and bees were flying around, and birds sang in the trees. It was a beautiful day full of sunshine and bird song.

We all walked further along; Philomena was chattering away; she talked about things she wanted to see in the gardens, and the duke had his own ideas. A bandstand was set up with colourful striped deck chairs surrounding it, and a band was playing. There were colourful stalls selling handmade fans and silk shawls, large bird cages housing parrots, love birds, budgerigars and other stalls selling ice cream and cool drinks. I stopped at one of the stalls with silk shawls and bought a beautiful one with a sky-blue background and colourful butterflies and flowers for Lady Mary. I hoped she would like it. The duke bought us all an ice cream, which was delicious. We ate it as we walked around and looked at the birds in the decorative cages. The parrots could speak, and when we walked past, they squawked, 'God save the Queen.' Beautifully laid out flower beds and peacocks were roaming around impressively, fanning out their beautifully coloured tails. Even a white peacock strutted around, fanning his tail for everyone to admire.

The duke pointed out the fireworks tower and other points of interest to us, but Philomena wanted to go back and look at the fans and the shawls again. Philomena pointed out a fan made of peacock feathers and said it would go perfectly with my ball gown for the evening. I told her I had a black lace fan that I had bought to go with it, never expecting to find a fan made from peacock feathers.

"Well, you go and look at whatever you wish, Uncle dear, and Julia, and I will go and see what we wish," she said to him.

The duke sighed in resignation, "Oh, very well, ladies," he said, walking around with us, not complaining about our female chatter. I believed that Philomena had persuaded him.

"Are you enjoying yourself, Miss Braemar?" The duke asked.

"Yes, thank you, although I do not think this is your ideal outing."

"You know me too well." He grinned at me, twin dimples on either side of his mouth, turning my insides to honey. "But I am used to my niece's ways, so I never expected to get my own way today."

I grinned, "Should I take that as a compliment or an insult, Your Grace?"

He laughed, "Oh, I would never insult a lady, Miss Braemar." We continued walking a little longer, and then Philomena turned, "Can we go home now, Uncle Robert? My feet are killing me."

The duke looked at me and shrugged. "Maybe when there is an evening function on, like firework displays, if Lady Mary is agreeable, I could escort you and Philomena again?"

"You will have to ask Lady Mary Your Grace, but I have never seen fireworks," I informed him.

"I am sure you would find them fascinating if you don't mind loud bangs?"

They dropped me off outside the door to Lady Mary's, and I went inside after thanking the Duke and Philomena.

Lady Mary was in the drawing room taking tea with Lord Melbourne. "Ah, Julia, did you enjoy your outing with Philomena and the duke?"

I told her that I had and then went to my room. When I came down again, Lord Melbourne was still there, but he looked ill, and I had to comment.

"Lord Melbourne, are you feeling quite well? Only you do look a little peaky?"

"Politics can be very tiring, Miss Braemar. After I see you make your debut, I shall return to Brocket Hall and rest for a few weeks. Thank you for asking."

"Well, I think that is the right thing to do. You need to keep up your strength, sir."

I knew that Lady Mary had told him the truth about my background, and I felt relieved that there were no more lies between us. I liked and respected him and couldn't help but worry about him. In Lord Melbourne, I felt I had a surrogate father and had a great affection for him.

Lord Melbourne rose from his chair. "Well, ladies, I will take my leave of you, and I will see you at your presentation, Miss Braemar." He bowed over our hands and then left.

"Lady Mary, I am concerned about Lord Melbourne," I said when I saw his carriage pass by the window.

She nodded, "Well, he, like me, we are not getting any younger, and my dear, immortality is not an option."

"Oh, I hope he and you still have many years ahead. I will be terribly sad if anything happens to either of you. I have found a new family in you both."

"And I genuinely believe you, my dear. He told me he had been leeched, which helped him somewhat."

"But they don't resort to that unless he is ill. I know that from my Gramps."

"Well, I am sure he will tell us if he needs to, my dear," Lady Mary said, patting my hand to comfort me.

I nodded, and then she asked me if I had enjoyed my afternoon. I told her that Vauxhall Gardens was very picturesque, but Philomena called an end to the afternoon as her feet were aching from all the walking.

"The Duke of Rochester did say that he would like to take us to an evening event there, when there is a fireworks display, with your approval."

"If Philomena is going with you, or you take Jane, I cannot see a problem."

I handed her the beautiful silk shawl wrapped in paper, which I had bought her from Vauxhall Gardens.

"What is this?" Lady Mary asked as I gave it to her.

"This is just a little something to thank you for all you have done for me. I cannot hope to repay you for your kindness, so this is just a token of my esteem. I hope you like it, Ma'am."

Lady Mary looked at the shawl, and I noticed that her eyes looked a little watery. "You need not have Julia, but I thank you. I can't remember the last time someone bought me a present."

"You don't know how much I appreciate everything you have done for me, Lady Mary."

She grabbed my hand and squeezed it. "Now, make a good marriage and be happy, my dear. That is all I want for you."

The next day, I received a parcel. I took it into the drawing room. "What is that, Julia?" Lady Mary asked.

I told her that it was a parcel for me. I opened it. "It's a peacock fan with a note from the Duke of Rochester."

"That's very kind of him."

"While Philomena and I were looking at the goods displayed on the stalls in Vauxhall gardens, I mentioned to Philomena that for the evening ball after our presentation, my dress would be in the colours of a peacock, but I already had a black lace fan for that. I imagine the duke must have overheard."

Lady Mary admired it.

"Lady Mary, I am confused?" I said and sat down opposite her,

"Why is that dear?"

"He does things to show that he likes me, but when I told him some months ago that I didn't have a dowry, he just made a hasty exit. Yet even now, he does things to please me, then the next minute he points out my mistakes, so I don't know if he is interested in me or not."

"I take it that you like him?" she said.

"Yes, but I don't think he will offer for me."

"You must be patient, my dear. You have not even been presented yet," Lady Mary said, leaning forward and patting my hand to comfort me.

"He did say something some time ago about any decent gentleman would not deny a young lady the excitement of having her season."

"Well, there you are then. Maybe he is waiting. As I said, Julia, be patient."

"But what if someone else offers for me before he does. If he does?"

"You can always thank them kindly for their offer, but you do not feel that they are the right person for you. Or you could say you need more time to think about it."

I greatly valued her advice, and although she was old enough to be my grandmother, there were times when I felt we were more or less the same age, or at least like mother and daughter. As I had never known my mother, I think I mainly looked at Lady Mary as a maternal figure. Maybe she looked at me as the daughter she wished that she had. How Mrs Trevelgue had treated me, I think that maybe something of Lady Mary had rubbed off on her. Mrs Trevelgue certainly hadn't been bad to me. I had much to thank her for, but not for making me lie to Lady Mary. That was now between Mrs Trevelgue and her mother.

Chapter Eleven

Now that I had told Lady Mary the truth about my past, I felt that I could fully enjoy and appreciate my new life. For the time being, apart from Lady Mary and Lord Melbourne, no one else needed to know my past, but I knew there would come a time if any man offered for me that I would have to tell him the truth.

The day came when my gown for my presentation arrived. It wasn't just me that was excited to see the finished product. Jane was as excited as I was.

Philomena came to view my gown, a beautiful cream with gold embroidery, and then I went to view hers, which was white with gold embroidery. Both gowns had a court-sized train. We practised curtseying to each other in preparation for the big day and our presentation to the Queen and Prince Albert.

I once would have been worried about lying to Lady Mary and not feeling I deserved the honour of being presented at court. I felt now that I belonged as Lady Mary's ward. We often talked about my real family, and it felt good that we had no more secrets.

I saw Mr Lamb, the Viscount Melbourne, once before the big day. He asked if I was excited about being presented. Of course, I told him that I was. Because he had taken such an interest in me, and Lady Mary had told him the truth about my background, and we talked openly about my past. He also knew about Lady Mary making me her heir and giving me a dowry. I didn't want that fact to be well known, as I expected gentlemen to offer for me because of the money, and I didn't want that, even if the Duke of Rochester wouldn't offer for me because he thought I lacked a dowry. I received a letter from Lord Waterford saying he would look out for me at my presentation and the ball in the evening. I tried to forget about the duke and tried to concentrate on the possibility of other suitors. I thought of Waterford as a golden Greek God and was pleased he would look out for me at the presentation. He was very good-looking, and we seemed to get on well together, but he didn't stir the feelings in me that I had when Rochester looked at me and grinned. Would I be happy to settle for second best?

When Philomena and I rode in the Row, we saw Rutledge again in his open carriage, this time with a different lady than I had seen before.

Philomena leaned over to me and said, "That is Miss Farnsworth. Rumour has it that he has already offered for her."

"She has my sympathy if she has accepted him. I doubt that he will remain faithful to his marriage vows. I have seen him with many different ladies riding here, never the same one twice."

"Uncle Robert also says that he has gambling debts that he hasn't honoured as yet."

"He tried to get me into his carriage one day. I rode away, then I heard horse's hooves following me, and I thought it was him again, and I screamed, then I realised it was your Uncle Robert. He has been like my knight in shining armour twice. The other time was at New Year when Davenport trod on my feet while we were dancing, and they were so painful that I limped off the dancefloor. After everyone had left, he carried me to Lady Mary's carriage, followed us home and carried me up to the front door."

"Uncle Robert likes you, Julia," Philomena said, which was very serious for Philomena.

"How do you know that?"

"He is always singing your praises."

I hadn't told Philomena about Lady Mary making me her heir or the dowry. There were certain things I couldn't tell, even my best friend. If I told her, I thought it might get back to the duke, and I didn't want him to know. I wanted him to continue to believe that I didn't have a dowry, so if he did offer for me, it would be for me, not my dowry.

We rode back to Philomena's house, where her mother gave us tea and biscuits. She asked me if I was ready to be presented. I told her that I was nervous about falling over when I curtseyed.

"Just find a point to fix your eyes on before you curtsey, and don't forget to smile, dear," she told me. I liked Philomena's mother and her family, including the Duke and Lady Virginia.

When I returned to Lady Mary's, I found another letter waiting for me. I thought it might be another letter from one of the gentlemen, but I found it was from Cornwall. Mrs Watson had replied to my letter. I explained it to Lady Mary, who told me to open it in the privacy of my bedroom.

"I have no secrets from you now, Lady Mary," I told her as I opened the letter. Mrs Watson's writing wasn't perfect, but I didn't mind. I was just pleased that she had written to me.

My dear Julia

I am so pleased that you reached London safely, and the Dowager Countess knows who you really are. It is not good to keep secrets from someone so kind. Now, you will be a real lady, and I am proud to say I know one. Your father and your Gramps would be proud of you, too.

I hope to hear that you have made a good marriage to a titled gentleman, but even if you don't, I am sure that you will find a nice young man who will love you for who you are.

Now that I know you are safe, I can rest easy. The new doctor has arrived and has been with us for a few months. He has employed me again as his housekeeper, and he says I know the ins and outs of the people around here. There has been trouble at the big house again. Master Richard has arrived home again in something of a scandal, but it seems all the family are tarred with the same brush. The mines are not doing very well, and there is talk of some of them closing. I don't know what will happen then. Whether we work on the land or at sea, we will survive.

Don't worry about the big house finding out about you. Your secret is safe with me. Thank you for the money. It will be put to good use.

Love and Kisses

Mrs W.

I was so pleased to hear that the village and Mrs Watson were well, but I wanted to help not just Mrs Watson but the whole village, especially if the mines were struggling as I doubted the Trevelgues would care about anyone but themselves.

"Lady Mary, I want to help the village. I have some money put to one side. Also, I still have some of Edwina's jewellery left that I would like to sell and send the village some money. Would you mind?" I asked her for advice.

"My dear child, it is your money to do with as you please. You have all my daughter's jewellery, so you don't need Edwina's. Sell the rest of Edwina's jewellery if you wish. It is good to know that you want to help others."

I must admit that I expected Lady Mary to say no, but I was relieved that I had her approval.

The next day, Jane and I took the rest of Edwina's jewellery to the pawnbroker.

When I opened the door, the little bell over the door tinkled. He had a welcoming smile on his face, which changed immediately when he saw who his customer was. I didn't even wait for him to say anything.

"If you prefer I go elsewhere, that is all very well. It will save us both time with haggling."

He grimaced, "Let me have a look, Miss."

"This will be the last time that you will have to deal with me, and I am sure you have made a good profit from the other items I sold to you," I said as I pulled the rest of Edwina's jewellery from my reticule.

I placed what I had on the countertop.

"You say I won't have to deal with you again?" he asked.

I nodded.

"Just remind me whose jewellery this was?"

"My late sisters."

He got his monocular out and looked at Edwina's jewellery.

"I saved the best till last," I told him.

"Hmm," was his reply.

He wrote a figure down on paper and slid it across the countertop to me.

"Double it, then less twenty percent," I told him.

"You said twenty percent?" he asked, shocked at my generosity.

"Call it a parting gift," I told him.

He wrote down what I said, less the twenty percent. "Do we have a deal?" he said.

"That is fine."

He counted the money, handed it to me, and held out his hand. "It's been good dealing with you, Miss?"

"Trevelgue. Edwina Trevelgue."

"Miss Trevelgue."

I said goodbye to him and left the shop with a wad of money in my reticule. After our haggling, it was still more than I had expected.

Jane and I went to the bank, where I drew most of the money out. Including the interest, I felt that it would be enough to keep the village safe, even if the mine closed. Then I gave Jane some of the money. "To add to your account, Jane," I told her. She looked at me, "Are you sure, Miss Julia? It's a lot of money."

"You took the same risk that I did when coming to London. Of course, I am sure," I told her.

Jane hugged me, then deposited most of it in her own bank account, keeping some back so that she could treat me to tea and a pastry. "My treat," she told me proudly.

Before going to a tea shop, we went to the post office, where I wrote a brief note to Mrs Watson telling her that the money was for the whole village so that they wouldn't starve if the mine closed. I enclosed the money and sent it to Cornwall.

When the money was sent, I breathed a great sigh of relief. I felt so much better knowing that all my childhood friends and families would not starve, due to the Trevelgues' neglect. I could finally do something positive for the people and village I grew up in and loved.

Jane and I went to the tea shop and had tea and cakes.

Finally, the big day came, and I am sure all the young ladies of the ton were getting excited and maybe apprehensive about their presentation to Queen Victoria and Prince Albert. Lady Mary was going to present me. For the big event, she wore a pale lilac gown, which she normally wore darker colours, so obviously, it was a momentous occasion for her, too. Lady Mary stood in the hallway as I walked down the winding stairway. Jane walked behind me, holding my train. I felt like a princess as I stood before her for her final inspection. She nodded her approval. We walked down the steps to her waiting carriage, where Jane helped me with my train. It was only a short journey to Buckingham Palace, and we followed the long line of carriages pulling up to the main entrance hall. It seemed to take ages. The longer it took, the more nervous I got and started to fidget.

"Julia, will you stop fidgeting, you will crease your gown," Lady Mary said.

I apologised, "I never in a month of Sundays thought that I would ever be presented at court," I told her.

"No, I suppose you wouldn't, even when you lived at the big house."

The waiting area was full of proud mothers primping and preening their daughters ready for royalty.

We all waited for our names to be called. Philomena was in front of me. She looked as nervous as I felt. She turned and gave me a weak smile before she walked through the big double doors with Lady Hiddleston. It was then me and Lady Mary next. I heard us announced.

"The Right Honourable Lady McKenzie, presenting her ward Miss Julia Braemar."

We walked through the door. People were standing on either side of the room, and straight in front of us on a dais were two thrones on which sat Queen Victoria and Prince Albert. Lady Mary walked beside me until I moved forward and curtseyed to the Royals. A footman handed me my train. I hooked it over my wrist, then took three steps backwards before turning and leaving. Then it was over. In less than a minute, everything that we young ladies had been waiting for was over.

We went home and rested, then bathed for the evening ahead and the first ball of the season at Lady Hemsworth's home, where the theme was exotic birds. As I hadn't slept well the night before with nerves about the coming day, I was glad to go home and catch up on some sleep before bathing in the lilac-scented bath that Jane had poured her own concoction of oils in after having been taught by Dorcas. Jane and I had changed so much in just over six months, and we knew we would never go back to our previous life.

I stepped into the peacock blue gown, picked up my peacock fan that the Duke of Rochester had bought me, and Jane placed the lone peacock feather among my curls, handed me my peacock mask, made of black lace and another peacock feather, and we were back out again. The massive ballroom housed dozens of cages accommodating all manner of exotic birds. I picked up my dance card and stood beside Lady Mary, waiting to be asked to dance. Philomena and Lady Hiddleston came and stood by us. Philomena was dressed in a bright yellow gown with gold ribbons and a yellow feather in her hair. She carried her yellow mask with another yellow feather incorporated into the design. She looked beautiful. "Are you sad that the presentation is finally over, Julia?" she asked me.

"All that fuss for what was over in less than a minute!" I said.

"Ah, but now the fun begins, the courtship," she said, grinning.

Lord Byron walked over to Philomena and asked for a dance, so she held out her dance card for him to put his name down. I noted that she did not go all starry-eyed after I had told her about Byron and Melbourne's wife. She smiled politely and then at Lord Waterford, who was behind Byron.

Lord Melbourne came to me and put his name down on my card, then Rutledge came and asked for a dance, which I felt tempted to decline but changed my mind and held out my card to him. I saw Davenport hovering in the background. He smiled at me but didn't come near me or any other of the young ladies for that matter. I think he still felt bad about injuring my feet, so he kept away from me. Byron came over and put his name down on my dance card. Behind him was the Duke of Rochester, then Lord Waterford. I was relieved that Rochester had put his name down, and I couldn't wait to dance with him. I sighed, and Lady Mary looked at me. She smiled. I couldn't help myself. Whenever I saw or thought of Rochester, I sighed uncontrollably. I kept telling myself it was ridiculous, but I still could not help it.

I felt sorry for Davenport, who stood at the side of the ballroom with a sad look on his face, so I walked over to him and smiled. "Lord Davenport, are you not dancing this evening?"

"Miss Braemar, how kind of you to come over and talk to me after what I have done. I am worried that I might permanently maim a young lady's feet," he said dolefully.

I truly felt so sorry for him. He was such a nice gentleman, but he didn't want to risk hurting anyone after what he had done to me. He couldn't help that he had big feet.

"Oh, come now, it wasn't as bad as that," I told him, smiling at him encouragingly.

"I hear you were indisposed for two whole days, Miss Braemar."

"Yes, but I am here today and none the worse. If you danced the dances where you weren't in close contact with your dance partner, you wouldn't have the opportunity to tread on their toes. May I put you down for a dance then?" I said, handing him my dance card.

"Are you sure, Miss Braemar?" he asked before putting his name on my proffered dance card.

"Quite sure," I told him. "Just dance the dances where you are not in close contact with the lady's feet, and I am sure you will be fine," I re-iterated.

"You are too kind, Miss Braemar," he said as he wrote on my dance card, a smile lighting his face, which I realised he was quite handsome.

"I look forward to our dance," I told him, then walked back to Lady Mary.

"Surely you are not risking your feet again, Julia!" she said in surprise.

"He looked so sad, standing at the side. He is concerned that he might injure another lady, so I told him to dance the dances where he wasn't in close contact with the ladies. I have him for one such dance. Apart from his big feet he is a really nice gentleman and pleasant looking."

"You are too kind, Julia," she said, and from her tone, I knew she meant it as a compliment.

"Well, he can't tread on my toes in that."

Lord Rothsay came along and added his name to my list of dance partners. "Lord Rothsay, I haven't seen you for a while," I said as he finished writing on my dance card.

"No, I had to return to Scotland for a few months, but travelling to and from there takes up so much time," he told me.

"It must take longer than travelling from Cornwall to London," I said.

"It certainly does. I shall see you later, Miss Braemar," he said, bowing to me.

I nodded and told him I looked forward to our dance later.

He bowed to Lady Mary, then left until it was time for him to claim his dance.

The ballroom was a blaze of vibrant colours as the dancers swirled around the floor. It was a beautiful sight, and the large gold-leaf-framed mirrors around the ballroom replicated it.

Lord Melbourne came to claim his dance with me.

"Did you enjoy your presentation, Miss Braemar?" he asked as he took my hand.

"Indeed, sir, but for something that all of the young ladies had been looking forward to for so long, it was over in such a short time."

"It is the event that opens the season. You looked beautiful and presented a perfect curtsey."

"You were there? I must admit I was too scared to look left or right. I never expected to be presented at court, yet it must be quite usual for you," I asked.

"I never miss it. I have seen debutants swoon, fall over doing their curtsey, and make a complete disaster at their presentation."

"Mr Lamb, I do believe that you look forward to those times." I smiled at him, flirting.

He laughed back at me, and I thought, once again what a handsome gentleman he was, even though he was advancing in years. It was a shame that he had never remarried and known true love and lasting happiness.

"And you, Miss Braemar. I believe you are flirting with me."

"Have you never thought of marrying again, Mr Lamb?" I asked him.

"Are you asking Miss Braemar?" he said with a devilish glint in his eyes.

I blushed. "I would never be so bold, sir," I told him, then fluttered my eyelashes at him.

He laughed out loud. "You are a tease, Miss Julia," he told me.

"I hate to see such a kind and caring gentleman alone," I told him.

"If I were ever looking for another wife, then you would be at the top of my list."

I blushed.

"I don't think that I have a good enough pedigree to marry someone of your position. After all, you know my family history."

Lord Melbourne gave my hand a brief squeeze, "My dear Miss Braemar, it isn't pedigree that makes a good young lady, but their kindness and their manners, and any man who saw you talking to poor Davenport would know that you are a lady." Then, he referred back to our conversation about marriage. "But I am too old for you, and after my first wife, I don't believe that I would like to take that step again," he continued.

"Such a shame, sir. You really need a wife taking care of you."

"I thank you for your compliments, though, Julia."

Our dance ended. He took my arm and walked me back to Lady Mary, grinning like a cat that got the cream.

"Melbourne, I do believe you are blushing," she said as he handed me back.

"Your ward has been outrageously flirtatious with me, Lady Mary."

Lady Mary scowled at me. "Julia!" she scolded.

"No, you mistake me. Miss Braemar was only doing it for fun, Lady Mary. It has brightened my evening," he said, then stood next to Lady Mary, talking.

A figure loomed over me, and I looked up to see Rutledge standing before me.

"My dance, I believe, Miss Braemar." He held out his hand to me.

We walked onto the floor. It was a waltz, so he put his hand on my waist and pulled me closer to him—too close for propriety. I tried to pull away, but his grip was firm.

I had no choice but to relax until he relaxed his grip somewhat, and we began dancing.

"I believe congratulations are in order," I told him as we waltzed around the ballroom.

"Are they?" he raised his eyebrows in question.

"I hear you are engaged to be married."

"Oh, that!"

"'Oh, that' is all you can say?" I scowled at him.

"I was compromised."

"I would say it was the other way round, sir, and you got found out. Your fiancé has my sympathy," I told him.

"If you had given me any indication that you were interested..."

"I would never be interested in you, as I hoped you realised after our last meeting. Do you remember?"

"How could I forget? Rochester gave me a right pasting after that." I could tell he was angry, but not at me—at Rochester.

"Well, it was justified." That was all I said, but then I thought I might have misjudged Rochester.

We continued to dance in a stressful silence.

I was relieved when the dance ended. If ever Rutledge asked me to dance again, I would refuse. I doubted that it wouldn't stop him chasing other women even if he were married.

Lord Davenport came to claim his dance. He was a bit sheepish as he stood in front of me.

"Lord Davenport, our dance I believe." I smiled as I spoke to him.

"Are you sure, Miss Braemar?" he asked me.

"Quite sure," I told him as I took his arm, and we walked onto the dance floor.

He still didn't look completely confident. We stood side by side, holding hands,

"I am positive. Now enjoy the dance, Davenport. Anyone would think you were going to the gallows."

He smiled at me as we moved around the floor. By the time the dance had ended, he was smiling again. We walked back to Lady Mary, where he bent over my hand and kissed it. "Thank you very much, Miss Braemar."

"It's my pleasure. Enjoy the rest of your evening," I told him with a smile.

"That was very kind of you, Julia, after what he had done," Lady Mary commented.

"He was mortified over it, Ma'am, and he is such a nice gentleman; he's just not for me," I told her.

"Miss Braemar, I believe you have me for the next dance."

I smiled as my heart did its usual flip when Lord Rochester took my hand.

"You look very fetching this evening in your peacock-coloured gown, it goes with..."

"My lips?" I teased him. Then, seriously said, "The peacock fan you bought after we visited Vauxhall Gardens. Thank you, Your Grace, it was most kind," I told him.

He laughed as if I had not thanked him, "You do realise that the male peacock is most colourful; the Peahen is very plain and boring."

"Then should I, perhaps, don a pair of trousers, sir?" I asked. Again, he laughed.

"They would probably suit you. I saw that you were dancing with Rutledge again."

"Yes, and I told him I felt sorry for his fiancé."

"Did you now?" the duke raised his eyebrows. "That was very brave of you."

"He told me that, in his words, 'you gave him a right pasting' after our meeting in the park. You told me that your knuckles were from boxing."

"Yes, boxing his face. He can't just play fast and loose with any female he fancies, especially you."

My heart flipped again. Especially me?

"I see you were risking your feet with Davenport again?" he said as if he had never said those words.

"I felt sorry for him, as he had, more or less, sworn off dancing after he damaged my feet. It seemed a shame, and as you see, I have survived."

"Very brave of you. Did you enjoy being presented to the Queen?"

"Yes, very much. Philomena was presented just before me."

"I know. I saw you both. You both looked very beautiful."

"We did?"

"Of course, I was biased." He grinned at me.

"Were you?"

"Well, Philomena is my niece." He grinned at me.

A little voice in my head was saying, 'And me? What about me?'

I never said anything, but I was hurt.

"Will you have the next waltz with me, Miss Braemar?" he asked, shocking me.

"Two dances, Your Grace?"

"Is there something wrong with two dances, Miss Braemar?"

"People will talk."

"Will they?"

"Are you teasing me again, Your Grace?"

He grinned, just grinned at me. The dance ended, and he walked me back to Lady Mary. Then he bent over my hand and kissed it. His lips were so beautifully soft and warm. Then he left. I saw him dancing with Philomena next, and I envied her.

The ball seemed to pass in a dream until he claimed his waltz with me.

"Are people talking?" he asked as his hand went around my waist.

I looked around the ballroom, and my heart seemed to stop momentarily. I thought that I saw Mark Trevelgue in the crowd.

I could feel the colour drain from my face.

"Are you feeling unwell, Miss Braemar?" he asked me, his voice full of concern as I nearly tripped. "You look pale," he said.

I shook my head and looked again, but who I thought might have been Mark Trevelgue had disappeared. Did I imagine it?

"No, Your Grace, I am quite well," I told him, but I felt my heart stop for that brief moment, and my past caught up with me.

"Do you wish to take the air? It is rather hot in here," the duke asked me.

I didn't think; I just nodded and took his arm as we went outside. The fresh night air hit me, and I felt better.

"You do realise people saw us leave, Miss Braemar?" That comment made me realise what we had just done.

"What does it mean?"

"Do you, really want to know?" he asked incredulously.

"That we…"

"Julia, are you feeling ill?" Lady Mary had followed us outside, too soon for people to realise I had been compromised.

"Umm. I just felt a little warm, Ma'am," I explained, fanning my face with the fan that had hung from my wrist.

She took my arm, "Dear girl, if you had been here alone with the duke, a minute longer, people would have thought that…"

"Lady Mary, Miss Braemar looked faint, so I offered her some fresh air. We were gone just seconds before you joined us, Ma'am."

"Surely you must realise what people would think if I hadn't followed so speedily," Lady Mary pointed out to us both.

"I apologise, Lady Mary," the duke said, then bowed.

"Unless you wish to offer for my ward, Your Grace?" she said, raising her eyebrow in question.

"No," I said, not wishing to push him into something he did not want.

"It's perfectly fine, Lady Mary. I will offer…"

"No," I said again, interrupting him. "There is no need for that," I told the duke.

The duke looked at Lady Mary again, ignoring what I had just said. "Lady Mary, I am quite prepared to marry your ward."

Lady Mary asked me, "Julia is that what you want, to marry the duke?"

I was confused. Yes, I wanted to marry the duke, but no, I didn't want to pressure him into proposing to me. He must want to marry me of his own accord if he offered to marry me."

"Miss Braemar, will you marry me?" he said, looking at Lady Mary.

I sadly shook my head, "Only if you want to marry me, Your Grace."

"Then that is settled," Lady Mary said. "I will put the announcement in the papers tomorrow."

It was done and sorted, very much like the presentation. I had been proposed marriage, and it was settled in less than a minute.

I should have felt great pleasure being engaged to the duke, but I didn't. I wanted to feel happy; I really did. He was the one I wanted, but not like this, not having his arm twisted into proposing to me.

"Now, can we go inside and finish our dance, Julia?" he said, taking my arm and steering me back into the ballroom. Lady Mary followed us back in.

The duke put his arm around my waist, and we waltzed.

"You didn't have to do that, Your Grace. It was quite unnecessary. Lady Mary was there to protect my virtue and my honour."

"I know."

"Then why did you propose to me when it wasn't necessary?" I asked him. Our cheerful banter had disappeared with his proposal of marriage.

"Maybe I wanted to. Did you never think of that?"

"But you swiftly left me when I told you I had no dowry."

"Is that what you thought? I didn't want to marry you because you had no dowry." His breath was on my face, warm and heady like champagne.

"Well, you certainly made a hasty exit," I replied.

"Because I wanted you to enjoy the excitement of your first season. I would have proposed to you, but not quite so early."

"But you know nothing of me."

After the waltz had finished, Rochester took my arm and walked me back to Lady Mary. I expected him to leave me then, but he sat beside me.

"What don't I know about you?" he asked, grinning at me like he was happy at the prospect of marrying me.

I went to speak, but the Duke of Waterford came to claim his dance with me.

Rochester looked at him, "Miss Braemar is already spoken for Waterford."

"The announcement will be in the papers tomorrow, Your Grace," Lady Mary told him.

Waterford blushed and apologised, then turned and left us.

"Does this mean that I won't be able to dance with another man, Your Grace?" I asked him.

Rochester grinned at me, "Not until you have my ring on your finger."

I looked over to Lady Mary, who smiled and nodded.

"I will call on you tomorrow at eleven, Miss Braemar, and we will ride in the Row in my open carriage. Will that be acceptable to you?"

I looked over to Lady Mary again. She nodded.

Shortly after, my first ball of the season ended, and I was already engaged to the Duke of Rochester.

Lady Mary and I rode back to Moldova Square. I was going to bed, but Lady Mary asked me to attend her in the drawing room, so I followed.

"You wanted to speak to me, Ma'am?"

"Come and sit by me, Julia."

I did as she asked.

"I will write your announcement and get one of the footmen to deliver it to the Telegraph this evening so that it will be in the papers first thing tomorrow."

I nodded. I didn't know what to say.

"You do not seem happy, my child? I thought that you wanted the duke?"

"I do, I did, but I wanted him to offer for me of his own volition. He doesn't even know who I really am."

"And who are you?"

"I am a nobody from a small fishing village in Cornwall, whose father was a manager for the Trevelgue tin mines and a grandfather who was the local doctor."

Lady Mary took my hand in hers. "My dear girl, you are also my ward and my heiress. You have as much right to be here as anyone. You are the granddaughter I never had. You are the grandchild that I should have had. You are the epitome of a young debutant with all the skills and abilities many of the young ladies presented at court today could only dream of. The Viscount Melbourne knows who you are, and he welcomes you. Does that not mean anything to you?"

I nodded.

She looked at me and said, "Tell me, why did you go outside with the Duke if you didn't want him to propose?"

"I...I thought I saw Mark Trevelgue, and I panicked."

"And was it him?"

I shook my head, "I don't know Ma'am. When I looked for him again, I couldn't find him."

"So, you were probably mistaken, then," Lady Mary said.

I nodded.

"Now, off to bed with you. Have a good night's sleep, as you will ride in the Row with your fiancé, the duke, tomorrow morning."

"I have to tell him who I really am. I don't think he will appreciate being duped."

"You must do as you think fit, Julia, but remember what I have just said: whether you are an earl's daughter or a mine manager's daughter, you are my ward and my heir, and you will be a duchess before the season is out."

I nodded and went over to kiss her goodnight. "Thank you for all you have done for me, Lady Mary. I do appreciate it."

"I know, my dear. Now, off to bed with you."

Wearily, I went upstairs to bed, where Jane was waiting for me.

"How was your first official ball, Miss Julia?" she asked me, dying to hear all about it.

"I am engaged," I told her. My voice held no sign of happiness, just resignation.

"Engaged? So soon? Who? Was it Lord Melbourne? I know he is a little older than you, but he is still handsome. Is that why he comes around so often?"

"It's not the Viscount Melbourne," I said wearily as she helped me undress.

"Lord Waterford. I hear he is golden, like a Greek god."

"Not Waterford," I told her as she brushed my hair out.

"Then who, Miss Julia?"

"Rochester," I told her. I felt so miserable. I was sure he would ask me to release him when he found out that I was a nobody.

"You are going to be a Duchess and live in that big castle we went to for the Easter weekend?"

"So, it seems," I told her as she helped me into my nightgown.

"But I thought that was who you wanted?"

"I did, but I wanted him to want me, Julia Beddoes from Porth. He will never marry me if he finds out the truth now."

"Then don't tell him; you are still Lady Mary's ward after all."

She sat down on the end of my bed.

"I can't start a marriage with a lie Jane."

"But it's not a lie, you are Lady Mary's ward."

"Jane," I sighed, too weary to discuss it then, "I'm so tired, and the duke calls for me to ride in his carriage at eleven o'clock."

Jane curtseyed and left me to sleep.

I didn't think any more about Mark Trevelgue. I was beginning to think it was just a case of mistaken identity. Still, I had disturbing dreams about Mrs Trevelgue coming to London and telling everyone that I was her daughter's companion and all the ton laughing at me. I tossed and turned, dreaming that even Rochester was laughing at me. It took me some time to drift off into a dreamless sleep.

The next morning was a beautiful summer day with tiny white fluffy balls of clouds skittering across a brilliant, near-cornflower blue sky.

Jane was a fluster of excitement as she carried in my breakfast tray and decided what I should wear for my carriage ride with my fiancé. She pulled out an emerald, green crepe morning gown with lily of the valley embroidered at the hem and sleeves and hung it outside the wardrobe, waiting for me to put it on.

I hardly touched my breakfast. I was nervous about being alone with the duke and telling him the truth about me.

Jane continued fussing over me and chattering away, but her voice seemed to provide background noise to my turbulent thoughts. Then I heard her mention the announcement in the newspaper that morning. "Do you want me to go down and fetch the newspaper for you to see it, Miss Julia?"

I nodded. Maybe seeing it in print would brighten my spirits. Jane didn't take long to run down the hallway and return the newspaper to me.

"It's in the notices, Miss Julia," she told me, handing me the newspaper.

I opened it up and scoured the notices. It looked like it was about someone else.

I washed and dressed, then went downstairs just as the duke knocked on the front door. I told the footman to wait to answer the door until I sat in the drawing room, which I noted was vacant.

I settled myself on one of the sofas and waited.

The footman announced the Duke of Rochester and showed him in. He looked around for Lady Mary.

"I see we are on our own," he said, sitting beside me. He immediately took my hand in his, which felt comfortable and comforting.

He turned it over and kissed my palm, then put his hand in his pocket and drew out a small box.

"I know everything was rather hurried last night, but I am glad we are alone today, and I can give you this." He slipped off the sofa and went down on one knee before me. "I wanted to do this right, so Miss Julia Braemar, will you do me the great honour of consenting to marry me?"

He opened the small red leather box containing an emerald and diamond ring. He removed the ring from the box and then put it on my finger.

"I should have known," he said, "It's far too big for you. We need to get the jeweller to reduce the size."

"I'm sorry, Your Grace," I said sadly.

A look of panic crossed his face, "Are you refusing me, Julia?"

I shook my head, "No, I didn't mean that. I am sorry that my fingers are so small."

He turned my palm upwards and kissed it again. "Don't be sorry for that." He grinned, relief showing on his face, "It is one of the reasons why I fell in love with you."

I looked into his eyes. "You love me?"

"My dear, darling Julia, I am not in the habit of proposing to young ladies I am not in love with."

I took a deep breath. My heart felt like it had ascended to my throat, making it difficult to breathe, let alone speak. I swallowed before I spoke. "I think there are some things that you need to know about me, Your Grace."

"Robert. My name is Robert, Julia."

"I am not who you think I am. My real name, before Lady Mary changed it, was Julia Beddoes. My father was a mine manager in Cornwall, and my grandfather was the local doctor. My mother died giving birth to me. I was invited to be Lady Mary's granddaughter's companion until she died."

"Oh." He hesitated.

"If you wish to withdraw your offer, Your Grace, I will understand."

"I have told you, Julia. My name is Robert. You think that telling me that will put me off, like you told me you have no dowry."

"I am not telling you to put you off. I am telling you the truth. I just wanted you to know who I really am—who you will be marrying if you still want to go through with it."

"Does Lady Mary know all this?"

"Yes."

"Is that why she's not here?"

"I don't know, possibly. I told her last night that I must tell you the truth about me before accepting your proposal," I said, looking down at our hands, which were still clasped together.

"Thank you for being so honest with me."

"I will release you from your proposal if you wish," I told him and took my hand away.

He took my hand again and looked at how my small hand fit within his. "I do not need a dowry, and I did not fall in love with you because you are Lady Mary's ward. I admit, I wasn't going to offer for you so early in the season. I wanted you to have the excitement of your first season in London, but things," he shrugged his broad shoulders, "just accelerated somewhat... but it does not mean I want you to release me from our engagement. Now that that is settled, we must visit the jeweller and make this ring into a child's size." He grinned at me. I liked the devilish glint in his eyes. I think that is what I liked most about him: how he made me laugh and how he made me feel. Maybe this could work out. I thought we might still go to balls, but I would be exclusively his. No more worrying about Mr Davenport damaging my toes. No more having to deal with Rutledge or Byron. I would miss dancing with Melbourne and Waterford.

Lady Mary came into the drawing room just as we were about to leave, first for the jewellers, then for a ride around Rotten Row together to be seen by the rest of the ton.

"Have you settled everything, Julia?" she asked after greeting Lord Rochester.

"Yes, Ma'am. We need to go to the jewellers to resize my ring, and then we are off to ride around the Row," I told her.

She asked to see the ring. "Ah, emerald and diamonds. It is a beautiful ring, Julia."

"I chose emeralds to match Julia's eyes," Robert said, still holding my hand in his.

"Did you see the announcement, Your Grace?" Lady Mary asked. "I thought to get it in the newspapers as soon as possible so that the proposal was the reason if you had been seen going outside together."

"Yes indeed. Now the whole of the ton will know, including my niece, who has been pestering me to offer for Julia, more or less, since we first met." He laughed.

We left Lady Mary, saying that we would be back later.

"Your niece will glory in calling me Aunt Julia," I told him as he settled beside me in his carriage.

"Oh no, that makes you sound old. No, I can't have that," the duke said, still holding my hand.

We left Moldova Square and rode to Bond Street, where the jewellers were situated, and the duke had already been earlier that morning. The duke helped me down from his carriage. He took my hand and placed it on his arm. Bond Street was nothing like the streets where the bank and the pawn brokers were; no urchins were running around barefooted, no man playing the barrel organ or monkey holding out his tin cup for money. This was a street where the rich and titled went, and I was here with my fiancé, a duke. I felt that I needed to be pinched.

The jeweller's shop window displayed not just rings and necklaces but tiaras and even coronets. Certainly not the sort of everyday jewellers. They only dealt with the rich, titled and the well-to-do, obviously. The duke opened the front door to the jewellers and held it open for me to go in first, then followed me.

The man behind the counter greeted us. "Your Grace, back so soon. Is the ring not to the lady's liking?"

The duke looked at me, "Is it to your liking, Julia?"

"Yes, it is beautiful," I told him.

"But there is a problem, Your Grace?" the jeweller asked.

The duke lifted my hand, "There is indeed. It is too big, as you can see from Miss Braemar's hand."

The jeweller looked at my hand briefly and nodded in agreement. "May I measure your finger, Miss Braemar?" He pulled out a chain from under the counter with rings of different sizes in a cheap metal. He looked at my finger, then picked one of the rings from the chain and slipped it over my finger. "No, still too big, let's try this one." He slipped another one on my finger, "Ah, we are getting there." He took another one and slipped that on. "Now that is better," he said, pleased with his success. "Is that comfortable, Miss Braemar, not too tight and not too loose?"

I nodded.

"Would you like to wait for me to resize your ring, or do you want to come back? It will take but a few minutes."

The duke said that we would wait.

"Then may I offer you some refreshments while you wait Your Grace?"

We were offered tea and biscuits brought to us on a silver tray. One of the shop staff poured, then left us.

I looked around us at the jewels on show. "It's a veritable Aladdin's Cave," I told the duke.

"All young girls dream of being surrounded by boxes of jewellery," Robert said as we waited.

"I think it would even outshine the modiste." I smiled at him. I felt more relieved now that I had told him the whole truth and he still wanted me.

"Now, that would be something. At some point, we will need to discuss the wedding arrangements. I would imagine that you will want plenty of time to prepare?"

"I have not had time to discuss anything with Lady Mary yet."

"No, of course not," he replied.

The jeweller returned to the shop, "There," he said triumphantly and handed the ring to the duke, "I said but a few minutes Your Grace."

The duke took my hand and placed the ring on my finger.

"There, that looks better," the jeweller said.

We left the jewellers, and the duke helped me back into his carriage, then we set off for Rotten Row.

The duke sat beside me as his footman drove us around Rotten Row.

"May I ask, Julia, how did you know about Lady Mary?"

"I was Lady Mary's granddaughter's companion, and we were tutored together. I moved into Seaward Manor. Edwina, Lady Mary's granddaughter was the bane of my life. She was a hateful bully, but I was getting a good education, which was all I wanted. One day, when I was nearly seventeen, I went to visit my grandfather and was told that he had died three weeks earlier. Notes had been sent to me, informing me, but I hadn't received any of them. I was going to return to Seaward Manor to tell Mrs Trevelgue, Lady Mary's daughter (but that is another story). When I arrived, I discovered that Edwina had been involved in an accident and was dead. I expected Mrs Trevelgue to tell me to leave, but she didn't. She proposed that I come to London posing as Lady Mary's granddaughter, and she would give me a season." I paused, "This is a very long story," I told the duke.

"I am not going anywhere, Julia; please continue."

"Mrs Trevelgue told me to get Jane to alter all of Edwina's clothes for me to wear them. She would pay for our journey to London and our stays at decent coaching inns, and she also gave me Edwina's jewellery." I paused for a breath.

"Why didn't this Mrs Trevelgue come with you to stay with her mother?"

"Lady Mary and her husband had disowned her when she broke off her engagement to her titled fiancé and married Mr Trevelgue, whose family owned several mines in Cornwall, and they had not spoken since."

The duke nodded.

"So, Jane and I came to London, posing as Lady Mary's granddaughter and maid. I hated lying to Lady Mary and eventually told her the truth when I couldn't bear the lies any longer. Lady Mary told me that she already knew what was happening in Cornwall and that I wasn't her granddaughter, but she wanted to keep me on because... well, we seemed to get on together, and I think she enjoyed my company."

"Where does Melbourne come into this?"

"He came to our rescue when the carriage overturned on our journey here; since then, I suppose he has taken me under his wing."

I looked over at the duke. "I can still release you from our engagement if you wish?"

"My dear Julia, I do not wish. What you have told me makes no difference," he said, holding my hand as we continued our journey.

We passed several people as we rode around, including Philomena, who had decided to ride with her groom. She waved and galloped over to us as soon as she saw us.

"Uncle Robert, Julia. Congratulations at last. May I see the ring, Julia?"

I removed my hand from the duke's and showed her the ring, which now fit my finger perfectly.

"Oh, lucky you, Julia. I am so pleased for you both. This is the first betrothal of the season. I shall be able to call you Aunt Julia soon."

"Don't you dare!" I told her, laughing.

"No, you won't, Philomena Hiddleston," the duke said.

Philomena pouted prettily at us, "You spoil all my fun, Uncle Robert."

"That is what uncles are there for, my dear girl," he replied, grinning at her.

Philomena's horse started to fidget, so she turned and left us, waving as she went.

When his niece left, the duke took my hand again, turned it, and kissed my palm. My heart skipped a beat again. I wanted to be completely happy, but something was holding me back, and I didn't know what.

"Well, we have been seen now, so what would you like to do?"

"Could we go to Vauxhall Gardens again or somewhere else?"

"How about a boating lake? Regent's Park has one, and I can flex my muscles for you," he teased me, trying to lighten the atmosphere that still didn't seem as easy-going as it once was between us.

"And have me swooning?" I said, trying to match his sense of humour.

He cocked his head to one side, "I really can't believe you are the swooning sort, Julia."

"No, I think I am made of sterner stuff, not like some of the females of the ton."

He leaned closer to me, "Shall I tell you a secret? A lot of the 'swooners' are just good actresses. I mean, look at your feet after Davenport nearly crippled you. Did you swoon? No. My lady is made of stronger stuff," he said proudly. "I haven't the patience for simpering misses, I am afraid."

"I must remember that then."

"What, not to swoon?"

"No, that I am your lady." I grinned.

We boated on the Serpentine, where Robert had taken off his jacket, rolled his shirt sleeves up and began rowing the little rowing boat, past swans, past ducks, past other couples. All I could see was him, his shirt undone a couple of buttons, and the muscles of his arms bulging as he rowed us around. He looked the same as he did the day that Copper was born, but now it was broad daylight, and I could appreciate the look of the man before me who would soon be my husband.

We were to go to a ball that evening, so the duke took me back to Moldova Square and Lady Mary. He came in with me and spent some time talking about our wedding. It was decided for the twenty-fourth of July, which didn't give us a great amount of time to arrange everything, but the duke told me that his mother, Lady Virginia, would help arrange things if needed.

He finally left us, saying he would meet us at the ball that evening. Then whispered to me, "I will be the one with a broad smile." Then he kissed my hand.

Now that we had a wedding date, Lady Mary said that we didn't have a moment to lose. She was sorry, but we had to go straight to the modiste to organise my wedding dress and my trousseau the following day.

I went upstairs to see Jane, whom I hadn't seen since that morning. She first asked me to see my ring and oohed and ahhed at its beauty. I gave it another look for what might have been the hundredth time that day. It really was beautiful, with an emerald as the main gem and diamonds on either side.

Not for the first time that day, I thought I needed pinching. How did Julia Beddoes, the daughter of a mine manager, get to become the future Duchess of Rochester?

"I will become the lady's maid to a real duchess." Jane was practically jumping for joy. "Who would have thought when we left Cornwall that we would end up like this?" Jane said. "Oooh, I would love to rub the noses of the staff at Seaward Manor in it," she said with glee.

"But you won't, Jane. It could stir up a real hornet's nest, and we don't want anything to ruin what we have." I warned her.

Jane hung her head, "No, Miss Julia."

I took her hand in mine, "I am not telling you off, just... I thought that I saw Mark Trevelgue yesterday, Jane. I don't want anything to ruin my happiness, but I feel I am being unfair to you. I am no better than you, Jane. We are equal, yet I feel bad that I will be a duchess, and you will be my maid. You deserve better than that."

"I have everything I ever wanted and more, Miss Julia. When we were in Cornwall, it was my dream to come to London and be the maid to a great lady, and thanks to you, I will be your maid as I always hoped. You have always been kind to me and treated me with kindness, and thanks to you, I have money in a bank account. What girl could want for more? I have more than I ever dreamed of, thanks to you."

After dressing for the evening, I sat with Lady Mary before the carriage was brought round.

"Lady Mary, I don't know how to repay you for all you have done for me. If it hadn't been for you, I wouldn't be engaged to the Duke of Rochester."

"My darling girl, I need no thanks. It has been my pleasure. You have brought happiness and laughter into my life again, and for that, I should be thanking you." She stood up, came over to me, and kissed my cheek. I felt the tears spring to my eyes; tears of joy and gratitude to this woman who had taken me in, not knowing who I was, and when she did find out, she never blamed me for the situation I had been put in. I saw Lady Mary also dash a stray tear from her face.

Several people came up at the ball and congratulated us, but no one asked me to dance, only Robert. He spent all evening by my side, talking to me and Lady Mary or dancing with me. He was so attentive, hardly letting go of my hand. I found that I was beginning to relax a little without the feeling that something bad was going to happen to me. I had Lady Mary, Lord Melbourne and now the duke behind me, supporting and protecting me. It felt comforting and reassuring. After dancing so much with my fiancé, he escorted us to Lady Mary's carriage. He gave me a chaste kiss on my cheek, squeezed my hand, and then went to his carriage.

I felt that I was glowing as I walked upstairs to my bedroom, giving my engagement ring yet another look to confirm that I was not dreaming and was engaged to Robert Beaumont, the Duke of Rochester.

I would ask Lady Mary, the next morning if I could cut out the announcement in the newspaper and send it to Mrs Watson. In the meantime, I let Jane undress me to prepare for bed, where I fell into a fitful sleep, ready for the following morning when Lady Mary and I would go to Madam Yvonne again.

After I had eaten my breakfast in bed, Jane helped me dress. So, Lady Mary and I went out again early that morning to see Madame Yvonne.

As we rode, I asked Lady Mary if she could use some of my dowry to pay for my trousseau. I said I didn't want to take any more money from her.

"My darling Julia, you have achieved all that I hoped for. You are to marry a duke. It is more than I could have hoped for. It will be my pleasure to pay for your trousseau. Now, I won't have you arguing. I have spoken," she said stoically.

She had that tone in her voice that I had come to know over the last six months that she would broker no arguments. I asked Lady Mary if I could cut out the announcement from the newspaper from the previous day and send it to Mrs Watson, as I was sure she would be delighted to know about the duke and me.

Lady Mary said that I could, of course, send the clipping to Cornwall for Mrs Watson.

When we arrived at Madam Yvonne's, she practically ran towards us with excitement. "Lady Mary, Miss Braemar, I read of your good news in the newspaper. Do you wish for me to make your trousseau and your wedding dress? I am honoured to make it for the future Duchess of Rochester. Congratulations, Miss Braemar. May I see your ring?" she asked, delighted that we had graced her establishment to provide all my trousseau. She was so excited that she hadn't given us time to speak.

I showed her my ring, and she gasped, "What a beautiful ring. It matches your eyes, Miss Braemar. The duke has chosen well."

Of course, she was over the moon to be asked to make my wedding gown and other gowns as befitting the Duchess of Rochester. I trembled at the thought.

I was involved in discussing my wedding gown and the gowns I would wear as a duchess. It was nearly the afternoon before we left Madame Yvonne's to go home and prepare for another ball that evening. I had not seen Jane all day since I left in the morning to go to the modiste. She was all a dither when I reached my bedroom. She asked me about my wedding gown and the gowns for my trousseau. There were so many gowns that we had ordered that day that I struggled to remember them all. I asked her if she would prepare a bath for me. She poured oil of lilacs in it to finish it off.

She chose a lemon gown with gold embroidery and suggested that I wear emeralds and diamonds to match it. The jewellery was all that Mrs Trevelgue had left behind, all of which Lady Mary had given to me on my debut.

I was back downstairs by eight o'clock, waiting for Lady Mary to appear.

Lady Mary arrived a couple of minutes later, followed by Dorcas, who also wanted to see my ring. "You are a credit to Lady Mary, Miss Julia," she said in her Scottish accent.

I thanked her, and then she told me that she would intensify Jane's training so that by the time I was married, Jane would be the perfect maid for a duchess. "As long as there is no ear piercing." She grinned at me, and Lady Mary laughed out loud.

"Poor Jane will never be able to live that down," Lady Mary said. I had never seen Lady Mary so excited and happy.

"Julia, you are a credit to me. I may even say I am glad you came to me."

I took Lady Mary's hand in mine. "Well, I am glad that I came to you. Your friendship has meant so much to me, and Dorcas's training for Jane has meant a lot to her. Thank you, both of you."

We travelled to the ball at the Bainbridge's, where the duke was waiting for us at the door. "I hope we didn't keep you waiting, Your Grace," Lady Mary said as we reached him in the doorway.

He looked appreciatively at me. "It was worth waiting for," he said as he took my arm. We walked into the ballroom, which was already full of ladies in a rainbow of coloured gowns, whisking around the room in the arms of gentlemen smartly dressed in their evening attire.

The duke took my arm and immediately led me onto the dancefloor.

"I haven't heard you use my name since we became betrothed, Julia."

"Rochester?" I asked, enjoying teasing him.

"No. Robert. Julia, my name is Robert. Let me hear you call me by my name, Julia."

"Robert. I am sure that I have," I told him.

"No, you haven't. Is it so hard?"

"I find it difficult. I never expected to be betrothed to a duke."

"Well, you are, and I am just a man, Julia. My name is Robert. Say it again, Julia."

"Robert," I said, and then I heard him give a satisfied sigh and dramatically clutch his heart in fun.

"You are ridiculous," I said to him.

"Robert," he added.

"You are ridiculous, Robert," I told him, laughing.

"But I am your ridiculous Robert." He grinned down at me possessively.

"My ridiculous Robert," I said again, and he gave another exaggerated sigh, which made me laugh.

"Are you happy, Julia?"

I nodded.

"Yes, Robert, I am extremely happy," he prompted me.

"Yes, Robert, I am extremely happy," I repeated, emphasising each word.

His arm tightened possessively around me as we moved around the floor. At the end of the dance, Lord Melbourne came over to us and congratulated us, then asked if Robert would allow him to dance with me. Robert nodded, "As long as you return her to me," he said.

Lord Melbourne took my arm and took me onto the dancefloor. "Well, who would have thought you would end up a duchess, Miss Braemar?" he said.

"Have I aimed too high, do you think, Mr Lamb?" I asked him, as I valued his opinion.

"Does the duke know of your past?" he asked me.

I told him that he did.

"Then no, not at all, my dear. I doubted that Rochester would let your past affect his proposal. I know Lady Mary is delighted," he said as we danced past Rutledge, who scowled at me.

"I asked Lady Mary if she would use some of my dowry to pay for my trousseau, but she refused, saying that it was her pleasure to buy it for me," I told Mr Lamb.

"She is very proud of you and how you have behaved in her care, and now, to be promised to a duke, it has made her day," Lord Melbourne said. "Have you decided on a date for your wedding?" he asked.

"The twenty-fourth of July," I told him.

An idea formed in my mind as we danced around the busy ballroom. "Apart from Lady Mary, I have no family. Would you give me away, Mr Lamb?" I asked him, feeling that it was a very good idea.

"It would be my pleasure, Julia," he told me.

When the dance ended, he handed me back to the duke. I told Robert and Lady Mary that I had asked Mr Lamb to give me away, then asked if that was alright. Thankfully, they both agreed.

Several people congratulated us again, especially Lord Waterford and Lord Davenport, who hadn't attended the previous ball.

Robert held my hand all evening, sometimes turning my hand over, kissing my palm, and occasionally dancing with me. He was very attentive and talked to Lady Mary about the wedding, explaining that because of the short amount of time, his mother had offered to help with the wedding planning. Lady Mary asked if his mother was in London, to which the duke replied that she was travelling up that day and would be with us the next day.

I looked forward to meeting Lady Virginia again after meeting her for the weekend party at Easter, which seemed so long ago now.

Before the evening ended, Robert asked Lady Mary if we could go out into the garden, and I was surprised when she nodded. Robert took my arm and led me through the open double doors into the garden. We were alone, and the garden was in semi-darkness. I looked across at Robert. "I hope you don't mind, Julia. I just wanted you to myself just for a minute or two."

He took my hand and led us behind a high box hedge. "I will not do anything until our wedding night, Julia, but I have been thinking since..." He hesitated. "May I kiss you?"

I nodded mutely; little did he know I had imagined him kissing me since our first meeting at the music concert.

He pulled me into his arms and put a finger under my chin, lifting it until I looked directly into his beautiful, grey, smiling eyes and gently touched his lips to mine. They were as soft and gentle, just as I imagined. I felt my lips moving against his as if they had a mind of their own. His tongue seemed to dart into my mouth, feeling my lips' contours. I could taste him, his very essence. He tasted of brandy, and it was heady. Would he think me brazen if I did the same to him? Tentatively, I moved my tongue to do the same, and our kiss deepened as he pulled me tighter to his strong, muscular body, and our kiss continued until we were both breathless.

He leaned his forehead against mine and groaned. "How long is it to our wedding Julia?"

"Six weeks," I told him.

"Oh God, as long as that?" he pulled me to him, and his hand cupped my head as if he was afraid that I would move it away again, but I welcomed his touch as we kissed again until he finally broke the kiss. "We must stop Julia; otherwise, I won't be able to control myself."

I didn't know what he meant, but whatever it was, I wanted more.

He tucked my arm in his, gave me a brief, chaste kiss on my forehead, and we walked back inside. Could people see that we had been kissing? I was concerned that Lady Mary would know and admonish me, but she smiled indulgently at us.

Robert took my hand and led me onto the dancefloor again. He gave a great sigh, "Ah, that's better." He looked down at me. "Are you all right, Julia?"

I smiled, "Never better."

"I didn't want to scare you, but I needed to kiss you. I have wanted to do that since the night of the concert."

"As long ago as that?" I replied, then thought, "But that was the first time we met."

"Can I tell you a secret?"

"Yes of course."

"So had I," I confessed.

"So had I what?"

"Well," I hesitated, "I had wanted to kiss you since the night of the music concert as well. I am not sure if I should be telling you this." I blushed.

"Well, then I am glad we both got our wishes. I wanted to be your first kiss and hopefully your last," he said, looking into my eyes, then kissing my hand.

We went back to Lady Mary and stood talking. It was decided that Lady Virginia would come to Moldova Square the next day to discuss the wedding plans.

Philomena came over with Lord Waterford in tow to discuss the wedding.

"I hope I shall be invited to the wedding, Uncle Robert," she said, grinning cheekily at her uncle.

"But of course," he said, "I doubt I could keep you and your family away." He grinned.

That night, I practically floated to bed on a pink cloud of happiness and slept a deep, dreamless sleep. I hoped I would dream about Robert kissing me, but it had been an extremely busy day that left me happy but exhausted.

Chapter Twelve

The following morning, I found Lady Mary reading the newspaper in the drawing room. She looked up as I entered and smiled, "You are in the newspapers again today, Julia. You and the duke are being called 'the love match of the season' and reports on your engagement ring and the wedding date." I never realised that there would be such publicity for our wedding.

"I imagine you will want to cut that out and send it to Mrs Watson. I will let you have the newspaper when I have finished it."

It was early afternoon when Lady Virginia came to Moldova Square to have "a council of war," as Robert called it.

As soon as Lady Virginia entered the drawing room, she kissed my cheek. "Julia, I am so pleased to be here with you and Lady Mary to discuss your wedding plans with my son. I couldn't have wished for a better bride for Robert," she told me, and I wondered if Robert had told her who I really was.

Robert sat on one of the sofas where I was sitting and took my hand in his, entwining our fingers. His thumb began stroking the back of my hand again, which I realised he often did when he held my hand in his. He never seemed concerned about demonstrating his love for me in public. I didn't think that I could be any happier. We left a lot of planning to Lady Mary and Virginia while we just sat listening, only speaking when our opinion was asked. At some point, the discussions between Lady Mary and Virginia about our wedding did not need Robert and me, so we excused ourselves and went into the gardens and watched the ducks waddling around. We sat on one of the benches, holding hands.

"Robert, does Lady Virginia know about my past?"

"What do you mean, Julia?"

"The fact that my father was a manager in the Trevelgue mines and Gramps was the local doctor?"

"Do you mind, darling?" he asked.

I noticed that he had started using endearments on me recently.

"No, not at all. I am glad that she knows. I have spent enough time with lies," I told him.

"My mother agrees that it doesn't matter what your background is. Your father and 'Gramps's, as you call him, held perfectly respectable positions. Who are we to argue if Lady Mary wanted you as her ward?"

"I hated lying, Robert," I told him.

"I know, and it is not a good way to start a marriage, Julia. I am glad you told me that."

I told him about Porth, the Lodge, Mrs Watson, and the village, and he often asked me about my previous life.

That evening we were invited to a musical concert. The music was by the composer Mozart "I don't know if you have heard the composer's music before? He is one of my favourites," Robert said.

We walked into the concert hall with my hand in the crook of his arm and took our seats. On the stage was a single piano, not a whole orchestra like the last time we attended a concert.

Robert and I took our seats as the pianist stepped onto the stage. Robert leaned over towards me as the first chords were being played. "Let me know what you think later," he whispered in my ear, his breath touching my cheek, sending tingles through my body.

I had never felt so happy. I had everything I could ever want and more, and I had no more fears.

Robert took hold of my hand again and turned it to kiss my palm. We sat and listened. The music didn't invoke the pictures that other composers did, but the music was still wonderful, very skillfully written, and played by the pianist. I looked across at Robert, and he had his eyes closed, letting the music flow over him. I did the same. It was magical. I always felt his hand in mine, rubbing the back of mine with his thumb. It felt so reassuring.

When the concert ended, Robert took my arm, and we walked back to the carriage and rode back to Moldova Square. "Would you like to walk in the gardens for a while before going inside, Julia?" he asked.

"I thought that the gates were locked at night?" I said, remembering what Mr Lamb told me the day I first arrived in Moldova Square.

"They put that about to stop people going inside, but usually they just close the gates," Robert explained.

"How did you know that?"

He gave that cheeky grin, touched the side of his nose, took my hand, and walked through the gate and into the gardens. I had never been in the gardens before, certainly not in the dark.

He led me to a bench underneath one of the large oak trees. We sat down, and he pulled me into his arms. Immediately, my heart began hammering in my chest, anticipating his kisses.

"What did you think of Mozart?" he asked me,

"Wonderful. I wish that I could play like that, but..."

"Your hands are too small to span the notes. I think many of the composers had larger hands than you Julia, but for me..." he said, leaving the obvious fact that he had larger hands than me, unsaid.

"I didn't know you could play the piano?"

"I can't tell you everything about me, or you might get bored and run away." He teased me.

I couldn't see his face, but I thought he was joking.

"I don't scare that easily," I told him.

"As I thought."

He gathered me closer to him so I could feel his breath's warmth on my face. I sighed as his lips met mine, and we kissed a deep, meaningful kiss that seemed to set my whole being on fire. His tongue began its exploration of my mouth, twisting and tasting my very essence, and I replied in kind, letting my tongue discover the contours of his mouth. I felt stirrings deep in my body that I had never felt before, and it wanted completion, but I didn't know or understand what that was. We kissed until we were both breathless, and he put his head against mine with a groan.

"I can't get enough of you, Julia. You are like a heady wine." I felt the same but dare not tell him. Was I brazen feeling this way about him? We were to be married. Would this change once the wedding night came?

"I must take you inside, or Lady Mary will think the worst of me. We must wait until we are married," he said finally. He took my hand and tucked it into the crook of his arm as we walked out of the gardens, carefully closing the gates behind us.

"Robert, what happens when one marries?"

He laughed. "Well, you will arrive at the church and walk up the aisle on the arm of Melbourne, who will then place your hand in mine, and the ceremony will begin."

I grinned and briefly swatted him on his arm. "I know what happens during the ceremony; what happens on the wedding night between husband and wife? I am ignorant."

Robert looked down at me. "Well, Lady Mary might give you a little talk, but it must have been many years," he grinned at me devilishly, "Many, many years since her wedding night, so she might not remember, and I am not at liberty to tell Julia. You will find out on our wedding night."

I quivered all over, but for what I did not know.

"You told me that you played the pianoforte, Robert. Would you show me?"

"Tonight?"

"Why not?"

The butler, Ritson, opened the door to my knock, and I invited the duke inside.

"Won't we disturb Lady Mary?" he asked.

"She will be in bed fast asleep. If we shut the door to the drawing room, it will stifle the sound," I told him. I did not want to let the duke leave: not just yet.

We walked into the drawing room, and I closed the door behind us so the music wouldn't reach upstairs.

He walked over to the piano and sat down on the stool. I sat beside him. I had left Beethoven's Piano Sonata No. 14 on the piano, which I had been playing earlier that day

He began to play, "Join me, Julia." He asked, "I'll play the top score. You play the bottom score."

We played, our shoulders, hips, and thighs touching, sharing our warmth as the beautiful music flowed from our fingers.

"Could we get nearer to heaven if we tried?" I said dreamily.

"I doubt it." He grinned down at me.

Only a few minutes later, the drawing room door opened, and Lady Mary came in in her dressing gown, her grey hair let down and tied in a plat. We stopped playing immediately and stood up, a look of guilt on our faces. I was the first to speak. "Lady Mary, I'm sorry if we woke you. I closed the door so that you wouldn't hear it."

"I apologise for waking you, Lady Mary. It was all my fault," Robert said, the perfect gentleman, prepared to take all the blame on himself.

"I am not complaining," Lady Mary said. "It sounded wonderful, and I had to come down and listen. Please do continue."

We sat down again and continued to play until we heard the clock in the hallway strike one o'clock. Robert and I stopped playing.

"I think it is time that I left, as pleasurable as it has been," he said to both Lady Mary and me.

"Please, Your Grace, come any time and play. It does my heart good to hear music as I am not gifted myself."

Robert kissed my cheek, then bowed to Lady Mary and left.

I slept and slept, dreaming of Robert holding me in his arms and kissing me. If only I could dream about him every night until we married. My life felt so perfect, almost too perfect. Did I deserve to be so happy?

When I woke up the following morning, I decided that Jane should benefit from my happiness. She had the money I had given her to open her bank account, but I thought that as she would be the lady's maid to a duchess, she should have a whole new wardrobe suited to her position. I sought out Dorcas and explained my idea.

"Do lady's maids have to wear a uniform, Dorcas, or can they wear normal clothes?" I asked her.

"You will be a duchess soon, Miss Julia. Jane can wear whatever you want her to; no one will argue with you over it."

I thanked her, went to find Jane, and gave her the good news. She was in my bedroom tidying up.

"Leave that and get ready. We are going out, Jane," I told her.

"Where are we going, Miss Julia?"

"To the modiste."

She didn't question me. When we arrived, Madame Yvonne came over with a big, welcoming smile on her face.

"Miss Julia, good morning. How may I be of service to you today?"

"With my forthcoming marriage to the duke, Jane's station will be elevated, so she must be clothed, suited to her new position."

Madam Yvonne looked a little strange at my request, but as Dorcas had told me, who would argue with the future duchess?

Jane looked shocked, then pleased.

I ordered her various-coloured dresses, remembering her favourite colours from our many chats at Seaward Manor. I also said that I wanted all her dresses to be en vogue.

Madame Yvonne hesitated, but I was the future Duchess of Rochester, and all my wishes must be obeyed.

Jane was overjoyed but did question me once we left the modiste.

"I'm not arguing with you, Jane. They will be your new uniform as befitting my ladies maid when I am the new duchess," I told her as we walked towards the little tea shop, we frequented on many of our little outings.

As we sat and waited for our order to be delivered, she couldn't stop smiling as she sat opposite me. "It was the best thing we ever did coming to London, Miss Julia. Thank you for everything."

"No, it is you that I must thank Jane. Without you I doubt that I would have had the courage to do what we did, but I didn't do this for your thanks. I've told you that you deserve this as much as I do. We are equals, Jane. Even if you don't remember it, I will."

She grinned all the way back to Moldova Square.

The next day was a glorious summer day; we had arranged to go horse riding in the Row. Robert came along on his massive black horse, which I found out he called Thunder, while I rode on Star.

It was good to be riding with him. The Row looked busy with many open-topped carriages. The female passengers dressed in their summer finery. We only went a short way when Philomena came riding up to us. "Uncle Robert, Julia, fancy meeting you here."

"Are you on your own, Philomena?" Robert asked.

"No, the groom is around somewhere," she said, laughing at the fact that she had managed to lose the groom yet again.

"Then you had better join us until he catches up," Robert said.

"Oh, Uncle Robert, you are no fun at all," she said as she rode between us. "Julia, have they finished your wedding dress yet?" she asked.

"Next week," I told her.

"Then I must be the first to see you in it," she insisted.

"You will see me in it on the day," I told her.

"Don't you want my opinion, Julia?"

I laughed "Philomena Hiddleston, you are incorrigible!"

"I do not permit you to see my bride's gown before I do, Philomena Hiddleston," the duke said.

Someone rode past us just then, and I thought it looked like Mark Trevelgue. My heart went into my throat. I knew I had to get home to Lady Mary. Thinking that I had seen him once could have been a mistake, but not twice. That was too much of a coincidence.

I must have gone pale because Robert asked if I was alright.

"I need to get back to Moldova Square, Robert. Please excuse me," I said, in my fear and haste. I didn't wait; I dug my heel into Star's side and galloped off.

I didn't know if Robert followed me or not. I was worried that if it was Mark Trevelgue, he might start slinging accusations about me killing his sister. I was scared, more scared than I had ever been since leaving Cornwall. My happiness could be crumbling down around my ears in moments.

"Julia, slow down. What is wrong?" Robert called after me.

"I just need to return home to Lady Mary, Robert."

"Why Julia? What has happened?"

"Don't ask me, Robert. Not now," I cried, so close to tears of fear.

When I reached the stables, I slid off Star's back, flinging her reins to William and ran into the house. I heard Robert following me but didn't stop until I was in the drawing room.

Lady Mary was sitting in her chair embroidering. She looked up as I burst into the room.

"Julia, what is the meaning of this, a young lady running?" she scolded me.

"Lady Mary, I think Mark Trevelgue is here." I was crying now.

"Sit down, dear, and catch your breath," she said calmly,

"Who is Mark Trevelgue?" Robert asked as he followed me in.

"Edwina's oldest brother. The last time I saw him, he accused me of killing Edwina," I said, trying to gulp in deep breaths.

"But Julia, you didn't kill his sister!" Robert stated.

I had already told him about Edwina and her antics and told him that I had been in the village finding out about Gramps dying when Edwina died.

"Of course, she didn't," Lady Mary told him. "He was trying to cover up the fact that his sister was eloping with the stable boy," Lady Mary informed him.

Robert took my hand and began rubbing the back of it with his thumb, trying to comfort me.

"Then there is nothing to be worried about, Julia. The truth will prevail."

"But he could call the police, and he would threaten all of the people in my village that they would lose their jobs at the mine if they told the police that I was with them in the village the day Edwina died; he threatened that after Edwina's funeral." I explained.

He put his arm around my shoulders and let me cry into his chest.

"If they want to keep their jobs, they must lie," I cried.

"The family also wants my money, Robert. My dowry and to also get you to buy into the mines."

"Me!"

"Whoever I married," I told him. "According to Mrs Watson, things aren't going well at the mines."

"And that is your fault, how?" he asked.

"No, but I will be blamed for everything," I cried again.

Lady Mary put her embroidery down and said, "If he sets foot here, he will get short shrift."

"Don't forget Julia. You are my responsibility now. I won't let anyone hurt you. I promise you that," Robert told me.

Lady Mary handed me her handkerchief. "Here, sweetheart, dry your eyes," she said gently, using a form of endearment that I had never heard her use on me before.

"I am not just crying for myself but for the people of the village and you, Lady Mary. I don't want any hint of a scandal coming to your door again," I said, drying my eyes.

"Julia sent some money to the people in the village not long ago to ensure they wouldn't suffer if the mines were struggling and they lost their jobs," Lady Mary told Robert.

"And you think they would lie about you after you have done that? I doubt it." He replied.

"But they could, to save their livelihood."

"Don't worry, darling. It won't come to that." Robert said, taking the handkerchief from me and drying my eyes.

"Are you positive you saw Mark, Julia?" Lady Mary asked.

"If it wasn't him, it was his double," I replied.

"Then let's just wait and see what happens," Lady Mary said.

Robert looked at me. After my tears, I started shaking.

"Lady Mary, do you have any brandy? I think Julia could do with a tot."

Lady Mary indicated to the sideboard, where a decanter of brandy sat with four crystal glasses. "Pour yourself one, Robert, and I think I will have one too. This has been very trying for us all, I think."

Robert poured the three of us a brandy and handed them around. I took a sip and felt it burning my throat as I swallowed it. I didn't like the taste, but it had the desired effect, so I took another sip and cringed. Robert looked at me and laughed. "I don't think you will ever be a despot, Julia." Then he kissed my forehead. He didn't seem to bother about Lady Mary sitting with us. He knew that I needed the comfort only he could give me.

Lady Mary tried to change the subject, hoping it might take my mind off it all. "You two played the pianoforte together beautifully the other evening. Would you do it again for me? That's if you wouldn't mind Your Grace?"

Robert smiled at her, knowing her ploy. "That would be a good idea, Julia," he said, taking my hand and walking over to the pianoforte.

"How about some Schubert Julia? You usually find that soothing," Lady Mary said.

Robert started to play the Schubert Piano Sonata, and I joined in. I was just beginning to relax when there was a knock at the front door. Once again, I blanched white in dreadful anticipation of who it might be.

Ritson, the butler, knocked on the drawing-room door and entered.

"Lady Mary, there is a Mr Mark Trevelgue with a policeman at the front door."

I gave a little cry and clutched Robert's sleeve.

He held my hand, trying to reassure me that all would be well.

Lady Mary sighed, "Very well, let's get this over and done with. Your Grace, will you stay during this meeting, please?"

Robert nodded, "Of course, Lady Mary."

Again, Lady Mary sighed, "Very well, show him in." She put down her embroidery, which she had picked up while listening to Robert and me playing.

The butler bowed and escorted Mark and the policeman in.

"What is the meaning of this?" Lady Mary demanded before the butler had shut the drawing-room door.

It was the policeman who spoke first. "Madam, this gentleman has said that the murderer of his sister is living here under the fraudulent name of Julia Trevelgue."

I looked briefly up at Robert and saw his jaw set with anger. Mark stood beside the policeman, looking very smug as if he thought he would win this, and after what the policeman said, I thought he might, too.

"Oh, he does, does he?" Lady Mary said.

Again, Mark gave a cocky nod.

"That girl there is a fraud," he said, pointing to me as if he had done Lady Mary a favour by pointing it out. "She has duped you right from when she arrived here." He pointed at me, and he smirked. "She is nothing but a girl from a fishing village near where I came from. Her real name is Julia Beddoes. Her father worked for us as a manager at our mine."

"Mines," I contradicted him. "It was your mines that killed my father, leaving me an orphan," I pointed out, trying to give as good as I got, but there are some wars that you just can't win.

Lady Mary looked at me. "Julia, please go upstairs and get your paperwork, dear?"

I nodded and flew from the room and up the stairs to my bedroom, where Jane was waiting. I went straight to my bedside table draw. "Miss Julia, you look terrible. What's wrong?"

I found my change of name documents and clutched them to my breast. "Mark Trevelgue is downstairs accusing me of being a fraud and of Edwina's murderer."

"Oh God, no." I think she went as pale as I had. My first thought was to remove my engagement ring and placed it on my bedside table in case I had to go to the police station.

I patted her arm to try to comfort her because if I were charged, I feared that she might be charged, too, so I went downstairs after telling her to stay in my bedroom out of the way.

I could hear men's voices as I went downstairs again to the drawing room.

I handed my papers over to the policeman, then looked at Mark, who was still smirking, as if he had already got me clapped behind bars.

"It says here that you legally changed your name to Braemar on the sixteenth of September last year, Miss Braemar."

"That is correct."

The policeman looked across to Mark, whose face had turned beetroot red with anger. That was one of his accusations scuppered.

"It also has the Dowager Countess's signature and that of her solicitor, Mr Woodbine," the policeman informed Mark Trevelgue.

"Mr Woodbine deals with all my legal matters and has done so for many years."

She looked at Mark, who, if looks could kill, Lady Mary and I would both be dead.

"And you are the grandmother who turned out my mother without a penny to her name," he gloated. "Well, she didn't need your money; my father had enough to keep them in the lap of luxury. You thought she would end up in the gutter, penniless. What sort of a heartless kind of mother would do that?"

"So, the family doesn't need my money? Then why does your mother want Julia to give her half of my money when I die?"

"Because it's my mother's birthright," Mark said raising his voice.

"Is it? Your mother gave up any right to my money the day she eloped with your father."

I think that I heard Mark call Lady Mary a heartless bitch under his breath, but I couldn't be sure.

"As it is my money, I will leave it to whomever I wish, not as your mother expects," Lady Mary argued.

"Well, that has dealt with the fraudulent claims," said the policeman, trying to carry out his duty regardless of the family row going on around him,

"Now, to the very serious crime of the murder of one Miss Edwina Trevelgue," he said, handing me back the legal documents for my name change.

Robert looked at me and took my hand. "Julia, I am afraid that I must leave for some time on urgent matters, but I will be back. I promise you." He winked at me and then excused himself.

What was he doing, leaving me at such a crucial time? He told me that he would stay and support me. Was he finally leaving me to the wolves? I grabbed his hand, my eyes pleading with him not to leave me.

He removed my hand from his. "I must go immediately." He bowed to Lady Mary, who also looked askance at him.

I looked over to Mark, who was smirking again. "Well, I don't think you will be a duchess now," he grinned.

"Miss Braemar, you have been accused of the murder of Edwina Trevelgue in Cornwall on the first of September last year."

"Edwina wasn't murdered," I told the policemen, "She died in an accident. Part of the cliff collapsed when she was running away with the stable boy," I cried. "I wasn't even there at the time. I was in Porth with the people I grew up with." Tears were beginning to run down my cheeks again, firstly because Robert had disappeared just when I needed him. The fact that I had told the policeman that

Edwina was running away with the stable boy, I knew that it sounded totally unlikely. "The people of the village will support my claim," I told the police officer.

"The people in the village of Porth were working in my tin mines when she claims she was there, so there is no substance. And the accusation that my sister would run away with a stable boy, of all people, is preposterous. We are a family well respected in Cornwall." Mark walked over and sat in one of the chairs, looking like he had made himself at home, as if he owned the house, not Lady Mary.

I could feel things turning horribly wrong and could do nothing about it. I could see that I was going to prison and probably hanging.

I could hear ringing in my ears, and I felt lightheaded, and then everything went black.

I don't ever recall fainting in my life before, but then I had never been accused of murder and facing the hangman's noose before.

When I came to I found myself lying on one of the sofas in the drawing room, Dorcas standing over me with a bottle of smelling salts. "Come on, lamb, that's right. Let's get you sitting up," she said in her soft Scottish accent. She helped me sit up and said she would stay with me.

I didn't expect Jane to come down as she might also be jailed for fraud. She was as innocent as I was in this, and I wanted to spare her.

"Miss Braemar, are you well enough to answer more questions?" The policeman asked me.

I nodded.

"Constable," Lady Mary spoke. "May I speak?"

"Of course, Lady Mary."

"Mr Trevelgue's mother sent Miss Braemar to me, with a letter telling me that she was her daughter, my granddaughter. Now, if Mrs Trevelgue thought that Miss Braemar had murdered her daughter, then why would she send her to me? Saying that Julia was my granddaughter?"

The policeman paused for a moment, then nodded. "Lady Mary has a point." Then looked across to Mark Trevelgue. "Why would your mother do that, Mr Trevelgue, if she believed that Miss Braemar had killed her daughter?"

"My mother was distraught at losing her only daughter, and she wasn't thinking straight," Mark supplied.

Again, the policeman nodded, thinking about all that he had heard. "Do you have the letter, Lady Mary?" he asked,

"Err, not here, of course not," she said, getting flustered about being challenged on her word.

"Where is it, Ma'am?" The policeman asked her.

"Well, I, we... I think that I threw it away," Lady Mary said, getting confused. I had never seen her look flustered all the time I had lived with her. She always looked so calm and in control.

"Because there was no letter," Mark said.

"You just said that there was a letter, and your mother had written it when she was distraught over your sister's death," I pointed out.

The policeman was getting to the stage where he didn't know who or what to believe.

"I think this is all very confusing, and to be quite honest, both parties have a point, and I am just a lowly police constable. I am afraid, Miss Braemar, I must take you to the police station for further questioning."

"Then I must get my solicitor to meet you at the police station," Lady Mary said as she turned to Dorcas, who still held my hand. "Please, get one of the footmen to get Mr Woodbine to meet us at the police station as soon as possible, Dorcas."

Dorcas left us, and the policeman was about to put me in handcuffs. "Surely there is no need to do that, constable. I shall escort Miss Braemar to the police station in my carriage."

"I'm afraid, Ma'am, that I must accompany Miss Braemar," he said, looking apologetically at us both.

"Then you may ride in the carriage with us." Lady Mary was going to broker no arguments.

Mark still sat in the chair with his legs crossed and that smug look on his face, as if he belonged there.

"And you can leave," Lady Mary said, not even giving him the privilege of calling him by his name. "You are never, I mean, never, to set foot in my home again, or you will find yourself in jail for trespass."

Mark shrugged and stood up, still with that smug smile on his face.

"Mr Trevelgue, you must meet us at the police station as well," the policeman said.

Again, he shrugged and walked out, still smirking.

"Julia, go upstairs and fetch your coat; it might be cold at the police station."

"I'm afraid I can't let her leave my sight, Ma'am, given the seriousness of the accusation," the policeman said apologetically.

By that time Dorcas had returned after asking one of the footmen to get Mr Woodbine to meet us at the police station.

"Dorcas, could you please fetch Miss Julia's coat from her room?"

Dorcas left the room and returned shortly after with my coat. She helped me with it, always tutting, saying that she always knew the Trevelgues were no good.

Chapter Thirteen

All through the journey to the police station, the policeman sat opposite Lady Mary and me, not saying anything but looking around the carriage appreciatively. I presumed Mark was following closely behind. I was still distraught about Robert leaving me just at the most crucial time of my life. I thought that I could rely on him. I would never have expected it from him, and it hurt more than I could say. If this all got out, as it would, bang would go my hopes of making a decent marriage. I didn't even expect Lady Mary to be around much longer. She had already had to endure one scandal with Mrs Trevelgue and now me.

Thankfully, I had never been to a police station before. It was a dull, dark place with ugly green walls and dark grey floor tiles. The smell of unwashed bodies and despair hit you as soon as you walked through the dark blue double doors.

Mr Woodbine was already there waiting for us. He smiled at us both reassuringly.

"Miss Braemar," the sergeant on the desk called. "Come this way," he said no polite remarks, just an abrupt order.

Mr Woodbine said he was my solicitor and followed us into a room with a table and four chairs. Lady Mary was told to wait outside for us.

"Sit down," I was told abruptly by a different policeman to the one who had come to Moldova Square.

I sat on one side of the table, and the policeman sat opposite me. Mr Woodbine took a seat beside me. I held my hands in my lap and used my thumb to massage the back of my other hand, like Robert used to do, hoping it would give me strength and courage to face what was before me.

"Right, Miss Braemar, you are accused of murdering Miss Edwina Trevelgue on the first of September last year in Cornwall."

"Miss Braemar is not guilty of the accusations laid against her," Mr Woodbine said.

"Oh, is that true Miss Braemar?" the policeman asked.

"I was in Porth village meeting my friends, whom I grew up with. I didn't know of Edwina's death until I reached Seaward Manor later that day," I told him.

"Seaward Manor?"

"Where I lived as Miss Trevelgues companion."

"And why were you in Porth?"

"I went to Porth to see my grandfather, who was the local doctor."

"And did you see him?"

"No. I found out that he was dead."

"And you didn't know?"

"No. The weather had been particularly bad over the previous few weeks, and I couldn't visit him. A message had been sent to me when he died, the day before his funeral and, also, when they were closing the house that I had been brought up in until I moved to Seaward Manor."

"And you didn't receive any of the messages. Why was that?"

"All three messages were given to Edwina, who didn't pass any of them on to me."

"And how did that make you feel? Angry?" the policeman asked, writing everything down.

"You are putting words into my client's mouth." Mr Woodbine interrupted.

"How did it make you feel?" the policeman repeated his question.

"Angry. I was going to have it out with Edwina when I got back to Seaward Manor and also inform her mother."

"Were you angry enough to kill her?"

"You are putting words in Miss Braemar's mouth again," pointed out Mr Woodbine again.

"I was angry, yes, and I was going to talk to Edwina and Mrs Trevelgue, but when I got back to Seaward Manor, I found Mrs Trevelgue in the library, with Edwina's dead body laid out on the desk there."

"You say you were in Porth at the time of Edwina's death. Who saw you there?"

"Everybody. When I found out about Gramps, I was distraught that he had died and been buried, and I knew nothing about it. I sat down on the ground and cried. Everyone in the village saw me, including Mrs Watson, who practically brought me up until I moved into Seaward Manor."

"Anyone else?"

"Her daughter and husband and everybody in the village, as I have just said."

"I understand that Mr Mark Trevelgue said all the men were away from the village working in his mines."

"They weren't because he had laid them off as there were problems at the mine."

"What sort of problems."

"As Miss Braemar was not involved with the mine, how could she know that?" Mr Woodbine again pointed out.

The questions continued and continued, and I was exhausted, emotionally rather than physically. Mr Woodbine did his best to get me returned to Lady Mary's, but because of the seriousness of the accusation. I was taken to the cells.

The cell was cold and dank and smelled, a six-foot square room with a wooden bench for a bed and a chamber pot. I felt so numb that I couldn't even cry. How could Mark do it? What had I ever done to him, apart from ignoring his advances? I was so tired. All I wanted to do was sleep and discover this was just a nightmare.

The only thing I could think was that they wished to cover Edwina's elopement with the stable boy, but surely Mrs Trevelgue wasn't party to this? Thoughts kept going around in my mind so that in the end, regardless of the uncomfortable bed, I fell asleep. I had pulled my coat over my shoulders and pulled my legs up so they would be covered and slept, but my dreams were plagued with pictures of Robert walking away from me. I woke up the following day with tears on my face. I dashed them away and sat on the bed, waiting, and waiting, and waiting. Porridge in a tin bowl and tea in a tin mug were brought to me. The porridge was lukewarm, looking like grey slime and barely edible, and the tea was so weak it was more like dishwater.

In the end, I pushed them all away, barely touching them.

I didn't even have a comb or brush for my hair. It was still up in the combs that Jane had dressed it the day before. I undid the combs holding my hair up, let it down, and tried to brush it with the combs, which kept breaking, apart from one which I managed to comb my hair a little, but then I had nothing to tie it back with. I had to clean my teeth with my fingers. I dreaded what Lady Mary would have said if she saw me in this state. Tears filled my eyes again at the hopelessness of the whole situation, especially with the disappearance of Robert. Why did he leave so swiftly? He didn't say where he was going. Nothing, yet only minutes before, he told me he would protect me and that I should trust him. Then he just... The tears were falling. I was doomed for the gallows, and Lady Mary would have another scandal on her hands, which was the last thing I wanted, and my fiancé had deserted me.

I didn't know what time it was, but someone came and told me to get out of the cell and follow him. There were no niceties, so I 'got out.'

I followed him to the room I thought I had been in the previous day. I found Mr Woodbine waiting for me. He smiled at me. "How are you holding up, Miss Braemar?"

I gave him a watery smile. "Tolerably," I told him. How could I say anything else? "Could you arrange for someone to bring me a hairbrush, Mr. Woodbine?"

"Hopefully, Miss Braemar, last night will be your last night here. I am endeavouring to see if we can find the letter from Mrs Trevelgue, but Lady Mary said she thinks she threw it away. I will argue that Mrs Trevelgue would not have done that if she believed you had killed her daughter, regardless of whether she was distraught after her daughter's death." He smiled at me reassuringly. "It will be irrefutable evidence. If Lady Mary just tossed it away and was picked up by one of her staff and put somewhere safe, but we will still have to find it."

I felt tears welling up again. Mr. Woodbine handed me his handkerchief, and I thanked him, drying my eyes. "What if you can't find it?" I asked him.

"Let us take one step at a time, Miss Braemar," he told me. He had a kindly look on his face. How could I not believe he would try his hardest to help me?

The policeman who interviewed me the day before came in. "Good morning."

It wasn't a good morning. I didn't return his greeting, but I sat with my head bowed and my hands clutched together.

"I believe Mr Woodbine has told us that Mrs Trevelgue sent a letter with you from Cornwall. May I see it, Mr Woodbine?"

"We don't have it yet, but we are continuing to search for it," Mr Woodbine said, looking apologetically at me.

"Why is that Mr Woodbine?"

"The Dowager Countess of Orkney believes that she threw it away but can't be sure, so we are still looking."

"But you are saying that this letter from Mrs Trevelgue says that you are her daughter and the Dowager Countess of Orkney's granddaughter. But you say you are not, Miss Braemar. Can you explain that?"

I looked to Mr Woodbine as it would be raking up old scandals of Lady Mary's family.

Mr Woodbine nodded and said that Mrs Trevelgue was Lady Mary's daughter. She had caused a scandal and eloped with the mine owner, Mr Trevelgue, after being betrothed to an earl. After the scandal, Lady Mary cut Mrs Trevelgue off without a penny, knowing that Mr Trevelgue was not penniless.

"Lady Mary said that Miss Braemar..."

"I would like Miss Braemar to explain Mr Woodbine." He looked over at me, "Well, Miss Braemar?"

"Mrs Trevelgue wanted me to pretend that I was her daughter so that Lady Mary would give me a dowry and make me her heir. Mrs Trevelgue wanted me to give her half the money Lady Mary would leave me so I could return it to Mrs Trevelgue to help support the mines."

"What if Lady Mary didn't do that?"

"Then she hoped I would marry well and persuade my husband to invest in the mines."

"How did you feel about lying to Lady Mary?"

"I hated it. Lady Mary was so kind to me. Mrs Trevelgue even lied to me about her mother, saying she was cold-hearted and a harridan. Then, before I made my debut, Lady Mary told me that she legally wanted to make me her ward, settle a dowry on me, and make me her heir. I told her I didn't want that, and then I told her the whole truth."

"When did you officially change your name?"

Mr Woodbine handed over his copy of my name change.

"Why did Lady Mary want you to change your name?"

"She told me that her daughter had caused such a scandal when she eloped, and the ton had long memories. She didn't want to remind them of the previous scandal."

"Didn't you mind?"

"I had no family living, and I knew that if I married, I would change my name anyway to that of my husband. Also, I would no longer be known fraudulently as Julia Trevelgue, so I didn't mind. Braemar was Lady Mary's family name, and I felt proud to bear her name."

"You have made quite a name for yourself, Miss Braemar, the talk of society, and you were betrothed to a duke, I believe, within a matter of days after your debut?"

Mr Woodbine spoke. "Lady Mary is very proud of her ward's achievements."

The policeman paused and re-read the name-change papers. He pinched the bridge of his nose in weariness.

"Well, Miss Braemar, if the original letter from Mrs Trevelgue to Lady Mary can be found, it might support your version of events. But without that letter or any witnesses to verify that you were elsewhere when Miss Trevelgue died, it will go to court. I shall have to keep these papers for the time being."

I sat silently crying.

"What if we cannot find the letter from Mrs Trevelgue?" Mr Woodbine asked.

"We must just hope that you can find it; otherwise, Mr Trevelgue has a case against you for murder, and it will go to trial, that is, as I said, unless we can find witnesses that you were where you said you were, I am afraid Miss Braemar you must go back to your cell. Also, the fact that you fraudulently posed as Lady Mary's granddaughter does not speak well of your character."

"But surely," I said to the policeman, "even if that letter can't be found from Mrs Trevelgue to her mother, why would Mrs Trevelgue send me to her mother. Surely if Mrs Trevelgue thought that I had killed Edwina, wouldn't she have called the local police while I was still at Seaward Manor, yet she fed me, she taught me all about what glasses were for which drinks, which cutlery to use when I arrived at her mother's home. Now why would she do that if she thought that I had killed her daughter? Why would she have paid for Jane and I to travel from Cornwall to London, staying at coaching inns. Why would she have given me all of Edwina's clothes? Why would she have given me Edwina's jewellery?"

"Mr Trevelgue has said that his mother has had a nervous breakdown after her daughter died, she might not have been in her right mind just after her daughter died. It proves nothing. You could have taken advantage of Edwina Trevelgue's death and stollen the jewellery. The letter will be the proof that we require Miss Braemar, that is unless you have any witnesses to you being in Porth at the time of Miss Trevelgue's death. I can't release you until we have proof of your innocence. You will remain in custody Miss Braemar. Murder is a serious crime and until what you say can be proved..." he left the rest unsaid.

Mr Woodbine leaned across to me to whisper in my ear, "Have courage Miss Braemar. Be brave. We will get you out of here as soon as possible." Then he turned to the policeman.

"Can Lady Mary see Miss Braemar?" Mr Woodbine asked.

"Just for a few minutes," the policeman said, "and I will have to leave a constable here."

He left us with a constable in attendance, and Lady Mary entered the room. She looked at me and held me to her. "Oh, my dear girl, was it terrible? It must have been," she said, answering her own question. She held me away from her and took in my appearance. "Oh, you dear child, you look dreadful. What can I get you?"

I told her that I hadn't eaten or had anything to drink. "The food here is awful, and I could do with a hairbrush and a ribbon to tie my hair back, please."

"How are you holding up, Julia?" she asked.

I tried to put on a brave face but couldn't speak for fear of breaking down in tears, so I just nodded.

"We will get you out of here as soon as possible," Lady Mary promised me.

"Have you found the letter from Mrs Trevelgue Ma'am?" I asked when I felt that I could speak without bursting into tears.

"We are still looking, Julia. I honestly can't remember what I did with it."

"If you burnt it. I have no proof of what she said."

Lady Mary looked confused. "I am sure I didn't burn it, but what I did with it... I have searched my writing desk, where I usually keep things like that. That is where I have kept all her letters to me, but I don't remember putting the letter there, so it must be somewhere else. Be patient, my dear." Then she sighed and squeezed my hand. "I am so sorry, my dear, that you are incarcerated here." She continued, and I could see tears gathering in the corner of her eyes. I hated to think that I had brought her to that.

"Have you heard from Robert at all? Do you know where he is?" He was my only hope, but I didn't know what he could do, even if he was here.

"No, my dear. He seems to have just disappeared off the face of the earth. Nobody knows. I am so sorry. Don't give up, Julia. Be strong, sweetheart," she said, then turned away before I saw her tears.

"Lady Mary, I am so dreadfully sorry for all this," I cried after her.

"I know Julia, none of this is your doing. It's the Trevelgues. I am sorry that they have brought this on you," she said with her back to me. I knew she was crying; I saw her shoulders shaking, and I thought that she might have put her handkerchief to her eyes.

As soon as she left, the policeman looked at me. "It doesn't look like you will be getting out of here soon, does it?" he said arrogantly.

I was led back to my cell to sit on the wooden bed and stare at the four walls. I felt totally numb inside. How could Mrs Trevelgue allow her son to accuse me of murdering Edwina when she knew full well that I was innocent, and Robert...? I dare not think of Robert, or the tears would flow. I couldn't help but think about my wedding gown. I doubted I would need it now, or the other trousseau clothes. Would Madam Yvonne be able to alter them for some other young bride? What would Lady Mary do when the news hit the newspapers that her ward was imprisoned for murder and would probably hang? I still couldn't feel anything. It was as if it was all happening to someone else. I heard my stomach growl with hunger. I would probably die of starvation before I got to the gallows.

That night, after I had decided that if I was going to hang, I wanted to write a will so that what money I had left in the bank would go to Jane, who, if I weren't around, would need to find an alternative position. That started me crying again. What about her new clothes that I had ordered from Madame Yvonne? I curled under my coat and tried to sleep on the wooden bed again. It wasn't so easy on my second night. The cell was cold and damp; I had got used to the smell, but the other inmates screamed and banged on the doors. I might have heard a rat scurry along the floor, but I couldn't be sure as there was little light in the cell. I had never felt so alone. Although I was an only child, when I was young, I had friends from the village whom I played with. When I went to Seaward Manor, I had Edwina, probably not a friend, but I also had Miss Frazer and later Jane. There was always someone in my life, but there was no-one to share my incarceration with. No-one to talk to.

No-one whose shoulder I could cry on. No-one. I was on my own. If I was finally charged with murder, much as she cared for me, would Lady Mary want her name linked to a murderer, whether I was innocent or guilty. Again, the tears flowed. I had never cried so much, and whenever I cried it always seemed to be, apart from the deaths of my father and Gramps, the Trevelgue siblings who had caused my despair. Of-course I also cried for the fact that my fiancé had deserted me in my time of need. I should never have aimed so high, I told myself, and at each bang or cry or scream from the inmates, I told myself again and again.

The following day, I could smell tea and bacon and toast, and I thought that I was beginning to hallucinate. The policeman opened my cell door and carried in a covered tray. Lifting the coverings, I found that I wasn't hallucinating. Lady Mary must have managed to get something decent, although simple fayre, sent to me to eat and drink. He left me with the tray, but I noticed no knives and forks, (probably in case I tried to injure or kill myself in desperation), so I had to make do with my fingers. Food had never tasted so good, even if I was eating with my fingers. I ate it all up. I was starving. After the one cup of tea with the breakfast, I had no more, but Lady Mary had arranged for me to have a flask of fresh water to drink, which was certainly better than even what they served as tea.

I tried to keep track of the days but ultimately gave up. I just knew that I had been in prison for quite a while.

Each morning, I had bacon or sausages, toast and tea on a tray and another flask of water. She also sent me a hairbrush, ribbon, and a thick blanket for the 'bed'. I knew that I had it a lot better than the other prisoners. One thing I missed, and there was no hope of getting it, was a hot bath. Oh, I even dreamed of it at night. A nice deep, steaming bath filled with sweet-smelling oils, then to get out, after bathing and washing my hair, to have a big fluffy towel warmed by the fire. Oh, it was a wonderful dream, even better than my dreams of Robert, where I woke the next morning crying.

Another thing I missed was privacy, to answer the call of nature. One of the smells in the prison was the smell of stale urine and other revolting body odours, which I had to steel my stomach from bringing back my breakfast.

I hated the nights the most when the other inmates were restless, and I would hear screaming, shouting, and banging on doors. At times like that, I was relieved we were all locked up separately. All the time that I was in prison, I never had to share my cell with anyone else. Whether this was normal or not I didn't know. But I think that Lady Mary might have paid for that as well.

I don't even remember how long I was there; every day crawled into the next. I began to wonder if I might be losing my mind. My body itched from not bathing, and my head itched from not washing my hair. I think that I had fleas, although I couldn't be sure.

One morning, I was called and told to follow the policeman. We went to a room laid out the same way as the one I originally went into. I found Mr Woodbine there, perfectly attired and clean. In contrast, I wore the same clothes I had worn the day they brought me into the police station (thankfully, I had the foresight that when I took my change of name papers from upstairs, I took off any jewellery I had,). Mr Woodbine looked at me, and I could see from his face that I must have looked a mess.

"Miss Braemar, how are you keeping?"

I couldn't speak. I was too emotional.

"We have found the letter," he said, triumphantly. "I have shown it to the police, and for the time being, they are satisfied that Mrs Trevelgue would not have written such a letter if she believed that you had killed her daughter," Mr Woodbine said.

"You are free to go, Miss Braemar, for now, but we still might have to call you to take you to court," the policeman said. "It could also be that Mrs Trevelgue wrote the letter when she was distraught from her daughter's death, as Mr Trevelgue said."

So, this wasn't the end of it? I still had the worry about a court case hanging over me and the torture of the prospect of the hangman's noose.

Mr Woodbine reached out to me. "Come along, Miss Braemar, let me take you home."

Those words had never sounded so good.

We walked to his carriage in the station yard. "Mr Woodbine, I cannot enter your carriage; I am filthy. Could you please order a public carriage to take me to the stables at Moldova Square? I would hate for people to see me like this," I told him. Surprisingly, he didn't argue but called a public carriage, which he helped me into and followed me back to Lady Mary's.

From the stables, I walked into the kitchen, keeping my head down and speaking to no one, then up the backstairs (that I had rarely used) to my bedroom. Jane was sitting quietly sewing. She looked up when she heard the bedroom door open and nearly screamed when she saw me.

"Oh my God, Miss Julia, you're back, oh thank God. Oh, you look terrible. I'll get a bath sorted, and we'll get you out of those clothes."

Jane was about to go downstairs and tell anyone who could hear that I was back. The next thing I knew, Lady Mary knocked on my door and entered my room. She gave one look at me, and tears filled her eyes. "Oh, my dear child!"

"Don't come near me, Ma'am. I am filthy, and I don't know what I have brought back with me from the prison." Dorcas stood at my bedroom door, holding her handkerchief to her nose and mouth. The little Scottish lady came bustling into my bedroom then, taking over from Jane and issuing her orders. "Lady Mary, get yourself downstairs while we sort out things up here. Miss Julia will come down to see you when she is more presentable. Jane, you go down to the kitchens; we want two bathtubs, one with carbolic soap to bathe Miss Julia first, then we will get you into the other bathtub with sweet-smelling oils to make you feel better."

Jane didn't argue; she knew that Dorcas was in charge then. Lady Mary looked at me before she left my bedroom, "Don't bother dressing, dear. Have your baths, and when you feel better, come downstairs in your nightdress and dressing gown, and we will talk. Bless you, my dear. I should never have left you in that awful place."

"There was nothing that you could do about it, Lady Mary. The law is the law. Is Mr Woodbine with you still?" I asked her.

"He is, but I shall tell him to return tomorrow," Lady Mary said, then left.

Dorcas came up to me and said, "Right, Miss Julia, let's get you out of those clothes and burn them all. God knows what we would find in them."

I had never felt so ashamed of my condition before. Even when I played with the children in the village I was never as filthy as I was now. Dorcas helped me out of the clothes, leaving me in just grey-coloured underwear, and left them in a filthy pile on the large hearth.

One of the baths arrived, then another, followed by an army of housemaids carrying buckets full of hot water. When the bath was full, Dorcas told me to remove my underwear and get into the first bath. "It might be a bit hot, Miss Julia, but we need it like that to kill off anything you might have on you. If you want it a bit cooler, I can add some cold water to it, but try to bear it as hot as you can, Lassie."

I stepped into the bath. It was hot, but I knew it would be the only way to feel clean again. She washed me with some strange-smelling soap and an abrasive sponge, then told me to lay back and soak my hair. I did that for a few minutes; then she told me to sit up and washed my hair with the strange-smelling soap. It wasn't unpleasant, but not as nice as the bath oils I usually used. She worked industriously on my hair and scalp until it felt fully clean. I exited that bath, feeling scrubbed clean and ready to be pampered in beautifully scented bath oils and creams.

The other bath was being filled with more hot water while the first one was being emptied. I sat wrapped up in a massive bath towel until the other bath was filled and fragrant lilac oil poured into it.

"Right, Miss Julia, into the other bathtub with you, and you lay back and have a good long soak. If you want more hot water, ask, pet," Dorcas told me. She left me to Jane's ministrations, then gave Jane instructions to cover me in the cream that she had given her for me. "That will make her skin and Miss Julia feel so much better. Leave the hair lotion on for a minute before washing it off."

"Yes, Dorcas," Jane said meekly, knowing that Dorcas was again in charge.

I lay back in the beautifully scented water when it was just Jane and me. "You don't know how many times I dreamt about this while I was in prison. This is all I wanted. This and a nice soft bed to sleep in."

"When we've got you out and dried and into a lovely soft nightdress and dressing gown, you can tell me all about it." She rubbed some sort of cream into my hair thoroughly to penetrate it all, waited, and then washed it off.

"There, that looks better; it will give it a lovely shine, according to Dorcas." She wrapped my hair in a towel and asked me if I was ready to get out of the bath. I told her I was. So, she helped me out, wrapped me in another large, thick towel, and told me to sit by the fire roaring in the hearth. She rubbed my hair dry, then brushed it until it had dried with a shine like silk. "There now. That's better. Let me rub this cream on your body now. Go and lie on the bed on your stomach, Miss." I was too weary to argue, so I did as I was told. Jane began rubbing some sweet-smelling cream over my legs, my arms, and my back, then told me to roll over.

I did as she said, too weary to argue. "You've lost weight, Miss Julia, while you were there." She couldn't bring herself to say the word 'Prison'. "I can see your ribs, and you have dark circles under your eyes."

When she had done my front, she helped me into a beautiful, soft silk nightdress, braided my hair in one long, thick braid that hung down my back below my waist, and then helped me into my velvet dressing gown. I knew it was still summer, but being in that cold, damp cell, I felt I couldn't get warm. I sat on the side of my bed, and my body shook with great wracking sobs. "I never thought I would ever come back here," I told Jane.

"And I never thought that I would see you again." She put her arms around me, and we both sat cuddling each other and crying on the side of my bed, crying until we were all cried out.

It felt so good, after I never thought I would be happy again.

Dorcas knocked and came in with a tray of food of bacon, scrambled eggs, tomatoes and a pot of tea. I had only one meal a day in prison, so I set to it like a starved man. Food had never tasted so good. Dorcas came in then with a glass of something and told me to drink it all up. Dorcas turned and said she was so pleased I was back home. Lady Mary had been inconsolable while I was away. She told me that Lady Mary was waiting downstairs for me. So, I put my feet in my slippers and went downstairs, leaving Jane to tidy my room after all the bathing and massaging me with creams.

I went downstairs to the drawing room, where I found Lady Mary. Her eyes seemed red as if she had been crying too, but I wouldn't dare mention it.

"Lady Mary, I am so sorry to have again brought more scandal to your door. It was never my intention."

"Of course it wasn't, dear, and thankfully there has been no scandal. Philomena called on you several times, but I told her that you were ill, and I feared it was contagious. Mr Woodbine has made sure that nothing reached the newspapers. Lord Melbourne called a few times. Obviously, he knows the truth, and he said that if he can do anything to help, we should call on him."

"Have you heard anything from Robert?" I asked her, expecting to hear that he had been seen somewhere in London.

"No, dear, and it's only a few weeks to your wedding day."

"I don't think that is going to happen now," I told her.

"Well, there is still time, and all your new clothes have been delivered here."

"I can't see that I shall need them," I told her sadly. I felt so lost. I thought that Robert truly loved me and would stand by me through thick and thin, but when the going got tough, my fiancé disappeared to God knows where and left me alone to face whatever would happen.

"I see you are not wearing your engagement ring."

"I could see no point in it when the man who gave it to me has disappeared," I said, dejectedly, hanging my head with disappointment.

"Well, you need to put your earrings in, or the holes will close up, and you will have to get Dorcas to do it again," she said, trying to bring some form of humour into the conversation.

"Yes, Ma'am," I said resignedly.

"You look tired, Julia. Go to bed and sleep, as long as you need to recover. If you need to stay in bed for a few days, that is no problem. I want you to recover from your terrible ordeal. I wish I could erase the last three weeks from your memory, Julia."

I thanked Lady Mary, then slowly walked back upstairs to my bedroom. I hadn't been downstairs for long with Lady Mary, but I felt exhausted. Jane pulled my bedroom curtains to and told me to get into bed. I noticed that she had warmed the sheets for me. I got into bed and snuggled down. My bed felt as soft as a cloud compared to the hard, unyielding wooden bench I had slept on in the prison. I crawled under the covers, and Jane pulled them up under my chin, then kissed my forehead, "Sleep well, Miss Julia."

I slept deep, but I was plagued by nightmares of Robert leaving me, then being led up to the gallows instead of up the aisle, and

Mark Trevelgue was standing laughing at me. I was screaming and crying that I didn't do it. Then I felt myself gathered in someone's arms and woke up to find Lady Mary cuddling me with tears streaming down her cheeks. "My darling child, I shall never forgive those Trevelgues for what they have put you through. It's inhumane." She cuddled me until I had calmed down. Little did I know that when she left me again to try and sleep, she had asked Mr Woodbine to call on her again.

After Lady Mary left, I went back to sleep again, this time in a deep, dreamless sleep. It was late afternoon when I woke up. Jane brought me a tray of sandwiches and cakes, which I ate with relish, and a pot of tea. Then she asked me if I could get up or stay in bed. I told her that if I slept anymore, I wouldn't sleep that night. So, Jane helped me dress and go downstairs.

I was surprised to see Lord Melbourne sitting by Lady Mary, holding her hand and comforting her.

"Ah, Miss Braemar," he said, standing and approaching me. He kissed my hand. "I hear that you have had quite a rough time of it. I am so sorry, my dear."

"Are you quite rested now, Julia?" Lady Mary asked me, her voice full of concern.

I thanked her and said I slept better after she left me.

"Lady Mary, I am so sorry for bringing more scandal to your door. I didn't mean to," I told her, yet again. Recently I seemed to have done nothing else but keep apologising to Lady Mary.

"Of course, you didn't, my dear. All of this will be kept out of the newspapers. Mr Woodbine has seen to it that it was a mistaken identity."

"So now you can continue as if nothing has happened," Mr Lamb said.

"I don't think I will ever do that again, Lord Melbourne. My fiancé has disappeared, leaving me to face the music alone, apart from Lady Mary and Mr Woodbine and yourself."

"I am sure Rochester had a perfectly good reason for leaving you, my dear. I have never known him to be less than honourable," Lord Melbourne replied.

"But where can he have gone? Has anyone heard anything from him?" I asked again.

Lady Mary sadly shook her head.

"I cannot see the marriage going ahead without the groom, and if that happens, my chances of marriage have gone for good," I told them, trying hard to cover the twisting, excruciating pain in my heart. After everything I told the duke about my former life, I thought he had accepted it. My revelations did not seem to bother him. Maybe with the words of 'murder' hanging over my head, it was more than he could bear. After all, he wouldn't want his duchess to be linked to murder, even if it was a lie. What would Lady Virginia think of me? She wouldn't want to be linked to me after I had been called a murderer, and I understood it.

"Rochester is not the sort to leave like that. I can't understand it," Lord Melbourne said.

I found out that the letter from Mrs Trevelgue had finally been found, after it had slipped down at the back of one of the drawers in Lady Mary's writing desk. One of the cleaning maids had put it there the morning after my first night in Moldova Square, not realising its importance or the fact that it had slipped behind the drawer.

Reflecting on my life as it was, I thought my best idea would be to buy a little cottage in the country and retire with Jane if she wanted to accompany me. Then, I could live the rest of my life quietly, in seclusion, and out of the public eye to bring no further scandal to Lady Mary. The more I thought of it, the more it became appealing, especially now that there was no duke to be seen, and no marriage.

Mr Lamb left us shortly after but returned a few times to see how I was over the next few days. I had forgotten that he was supposed to return to Brocket Hall to try and rest, as he looked as bad as I felt.

I had not left the house for days, worried that I would either get accosted by Mark Trevelgue again or the police or the newspapers. I played the piano for Lady Mary, read, and did needlework, but I never left the house, even though Lady Mary tried to persuade me to go out riding. Philomena came to see me, but I told Jane to say that I was still ill and couldn't see anyone. No doubt if I saw Philomena, she would chatter about my forthcoming nuptials to her uncle, who had left me just when I needed him. I couldn't face that. I discovered that Lady Mary had told Dorcas to store my wedding dress and trousseau in one of the spare bedrooms, along with Jane's new clothes that had arrived as well. I thought that if I did buy us a small cottage in the country, at least we would both be well dressed and Jane could finally be seen as my equal.

Apart from Lord Melbourne and Philomena, who I still told Lady Mary to tell that I was still ill, albeit slowly recovering, we had no further visitors until one day, as I was sitting in the sunny drawing room, a knock came on the front door. Ritson already had instructions from me that I was not receiving anyone, but he came into the drawing room and announced the Duke of Rochester and guests. My eyebrows drew together in a frown. I couldn't understand why he should come to me now and who were his guests? Lady Mary told the butler to show them in. I rose to leave the room and run upstairs. I couldn't stand to see him after what he had done to me. I felt hurt, and I felt angry. He had disappeared when I needed his love and support, and he had not even the decency to contact me to apologise or explain.

Lady Mary told me that I should stay and face him. I hesitated, but Lady Mary said that I had more spirit in me than to go running to my room and hiding. I felt that that spirited young lady had left when the duke did, but I sat back down.

"The Duke of Rochester and guests," Ritson announced. I gathered by his tone that he wasn't very happy with the duke's disappearance either, although it was not an employee's position to voice their thoughts or show their feelings, certainly not a butler. Although it was all around the servant's quarters as common knowledge what had gone on.

The duke walked into the drawing room, and three other people stood behind him. I couldn't see them without lifting my eyes from the book I was trying to hide behind.

"Lady Mary, Julia, firstly, I must apologise for my state of dress; we have been on the road for days on end with little rest, only we wanted to get here as soon as possible to spare Julia any further distress or imprisonment."

It was no good. I had to look up. The duke certainly looked unkept, with several days of growth of a dark, nearly black beard, and his clothes were travel-worn and creased. What took my breath and speech away was who stood behind him. I saw Mrs Watson, the woman who had practically brought me up, and behind her stood her daughter Elsie and son-in-law Jethro. I stood, and tears started coursing down my cheeks as I stood and ran towards Mrs Watson, completely ignoring the duke, flinging my arms around her.

"Oh, bless you, sweetheart. You've been through a rough time because of Mark Trevelgue, but I'm here now, pet." She kissed my forehead, then held me away from her to take a good look at me. "Whatever happened to that spirited young girl that I knew?"

"She left when I was imprisoned," I told her, not daring to look at the duke.

"There are another three carriages full of miners and their families from the village," Jethro said. "When we heard what Mark Trevelgue had accused you of, we didn't want to work for him a minute longer; he thought he could blackmail us with our jobs if we said you were with us when Edwina died," he continued, clutching his cloth cap in his hands.

"Those Trevelgues think they can get away with anything," Elsie said.

I finally looked at the duke, "What will happen to them now?" I asked referring to the people from Porth.

"Well, they are prepared to stand and tell the police that you were with them when Miss Trevelgue died, and Mark Trevelgue had lied."

"Yes, but then what?"

"I have plenty of properties to offer employment to the people from the village, and they will have permanent, healthy employment from that of working down in the mines," the duke said. "I am sorry that I ran off without any explanation, but I knew I had to get the people here before they imprisoned you."

"They did imprison Julia," Lady Mary spoke using an accusing tone. "She was only released a few days ago after over two weeks in prison," she continued.

Robert came over and put his arms around me. "Oh, my darling, I am so sorry; I didn't know what to do for the best. I thought that if I brought the witnesses against Mark Trevelgue's words, that was the most important thing. I only stopped to change horses on the way there, and we did the same back. I couldn't say what I intended to do while Trevelgue was here."

"Julia thought you had left her in the lurch, never to be seen again; I thought so as well," Lady Mary spoke again.

The duke looked down at me again, "Julia, I would never leave you. I thought you knew how much I love you."

I had forgotten that we had an audience. "I didn't know what to think when you left without saying where you were going and what you would do."

"I thought time was of the essence, Julia. I am sorry that you had to spend even one night in prison, let alone over two weeks. It must have been dreadful for you."

I could not talk to him about us, and I was still unsure whether I wanted to marry him. The thought of a little cottage somewhere was still very appealing to me.

"What will we do with all the villagers for now?" I asked him.

"I thought that we could spread them around our three houses in London until the police have finished with them. I think the first thing is for me to see the police and get all the charges against you dropped," he told me.

"Woodbine took the letter from Mark Trevelgue's mother to the police, and it was then that they released Julia, but I don't know if the charges have completely been dropped or Julia will have to appear in court," Lady Mary explained.

"Well, let me get all the people from the village to the police station to give their statements," Robert said.

"I will arrange for bedrooms for Mrs Watson, Elsie, and Jethro here and maybe one other family," Lady Mary said.

"Attic rooms will do us very well, Ma'am," Mrs Watson said.

"No, Mrs Watson. You and your daughter and son-in-law will take two guest bedrooms, and we will put another family in the attic rooms."

"But we don't want to put you to any trouble Ma'am," Mrs Watson said.

"It's no trouble at all, Mrs Watson, after what you have done for Julia," Lady Mary said.

"What Mark Trevelgue is trying to do to Julia is unforgivable. It's dreadful. He should be imprisoned for lying or at least horse-whipped," Mrs Watson said.

I think Elsie and Jethro were dumbstruck being in the house, which I must admit, compared to their home in the village, was a palace, and I didn't want them to be overawed, not after what they had been forced to give up, to travel to London and help me.

"Well, let us forward to the police station, then we can get you all settled for the time being," the duke said, "Then I will go home and clean myself up. We have been on the road, more or less, nonstop. I will call on you tomorrow, Julia, when I am more fit to present myself to you." He came over to me and placed a chaste kiss on my cheek. Then looked at my hand. "You're not wearing your engagement ring, Julia."

"I didn't think I was going to get married," I told him.

"Of course we are, Julia. That is all I have been thinking about since I left here. It is all that has kept me going on the road."

"If you are sure, Robert." That was all that I could say.

"Never surer, Julia."

I told him that I would go upstairs and put it on again.

He left us, taking Mrs Watson, Elsie, and Jethro with him, to give their statements to the police. I couldn't help but grin at the thought of the Duke of Rochester traipsing into the police station with about twenty people from the village following.

"That is the first time you have smiled in nearly three weeks, Julia." Lady Mary noted.

"I had nothing to smile about until now, Ma'am. I was thinking of Robert going to the police station like the Pied Piper with all the families from the village following behind him," I said, beginning to giggle at the mental picture it invoked. Lady Mary joined in, and I started crying again, great gulping sobs.

"What on earth is wrong, dear?" Lady Mary asked, concerned, as she sat beside me and gathered me into her arms to cuddle me.

"I am so happy."

I could feel her laughing as she held me and stroked my back. "Oh, my dear Julia, you are a joy," she told me.

"But I have brought another scandal to your door."

"No, you haven't. Mr Woodbine is seeing to that. Of course, if it still goes to court, we can weather that storm if it comes." She gave me her handkerchief and told me to dry my eyes. My fiancé was back with proof of my innocence.

"And half the village in his wake." I grinned.

Two days later, I had to present myself to the police station. I started shaking again, thinking that I couldn't spend another night in the cells. Robert came with me and Lady Mary.

I was taken into a room and saw the policeman who had initially dealt with me. This time, he invited me to take a seat.

He took a deep breath and began, "Well, Miss Braemar, it seems that nearly all the village where you were brought up has come to support your statement, so it certainly looks like Mr Trevelgue was lying all along. You do realise that you could bring charges against him for defamation of character, and he would get a custodial sentence." He looked across the table at me in question.

"I just want to put the whole terrible thing behind me," I told him, relief filling my body. I just wanted to start my life afresh.

"So, you don't want to press charges?" he asked again.

"No," I replied.

Deep down, I would have loved to see Mark Trevelgue behind bars. Still, I didn't want to bring any more trouble to Lady Mary's door, and if I had Mark Trevelgue imprisoned, everything about him and his mother would come out, and Lady Mary's name would once again be aligned with another scandal. So, I said to leave things alone. I just wanted to get on with my life and my marriage to Robert, for which preparations were again in full swing. My trousseau had to be altered and taken in before being transferred to my bedroom and packed in my trunks, ready for the honeymoon. Once again, Jane worked day and night along with Dorcas to finish them before they were taken to Knole Castle, and Jane also couldn't wait to wear her new uniform finally.

Now that Robert was back and things were set right again, I started going out once more. Robert had sent the people from the village to his various properties around the country. Mrs Watson, Elsie, Jethro and another couple were sent to Robert's property in Kent at Knole castle, where we had had the weekend party. Knole

Castle was massive, so I did not doubt there would be enough room for them and enough work for them all. Robert wanted Jethro to work in the stables with him. At least it was above ground, compared to the mine, and he had honest work without the threat of losing his job. Mrs Watson and Elsie also found work. Mrs Watson would oversee and train all the housemaids, and Elsie would be in the kitchens. Robert again exhibited his caring feelings towards me by keeping Mrs W, Elsie and Jethro close, knowing I would want them to be nearby. I hoped they would all be happy in their new positions, but I would have plenty of time to find out when we reached Knole Castle to begin our honeymoon. Lady Virginia, Robert's mother, was staying in London for the time being at Robert's townhouse on Berkley Square so that she could spend time with her brother and family. Some more of the families from Porth were employed in Robert's townhouse, and even the Hiddleston's came to the rescue and offered employment for some of the people from the village to work on their property.

Slowly, bit by bit, the people of Porth village, who had originally worked in the tin mines near Porth, had found meaningful employment in all of Robert's and his family's properties, which was more secure and healthier than their lives in Cornwall.

I had asked Mrs Watson how the new Doctor would manage without her, and she told me that he had a wife who would help him at the Lodge. "If not, plenty of women are still left in the village to help out," she explained before being sent to Kent. Mrs Watson said she would have liked to see me get married, but I told her she would see me when I was a duchess.

"Who'd have thought, all those years ago, that you would ever become a duchess?" she told me. "Your father and Gramps would have been so proud of you, sweetheart," she said, then kissed me.

Philomena started to come over to visit me and discuss my wedding. She told me that she had seen quite a lot of Lord Davenport during my illness. "I know that he is not the world's best dancer; in fact, he will not waltz with me, but only the dances that we are not close together; he says that he would hate to tread on my toes. Apart from that, he is very handsome and charming. I know he likes me. He visits nearly every day and brings me some token or other of his esteem: flowers, chocolates or a book."

"I am pleased for you, Philomena," I told her, then asked about Lord Waterford.

"Oh, I know he is handsome, but his home is in Ireland. If he proposed and I married him, I would be miles away from my family and my new aunty," she teased me.

We had not heard anything more about Mark Trevelgue, so I presume he returned to Cornwall with his tail between his legs and no workforce in the mine.

Robert told me he hated bullies, and Mark Trevelgue fell into that category. Lady Virginia and Lady Mary's staff worked tirelessly to complete the wedding and reception on time and surprisingly managed it.

Jane was getting excited about becoming a lady's maid to a duchess, but I was concerned that I didn't have the training to become a duchess and run a large household like Knole Castle. I had no idea how many staff were employed at the castle, let alone Roberts London house and the others scattered around the country. I voiced my concerns to Lady Virginia one day when she came over to Lady Mary's for another 'council of war,' as Robert called it.

"Julia, don't worry, my dear. After your honeymoon, I will be back at the castle and be able to teach you everything you need to know," Lady Virginia said, "Robert tells me you are a quick learner; I am sure you will pick it up easily."

"But I have never had a large number of staff before. In fact, I have never run a household before," I told her. "What if they don't like me?"

Lady Virginia put her arm around my shoulders and hugged me, "If you can get the love and support you have with the people from

Porth, I am sure you will do well with all your staff. Just be your kind and caring self."

Philomena took me to one side and whispered, "Julia, do you know what to expect in the marriage bed on your wedding night?"

I shook my head. Lady Mary was lovely, but I could not ask her that question.

"My mama told me that my husband will know, and I just have to listen to him and do what he says," Philomena told me.

I looked at Philomena. "Well, that doesn't tell us much," I said.

"I even asked one of my brothers, but he would not tell me. He just said to wait until I get married. I did not even know about 'monthlies' until they happened, then Mama told me. She could have warned me!" she told me with mock anger. "Will you tell me when I next see you, Julia?" she begged.

I laughed at her. "Why can't you wait? You will know when it is your time. If I can go to my marriage bed, ignorant, why can't you?"

"Because I am nosey," she told me, and we both laughed.

I looked at my wedding gown, now hanging outside my wardrobe. Jane had taken it in since I had lost weight during my imprisonment, even though my imprisonment was for only just over two weeks. The next day, I would wear it and return from the church as Julia Beaumont, Duchess of Rochester. I was overawed at my lofty elevation from a normal girl in a fishing village to a debutant and, finally, a duchess. I was not prepared to be a wife or run a home, not just a house but a castle.

When I voiced my fears to Robert, he kissed my hand. "Why do you think I wanted to keep Mrs Watson near you? So that she could help you and my mother is keen to help as well."

Chapter Fourteen

Jane came to my room at nine o'clock the next morning. She opened the bedroom curtains to a beautiful, sunny summer morning. The sky was a beautiful cerulean blue with the occasional tiny white fluffy clouds daring to show their faces.

She placed my breakfast tray on my lap. I looked at it and realised I couldn't face sausage, bacon, scrambled eggs, toast, jam, and tea; I was too nervous.

I told Jane to take it all back to the kitchen.

"I can't do that, Miss Julia. Cook has made it especially for you."

"Well, you eat it," I told her. "I will just have tea and toast."

Jane didn't take asking a second time and began eating it while I took some of the toast, spread butter on it with the apricot jam and drank my tea.

After Jane finished eating, I asked her if she could prepare a bath for me. She put my tray and finished breakfast outside my bedroom door, then prepared my bath and washed my hair. She put the cream that she had used after I returned from prison, on my hair. When I was dry, she massaged another cream into my body, smelling of my favourite flower, lilac.

"Have you packed all your clothes, including your new uniforms?" I asked her as she began brushing my hair out, which I was ready for her to style.

Jane's new dresses, which I had told her was her new uniform, consisted of dresses in deep lilac, dark green, a deep blue, and dark scarlet, which she fell in love with, plus the usual black, as she had always had to wear a black dress with a white cap, collar cuffs and pinny in Cornwall. Still, as a duchess's lady's maid, she could dispense with the pinny and cap. I wanted to bring more colour into her clothes as she was elevated from the position of my maid as a commoner to that of a Duchess's ladies maid. When her new uniforms were delivered from Madame Yvonne, she clapped her hands in glee. "I will certainly stand out against the rest of the staff at the castle. I dreamed, but never thought that this day would ever come," she told me. "I will leave you for the castle once I have dressed you in your wedding gown, so I will be there when you arrive."

Once I had put on my wedding dress and veil, I looked at myself in the large bedroom mirror. My gown was an empire-line, fitted with short puff sleeves. It had a six-foot train, and my veil was the full length of the train. I looked every inch a Duchess.

Lady Virginia had visited the day before to give me the family diamonds to wear on my wedding day; they consisted of a diamond tiara, necklace, and earrings. My wedding dress was ice white satin, and the train was edged with Brussels lace to match my veil. Yes, if not a Duchess, then a Princess. I thought as I looked at myself in the mirror. I wondered what my father and Gramps would have thought, and I wished that Mrs Watson were here to see me, but she was busy in her new position at Knole castle, ensuring that all the maids were doing their jobs correctly.

Lady Mary came to my room just before I was due to go downstairs.

"Julia, you look beautiful, my dear. Transfer your engagement ring to your other hand so the duke can place the wedding ring on your finger." She paused, then took a deep breath. "What happens on the wedding night, your husband will instruct you, dear, and what happens between husband and wife is strictly between a husband and his wife, and it is not to be discussed outside the marriage bed. So, no telling Philomena what happens, even though I know she has been pestering you to find out. Dorcas will help you out of your wedding gown and into your travelling dress for going away." Again, she paused, "I am so proud of you, Julia; for the woman that you have turned out to be, no true grandmother could be any prouder than I am at this moment," she said, then dabbed away a tear that had escaped from the corner of her eye. "I shall miss you. Your presence has been a joy to me, from playing the piano and reading to the times you made me laugh until I cried. It will certainly be quiet around here without you." She sniffed, dabbed her eyes again, and took a deep breath, "Melbourne is downstairs waiting for you. Your bouquet was delivered about half an hour ago. It smells beautiful." Lady Mary kissed my forehead. "Be happy, my dear." Then left me to go downstairs.

All the staff were gathered in the hallway to see me and wish me well. Dorcas handed me my bouquet and looked at me. "You look perfect," she said, then kissed me and blushed at being so informal.

Lord Melbourne approached me, offered me his arm and we walked out to the open-topped carriage, pulled by four white horses. He sat next to me, as the carriage pulled out of Moldova Square.

"If you were my daughter, I would be so proud of you," he said, smiling at me. "As it is, I should have offered for you myself, and indeed I would have, if Rochester had not returned..." he teased me. "Rochester is a lucky man."

"I know you are married to your work, Lord Melbourne. Thank you for all you have done for me and for being my friend," I told him.

"Who would have thought that day that you and Jane shared my coach to come to Moldova Square, that I would be escorting you to your wedding to a duke? You have certainly come a long way Julia in a relatively short time. As Lady Mary and I are proud of the young woman you have become, you should also be proud of yourself. You have become quite a celebrity among the ton for your piano playing."

Then, it was time for us to leave the carriage and go into the church.

I walked down the aisle on Lord Melbourne's arm. Then he handed me over to Robert, who looked splendid as I stood beside him at the altar. I looked across at him, and he smiled down at me. "You look beautiful," he whispered.

The ceremony began, but I don't remember saying my vows or Robert saying his. The next thing I remember is looking at the wedding ring on my finger and transferring my engagement ring back on top of it. Robert kissed me chastely as we were pronounced husband and wife, and arm in arm, we walked back down the aisle. It was all over in what seemed to be a matter of minutes, and I wished I could have just stopped time so that it would all be imprinted on my memory, to enjoy the happiness of the moment after all the pain that Mark Trevelgue had put me through.

We returned to Moldova Square, where the wedding breakfast was being held. Dorcas came and took my wedding veil off me and congratulated me. She was the first person to call me 'Your Grace,' and it felt surreal. I was now the Duchess of Rochester. What would my father and Gramps have said? Even Lady Mary called me 'Your Grace,' I told her I did not want her to call me that. I was Julia to her, and I always would be.

"I cannot thank you enough for everything you have done for me, Lady Mary. Since telling you the truth, and maybe before, I have looked at you like the grandmother, or even mother that I never knew," I told her. She just kissed my forehead and told me it had been her pleasure.

Lord Melbourne came over, took my hand, kissed it, and shook Robert's hand. "Congratulations, Your Grace," he said.

"Thank you for all you have done for me, Mr Lamb. I owe you and Lady Mary so much for taking me in and making me feel like a family member," I told him.

"It has been my pleasure to see you grow and develop into a young lady of the ton and now look at you, a duchess."

"You will be welcome in any of our homes Melbourne," Robert told him, shaking his hand again.

Lord Melbourne thanked us both, said he could not monopolise the happy couple and moved off.

Philomena came over to us, full of enthusiasm as usual. "Uncle Robert, Aunt..."

"Don't you dare," I said, interrupting her, knowing full well what she would call me. "I am only your aunt by marriage, so don't you ever call me Aunt Julia, Philomena Hiddleston," I said, laughing.

"Oh, you spoil all my fun," she said, kissing us both. "Congratulations, Your Grace," she said as she kissed me.

"Your turn next, Philomena. Anyone in the offing as a potential suitor?" Robert asked.

"Didn't you mention Lord Davenport, Philomena?" I asked her.

Her eyes were dreamy, "Oh, he is so attentive," she spoke.

Philomena had that glint in her eye whenever Lord Davenport's name was mentioned, the same as I had whenever I had mentioned Robert.

"I hope you move your feet fast," Robert teased her.

"Uncle Robert, don't you start. He still talks about how he trod on Julia's feet, and you were laid up for a couple of days. He still feels bad about it and never dances the waltz with me or any other dances where he might tread on my feet."

"You really like him, Philomena? I am so pleased for you. Would you accept if he proposed to you?" I asked her.

"In a heartbeat." She paused, and I could tell she was thinking about her own wedding to Lord Davenport. "Your wedding gown and your veil are beautiful, Julia. Is that Honiton lace that your veil was made from?"

"Brussels lace," I told her.

"Oooh, Brussels lace. Well, I suppose it's only fitting for a Duchess," she laughed. "Oh, and you have the family diamonds, Julia; they are beautiful."

"I was surprised when Lady Virginia brought them over for me," I told her.

"Julia, we must circulate," Robert prompted me.

"Sorry, Philomena," I apologised.

"No worries, Julia. I know you must do your duties to your guests."

Robert and I circulated among our guests.

I went and spoke to Lady Mary. "Your Grace," she said, grinning at me.

I kissed her cheek. "Never call me that, Ma'am. I am, and always will be, your Julia," I reminded her again.

I went over to my mother-in-law and said, "Thank you for the use of the tiara and diamonds, Lady Virginia."

"Use, my dear Julia? They are yours. You are the Duchess of Rochester now, so the family jewels are yours."

Robert and I spoke to more guests, and then Robert told me it was time for me to go upstairs and change.

I went upstairs to my bedroom, and Dorcas waited for me. "Are you going to leave now, Your Grace?" she asked me.

"It will take some getting used to being called 'Your Grace,'" I pondered. "Yes, Dorcas. I need to change," I told her, giving one more look in the mirror at me in my wedding gown. It was so beautiful, and I had only worn it for a few hours.

"It really is beautiful, Miss Julia, and you looked the perfect wee bride," she said as she unbuttoned my dress. "It has been a pleasure getting to know you," she said, forgetting my new title, and I couldn't contradict her. To Lady Mary, Dorcas, and others who knew Julia Beddoes, such as Mrs Watson, I would always be Julia to them, and would never push my elevated position on them. I wanted them to keep me grounded, as still the young girl from the little fishing village of Porth. Then I thought of the smug look on Mark Trevelgues face after Robert had left me, saying that I would never be a duchess. I hope that was the last of my dealings with any of the Trevelgues.

I brought myself back to the moment and my conversation with Dorcas, "Well, I would never have gotten my ears pierced without you, Dorcas," I told her, and we both laughed.

"Jane has turned out to be a very good lady's maid. She picked up everything quite easily, really... apart from ear piercing." She laughed as she finished buttoning my travelling gown.

"Dorcas, you must let Lady Mary know she is always welcome in my home. Let me know if she ever needs me, and I will come immediately."

"I'll do that, Miss...Your Grace."

"Thank you again, Dorcas." I kissed her cheek.

"Be happy, Miss Julia."

I smiled, then turned to leave.

Robert was already waiting in the hall downstairs.

"Are you ready, Julia?" he asked as he took my arm.

I nodded.

Our guests came out to the front of the house to see us off. The wisteria Lord Melbourne had once told me about when I first arrived in Moldova Square was out in full bloom. Robert handed me into his carriage, then got in beside me and closed the door.

"Alone at last," he said, grinning. His two dimples appearing either side of his lips.

"I honestly didn't think this day would ever come," I told him.

"We have the rest of our lives together, starting from now," he told me, holding my hand and stroking it with his thumb. "We can't make the journey to Kent in one go because of the lateness of the day, so we will stay overnight at a coaching inn and reach the castle tomorrow."

All of our guests stood outside the house on Moldova Square to wave Robert and me off on our honeymoon.

Robert pulled me to him as the carriage rolled away from Moldova Square. He gently placed his lips to mine, and I found that my lips had a mind of their own as they began to move under his until his tongue invaded my mouth, searching and discovering. My tongue moved involuntarily to his, tasting and feeling the texture of his mouth. I heard him groan, "Oh God, how I have thought of this moment every day since we first kissed." He rested his forehead against mine as he cupped my head, bringing me closer as if scared that I would disappear. His other hand moved from my waist to my breast as he cupped it, and his hand, feeling my nipple peak and harden, began running his thumb over it. I felt my breathing become faster as if I had been running, and I arched my back, thrusting my breasts deeper into his hand, wanting more. He moved his other hand from behind my head to cup my other breast. I felt a tingling deep inside my body, wanting fulfilment, but how Robert or I was to achieve that, I didn't know. All I did know was that I did not want him to stop this exquisite torture. He kissed me again with more urgency until we were both breathless. The amazing tingling had spread to my most private parts, demanding relief. Robert rested his head on mine again.

"We must wait until we get to the inn, my love. We have waited a long time already. We must wait just a little longer." He sat back and held my hand again, rubbing his thumb over the back of my hand. It felt so comforting. I rested my head on his shoulder, and I think I must have closed my eyes and let the carriage rocking relax me. I had everything I could ever want and more. I, Julia Beddoes of the Lodge, Porth, near Newquay in Cornwall, was now Julia, Duchess of Rochester, and I would be living in a castle, Knole, in Kent. What would Gramps and my father think if they saw me? I had not meant to fall asleep, but I had not slept well the night before, wondering if anything more could come along and spoil my happiness.

Robert gently stroked my face, "Hey, sleeping beauty, we have arrived at Croydon,"

"Oh, I am so sorry, Robert; I didn't mean to fall asleep; it's just..." I was quite flustered.

"Don't tell me you didn't sleep very well last night. Were you worrying about our wedding night?"

How could he know me so well after such a brief time? I nodded.

"Darling, it is nothing to worry about, I promise you. I don't suppose Lady Mary told you anything?" he said, stroking my cheek.

"She just told me to do what you wished of me," I said, almost apologetically.

"Typical." He scoffed.

"Well, as you have said before, it has been many years since Lady Mary's wedding night," I reminded him.

"Many, many, many years," he joked.

"Robert, you are awful." I laughed.

"We're here, Julia, at the Coach and Four," he said.

"Do you usually stay here when you are travelling to Knole?"

"Most times. They already know me."

"I don't remember Lady Mary and I stopping here at Easter."

"No, there are several different routes to Knole."

The duke's coachman came and let down the step to help us alight. Robert went first, then held his hand to me to help me. He tucked my arm into his, as we walked into the inn.

The Innkeeper approached us with a welcoming smile on his chubby, rosy face. Looking at his heavy build, I thought the food must be good here if he was anything to go by.

"Your Grace. Welcome. It is good to see you again," he said, bowing to us. "And you, too, your Grace, congratulations on your marriage. We have been expecting you, so your rooms are ready, as requested."

He took us up the wooden stairs to our bedroom, which was attached to our dining room, where we would eat.

"I hope this will suit you both. Would you like my wife to act as your maid, Lady Rochester?" he asked me.

It was my first time being called 'Lady Rochester', which seemed strange.

"There is no need for a maid Kirby. I shall act as my wife's maid this evening."

I could feel myself blushing. Robert winked at me behind Mr Kirby's back.

"Dinner will be served at seven o'clock. Do you wish to go to the dining room, or will you have it served up here?" Mr Kirby asked before leaving.

"Oh, I think we will have it here, Kirby," Robert said.

"Very well, Your Grace." Mr Kirby bowed.

The innkeeper left us then.

Robert approached me, "Right, where were we in your education?"

He gently touched my lips with his, and then they moved to my ears, kissing and nibbling. His lips moved from my ears to my neck, and his hands cupped my breasts and began to knead them gently under the cover of my gown.

"No, this is not good enough." He put one of his arms under my knees and scooped me up and held me against his powerful, strong body. His kisses continued until we reached the bedroom, where he turned, kicking the door closed behind us, "We don't want any interruptions."

He put me down gently beside the bed, returned to lock the door, and then turned to me. His hand went behind my head. I thought he would kiss me again, but his hands removed the pins from my hair, setting it free until it tumbled in a dark mass over my shoulders and down my back. "Oh, my darling, it is glorious."

His fingers began running through my hair, then kissing my lips and my cheeks, pushed my hair from my shoulders and made his way down to my breasts. His kisses brought little gasps of pleasure from me. I didn't realise that his fingers had been deftly undoing the tiny buttons at the back of my gown so that he pushed it from my shoulders, and it fell to the floor in a pool of peach silk around my feet. His eyes devoured me. I felt stupid just standing there, and I couldn't get out of my mind how he looked that night when Amber gave birth to Copper, so I thought that I would do the same. I undid his necktie and slowly undone the buttons on his shirt, showing me the dark hairs of his chest. He caught his breath as I ran my hands through them, and I was amazed at how silky soft they were to my touch.

He grinned at me, "Well, well, well, I never realised that I had a brazen hussy for a wife."

I felt my body blush as I lowered my head in embarrassment. "I'm sorry, Robert, but I just couldn't stand around..."

He kissed the tip of my nose. "I am certainly not complaining, my love. I was teasing you. Feel free," he prompted me and opened his arms, inviting me to continue.

I looked at his face as I continued. With each button I undid, his breath seemed to hitch, and then he began removing my undergarments until I stood naked before him. He cast off his shirt and began to undo the buttons on his trousers. I lay down on the bed and watched. His broad chest practically rippled with muscles, and I felt that strange tingling deep down within me at just seeing my husband stripped naked. Robert lay down beside me. He began kissing and teasing my body using his tongue and his hands until my body started moving of its own volition, arching, wanting more. We came together, and our bodies moved in a dance as old as time. He did things to my body that lifted me higher and higher into the sky until my body exploded into a million stars, and slowly, I came back down to earth, fully sated, to lay down next to him with a satisfied grin on my face. I never knew that a man's body could be so beautiful, from his muscular, solid arms to his broad chest and trim waist to his firm thighs and legs. I lay my head down among the soft hair of his chest and sighed with contentment. "Are you alright, Julia? Did it hurt you?" he asked me, concerned.

I smiled, "I never knew pain could be so exquisite." I sighed.

"It won't hurt at all from now on, darling," my husband told me.

"Oh, my Robert, my heart is full of love for you. No wonder mothers never tell their daughters about this. Otherwise, they would all be clambering to lose their virginity," I whispered.

I could feel his body shaking with laughter. "I always thought that our life would be filled with joy and laughter, and I don't think you will disappoint me, my little love."

I hoped not. "Will you teach me how to please you, Robert, as you please me? Or am I being a brazen hussy again?"

"All in good time," he told me. "Are you hungry? I know I am."

I nodded. At some time since we had arrived at the inn food had been delivered to our dining room. We sat in the dining room, next to our bedroom, wrapped in sheets from the bed, then when we had eaten, we went back and lay down again, and our ecstatic bodies moved as one. This time, there was no pain, only pure pleasure and joy as we enjoyed each other's bodies once more. Apart from Jane, I had never shared a bed with anyone before, and it felt strange to go to sleep with my husband's arms wrapped protectively around me. I woke the next morning in the same position, and it felt comforting to think that I would never wake up alone again.

After a hearty breakfast, we boarded the coach the following day and made the final part of our journey to Knole Castle. I sat beside my husband, looking forward to what the night would bring. I had a feeling that it would only get better. It seemed only a short journey to the castle. The carriage pulled up into the courtyard, and Robert helped me down.

All the staff had lined up in the courtyard to greet us. The first people I noticed were Mrs Watson, Elsie, and Jethro. I know it had only been a short time since they moved here after their long and hasty journey from Cornwall, but they all looked happy. Mrs Coleman, the housekeeper, stood at the top of the line of female staff, and Mr Jenkins, the butler, stood at the top of the line of male staff. As I went to each one, they bowed or curtseyed and called me 'Your Grace.' I knew getting used to being called that would take me a long time.

I needed to talk to Mrs Watson to determine whether we had done the right thing by bringing her and the others to London and then to Knole Castle.

After introducing me to our staff, Robert picked me up and carried me over the castle's threshold into the regal reception area.

"I never expected to be back here so soon," I told him.

"Are you disappointed you didn't have more time for your season than you did?" he asked me.

"No, because as soon as I first met you, I hoped you would offer for me, but I didn't think you would."

"Oh, so it was love at first sight then?" he grinned at me, his eyes twinkling in devilment.

"Do you expect me to answer that and give you a swollen head, as well?" I teased him.

"As well as what?" he asked, raising an eyebrow, and his eyes sparkled with devilment. He knew what I meant, and I certainly knew what he meant. I tapped his arm playfully. "Robert, you are incorrigible." I laughed.

He pulled me into the protective curve of his body. "Do you want to know a secret?" he whispered. "It was love at first sight for me." Then he kissed me and carried me up the long staircase to his bedchamber, our bedchamber, which looked fit for a king. Our bedchamber was in blues and golds with great tapestries hanging on the walls. Our four-poster bed actually had a crown picked out in gold leaf above it. The huge cream marble fireplace had a fire roaring and crackling in it despite the warmth of the summer weather. Robert explained that although it was the height of summer, because of the size of the staterooms, they still needed to keep the fires going. "But, once we get in that bed and the curtains drawn around it, we won't need massive fires to keep us warm. We will be generating our own heat."

"Robert!" I said, embarrassed.

"What happens in the bedchamber stays in the bedchamber, Julia," he grinned at me, setting my pulse racing in anticipation of what the night would bring.

I looked about the room, "Is this where you usually sleep?"

"Why, is it not grand enough for a duchess?" he teased me.

"What was good enough for a duke is good enough for a duchess. So, is this where you normally sleep, Robert?" I asked him again.

He grinned at me and pulled me to him, "Do you want to see where I slept before I married you?"

I nodded. He took my hand, and we walked away from the massive state apartments to another wing of the house, which, although grand, was not as ostentatious as the royal apartments. Once again, the bedroom was all blue but with velvets and silks and no crown over the bed. It was more modern, whereas the other bedroom looked like maybe King Henry VIII had stayed in it. Robert's bedroom was more 'Robert'. It still had tapestries, but there were paintings of horses on the walls. I saw a painting of a horse resembling Star, who I had ridden at Lady Mary's. At that moment, I wondered if Lady Mary was missing me. I had been with her for less than a year, but during that time, I became very fond of her, and I think my presence with her had somewhat brightened her life.

"Why did you decide to move to the state apartments?" I asked him.

"Don't you want to sleep in the bed Henry VIII slept in?"

I snuggled up to his body as I looked around his old bedroom. "I would rather sleep in the bed that Robert Beaumont, Duke of Rochester, slept in," I told him.

"Henry would be very hurt." His eyes twinkled as he teased me.

"But thankfully, I am not married to Henry. I am married to you. Could we please move back in here, Robert? You forget I am just a simple girl from a fishing village in Cornwall. I am overwhelmed by the fact that I am sleeping in the bed Henry VIII slept in."

He kissed the top of my head. "Darling, your every wish is my command," he told me. Then he called for Jenkins, the butler, and told him to arrange for our things to be moved into his old bedroom.

"Yes, your Grace," Mr Jenkins said, bowing to us.

"Where does your mother usually sleep?" I asked.

"Oh, she lives in the West Wing on the opposite side of the castle, but she won't be moving back here for a month to give us total time together alone."

Within minutes, a trail of footmen paraded into our new bedroom with our trunks. I was surprised that the bed was already made.

"Oh, most of the bedrooms are kept ready for guests, just in case," he told me, then ordered the footmen to leave and told them to tell my maid, Jane, and his valet, Andrew, to leave unpacking until we went to dinner.

The footmen left, and Robert went over to lock our bedroom door. "We have some serious honeymooning to do now," he told me as he bent and put his arm under my legs and swept me up in his arms to unceremoniously dump me on the bed, laughing. He began practically ripping off his clothes, then came over and began undressing me. I could tell that he wanted me all to himself, and our lovemaking began as he began kissing and nibbling me from my neck to my toes, causing me to give little squeaks of pleasure as he brought me to fulfilment time and time again. He knew how to play my body like we played the keys on a piano.

That evening, we dined in the small, intimate dining room. Robert asked me if I wanted to dine in the main dining room, which could seat over one hundred people, but I declined, saying that I didn't want to shout to the other end of the table to talk to my husband. That arrangement was acceptable for house parties but not for a newly married couple.

Robert was so loving and attentive, and I thought my life was perfect. We loved, we laughed, and we roamed around the rooms of the great castle, where Robert told me of the family's history and that of Knole castle, and I had to keep pinching myself to make me realise that this was not a dream. This was my home or one of them. I had not seen Robert's house in London or any of the others scattered around the country. How did he share his time with all of them? He told me as he touched my nose playfully, "You have all the time in the world to ask your questions and for me to give you your answers. Patience, my dearest girl."

Robert showed me the castle's various wings, which were much more homely than the wing with the State apartments. That wing was very regal and impressive, but it wasn't homely, and I doubted I would ever feel comfortable in such grand surroundings as the wing in which Henry VIII stayed. It had been a significant change for me when I left the Lodge in Porth to move to Seaward Manor. Then, there was another significant change when I left Seaward Manor to stay at Moldova Square in London. Although Lady Mary's home was large, it was not nearly as large as Seaward Manor, but I felt comfortable with its size. Now, I was here in this magnificent castle with hundreds of years of history, which was now one of my homes as the Duchess of Rochester. Now that I had got over being accused of murdering Edwina Trevelgue, I felt that I had a chance to truly be happy with the man who it was love at first sight.

We spent much of the time horse riding and exploring Knole Castle's grounds. We often went to the stables to look at Copper, Amber's foal, whom I had watched being born. But most of all, we spent our time loving each other.

I felt truly blessed in the life I found myself in. I had a husband who loved me, I lived in a castle, and I was a titled lady. What more could I want?

I had been happily married for three weeks. For three weeks, I had been the Duchess of Rochester, and then I had a message one day from Lady Mary, saying she was seriously unwell and asking me to go to her but not to tell Robert. I couldn't understand it; she had been perfectly well at our wedding; how could someone so vital be suddenly struck down? Why did she not want me to tell my husband? Because I cared for her so much, I did as she had asked me. Robert had reluctantly gone into Sevenoaks on business and had left me in bed. As soon as I received the note, I hurriedly dressed and ordered the coach that was waiting in the courtyard to take me to London. I knew that I didn't need to take money with me. As soon as I told Inn keepers that I was the Duchess of Rochester, they would send the bill to Robert for payment. I had hurriedly packed my faithful carpet bag and hurried to the carriage. I had not seen Jane so far that day because I was on my honeymoon; she had little to do because Robert used to tell her that he would act as my lady's maid. I had meant to catch up with Mrs Watson, as Robert said he would be away most of the day, but with Lady Mary's urgent message, everything was forgotten in my haste.

I told the coachman to make haste for London and to keep going as long as we had daylight, then look for a coaching inn, and we would continue early the following day. I didn't take notice of the coach driver. I was just so worried about Lady Mary. I felt that she was now my family, and after all she had done for me, whenever she called, I would go to her, regardless of where I was or what I was doing. It must be serious for her to interrupt my honeymoon.

We had been travelling for about two hours when the coach slowed down and came to a stop. I couldn't understand why, as I had told the driver to keep driving. I went to get out of the carriage when I heard a gunshot. At the sound reverberating through the woods we were driving through, my heart began to beat a tattoo of fear against my ribs. I had not heard of highway robbery recently, but I thought it best to stay inside. The carriage door was flung open by a masked man dressed all in black, who came inside the carriage and, without saying a word to me, placed a wad of something over my mouth and nose, and I immediately lost consciousness.

Chapter Fifteen

I do not know how long I was unconscious for; I know when I came to, I felt dreadfully ill, probably the after-effects of whatever drug I had been administered.

I regained consciousness, lying on the floor of what I thought was still the same carriage, but I was so woozy that I couldn't be sure. My hands and feet had been tied. I felt sick, but I had nothing in my stomach, so I just rolled on my side and retched.

A man wearing a black mask that completely covered his face, and head entered the carriage again when it had slowed down to a stop and, without speaking again, put another wad of something over my nose and mouth, and again, I lost consciousness. I didn't even have a chance to ask why they were doing this to me. Nothing. With the complete covering of his face and head, I had no idea whatsoever who the man might be. He could have been known to me, or he could have been a complete stranger. I didn't know, and before I could even try and think, darkness overtook me once again.

I don't know how often this happened, but I think it was quite a few times. Until one time, I came to, and my hands and feet were untied, but I was not in the carriage. I was in a room. I looked around, and the room looked strangely familiar, but with the effects of the drugs, I was so confused and felt so ill that my woolly brain wouldn't allow me to establish where it was. I staggered over to the door and tried to open it but found it was locked and the windows had been blacked out. When my head started to clear, I wondered who could have done this to me. There was a thought somewhere in the back of my mind, but my mind couldn't grasp it. The thought kept drifting just out of my reach to grab it mentally. I don't think I had ever been so scared in my life. At least when I was in prison, I was lucid, although the thought of the hangman's noose was still in my mind. I had the hope that Mrs Trevelgue's letter would be found, and I would be released. But with this abduction, I didn't know who would know that I had even left Knole Castle or why. Jane hadn't come to my room as Robert, and I were managing ourselves while we were still on our honeymoon. What had I done with the note? I hoped that I hadn't tossed it in the fire. I didn't know. My brain just refused to work.

I heard the bedroom door being unlocked, but I couldn't get my legs to function properly—not enough to attack whoever was at the door. So, I lay curled up on the bed and waited to see who it was. Maybe I could reason with them?

I think it was the same man who had placed the pad of something over my nose and mouth, but I couldn't be sure as he was still completely covered. Whoever he was, he brought me food. I don't know when I last ate. I had left Knole Castle on the morning of the day I received the letter from Lady Mary, which I now realised was not from Lady Mary.

I had been kidnapped. I had the proof. I was the proof. The thing was, who had kidnapped me and why? The only people that I could think of were Mark Trevelgue, or his brother Richard, or could it have been Rutledge for me refusing his attention? If it was Rutledge, what did he intend to do to me? I didn't know. If it was Mark, surely Mrs Trevelgue would have stepped in and stopped it?

My captor left a tray of food, a beaker and a jug of water. He didn't say a word to me. I tried to ask him why he was doing this and what I had done to deserve this, but he ignored me and locked the door behind him when he, once again, left me on my own.

I started eating the food, which was simple fayre, but I was so hungry I didn't mind. After all, when I lived in the Lodge, Mrs Watson's food was nourishing but not fancy like the food I had eaten at Seaward Manor, Lady Mary's, or Knole Castle.

Not long after I had eaten, I began to feel drowsy again. How could I feel so tired now after all the sleep I had already had? I was too drowsy to think about it.

I lay down on the bed. It might not have been as comfortable as the bed at Knole Castle or Moldova Square, but it was certainly better than the police station, so I closed my eyes.

How long I slept, again, I didn't know. What drugs I thought might have been used, I didn't know. Even when I was awake, I was in a drugged state, woolly-headed and unsteady. At least I had food and drink, although the food was only once a day; I had a jug full of water and drank thirstily.

I spent my days and nights, (how many they were, I didn't know), in a drug-induced state, unable to tell which was drugged, the food or the drink, but without either of them, I would starve to death, and even in that drug-induced state, I knew that I had to keep up my strength.

My life in London with Lady Mary and my marriage to Robert seemed to be long-ago dreams. In fact, at times, I even began to think that the trip to London and my marriage was a dream. In my low moments, I doubted I would ever see my husband or Lady Mary again. Wherever I was, I could see no way of getting out. My jailer was fastidious in his imprisonment of me. He never spoke. He delivered my food and drink, then locked the door behind him and made sure that I was kept completely drugged. I still had no idea where I was. I had tried in my more lucid moments to try and scrape off the blacking on the windows of my bedroom or my prison, but it seemed that it was on the outside. The windows had also been locked, so I couldn't open them. All I knew was the passing of the seasons. I knew that I had been delivered the letter that had started all of this, and it was still summer, early August. It was now cold in my bedroom, so cold that I could see my breath in clouds as I breathed. For the first time, I broke down in tears. I wanted Robert. I wanted my husband to feel his strong arms around me, telling me he loved me and everything would be alright. I wanted to carry his baby and watch our children grow together. I had hoped that after three weeks of marriage, I might be carrying Robert's baby inside me, but I had continued to bleed normally. Did Robert think that I had just run off and left him? I tried to remember what I had done with the letter. Had I thrown it away? Had I burnt it? I couldn't remember whether a fire had been burning in our bedroom's hearth. Did anyone see me get into the carriage? Did anyone follow me? I doubted it. Where was Jethro? Was he in the stables? Did he prepare the carriage? What had happened to the original carriage driver? I heard a gunshot. Had he been shot dead?

Whoever my kidnapper was, this had been planned meticulously, possibly over quite a long period of time. Was it just one man or more? Surely, it had to be more than just one.

My masked jailer brought me another meal. "Where am I?" I asked. "Who are you? What do you want me for?"

Nothing. He just pointed at the tray of food, turned, and left. I picked up the tray and threw it at his disappearing back. It splattered against the heavy wooden door and lay on the floor. I cursed myself for my own stupidity. Now, I would have nothing to eat until tomorrow. I still had the jug of water, which he had taken from the tray and placed on the small table.

I had picked up and placed the now destroyed tray with the plate of food on it.

On the bed, I lay berating myself for stupidly picking up and throwing away the only meal I would have that day. What an idiot! Did I really think that throwing the tray full of food at the disappearing back of my jailer would help me get out of the place?

Even if I did get out, I didn't know where I was or how to get back home. I thirstily drank some of the water in the jug. It was a mistake; I know that now. The water was drugged. I collapsed to the floor. I didn't even make it to the bed. When I next came to, I was lying on the cold floor, shivering and with a dreadful headache. What was in the water jug must have been stronger than usual to knock me out where I stood and give me this banging headache when I came to. I crawled over to the bed, wrapped the blankets around me and slept.

I had no idea how long this went on, as by now, I was spending all my time in a drugged state, not knowing if it was day or night or what time of the year it was. I didn't know how long ago it had been since I had initially received the letter from Lady Mary. I knew now that it hadn't come from Lady Mary. I hadn't recognised the writing.

In my drugged dreams, I dreamt that I heard Robert calling my name, but it was obviously just another of my drug-induced dreams. I had heard him call my name several times before, and I always awoke with tears still damp on my cheeks. I just snuggled into the blankets and tried to sleep again.

The next day, when I came to, I found a tray of food and another jug of water on the table. I must have still been unconscious when it was delivered to my jail. My stomach was growling with lack of food. I ate, even suspecting that it might be drugged, but I still ate. I slept, I ate, I slept again. I knew that if the food wasn't drugged, then the water was, or maybe they both were, and so my days blurred into one another until I knew that I needed to have whatever it was concealed within the food, water, or both. If I didn't eat or drink as much as I needed, I became sick, shaking with a fever, and the pains in my body were unbearable. I ended up crying for the relief which only more of the drug could bring. I didn't care anymore; I just needed the drug to help me to feel better, well, better than I did without it.

I was an addict.

I couldn't even think about Robert anymore. All I wanted was the drug and the relief it brought. I didn't know who brought me the drugs any longer. I don't even remember when it was brought into the room, as long as they brought me the drugs that my now-addicted body craved. Sometimes, in my drugged dreams, I remembered the first concert I had attended in London, and the music went around in my mind. Other times I thought back to my time in prison and the smell of urine and unwashed bodies. All thoughts were muddled in my mind.

One day, I felt myself lifted and carried somewhere. I could feel a breeze on my face. I must have been dreaming again as I heard Robert's voice coming at me down a dark tunnel. I remember saying his name, and I felt his kiss on my lips, and I cried because I knew it was just a dream, a dream sent to haunt me of my past life, a life full of love and happiness. How many times had I dreamt of him holding me? I couldn't guess. He seemed to be the one constant that I clung to in my drugged state. I dreamt of Mrs Watson and how she used to call me sweetheart, and I cried. I dreamt that I was in a lovely warm bath with angels gently bathing me and washing my hair, then they carried me to a soft, warm nest, and I dreamt of Robert holding me and kissing me, trying to feed me soup, but it was all just a wonderful dream, that I didn't want to wake up from. I dreamt of Robert's sandalwood cologne, and my heart was filled with love for him. I wanted Robert. I remember calling his name, or I think I called his name, and I dreamt that he responded and kissed me. Oh, what a lovely dream it was. I didn't want to wake up.

I slept and dreamt, and slept, and dreamt, and every dream I had contained Robert and sometimes Mrs Watson.

Very slowly, my nightmarish dreams started turning into happier dreams, and I wanted them to continue, but all good things must come to an end, and I felt myself wake up, if only briefly. I was given warm soup, and then I curled up and went to sleep. I didn't know who had given me the soup; my eyes wouldn't stay open to see. When I woke up again, I was given some more soup. I could feel someone's arms around me, supporting me while someone spooned more soup into my mouth, and then I slept and dreamt that I was snuggled up in Roberts's arms. It was heaven, but I thought, again, only a wonderful dream. I had given up any hope of Robert ever rescuing me. I don't know how long I had been imprisoned, but I know that it was a long time. My body wasn't allowed to crave the drug now because if I didn't get it, sickness, shaking of my whole body or terrible cramping pain would take over me.

One day, I woke up briefly and recognised Mrs Watson. Had I been ill? Had I dreamed that I had gone to Seaward Manor, then dreamed of Lady Mary and Lord Melbourne and Robert? Were they all people from a fevered sleep? I managed to look around briefly and thought I was back in my old bedroom at the Lodge and Gramps would be coming to check on me soon. Mrs Watson told me that I had been very ill, but I was slowly getting better. She fed me some soup and then laid me back down to sleep. I must have come round slightly as I felt wrapped in strong arms, and I went back to sleep with a smile on my face.

I slowly became more lucid each time I woke up, but still, I had not seen Gramps. Was it an epidemic of some sort that kept him so busy? Again, I slept, but I felt wrapped up again in someone's arms. I thought it might be Gramps cuddling me to sleep, so I slept again with a smile on my face. I was home, and that was all that mattered.

Chapter Sixteen

Each day, I became more and more lucid. Yes, I was back in my old bedroom at the Lodge, but Gramps was dead and had been for some time. I was married to Robert, who spent what time he could with me but was busy setting up farms and buying land for the people of Porth so that those who wanted could farm the land for their own means.

I found out that Mark and Richard Trevelgue had kidnapped me, and Mrs Trevelgue had also taken part in it, sending ransom notes to Robert, throwing him off the scent of my whereabouts. I had been captive for months at Seaward Manor, where I was kept. They were all now in police custody. The new doctor at the Lodge was Doctor Meadows, and he had a wife, Constance. When they discovered all about me, the doctor and his wife gave up their bedroom, which was my old room. It was under Doctor Meadow's instruction that I was being slowly weaned off the drugs that the Trevelgues had been feeding me, until I was addicted. Luckily, Robert, Jethro, and Mrs Watson, with the help of the police, finally tracked me down to Seaward Manor, where they found me in a terrible state. They never said what that state was for fear of upsetting me. The Trevelgues had sent Robert zigzagging across the country with their ransom notes, even suggesting that I might be found across the sea in France.

It was a long journey back to Knole castle, and I was in no fit state to undertake such a long journey for several months. Because of the addiction and the fact that the Trevelgues only fed me one meal a day, I had lost an awful lot of weight, so I looked near skeletal. My eyes were sunk into my skull, and my cheekbones protruded at sharp angles. Robert hardly recognised me when they finally broke into the room I had been locked in for months. Doctor Meadows had been called to me and said that I had to be slowly weaned off the drugs, which would probably take as long, maybe even longer, as it had taken to get me addicted in the first place, maybe longer because of my emaciated condition. The Trevelgues butler Mr Masters, who, after the Trevelgues had been arrested and carted off to prison, had offered us the use of any of the decent bedrooms in Seaward Manor, but Doctor Meadows had said that he needed to keep a close eye on me, so they had transported me back to the Lodge. Firstly, I spent time in what Gramps had kept as his hospital, occupying one of the single beds, but as I slowly improved, Robert carried me to what had been my old bedroom and had spent most nights curled up on my old bed, cuddling me off to sleep. Mrs Watson had taken over in the kitchen, preparing good, wholesome soups to feed me along with smaller and smaller amounts of drugs.

After I had been back at the Lodge for three months, Doctor Meadows told Robert and Mrs Watson that we could return to Knole Castle if we took it slowly. The journey back to Knole wasn't as far as it was to London, but it still took us ages to get home, mainly because we only travelled a few miles a day before stopping at Coaching Inns. During the journey Robert let me curl up and sleep on the carriage seat with my head on his lap, while Mrs Watson sat opposite. Jethro sat on top and drove the carriage. At each inn, Robert carried me upstairs to our room while Mrs Watson supervised my meals in the kitchens. Although Doctor Meadows said that I was well enough to travel, according to Mrs Watson, I was still extremely ill, and it would take me many months to get back to my old self.

The day we drove up the large, winding driveway to Knole Castle, I cried tears of joy, thinking often during my incarceration that I would never see it again. Robert carried me up to our bedroom, and Mrs Watson supervised the maids, including Jane, who cried when she saw me all wrapped up in travel blankets being carried to my bedroom. Mrs Watson supervised me having a bath, then dried me off, and Robert carried me over to our bed, which had been warmed for me. Jane came into our room carrying another tray with a bowl of soup for me. I had been asleep after I had had my bath. Just a simple thing like sitting in a bath and lying in warm, scented water and having my hair washed had left me as weak as a kitten. Robert sat on the bed and fed me until I said that I had had enough and then handed my tray back to Jane to return it to the kitchen, where Mrs Watson was supervising all my food and putting less and less of the drug in it.

Lady Virginia had moved back to the castle into her wing but was a regular visitor to my bedside. Even Philomena, soon to be Lady Davenport, had sent flowers and chocolates.

Lady Mary came to stay with Dorcas, who came bustling to my bedroom, calling me her 'wee lamb'. Lady Mary shrugged her shoulders, which was a very unlikely gesture by Lady Mary. Once Dorcas had left the room, Lady Mary apologised for Dorcas, "But she insisted that when we arrived here, she came to see you, and I didn't have the heart to deny her. Oh, my dear Julia, what has my family done to you? You look dreadful." She didn't try to mask the tears in her eyes.

I couldn't help but give her a weak smile, "Lady Mary, it is so good to see you. I never thought..." Then the tears started again. It took so little to make me cry now, but Doctor Reynolds, Robert's family Doctor at Knole Castle, told me that because I was so low due to the drugs, I would be like that for quite some time until I managed to get them totally out of my system. Robert and I had also been advised that I should not try to get pregnant until I had been completely free of the drugs for twelve months, "Otherwise, the baby could be born dependent on the drugs in your system and may not survive for long." That statement had dashed my hopes and dreams of carrying Robert's baby, and again, I apologised to Robert for not being able to have his baby. I told him that was all I had ever dreamed about during my incarceration, "And now I can't have your baby." I burst into tears again.

But I digress. Lady Mary said that I had lost so much weight. "Julia, you look absolutely skeletal. We must put some weight back on those bones. I hope your cook is giving you good, nourishing food."

"Mrs Watson is supervising all of my meals as she used to help Gramps when he had patients in his hospital, so she knows all about nourishing foods, but at the moment, they are still weaning me off the drugs given to me."

"You mean you are still on the drugs, Julia?" she asked, shocked.

"The doses are slowly being reduced," I explained to her.

"But why do they still keep giving you the drugs, darling?"

"Because her grace would get withdrawal symptoms if they stopped the drugs completely," Jane told Lady Mary as she bustled around my bedroom, tidying things away.

"Julia, my darling girl, I can't apologise enough for what my family has put you through." Tears of regret filled her eyes.

I took her hand in mine. "None of this is your fault, Lady Mary."

"I regret the day I gave birth to my daughter; after all that she has put not just me, but also you through. You never asked for any of this, Julia; she and her family have used you to their own cruel means," she told me.

"But if it hadn't been for Mrs Trevelgue, I would not have had the education I did, and I would not have gone to live with you and married Robert, so I still have a lot to thank her for, however misguided."

"Misguided, ha! Greed, more like! Driven by greed for money!" Lady Mary said, anger showing for not just her daughter but also her grandsons, who had been the main instigators in my kidnapping. I had never seen Lady Mary so angry before.

"I understand that the court case cannot go ahead without you, my dear, so they are languishing in prison still. That alone will make them think again before trying anything like that. That's if they ever get out of prison."

"Don't you feel anything for them, Lady Mary? After all, they are your flesh and blood," I asked her.

"Julia, I don't know them, well, the boys certainly. My daughter has just proved that cutting her off without a penny was right, and nothing you can say will change my mind, Julia."

I was tired and struggling to keep my eyes open. Lady Mary's hand was on mine. "Darling girl, you are getting tired. I will leave you to rest. Is there anything I can get you before I leave?"

I told her that I had everything that I wanted.

"You will stay here at Knole until I am recovered?" I asked her.

"As long as you want me here, Julia." She kissed my forehead and then left, closing the door behind her. Jane fussed about me, fluffing my pillows, then told me to close my eyes, and she, too, left. I closed my eyes and slept.

When I next woke up, Philomena sat beside my bed in a chair. When she saw me open my eyes, she started chatting about her engagement ring and her fiancé. For some reason, I envied her. She still had youth on her side, but the Trevelgue family had stolen what was left of mine away from me. I lay there feeling old, feeling that I had cheated Robert of our honeymoon, and again, I started crying. I sniffled, trying to apologise to Philomena, who gathered me to her and cuddled me for a while. Then, when I finished crying, she held me away from her, "Now, what is all this about? You are home safe and sound. Those brothers and their mother are all in prison, and Uncle Robert adores you. Over the months that you were kidnapped, he was going nearly mental, trying to find out where you were, and he never gave up, Julia. He never gave up on finding you.

Between him, the police and some man, they eventually tracked you down to Cornwall, and Uncle Robert, your Mrs Watson and her son-in-law, along with the police, none of them ever gave up on you. Uncle Robert said that if they had been delayed by another few days, you would have been dead. You have much to be thankful for, so no more tears, Aunt Julia," she told me sternly. I thought that Philomena calling me Aunt Julia would get a rise from me, but I was too weary.

"I hear you are getting better daily, and you will soon return to your old self, Julia. Don't give up. I hope to see you at my wedding to Arthur at Christmas."

I didn't even know what time of the year it was. It hurt my brain to try and work it out. I had married Robert on the twenty-fourth of July. I had been married just three weeks before I got kidnapped, which took me into the middle of August. It had been three months before I had been rescued, which made it November. I had been taken care of in Porth for three months before Robert, Mrs Watson and Jethro were allowed to bring me home to Knole castle, which took it to March of the next year, and I had been here at the castle for two months, or so I thought, which made it May. I thought. I asked Philomena, "What month is it?"

"What month? It's July, Julia. We have been out for over twelve months now."

"It seems like another life to me," I told her, trying to give her a weak smile.

"I'm not surprised. From what I gather from Uncle Robert, you were kept permanently drugged for months. God, I could kill that family for what they did to you. I gather that they had to hold Uncle Robert back from killing them. Uncle Robert has changed from that devil-may-care gentleman you married nearly twelve months ago," she told me.

"And that is all my fault," I cried.

"No. No, Julia, it's not your fault at all. It is that family who kidnapped you. I hope they lock them all up and throw away the key. Do you know they even gave Robert the impression that you had left the country? France, I think. No wonder they took so long tracking you down." Philomena said vehemently. Robert came into our bedroom then and, more or less, shooed Philomena out. "Let her have a rest, Phil, then you can come back another time," he told her.

"How did a kindly old lady like Lady Mary give birth to that woman?"

Was Philomena's parting remark before she came and kissed me. "I'll be back, Aunt Julia," she said, then winked devilishly at me. I laughed.

When Philomena left, Robert sat on the bed beside me. "That is the first time I have heard you laugh since... well, before you got kidnapped."

"I haven't had much to laugh about recently, but it felt good to laugh, Robert. I wish we could go back to our honeymoon."

"When you are better, darling, we will have our honeymoon all over again, and we will be making love all over the place, making up for lost time. Before that, though, we have to get the court case over with."

"Why can't they do that without me?" I didn't want to see the faces of the Trevelgues, be it across a courtroom.

"Julia, you are the key witness. Only you can tell what went on. Doctor Meadows will have to come up from Porth to give evidence. I told him we would have him, and his wife stay with us in Berkley Square."

"His wife as well?" I asked.

"Well, he might not want to leave her behind in Cornwall, but I will leave that up to him."

"Robert, I want to dress up and be able to dance. I want you to take me to the stables and tumble me in the hay. I want to have your baby, to feel it growing inside me."

He cuddled me against his chest, "Darling, we will do all that, some sooner than others."

"I don't feel that we are even married anymore, Robert. Will you come back and share our bed again? I know you are sleeping only a few steps away from me in your dressing room, but I want to fall asleep in your arms and wake up in them. I know you cuddle me off to sleep, but you have your clothes on, and I am wrapped up like a 'born again' virgin in my nightdress," I said, trying to make a joke

"Lady Rochester, you brazen hussy!" he said, smiling at me. A little of the Robert I fell in love with at first sight showed itself briefly.

The Trevelgues had not only stolen my youth from me, but they had also taken the man I had fallen in love with away from me. He was no longer the cheeky, carefree man who had stolen my breath away whenever he smiled at me.

"Will you take me downstairs so that I can play the piano, Robert, and you can play with me?"

"Your Grace," that twinkle in his eye came, and for the first time in however long, the dimples came on either side of his smiling mouth. "I would love to play with you." I gave him a weak, playful tap, knowing that he meant something totally different from what I meant.

"Do you want to go downstairs now, sweetheart, or after you have had a nap?"

"If you would hand me my dressing gown and slippers."

I had hardly finished speaking when he handed me what I had asked for. He helped me into my dressing gown, then bent down and slipped my slippers on my feet as I swung them out of bed.

I went to stand, but he swept me into his arms to carry me downstairs. What staff we passed stopped and stared at me, then smiled. Robert carried me into the music room, put me on the piano stool, and sat beside me.

My fingers glided over the keys as I played Brahms. I closed my eyes and let the music drift over me, and then I heard Robert joining me. For the first time in a long time, I felt my soul lifted, and it felt beautiful. I wanted to sing and dance, but I knew my strength would desert me if I tried to dance. It was as if Robert could read my mind as he stopped playing, lifted me in his arms again, and waltzed around the room as he carried me, humming the tune.

"My heart is full of love for you, my Robert," I whispered in his ear.

"And me," he said as he began kissing me. My heart felt full. Maybe there was a normal, happy future for us, eventually.

He looked down at me, "Are you tired now, darling?"

Reluctantly, I said, "A little."

"Come on, then. It's back to bed with you." Again, he picked me up and carried me back to our bedroom.

"Will you sleep with me tonight, Robert?" I asked him as he stood me up and helped me off with my dressing gown. I stepped out of my slippers.

"Yes, my love."

I lay on my bed while Robert pulled the sheets over me. He kissed me on the tip of my nose and said if I had a sleep now, maybe I would like to join everyone downstairs for dinner that evening. I felt like an excited young girl at such a simple thing. "Really? Oh yes, please, Robert. Can I wear a dress for it?"

He made a dramatic gesture, "Yes, my Lady."

"With Jane dressing my hair and me wearing some of my jewellery?" I asked.

"If you are sure that you will feel up to it?" Robert asked tentatively.

"Yes. If I sleep now, I am sure that I will feel up to it," I told him excitedly. I felt like a young child being given a birthday present.

"And you still need to have your medication," Robert reminded me.

"How much am I on now?"

"Doctor Reynolds has changed the other drug, now to laudanum, and you are on three drops, watered down," he replied.

"When does he think I can come off the drugs completely?"

"Another few months yet."

"So, September then?" I asked.

"Julia, don't try to rush things. Doctor Reynolds knows what he is doing. Doing it slowly gives your body a chance to recover properly."

"But I want to get the drugs out of my system so that we can have a baby Robert," I replied impatiently.

"Julia, stop trying to rush everything. I can wait," my husband said, taking my hand and kissing my wrist.

"But I don't want to wait. I am getting older, Robert," I sounded like a whining child.

He laughed for the first time since before I was kidnapped. "My love, you will be twenty this year. Hardly an old maid."

"I feel like an old maid," I told him, giving him a childish pout. "I feel the Trevelgues have stolen my youth, firstly by having me imprisoned. I could have come back from that, but what they did to me back in Cornwall nearly killed me. It certainly killed my youth." At that moment, I felt genuine hatred, even more so than when I found out that Edwina had kept the letters about Gramps from me.

"Well, I can assure you that I don't think of you as an old maid. Your body still drives me wild with wanting you, but I can be patient, unlike some people," he said, meaning me. He kissed my nose again and told me to sleep.

That evening, Jane helped me dress in one of my gowns. She tutted at how it hung on me. Then she had me sit on a chair in front of my dressing table to enable me to relax against the back of it while normally I would have had to sit up straight on the stool. Everything was done for my comfort as the Duchess of Rochester, and according to Jane, I was still terribly ill. Looking at the face that looked back at me from the mirror, I did not recognise the woman with the dark circles around her eyes, the sunken cheeks or the pale lips, which was now myself.

Jane had picked out an emerald gown and done my hair in a simple chignon. I wore emerald and pearl earrings and a five-string pearl choker with an emerald clasp. Robert told me I looked beautiful, but I had seen my gaunt face in my dressing table mirror and wondered if I would ever return to my old, vigorous self. If I did, how much longer would it take? I was not used to being ill and bedridden as I had never been ill in my life, apart from the odd cold, but nothing like this and the inactivity were uncommon to me.

Lady Mary, Virginia, Philomena and her parents, Mr Davenport, Philomena's fiancé, Robert, and I sat down to dinner that evening. This was the first time I had eaten in the small dining room since I had been kidnapped. Then, it had just been Robert and me, so it was a happy welcome party. Wine had been ordered to go with the meal, but I was not allowed it because of the drugs I was still on, so I drank water. I ate the meal, enjoying something different from Mrs Watson's soups.

I enjoyed the meal enormously and the desert afterwards. Usually, after the meal, the ladies would retire to the drawing room alone, while the men normally stayed in the dining room for brandy and cigars for those who smoked. However, Robert said that the gentlemen would join us for coffee. It was lovely to feel that I was slowly beginning to regain some semblance of normality in my life.

Everyone was saying how good it was to see me downstairs again, but after half an hour in their company, I was beginning to flag. Robert picked me up and told me that I had had enough excitement for one evening and carried me off to bed, where Jane was waiting for me.

"Robert, could we invite Lord Melbourne? I haven't seen or heard anything from him since he gave me away at our wedding."

I saw Robert look across to Jane, "Julia, Lord Melbourne went back home to Brocket Hall after the wedding." Robert seemed to be holding back, and I sensed that something was wrong.

"I remember he was going to retire to Brocket Hall to rest and recover from the stress of politics," I told him.

"Darling, he was taken very ill while he was there."

"I told Lady Mary it would be more serious if he had to be leeched. How is he doing? I shall write to him and invite…"

"Julia, Melbourne died two months ago. He had been ill for quite some time," he told me as gently as he could.

I just felt my whole body crumple at those words. Not only had I missed my Gramps's funeral, but now, because of the Trevelgues, I had missed Lord Melbourne's funeral.

Robert knelt in front of me and gathered me into his arms so that I could cry against his shoulder. "Darling, he was old. None of us can last forever," he told me, kissing the top of my head.

"Lady Mary always said that immortality was not an option," I said between sobs.

"And she was right. Melbourne would have been seventy next birthday. He served this country well and will long be remembered."

"But I missed…," I said into his shoulder.

"Darling, you could not be responsible for missing his funeral. I know that he was as worried about us finding you as Lady Mary was. At least he heard that you had been found before he died."

"Could we send flowers to his grave, Robert?"

"Of course, darling, and when you are well enough, we will visit his grave."

Robert kissed my forehead, then left me to Jane's ministrations.

"Oh, Miss Julia... sorry, Your Grace, you look exhausted." She helped me out of my gown and into a clean nightdress, then sat me down in front of my dressing table. There, she removed my jewellery, including my earrings, which made me smile. "Dorcas would be so proud of you, Jane," I told her.

"There's no blood now, Ma'am." She grinned at me. She undid my chignon and began brushing my hair, then was going to plat it, but I thought if Robert were joining me, I would leave it down, as he loved my hair.

Thankfully, it was only a few steps to our bed, but I had to lean on her. I flopped on the bed, and she pulled the sheets under my chin. "Good night, Lady Julia," she said, then left me. I intended to stay awake and wait for Robert, but after the efforts of sitting downstairs for so long, I fell asleep.

I didn't wake when Robert came and joined me in our bed, but when I woke the following day, he was lying next to me, with his arm draped over my body. I began kissing his cheeks, then his forehead, and he woke with a grin. "Now that is what I call a good morning wake up." He kissed my cheeks and my eyes, then my lips. Recently, all our kisses had been chaste, but I let my tongue invade his mouth this morning, deepening our kiss until he responded. For a few short moments, I could entice him to take it further, but although my mind was willing for him to make love to me, my body was worn out with just that little bit of exertion. Once upon a time, he made my body tingle with his touch, but he could see that I was tired again, so he kissed my nose and got up. I lay back and watched as he dressed, enjoying looking at his body, which I always found enticing. That morning was no different. I watched as he stripped off his nightshirt until he stood naked before beginning to dress.

"Now, that is what I call a good start to the morning," I whispered.

He turned to me with a devilish grin on his face. "Be patient, Julia. We will get there. Today was better than yesterday, but not as good as tomorrow will be." He finished dressing and told me to go back to sleep and dream of tomorrow. I did fall back to sleep for another hour or so with a smile on my face.

Jane arrived carrying a tray with my breakfast on it. "I thought you might like steak and eggs, Lady Julia, to build strength. I have also brought you toast, plum preserve, and coffee. Eat what you can and leave what you can't, Ma'am," she said, plumping my pillows behind me and placing the tray on my lap. The food smelt wonderful. Until then, I had been having scrambled eggs and porridge.

I attempted to eat as much as I could, as I knew that it was the only way to get on the road to recovery.

When Jane returned to collect my tray, she smiled, impressed with what I had managed. "Well done, Miss Julia. Keep it up, and you will soon return to your old self. Is there anything else that I can get for you?"

I thought momentarily, "Could you ask Lady Mary if she could pick me out a book from the library? She knows what sort of books I like."

Jane curtseyed and took my breakfast tray out with her. I could see that what I had eaten, I had made her happy. Unlike the Trevelgues, who lusted for money, it took little to make Jane, Robert, or myself happy.

I lay back on my pillows and closed my eyes for a while. The next thing I knew, Lady Mary had come into my room with a book.

"Ah, Julia, did I wake you, my dear?" she asked.

"No, Lady Mary, I was just resting my eyes. What have you picked out for me?" I asked her.

"Your husband has a very good library, so I was spoilt for choice. But I know that you liked Homer, so I chose something in the same vein. Would you like me to read it to you, my dear, or would you like to read it yourself?"

"I will read it later, please, Lady Mary; just talk to me and tell me everything I missed during my incarceration. I found out about Lord Melbourne's death. Robert told me last night. I was so sorry. He was like a father to me."

Lady Mary settled herself in her chair, ready for a good gossip, which I think she must have missed since I married. "He talked of you very fondly, and I think you asking him to give you away at your wedding meant a great deal to him. He told me that he looked at you as a daughter.

"Do you know, many years ago, when I had my debut, William Lamb, as he was then, was one of the gentlemen who courted me?" she continued. "He was a very attractive man, then along came Caroline Ponsonby, and he was smitten. I never stood a chance against her. They married and were, I think, happy for a short while, but her behaviour was getting more and more erratic, and then she and Byron met. At first, I think Byron chased her until she caught him, then wouldn't let him go. She became obsessed with Byron and also very possessive. Byron, tired of her possessiveness, eventually tried to cast her out, but she tried everything she could to keep him. When he ignored her, she slit her wrists at a dinner party; luckily or unluckily, they saved her, and she retired to Brocket Hall to recover. Melbourne was still just William Lamb at the time. When Caro returned to society, she tried to have a public affair with the Duke of Wellington, but that didn't last long. Wellington wanted it all hushed up, and she wanted him to publicly acknowledge her as his mistress; once again, she retired to Brocket Hall alone. Her actions became increasingly erratic, and Melbourne stayed away, as he had politics to occupy his time by then. He returned occasionally to Brocket Hall, but by then, Caro stayed in her room, sitting in a corner as if ashamed of her actions. In the end, she died. After her public humiliation of William, he stayed out of the eyes of society for some time. Then, after Caro's death, he immersed himself in politics, and his political career seemed to take off, but he never wished to marry again. I don't think he ever dared to love again, so he never married. Of course, when his political career took off and he became Viscount Melbourne, he became Prime Minister. Queen Victoria had him advise her on many things regarding her reign until he became invaluable to her, but with that came gossip about their relationship. Melbourne lost his position in the elections and retired to Brocket Hall until you came along. I think he might have offered for you if there hadn't been the large age gap." She sighed. I think Lady Mary also had stronger feelings for Lord Melbourne than she would ever admit to.

"Would you tell me about your husband, Lady Mary? You've never talked about him."

A smile touched her lips as she recalled her marriage to the Earl of Orkney. "My Edward," she said and sighed. "I met my Edward in my first season, much as you and the duke. Edward whisked me off my feet. He loved to dance. He was so handsome that just seeing him made my heart beat faster. For a couple of weeks, at every ball I attended, he would have a maximum of two dances with me. Of course, even then, two dances with the same person would start the gossip, chattering like a pen full of chickens. You think William Lamb was good-looking in his way, but my Edward... there was no comparison. As soon as he entered a room, all the young ladies would flock around him, but he only had eyes for me. You might look at me now and not believe it, but when I was seventeen, I was very attractive, enough to have a queue of young men wanting to fill my dance card, but I only had eyes for Edward. We married halfway through my first season, which was a great accomplishment, and he took me back to the Orkneys for our honeymoon. We stayed there for several months until I got pregnant with our first child. We were both delighted, but I lost that baby after three months. We were both devastated. Six months later, I got pregnant again, but after eight months, he was stillborn. Edward said we should return to London, where the doctors were more advanced than our local doctor, so we moved back south to London again. The journey to the Orkneys seemed long when I travelled there as a bride. It seemed even longer on the return journey. Anyway, once back in Moldova Square, I got pregnant again with my daughter. Her father danced for joy the day she was born, and we decided to name her Joy."

"So, Mrs Trevelgue's name was Joy?" I asked. "I had never known her given name, even when I lived at Seaward Manor."

"Yes, and she was the apple of her father's eye. His little princess. Unfortunately, as she grew older, she became very wilful. Oh, she was beautiful, and she knew it. When she had her first season, she had gentlemen queueing around the square. She became engaged to the Earl of Alvechurch; he was a nice young man but wasn't strong enough to stand up to her demands and gave in to her every whim. She met Trevelgue. He didn't have a title like Alvechurch, but he had several tin mines in Cornwall, and the family were like the first family of Cornwall. There was no family to match the Trevelgues financially. She persuaded Trevelgue to elope to Gretna Green and consummate the marriage, so we couldn't get it annulled. In the meantime, when Alvechurch found out about the marriage, he was distraught. They found him hanging in the stables."

I was shocked. I knew from Lady Mary, that Mrs Trevelgue had been engaged before, but I didn't know that the gentleman had committed suicide. A lot of what Lady Mary had told me about her daughter reminded me so much of Edwina.

"When she and Trevelgue returned to London after consummating the marriage, she wanted her father and I to buy them a house in London so that she could spend the season here each year. After the news of Alvechurch's suicide was in all of the newspapers, her father felt that she had used us, and he decided that he would cut her off.

"So now you know the full story, Julia," Lady Mary concluded. Then, she changed the subject.

"Well, as you know, Philomena is engaged and will be getting married at Christmas. I know that she really wants you and the duke there, so you must hurry up and get better. Jane returned after bringing your breakfast tray down, telling everyone how much you had eaten. If you keep that up, you will soon be back on the road to recovery. Mrs Watson, up until now, has been organising your food, but after last night and this morning, I think you will be eating more normal food. I understand the doctor is due today to see how you are." Then, a shadow seemed to cross her face. "It was a good job that Robert found you when he did. The Trevelgues had laid down so many false clues, which was why it took Robert and the police so long to find you. Mrs Watson insisted she go along with him, as they knew the village people and the doctor better than the duke, and Jethro also insisted on going. I understand he felt guilty about not giving you Mrs Watson's notes directly instead of handing them over to Edwina."

I didn't want further reminders of that awful time. I changed the subject again.

"What other news? Has Lord Rutledge married the girl he was forced to offer for?"

Lady Mary's eyes lit up with glee, "Ah, now there lies another bit of scandal. Rutledge was going to back out of the marriage, but the young lady's brother challenged him to a duel. Oh, I know it is illegal, but what could the poor man do to save his sister's honour? Well, they duelled with pistols. Rutledge was shot, not fatally (more is the pity), but he was badly injured, and the marriage was called off." Lady Mary's voice dropped, " I don't think he will be chasing after the young ladies for a long time. As I said, the shot didn't kill him, but... well, we are ladies of the world now; Rutledge will not be able to father any children."

"Never?" I asked.

"No, my dear," Lady Mary said, shaking her head.

"Ooh, well, I suppose you could call it poetic justice," I said. "What about Lord Waterford? Has he found anyone? He looked like a Greek god with his blonde hair and tanned skin. I should imagine all the debutants falling over each other for him."

"And yet you married Rochester?"

"Robert makes me laugh. We have the same interests, and it was love at first sight for me anyway. I wonder if he knew then what he knows now about the trouble I have brought into his life, he would still have offered for me."

Lady Mary stretched her hand out to me. "Julia, your husband adores you. He never gave up looking for you, and when he found you, Jethro and the policeman had to physically hold him back from murdering the Trevelgue brothers. Although not quite as tall as others, your husband is very strong. He nearly got the better of them both."

Lady Mary never referred to her daughter or grandsons as anything other than the Trevelgues, as if she had completely blocked them from her life.

"Anyway, you were telling me about Lord Waterford?"

"He has been seen in the company of Cissy Wellington. Gossip says that there will be a marriage there soon," Lady Mary told me.

"I hope he makes a happy marriage." I sighed, "Oh, Lady Mary, I feel my youth has been stolen. While the Trevelgues had me imprisoned, I should have been dancing and laughing, and maybe by the end of my honeymoon, I would be carrying Robert's baby. Now, the doctor tells me that I must be completely free of the drugs before I get pregnant, as the baby could be addicted to the drugs. They have stolen so much from me." Tears of self-pity began to gather in my eyes at the unfairness of it all. I knew that it was all because I was still so weak.

Lady Mary noticed. "Now, I think enough gossip for a while. You need to sleep."

"You won't be returning to London for a while yet, Lady Mary, will you?" I asked her again, scared of losing her back to London.

"I will stay as long as you want me to, my dear." She leaned over and kissed my forehead, then left me. I lay my head back on my pillows and slept. I dreamt of waltzing in Robert's arms and knew I was smiling. Then I dreamt of Lord Melbourne, as he came to me just before I married. Whether it was wishful thinking, the drugs still, or whether the dead do visit the living, I didn't know, but we had a good conversation. I suppose in a way I did love him; after all, it was due to his generosity, taking us in when we left Cornwall and were lost in the fog, he also introducing me to Lady Mary, in the hope that if he made the introductions, she would not turn me away. In my dream, Melbourne looked at me sadly. "The Trevelgues have a lot to answer for, not only for the incarceration in Cornwall, but for Mark Trevelgue getting you wrongly imprisoned. I should have advised you to take him to court for slandering your name. If you had done that, you might have been spared the kidnapping. My dear Julia," he took my hand in his, "You did not deserve any of this. The family is corrupt."

In my dreams, there were no honorifics. We were just good friends, William and Julia.

"Hindsight is a wonderful thing, William, and like it or not, they are Lady Mary's family."

He nodded. "She feels dreadful about that and the fact that they have caused you such suffering, and you had done nothing to deserve it." Lord Melbourne's wraith told me. "I think it all stems from Mrs Trevelgue being cut off without a penny after she eloped with her husband, with no decency to end her engagement beforehand. It caused a terrible scandal, which made Lady Mary ill at the time," he said in my dream. "I think it was a part of her life that she wished to forget, knowing that her daughter caused a man to commit suicide. Anyway, the Trevelgues are all behind bars, which is as it should be. The courts are waiting on your recovery before they start proceedings."

"I wish I could go now and get it over and done with. I shall miss you not being there with me," I told his spectre.

"I shall be with you in spirit, and you have your husband now. I know that you are in good hands with him at your side. When the doctor decides you are well enough, you will return to London." His ghost told me.

"Oh, I want to go back to London and dance and go to concerts, dance and ride in the Row. The season is in full swing now, isn't it?"

In my dream, I could hear his voice telling me that I would have many years to enjoy the season's excitement again. "Lady Mary, she loves you like the daughter she should have had, and she is so proud of your achievements and the fact that you made a brilliant marriage. Rochester is a good man who adores you, as do I, Julia. You were the daughter that I never had."

Although I was still sleeping, I could feel tears trickle beneath my closed eyelids. I knew that I would miss him as much as a family member. Then my dream faded, but I felt I had talked to Lord Melbourne, even if he was in the spirit world. It was probably Robert telling me of his death that sparked the dream, and it must have been the effect of the drugs that I still had to use. I slept then with no more dreams.

Philomena was sitting next to me when I woke up.

"I have just heard my father talking. You know that he went with Uncle Robert to Cornwall."

I shook my head, still half asleep.

"He said that Uncle Robert aged nearly ten years when they couldn't find you."

My breath caught in my throat in shock.

"The police and Jethro had to hold him back from killing Mark Trevelgue when he saw the state you were in when they found you. Mrs Trevelgue offered to have you moved to a decent room at Seaward Manor after they found you, but Uncle Robert turned on her and said he wouldn't allow his wife to spend another second longer under her roof. I know the Butler; Masters was shocked at what the brothers had done, and neither he nor any of the staff knew anything about what was happening."

"But how could that be?" I asked her.

"The Trevelgue brothers had been very devious, explaining that you were Mark's ailing wife, and he wanted to look after you himself. He brought up food from the kitchens and, between him and Richard, did everything between them. Their mother knew what they were doing but didn't stop them or improve the conditions you were in." She shook my hand, "Anyway, enough of this. We don't want you to think about that. You must concentrate on getting better. I have missed you in London."

I asked Philomena who was staying at the castle.

"It's just me, my parents, Lady Mary, oh, and Lady Virginia, but of course, it's her home as well as yours."

"You won't go back to London yet, will you?" I asked her very selfishly.

"Not if you don't want me to, why?"

"I need some light-hearted conversation to cheer me up. At the moment, all I seem to hear is about me, drugs, and Cornwall. I hear that Lord Melbourne is dead, and I feel that my life is over before it's really begun. I'm going on twenty, and I feel about ninety. Talk to me of balls, fashion, and dresses, anything that is not doom or gloom, Philomena."

She sat and held my hand, telling me about how Davenport proposed to her, the ball they were at, her wedding dress, and all the things that I wanted to hear to cheer me up. Ultimately, I lay back against my pillows and closed my eyes after Philomena had left, telling me she would get into trouble for being with me so long.

Jane brought me a nourishing soup for lunch and a milk pudding for my dessert. She then told me that if I felt up to it, she would arrange a bath for me after an afternoon nap. After the bath, she let me rest again before preparing me to go downstairs for dinner. Since we had moved to London and she had become my lady's maid, she had put on a little weight with all the good food that we made sure our servants had. With the extra bit of weight and her new uniforms, she looked different from the young girl who came to my room at Seaward Manor and told me all the gossip below the stairs.

I teased her about looking better than me, and she laughed, "I would never be as beautiful as you. I am content as I am Your Grace, and that is all thanks to you."

Robert came in briefly after Jane had collected my lunch tray.

"Sweetheart, I feel I have been neglecting you, but with all your visitors...It has enabled me to attend to things down in the stables. Oh, and Jethro sends his regards. He did say love first, then thought he was being a bit forward, considering your position, so changed it to his best wishes." He grinned. "I shall be getting jealous, with..."

"Robert, you are the only man for me from the moment I first met you. My heart is full of love, my Robert," I told him. He sat on the bed beside me and gathered me in his arms. "And I want to show you how much I love you too, but I am patient, and it will be all the sweeter for the waiting. Now close your eyes and sleep again."

"Will you lie down with me, Robert, or am I keeping you from something?"

"Nothing is more important than you," he said, pulling off his boots and lying down beside me. Then he pulled my body into his and kissed and cuddled me.

As I snuggled up to him, I could smell his Sandalwood cologne and the warmth of his body. I slipped into a blissful sleep.

Chapter Seventeen

With all the good food and rest, I was beginning to feel well enough to travel to London. After two more weeks, the doctor permitted me to travel, but once I reached Berkley Square, I had to rest completely for at least a few days.

The journey back to London, which generally took two days, took four this time, with us staying overnight at very good coaching inns. I think if Robert could have put our large bed from Knole Castle on wheels and travel that way he would have, He was so mindful of my condition.

When we reached Berkley Square, Robert held me in his arms and carried me straight upstairs to our bedroom. This was my first time in Roberts town house, which was magnificent. I wished I was up to walking around it and acquainting myself with my new home. Our bedroom was beautifully decorated in creams and pale greens, with an en-suite bathroom, running water and a dressing room off it. It had modern touches to it that the castle did not have, but Robert was saying that he would get the castle modernised over a period of time. I was just happy to be back in London, where I might be able to attend some events. Robert instructed that I had a wheelchair at my disposal, and that Jane should push me around in if he were unavailable. Mr Meadows, the butler, had informed me that there was a lot of news in the newspapers about me, and several people had called by leaving flowers for me. I was told that the drawing room looked more like a florist's shop than the room of a house; there were so many bouquets. I think Robert had tried to spare me from the horrible truth in the tabloids, but I had insisted that he let me read the newspapers and see what was being said. With our return to London, Lady Mary returned to Moldova Square. I hoped that Lady Mary had been spared any part of this scandal.

With Robert being back in the city he had things to do which took him away from the house, so I was, more or less, left to my own devices. The following morning, Mr Meadows came into the drawing room to say that a gentleman had asked to see me.

"Did he say who he was, Meadows?"

"Only that he did business with you last year, Your Grace."

My brow creased as I tried to think who it might be. "Very well, show him in, please, but stay just outside the door if you would," I told him. I didn't realise that the past had affected me so much that I was very cautious to meet anyone alone now, only people I knew.

"Mr Rosenthal, Your Grace," Meadows said, announcing the guest.

My eyebrows creased in confusion. I looked up and was shocked to see the pawnbroker to whom I had sold Edwina's jewellery.

"Mr Rosenthal, how nice to see you," I told him and asked him to sit. I was dressed but propped up with plenty of cushions on one of the sofas in the drawing room.

He shook his head, "Oh no, Your Grace, I couldn't do that. I hope you don't mind me being so forward, but I read about you in the newspapers, saw your picture, and thought you had been the young lady who had come to my shop last year. I just wanted to bring you these," he said, pulling a bunch of flowers from behind his back and giving them to me. "I never knew that you were a duchess, Your Grace."

I took the flowers from him and thanked him, then rang the little bell left on a side table beside the sofa. Jane came in. "Jane, can you put these lovely flowers in some water and bring the vase here for me to look at them? Can you also order tea for Mr Rosenthal and me, please?"

Mr Rosenthal looked shocked.

"I was not a duchess when we met Mr Rosenthal," I told him as we waited for our tea to be delivered. "Thank you for the beautiful flowers. After your very kind gesture, I would like you to take tea with me. Please sit and spend a while with me. I would so much like it."

He sat on one of the chairs, holding his hat and nervously passing the rim around in his hands.

"How is your business, Mr Rosenthal?"

"I'm pretty busy still, Your Grace, although I might say I have not had anyone as..."

"Difficult as me?" I prompted him with a grin.

"Oh, I wouldn't say that, Your Grace; you might have been hard to strike a bargain with, but it was all good fun. It certainly kept me on my toes."

I grinned at him, "So if you saw me coming towards your shop again, you would not put up the 'closed' sign?" I teased him.

He smiled and blushed, "Oh no, Your Grace. As you guessed, I made a tidy sum off the pieces you sold to me. I came because I thought what happened to you was terrible. Those men ought to be hung for what they did to such a nice lady as you."

I told him that was very kind and asked him how he took his tea.

"Oh, milk and three sugars, please, Your Grace."

I smiled as I poured his tea and handed it to him. "Do you have family, Mr. Rosenthal?" I asked him.

He told me that he had a wife and three children in England. He was Jewish, and he had other family in Israel.

"So, when did you come to England, Mr Rosenthal?"

"Oh, my oldest son is now fourteen, and my wife was expecting him when we left Israel, probably about fifteen years ago."

"Were you a pawnbroker in Israel?" I asked him, enjoying the conversation. The subject of our talk was so far removed from what had happened to me, and it was refreshing.

"No, Your Grace, I was a cantor, but that does not pay much, so I opened the pawnbrokers. It took a few years to start making money, but I am doing quite well, thanks to you."

"I'm sorry to sound ignorant, Mr Rosenthal, but what is a cantor?" I asked him, interested in the Jewish faith.

He laughed, "Unless you are Jewish, Your Grace, I doubt anyone would have heard of a cantor. I sing in the synagogue. We get paid a little, but nowhere near enough to feed and clothe a growing family."

"I must admit that I was surprised to see a pair of false teeth in your shop window." I laughed with him, "Where on earth did you get those from, or shouldn't I ask?"

"Ah, now. I got those from an old man, who told me they were made of old, dead soldier's teeth."

I shivered and laughed at the thought. "How dreadful," I told him.

"Believe it or not, I sold them just the other day."

"Oh no!" I cried.

He grinned, "It is amazing what some people will buy," he told me.

After he had finished his tea and eaten some biscuits, he stood and told me that he wouldn't outstay his welcome, and it was time for him to leave.

"Well, thank you very much, Mr Rosenthal. I have enjoyed your company," I told him sincerely, "If you are ever in this vicinity, please call again." I had genuinely enjoyed our time together, and I was not so 'high on the instep', as they say, that I thought I was any better than him.

"Well, thank you very much for the tea, Your Grace, and I hope those men get put behind bars for at least a very long time," he told me, then bowed over my hand and kissed it. "You are a lovely and gracious young lady. Get well soon, and anytime you are in my vicinity, do pop in for a cuppa. It will not be as grand as this, but you are very welcome," he told me and then left.

I lay on the sofa grinning about my enjoyable time and how Mr Rosenthal made me laugh.

"Well, someone looks happy," Robert said as he joined me about half an hour later. "I understand you had a gentleman caller, and you were laughing with him." He looked at me with a cheeky glint in his eye. "Should I be jealous?"

"Oh, Robert," I said, enthusing over my visitor. "You would never guess who he was?"

My husband raised his eyebrows in question.

"He was the pawnbroker to whom I sold Edwina Trevelgue's jewellery. He said he saw the newspaper with a picture of me and wanted to come and see me. Isn't that nice of him? And he brought me some flowers."

"A pawnbroker?"

I nodded. "When I went to his shop, he had a pair of false teeth in the window, and he told me that they once belonged to an old man, and they were made from the teeth of dead soldiers."

"How gruesome."

"But apparently, he sold them just the other day. Would you believe it?" I grinned.

"Good lord. Well, his visit has cheered you up, Julia; you look more like your old self."

"I feel better than I have in ages, Robert. I think I am on the mend," I enthusiastically told him.

"Well, I am glad about that, my love, as our solicitor wants to come this afternoon to talk to you about what went on. Do you feel up to it?" He sat on the sofa beside me and took my hand in his.

"What time?" I asked him.

"About two o'clock. Will you feel fit to receive him and discuss it?"

"Will you stay with me, Robert, while he is here?"

Robert assured me that he would. "But I think you should have a nap before then. Should I carry you upstairs, Julia, or will you have a nap here?"

"I think I can sleep better upstairs, Robert. Do you mind?"

He bowed to me, "Your wish is my command." He picked me up and carried me upstairs. "Do you want me to cuddle you?" he asked, knowing I would say 'yes'.

I don't think I slept much, but I was thoroughly kissed as we snuggled on our bed. "Will you make love to me tonight, Robert?"

"If you feel well enough."

"And show me how to please you?"

"I think one step at a time, darling," he said, kissing my nose.

I slept for a while and woke of my own accord to see Robert looking down at me. "Don't tell me I snore?" I grinned at him.

"No. I like watching you sleep and knowing that you are getting better and better with each sleep." He looked at his pocket watch. "It's only one thirty. Do you want to go back to sleep for a while longer, and I can come and get you when the solicitor arrives?"

I told him that when he did, I would immediately get up and go downstairs.

The solicitor, Sir Roger Ellingham, arrived promptly at two o'clock with another man who, he explained, would be taking notes. They sat down when offered, and Sir Roger asked me how I felt.

"Thankfully, better than I was, but not as well as I would like," I replied.

"My wife is still very ill, Ellingham. She spends most of her time sleeping still. The effects of the drugs given to her by the Trevelgue brothers." Robert told him. I could tell by his tone that if Mark and Richard had been standing in front of him, he would have killed them, even now.

"I will try not to tire you, Lady Rochester. Let me know when you've had enough, and we will finish for the day."

I thanked him. Robert gave me another cushion behind my back to relax while the solicitor questioned me.

"Could you tell me the line of events that led up to the kidnapping?" Sir Roger asked. As soon as I started speaking, I could hear the other gentleman taking down my answers, scratching away with his pen on his notebook.

I told him I had received a note, supposedly from Lady Mary.

"That is Lady Mary McKenzie, formerly the Dowager Countess of Orkney?"

I nodded. "I left the note at Knole Castle and got in what I thought was our carriage, and we started on our way back to London. Do you have the note?" I asked Sir Roger.

"Yes, Lady Rochester. When or where were you kidnapped?"

"I'm not sure. All I knew was that the carriage started to slow down after some time and then stopped. I heard gunshots, but I don't know who fired the gun and who was shot at. Someone, I don't know who, because they wore a mask and never spoke, but they opened the carriage door and put a pad of something over my nose and mouth, and I went unconscious. I don't know how long for. When I came to, I was lying on the floor of a carriage with my hands and feet tied. I don't think it was long before someone returned and put another pad over my nose and mouth. I don't know how many times this happened and how long it had been since I was initially kidnapped."

"Did you, at any time, see anyone's face?"

"No. I don't know how long it was before I was put in a room, but I came to, one time and my arms and legs were untied. Someone, again masked, came in with some food and water in a jug. I don't know how long I had gone without food, so obviously, when I was given food and drink, I ate and drank it. I did not know that it was drugged or whether it was the food or the drink that was drugged." I sat up on the sofa to answer the questions, however much they taxed me.

"Can you remember anything about the room that you were in?"

"It seemed familiar, but I couldn't think from where I thought I would know it. My brain was very foggy. The windows had all been blacked out, and the windows were screwed shut and locked so that I couldn't even open them. There was a bed, table, and a chamber pot, but I can't think of anything else. Once I was in the room, I was constantly kept drugged. I was brought one meal a day, but I think it was pretty basic, some stew." I stopped and found that I was shaking.

Robert looked at me. "Do you want to go on, Julia, or have you had enough for today?"

"I want to get this over and done with Robert," I told him.

"Well, put your feet back on the sofa, and I will put some more cushions behind your back. Then you can relax."

I did as Robert said and felt a little better.

"I am sorry, Lady Rochester, but we need to get your version of events, however painful they might be," Sir Roger apologised.

"I understand," I said. "Because they were only giving me one meal a day, I knew that I had to eat to keep my strength up, but every day, the food or water or both were drugged, and the days began to get hazy so that I was completely lost. I knew that I was getting addicted to the drugs. One day, I flung my plate of food at the door, so that day, I went without food. I started to shake, vomit, and sweat, and the pains in my stomach were so bad that I just wanted to die, so when they brought me food and water the next day, I ate and drank it. I think I knew that it would be drugged, but the withdrawal effects were so bad by then that I knew I couldn't do without it. After that, I don't remember much because I was permanently drugged, and I knew that I was addicted. It wasn't until I was found, and I was back at the Lodge in Porth that I started getting some lucid moments, but most of the time, I was still kept drugged because I was so addicted to whatever they were giving me. That is all I can tell you I am afraid," I said wearily.

"Lady Julia, you said that you knew that you were addicted. How did you know that?"

"My grandfather was a doctor, the local doctor. He often talked to me about medical things, drugs and addiction, among other medical terms. After my father died, I spent much time with my grandfather, and we often talked about such things."

"And why was that? Why did you talk of such things?"

"I was interested in all things. I used to think that if I married when I got older, it would be to a doctor, and I could help him in his work as my mother did with my grandfather. My grandfather often used to say that if women could become doctors, I would be one of the first. I enjoyed learning."

"Thank you, Lady Rochester, that has been most helpful," said Sir Roger Ellingham.

I leaned back into the pillows and closed my eyes briefly.

"Lord Rochester, I gather it was you and your groom, Mrs Watson and the police that finally found your wife at…" he looked at some notes. "Seaward Manor in Newquay, is that correct?"

"That is correct," Robert said. His strained voice told me he was still furious with the Trevelgues.

"Can you tell me your wife's state when you found her?"

"Emaciated. I don't think she had been washed or anything, and she was drugged. We sent for the Doctor from Porth, who told us that if we had left it any longer, my wife could have died. We removed my wife to the Doctor's house in Porth, which had once been my wife's childhood home. As my wife said, her grandfather had been the local doctor there until he died."

"Ah, yes. I understand that Mr Trevelgue, Mr Mark Trevelgue, had accused you of killing his sister before you were married to the duke. I believe that you were in Porth at the time, and Miss Trevelgue's death was accidental." Sir Roger looked across to me, "You were imprisoned for quite some time until a note from Mrs Trevelgue to Lady Mary had been found. May I ask Lady Rochester, why didn't you have Mr Trevelgue imprisoned for falsely accusing you?"

I was lying on the sofa with my eyes closed, but I could still hear what was said.

"I did not want to cause any further scandal for Lady Mary. Mrs Trevelgue had caused a terrible scandal for Lady Mary several years before, so I didn't want her to suffer any more. I thought that Mark Trevelgue would leave me alone after the false imprisonment. I never expected this to happen."

"I understand that the Doctor who initially treated Lady Rochester in Porth is coming to London for the trial?"

"He will be here tomorrow and stay with us until after the trial," Robert told him. "How long do you think the trial will last, Ellingham?"

"As far as I can see, it is an open and shut case. Lady Rochester was found under Mr Trevelgue's roof, in an emaciated state and heavily drugged. The opium that he had been using and the ether that he initially used to kidnap Lady Rochester were all found in his bedroom, so I can't see how he can get away with it. Also, the younger brother was involved in the kidnapping as he was driving the coach with Lady Rochester inside, drugged. The mother knew that they were keeping Lady Rochester incarcerated and did nothing to stop it. It was the mother who wrote the ransom notes. We have a sample of her handwriting from the initial letter she sent to Lady Mary, so none of them have a leg to stand on. They are all guilty of kidnapping, incarceration, and misuse of drugs. It will be up to the judge to decide the sentence, but it will certainly be custodial."

"Even Mrs Trevelgue?" I asked wearily.

"Yes, why Lady Rochester?"

"Mrs Trevelgue also educated me and took me under her roof to be her daughter's companion. She fed me, clothed me, and gave me the opportunity to become a lady," I told Sir Roger.

"Yes, but at what cost, Lady Rochester? She knew that you were being kept upstairs by her sons. Did she ever check to see that you were alright?"

"I... I don't know because I was drugged," I supplied.

"Even if she did check on you, why didn't she tell her sons to stop or call a doctor for you?"

I let the tears that I had been trying to hold back trickle slowly down my cheeks. I had always hoped that Mrs Trevelgue liked me, which was why she took me in, but it was all to try and keep Edwina in line. When she sent me to Lady Mary, I thought she was again doing me a favour, but that was all for her means and hopefully to get money from either Lady Mary or Robert. Still, it was never for my benefit, and I felt terribly betrayed. What had I done to the Trevelgue family that they should hate me so much and do what they did to me?

"If you have finished questioning my wife, Ellingham, I think she needs to be taken upstairs and put to bed. This has all been very stressful and tiring for her, and she is not in the best of health, thanks to the Trevelgues. If you want to talk to me further, I will be down shortly once I have ensured Julia is settled."

"Yes, I would like to discuss this further with you, Your Grace," said Sir Roger.

"Very well, I will be back shortly. In the meantime, can I order some refreshments for you and your colleague?"

I don't remember what Sir Roger said. I was too exhausted and upset to care. I snuggled into Robert's shoulder and cried as he carried me upstairs to our bedroom.

Robert gently placed me on our bed and instructed Jane, who was waiting, to help me undress and put on my nightgown.

"I will be back to check on you when they have gone, darling," Robert said, kissing me.

Jane undressed me like I was a child, hardly speaking. I looked at her and saw that she was crying. Tears were silently trickling down her cheeks.

"Why the tears, Jane?"

"Those Trevelgues have a lot to answer for. I hope they imprison all of them and throw away the key," she said vehemently.

"Were you listening at the door, Jane?"

"I'm sorry, Miss Julia, but I had to find out what those devils had put you through."

"I am so glad you came with me when I left Cornwall to come to London," I told her.

"You have always been so good to me, giving me money from Edwina's jewellery and helping me open a bank account and all my new clothes."

"I did that to give you independence, Jane."

"Independence to do what, though?" she asked me.

"To do whatever you like. Maybe stop working for me and do something that you want to."

"I am doing what I really want to do: looking after you. Without you, I wouldn't be a lady's maid to a duchess, and you are so kind to me. I don't want anything more. I feel that you are my family, and I never want that to change. I owe you everything."

"I am lucky to have you. You are not just my personal maid. You are my friend Jane, and your friendship means a lot to me. When I am better, we will go into the city and have tea in a tea shop again or something similar for our treat," I told her.

"I would like that. You are a good person, Miss Julia, not just to me but to Lady Mary. Even that pawnbroker thought you were lovely."

"You were listening at the door then as well?" I asked her.

Jane just grinned and shrugged her shoulders. "I've got to make sure nothing bad happens to you ever again."

I couldn't help but laugh, "Jane, you are my maid and my friend, not my guard dog."

"If I had been with you when you received that note from Lady Mary, you wouldn't have been kidnapped."

I took her hand, "Hindsight is a wonderful thing, Jane," I told her.

"What does that mean?"

"It means that if we knew what was going to happen, we wouldn't do many things," I explained to her.

"Ooh," she said, but I wasn't sure she understood. "Well, you look tired now, so you should sleep," she said.

It had been a very tiring and emotional day. I was exhausted. I slept.

A week later, Robert wheeled me in my wheelchair into the very busy courtroom, where it was a cacophony of people talking. When we entered, a hushed whisper went around the room. I looked to see Mrs Trevelgue and her sons in the dock, and I felt sick. Robert looked at me.

"Julia, are you alright?"

I nodded my head. How could one human being do what they had done to me, and for what reason?

He took my hand, and his thumb began to rub the back of my hand like he always did, trying to give me some of his strength to face this terrible ordeal.

Lady Mary was also in the courtroom. I think it was the first time she had seen her daughter since she had banished Mrs Trevelgue without any of hers or the late Earl of Orkney's money. I wondered how she must feel now to see her daughter and grandsons in court.

Sir Roger Ellingham looked across at me, then at Robert, and came over to where Robert had placed my chair.

"Lady Rochester, are you feeling strong enough for this?" he asked, looking at my pale face.

I squeezed Robert's hand. "Yes."

"I will try to make it as painless as possible. Will you feel able to take the stand if I call you up first, Your Grace? Get it over and done with, then if you want to return home to rest..."

I took a deep breath, "Yes, if you could, please." I didn't know how I would fare during the court case, and I refused to let any of the Trevelgues reduce me to tears. I lifted my head and stared at the three Trevelgues in the dock. I wanted them to see that I would stand up and watch their downfall despite what they had done to me.

Sir Roger noted what I had done and nodded. Robert looked at me and smiled proudly. Then I looked across to Lady Mary, who had a look of pride on her face as she, too, looked at me. I was determined the Trevelgues would not cower me down.

Firstly, the charges against the Trevelgues were read out, and they were asked how they pleaded. Considering all the evidence against them, they all pleaded not guilty.

I looked at Robert, who raised his eyes to heaven.

Sir Roger explained that he would like me to take the stand first due to my poor health. The judge nodded, so I was wheeled to the stand.

After I was sworn in, the judge looked over to me.

"Lady Rochester, if this gets too much for you, please let me know, and I will stop the proceedings until you are feeling better," the judge said, looking at me, seeing my pale face, and smiling sympathetically.

I thanked him.

Mark Trevelgue, standing opposite me, raised his hands to heaven, "Oh, for God's sake, she was just a servant girl until she entrapped the duke. She can face anything. Stop treating her like a delicate flower!"

I looked at Robert and could see that he was gritting his teeth. I could imagine that he would have liked to murder Mark Trevelgue.

The judge banged his gavel, "That is enough, Mr Trevelgue, or I shall have you removed from this court."

Obviously, his spell in prison hadn't broken his arrogance. He just grimaced, then shut his mouth.

"Lady Rochester, firstly, let me clarify that this was not the first time Mr Mark Trevelgue had dealt with you. Is that correct?" asked Sir Roger Ellingham.

I nodded, "Yes, that is true."

"Could you tell us about that first of all?"

I took a deep breath and told of the time that Mark Trevelgue had accused me of murdering his sister Edwina.

"It was found out after over two weeks in prison that Mr Mark Trevelgue had lied, and you were nowhere near his sister because you were in Porth village where you had been born, finding out that your grandfather, your only remaining relative, had died and had been dead and buried three weeks previously. Is that correct?"

The Trevelgue's solicitor stood up and said that that was irrelevant to this case.

"Sir Roger?" the judge looked over to Sir Roger Ellingham in question.

"Your Honour, I wish to show what outright lies Mark Trevelgue has previously laid against Lady Rochester."

"Objection over-ruled," said the judge. "Proceed."

"Why did you not find out about your grandfather's death?"

"For several weeks, I had not been able to leave Seaward Manor because of the terrible weather, so I went and saw my grandfather when it improved somewhat.

"On the day of Edwina's death, she was supposed to have been having a dancing lesson, so I thought I would take that opportunity to visit my grandfather. When I got to the village, the people I had known all my life and who had been my friends gave me an icy reception, and I couldn't understand why. I had called at the Lodge where my grandfather lived, and it was all shut up. The housekeeper, Mrs Watson, was nowhere to be seen, so I looked for her in the village, and that was when I found out. Mrs Watson had sent notes to me, firstly informing me of my grandfather's death, then another to inform me that his funeral was being held the next day, then the third one she sent was to inform me that she was shutting up the Lodge and to come and take what I wanted."

"Did you receive any of those notes from Mrs Watson?" asked Sir Roger.

"No, which was why I was so upset when I was in the village."

"What had happened to those notes?"

"Mrs Watson said that she had given them to her son-in-law, Jethro, who had given them to Edwina, who never passed any of them on to me."

"Why was that?"

"Jethro, Mrs Watson's son-in-law, said that Edwina was otherwise engaged with the stable boy."

Mark Trevelgue shouted, "That's why she killed my sister."

There was a loud gasp around the court. The judge banged his gavel again for silence. "I have told you, one more outburst like that, and I will remove you from this court."

The court went silent.

"Where were you when Edwina Trevelgue died, Lady Rochester?" Sir Roger asked once silence had been restored. The Trevelgue's solicitor went to Mark Trevelgue and whispered something to him.

"I was in the village finding out about my grandfather's death. My Gramps was the local doctor and my only relative left," I continued.

"When did you find out about Miss Trevelgue's death?" Sir Roger asked me.

"When I returned to Seaward Manor. The staff were all standing around; some were crying, but all were in shock. I found Mrs Trevelgue in the library with the body of her daughter, Edwina, laid out on the library desk."

"When did Mr Trevelgue accuse you of his sister's death?"

"On the way back from Edwina's funeral."

"And what did you say to that?"

"I told him that I was nowhere near her, as I was in Porth village, and I had plenty of witnesses."

"What did he say to that?"

"He said that he owned the mines, which many of them worked in, and he would sack anyone that said I was in the village."

"So, Mark Trevelgue was lying about you and holding the villagers to ransom, if we could call it that."

I nodded.

"Mark Trevelgue later came to London to Lady Mary McKenzie's home where you were living as her ward and accused you in front of a policeman of killing his sister."

"Yes."

"And you were imprisoned until your now husband came back from Porth with witnesses that you were in the village at the time of Edwina Trevelgue's death?"

"Yes, er no," I stumbled. "Lady Mary found the original letter from her daughter, introducing me as Lady Mary's granddaughter, which they said more or less, proved that Mrs Trevelgue would not have done so if she thought that I had killed her daughter. I had been back at Lady Mary's for a couple of days when Robert, sorry the duke, returned with people from Porth village who could attest that I was with them then."

Sir Roger turned to the judge then.

"Your Honour, this proves the steps Mark Trevelgue took to get revenge on Lady Rochester."

Sir Roger looked at me, "Do you still feel able to carry on, Lady Rochester?" he asked.

I nodded.

"Then let us move on to the day of your abduction."

"Objection, Your Honour," The Trevelgue's solicitor stood up and spoke.

Sir Roger looked at the judge, who scowled at him as if to say, you can't say that as it's not been proved.

"Objection sustained," the judge said.

"The day you left Knole Castle, Lady Rochester. Why did you leave?" asked Sir Roger.

"I received a note, supposedly from Lady Mary, saying that she was ill and needed to see me urgently but not to tell anyone."

"Who did you take it to mean when it said 'anyone'?" asked Sir Roger.

"My husband."

"So, what did you do?" Sir Roger asked.

"I packed a few things in a carpet bag and got into the coach waiting for me."

"Did you see who was driving the coach?"

"I didn't notice. I was too intent on reaching Lady Mary."

"Why was that, Lady Rochester?"

"Lady Mary had been very good to me since my arrival in London, and I had grown very fond of her."

"Then what happened?"

"We drove away from the castle, and as we were going through a forest, the coach came to a halt. I was going to get out and ask why the carriage had stopped, then I heard a gunshot and thought better of it. A man in a mask opened the carriage door and placed a handkerchief over my nose and mouth. I presume that it was ether on the handkerchief, and I went unconscious."

"What makes you think that it was ether?"

"My Grandfather was the district doctor when he was alive, and he used ether when he did any surgery on people. He had shown me and told me what it did, so I recognised the smell."

"Thank you for clarifying that, Lady Rochester. So, you were unconscious, then what?"

"When I came to, I was on the floor of the carriage, and my hands and feet were tied. The carriage stopped again, and a masked man came and put the handkerchief over my nose and mouth again, and I lost consciousness again."

"Did you see whether it was the same coach?"

I shook my head, "I don't know. I was still too dazed from the first time."

All the questioning brought back the terrifying events, and I struggled to keep going. I could hear my heartbeat ringing in my ears, and my mouth had dried out. Once or twice, I felt so weak that I didn't think I could carry on. Then, I looked across the courtroom at Mark Trevelgue's arrogant face and steeled myself to carry on and answer the questions Sir Roger put to me.

"Did you struggle against this?" Sir Roger asked me.

"No, I was still too dazed, and I felt very sick."

"At any time did the masked man speak to you?"

"Not that I can remember." Then I shook my head. "I think that if they did, I would have known that it was one of the Trevelgue brothers."

"Then what happened?"

"I was kept constantly drugged, but I don't know how long for."

"When do you remember after that?"

"I think the next time I returned to consciousness, I found myself in a room. It looked familiar, but I was still too dazed to get my brain to function. My hands and feet had been unbound so that I could struggle to walk around, but I was unsteady. The windows of the room were blacked out from the outside and also screwed and locked, so I couldn't see where I was. A masked man brought me food, a jug of water, and a beaker. As I had not eaten for so long, I was starving, so I ate all the food and drank the water, but I know now that one or the other was drugged, maybe both, and I fell unconscious again."

"Did this continue?"

"Yes. Every day, I was brought food and water, and every day, I was drugged. It continued, I presume, for some time to the extent that I couldn't do without the drug, whatever they were giving me," I said and started to shake; I wanted to get this ordeal over with as soon as possible, so I gripped my hands together to try to stop the shaking.

"At any time did you go without the drug, and if so, what happened?"

"One day, I was brought food and water, and I angrily threw the plate of food at the door, so I only had water to drink until the next day. By that time, my body had become used to the drug and dependent on it to the state that when I didn't get it, I was sick. I had shivers and terrible stomach pains, so the next day, when food was brought to me, I knew that I had to eat it to stop the adverse reactions, which I did, and I became unconscious again."

"So, you became addicted to the drug that your captors were giving you?" reiterated Sir Roger.

"Yes."

"As we know, eventually, your husband and your old housekeeper, Mrs Watson, found you, but you were now addicted to the drug. Can I ask you how you feel about the whole episode?"

"Angry."

"Why is that?"

"Because I was made into a drug addict, and I lost my youth. I have been bedridden for months, being slowly weaned off the drugs, and it has only been the last week or so that I have managed to leave my bed, but I have lost any strength that I had; hence, I had to be brought here in a wheelchair." I explained. At that moment, if I had been fit and healthy, I think that I would have gone to Mark Trevelgue and scratched his eyes out; I was so angry and he just smiled so smugly as if he had won.

"Thank you, Lady Rochester. I have no further questions."

The judge looked across at the Trevelgue's solicitor.

"Mr Penberthy, do you have any questions for Lady Rochester, bearing in mind that Lady Rochester is still very frail?" the judge asked.

I looked at Robert, who smiled at me and mouthed, "Well done. I love you."

"Lady Rochester, you really have no claims to being a lady. Your father was a mine manager, and your grandfather was a village doctor."

I nodded, "That's correct."

"And yet here you are now, a duchess."

"Yes, Lady Mary made me her ward and had me presented at court."

"Were you overwhelmed by your... elevation?"

"I suppose I was at first, but Lady Mary welcomed me into her home, and I felt privileged by her faith in me."

"And when you became a duchess, how did you feel then?"

"I loved my husband. He knew my past and never held it against me."

"So would you say you are happily married?" asked the Trevelgue's solicitor.

"Yes, very."

"Yet your husband found you in prison?"

"Objection, Your Honour!" Sir Roger said, standing up. "Lady Rochester was wrongfully imprisoned, which has been proved."

"Mr Penberthy..." The judge scowled at the Trevelgues solicitor. "Objection sustained."

"I put it to you that your husband did hold the fact that you had been in prison against you, and you argued, so you took a coach back to where you were born and lost yourself in drugs to blot all out..."

"If the duke was unhappy about me being imprisoned," I interrupted the Trevelgues' solicitor, "then why did he marry me after that?" I asked.

"Your Honour, we have the letter that caused Lady Rochester to flee from Knole Castle as evidence," Sir Roger pointed out.

"Mr Penberthy, do you have anything more you wish to ask, bearing in mind that there is proof of the reason why Lady Rochester left Knole Castle? Otherwise, I think Lady Rochester has answered the question," the judge said.

"One more question, Your Honour."

"Proceed."

"Lady Rochester, didn't you go to Lady Mary, posing as her granddaughter?"

"That's correct."

"So, you fraudulently posed as Lady Mary's granddaughter."

I began to worry that Mrs Trevelgue's past scandal would be brought up again, and I didn't know how to answer. I looked at Lady Mary, who smiled at me and nodded, knowing that her past scandal would be brought up, but it was alright for me to tell the truth.

"Lady Rochester, I ask you again, were you not, initially, fraudulently, posing as the granddaughter of the Lady McKenzie?"

"Lady Mary knew that I was not her granddaughter when I first arrived in Moldova Square."

"But did not Mrs Trevelgue give you a letter to her mother telling her that you were her daughter and, therefore, Lady Mary McKenzie's granddaughter?"

"Yes, but Lady Mary was aware of her daughter's life in Cornwall, so she knew I was not her granddaughter."

"You changed your name to Lady McKenzie's family name of Braemar. Why was that?"

"Lady Mary asked me if I would." I shrugged, "I had no family living and thought that if I were lucky enough to marry, I would change my name again anyway, so I saw no problem with that."

"No more questions, Your Honour," said the Trevelgues solicitor.

The judge looked at me; I was both emotionally and physically exhausted, and it must have shown.

"Lady Rochester, thank you for leaving your sickbed. You may leave the stand now," he said to me.

I heard Mark Trevelgue groan.

I sighed in relief, and Robert came and wheeled me away from the stand.

"Do you want to go home now, Julia?" Robert whispered to me as he wheeled away.

"I want to stay and see who Sir Roger calls next," I told him.

"Very well but tell me when you want to go home. You did so well, Julia. I am proud of you." He took my hand and kissed it.

"I call now Doctor William Meadows," said Sir Roger.

Doctor Meadows went to the stand. He had been staying as a guest at our home. It was the least we could do after the way he had taken care of me, but we were told never to discuss the case. Sir Roger had expressly told us all not to, so Doctor Meadows just restricted our conversations to how I was feeling now. I found out that he and his wife were in their forties, and the doctor had previously worked in the midlands, where he was looking after men who worked in the coal mines and foundries who suffered from lung problems. He told me that when he and Mrs Meadows moved to Porth, many residents often talked about me as a child and Gramps as a good and caring doctor. It pleased me that the Porth residents forgot neither Gramps nor me. Doctor Meadows commented that I looked better than I had when I was initially brought to him, but he could say no more because of the court case. While they were in London, Doctor and Mrs Meadows spent their free time seeing the sights of the big city.

"Doctor Meadows, you were the doctor who initially treated Lady Rochester after she was found at Seaward Manor, the home of the Trevelgue family."

"That's correct."

"Can you tell me the condition of Lady Rochester when she was brought to you?"

"Lady Rochester was emaciated and heavily dependent on drugs. If she had been left any longer, she would have died," Doctor Meadows explained.

"She was addicted to the drugs that had been given to her?" Sir Roger reiterated

"That is correct," said Doctor Meadows.

"So, if Lady Rochester hadn't been found when she was, you are saying that this would have been a murder trial."

The Trevelgues solicitor, Mr Penberthy, jumped up, "Objection, Your Honour. It has not been established that the Duchess did not do this to herself."

The judge just scowled at Mr Penberthy.

"That is correct." Replied Doctor Meadows after the outburst, ignoring the Trevelgue's solicitor and answering Sir Roger's question.

"How did you treat Lady Rochester?" Sir Roger asked him.

"Because she was so heavily dependent on the drugs, we had to slowly wean her off the drugs. It would be a long, slow process. Because she was on these drugs, even when she was well enough, which would be some considerable time, Lady Rochester and the duke were advised not to try for any children because they would also be addicted to the drugs in her system, so after she had been clean of the drugs for twelve months, then she should be able to conceive. The child should be born healthy."

"So, in Lady Rochester's words, not only had she had her youth stolen from her, from the kidnapping, but also, the chance of having a child as well?"

"For the time being, yes," Doctor Meadows agreed.

"Objection, Your Honour. There is no proof that Lady Rochester was kidnapped."

"Mr Penberthy!" the judge said and again scowled at the Trevelgue's solicitor, who then sat down again.

"Doctor Meadows, do you know what drugs had been administered to Lady Rochester?"

"I cannot be sure as I have not seen the evidence of what drugs they were, but they were opiate-based."

"Opiate based?" asked Sir Roger to clarify.

"Containing Opium, if not actual opium."

"So how did you 'wean' Lady Rochester off these drugs?"

"She was given reduced amounts of an opium-based drug over a matter of months."

"You are saying that she was still dependent on these drugs for several months, even in lower doses?"

"That is correct."

"Do you know where these drugs initially came from?"

"No, but they certainly were not from me," Doctor Meadows said.

"Thank you, Doctor Meadows. Can you tell me if you are still Lady Rochester's doctor?"

"No. When Lady Rochester was well enough to be transferred to her home at Knole Castle, Lady Rochester's care was taken over by the Duke of Rochester's own doctor."

"Thank you, Doctor Meadows. No further questions."

The Trevelgue's solicitor stood up then.

"Doctor Meadows, do you keep opium-based drugs in your surgery?"

"Some, but not many, and they are all kept under lock and key."

"Do you carry out surgery on your premises?"

"Yes. Occasionally, when it is needed."

"What drugs do you use for the surgery?"

"Ether, in measured doses."

"So, you also keep ether on your premises?" Mr Penberthy asked Doctor Meadows again.

"Yes, but like the opiates, they are all kept under lock and key."

"So, did you, at any time, supply the Trevelgue family with either the opium-based drugs or the ether?"

"No."

"If someone didn't get these drugs from you, where would they go to get these drugs?"

"I should imagine Truro. That is where I go to get further stocks of medication."

"Are these stocks of drugs registered in Truro?" Mr Penberthy asked.

"Well, I have to sign for everything I purchase, so yes, I presume so."

"Your Honour, I put forward the drugs register of the druggist in Truro, showing the drugs received by Doctor Meadows."

He handed a copy of the list to Doctor Meadows. "Is that your signature, Doctor Meadows?"

"It is my signature against some of the drugs, but although it is my name next to some, it is not my signature against all of them. It looks like someone has tried to forge my signature against the ether and some of the opiate-based drugs."

"Are you sure, Doctor Meadows?"

"Yes, I am positive. I would never have purchased them in such large quantities. I do not need them. Even the ether, I admit that I use some, but I would never collect it in such large quantities."

"Why not?"

"I have no need for such large quantities for my surgery."

"Thank you, Doctor Meadows. No further questions."

The Trevelgues solicitor stood up and said, "Doctor Meadows, who do you think forged your signature?"

"I have no idea, but it certainly wasn't me."

"Could it have been Lady Rochester?"

There was a gasp went around the court at this.

"It could have been anyone, but it wasn't me," Doctor Meadows reiterated.

"No further questions."

Robert looked at me and said, "Have you seen enough, Julia? Do you want to go home?"

I nodded. I was weary, but then I heard Lady Mary's name called and told Robert I wanted to stay. He looked at me, concern creasing his face as I had not sat up for so long since I had been kidnapped.

Lady Mary took the stand.

I looked at her and said, "I am so sorry." Knowing that the previous scandal would be brought forward, she smiled and nodded to let me know that there was nothing to be sorry about.

Sir Roger looked at Lady Mary, "Thank you for coming along today, Lady Mary."

Lady Mary just nodded.

"Lady Mary, when did you first meet Lady Rochester, and how long have you known her?"

"I met Lady Rochester when she turned up on my doorstep after arriving from Cornwall? It's going on two years now."

"Did you know who she was?" asked Sir Roger.

"I knew who she wasn't, which was my granddaughter," Lady Mary said, looking across the courtroom to her daughter.

"How did you know that?"

"Because she looked nothing like my side of the family."

"Did you challenge her on that?"

"Yes, I did."

"And what did she say?"

"That she looked more like her father's side of the family. My daughter had told her to say that if she was challenged."

"And you believed her?" asked Sir Roger.

"No."

"Yet you still took her in. Why was that?"

"Although I had received a letter from my daughter, Mrs Trevelgue, saying that Lady Rochester was my granddaughter, I wanted to find out my daughter's intentions."

"Why did you ask Lady Rochester to change her name to yours?"

"Because, if my daughter was up to something, with Lady Rochester changing her name to my family name of Braemar, she posed no relationship to my daughter and would therefore be free from my daughter's machinations, or so I thought."

"And how did Lady Rochester react to changing her name?"

"She accepted it."

"Why was that? Did she explain to you?"

"Not at first, but when we had become better acquainted, she did, and she told me that her real family name had been Beddoes."

"When did she tell you the truth of her birth?"

"When I said I wanted her to become my legal ward and heiress."

"How did she react to that?"

"She was in floods of tears, begging me not to do it. I knew she had never felt comfortable about lying to me from the start. She said at the very beginning that she would completely understand if I didn't want her to stay with me; she would leave and look for a position as a governess or a lady's companion, so I decided to treat her partly as my companion. When Julia, Lady Rochester, told me the truth, she tried to tell me that she would be quite happy to become a governess to a family or a lady's companion. Then she told me the full story."

"And what was that?"

"That my daughter, after I died, wanted Lady Rochester to give my daughter half of her inheritance, or if that failed and she married well, to persuade her husband to invest in the mines."

"Was that the Trevelgue mines?"

"Yes, that is correct."

"Yet you still proceeded to make Lady Rochester your heir and also to give her a dowry. Why was that?"

"Because by then, I had grown very fond of her; she was like the daughter I hoped I would have had." Lady Mary's eyes seemed to fill up, and I saw her brush a stray tear away.

"You say that you were fond of her, 'like the child you never had.' Can I ask you what you mean by that?"

I saw Lady Mary take a deep breath. "My daughter and I have been estranged for many years. Lady Rochester was a very accomplished young lady. She had a glowing letter of reference from the governess who had taught her and Edwina Trevelgue. It said that Julia, Lady Rochester, had been a good studious student and had excelled in maths, geography, history, English, French, Latin, and piano. Any parent or grandparent would be proud to have a child like that. I took Lady Rochester in, probably as a companion to me. For my part, I thought that she deserved a future. A future in a world of the privileged classes, regardless of her roots. When I first decided to take her in, I told her that I wanted to be addressed as Lady Mary or Ma'am, so she really became my companion and not, as Mrs Trevelgue wanted her to be, fraudulently, my granddaughter."

"As a companion, what were Lady Rochester's duties?"

"She had no real duties as such; she was free to do as she wanted, but she would read aloud to me or play the piano for me. While she played, she would tell me what pictures the music would evoke in her. She was a pleasure to be with."

"You paid for her to have a new wardrobe, and she attended functions with you."

"That is correct."

"May I ask why you were estranged from your daughter, Mrs Trevelgue?"

"My daughter was a wilful child, and from what Lady Rochester told me, so was my granddaughter. My daughter, Mrs Trevelgue, was presented at court and had her season, where she became engaged to the Earl of Alvechurch. She met Mr Trevelgue, and they eloped to Gretna Green in Scotland, not even leaving a message to her fiancé or her father and me. They returned from Scotland, Gretna Green and told us that they would not go through an annulment, as the marriage had already been consummated. The scandal of my daughter was published in the newspapers, and her fiancé, the Earl of Alvechurch, committed suicide shortly after. Her father and I cut her off without a penny. No dowry, nothing. We knew the Trevelgue family had money from the tin mines they owned in Cornwall, so I knew she would not be penniless."

"Have you ever regretted your actions towards your daughter, Lady Mary?"

Lady Mary looked at her daughter standing in the dock with her grandsons. She looked the three of them straight in the eye, shook her head, and said, "No, and going by how she and her family have behaved in recent months, leading to this, no. Her father and I did the right thing. I have no regrets, only the regret that I could not spare Julia... Lady Rochester from the suffering that they have put her through."

"Objection, Your Honour. Lady Rochester or my learned colleague has yet to prove this."

"Very well. Do you have any further questions, Sir Roger?" asked the judge.

"No, Your Honour." Sir Roger sat down.

"Mr Penberthy?"

"Lady Mary, do you know how Lady Rochester knew your granddaughter?"

"She told me that she had been brought from the village to be a companion to Edwina Trevelgue."

"Was she jealous of Edwina Trevelgue?"

"Not that she had ever told me. In fact, she was grateful to Mrs Trevelgue for giving her a good education. I understand that my granddaughter was not kind to her. She was spiteful."

"Your Honour, surely Mr Penberthy should have been asking Lady Rochester that, not hearsay from Lady Mary?" Sir Roger said, standing up.

"Yes, Mr Penberthy," the judge said.

"No further questions then, Your Honour," said Penberthy.

Mr Penberthy sat down.

The judge instructed Lady Mary to leave the stand. I waited to see if she was all right after her ordeal and invited her back to Berkley Square so we could sit down and talk.

Robert wanted me to go upstairs and rest, but I said I would be quite comfortable on the sofa, so he propped me up with plenty of cushions. I was this way when Lady Mary came in. I went to stand and go over to her, but she told me to stay where I was.

"Lady Mary, I am so sorry for bringing another scandal to your door. It was never my intention." I felt tears well in my eyes at this lady who had never done anything to hurt me. I think I could even say that it was a form of love, a love that I was never able to give my own mother due to her dying at my birth, and I think that Lady Mary felt a similar feeling to me, as she could not give that to her, own, undeserving, daughter.

Lady Mary came over to me and took my hand, kissing it. "Julia, my dear girl, you have not done this. They have. My daughter has used you. My grandsons have used you, but you have not done this, my darling girl. They have done this," she repeated.

"But the scandal will come out again. What are you going to do?"

"I have done nothing wrong, Julia. They have brought all of this on themselves. I know that you are grateful to my daughter for your education. Still, it was all done for her own ends, whether to try and get her daughter interested in her education or to get money from you when I die, but it was all for her own ends, Julia. She never did anything for anyone but herself."

"Do you really have no feelings for her? No compassion that she could end up in prison with her sons?" I asked her.

"I have steeled myself against any feelings that I might have had for her, and now that she has been involved in what happened to you. No, I have no feelings whatsoever for her. She wanted to get money from me by fair means or foul. She and her sons decided to do so by foul. What they did to you, Julia, was inhuman. You had done nothing to hurt them, and yet they did such a terribly cruel thing to you. In fact, you lost the only two members of your family to the Trevelgues', your father to their mines, and your grandfather to her daughter."

"I always thought that that was why Mrs Trevelgue did what she did for me, by giving me an education after my father was killed and the chance of a good life with you after Edwina withheld news of Gramps death from me."

"But she still wanted something from you, Julia. A way of getting either my or your husband's money to support their mines. Why couldn't she have just been honest with you, with us? I might have felt some compassion for her then, but for her to be part of your abduction and treatment, which was unforgivable and cruel." She sighed. "Now, do I have to go and make some tea myself, or will you ring that little bell on your side table and order some?" She smiled at me.

I rang the little bell and ordered our tea and biscuits. "After what we have been through today, tea and biscuits are the least I can offer," I told her.

When the tea was brought to us, Lady Mary insisted that she pour, as I had done it enough times while I was living with her.

"Let us hope that once we have resolved this court case, we can return to finding some form of happiness. I must say that my house is quiet without you."

"Are you lonely, Lady Mary?"

"I did miss you when you first left, but I managed before you came into my life, and I will do so again," she told me.

"You are always welcome to my home, Lady Mary," I said, grinning. "All six of them."

She laughed. "I do miss this." I looked at her in question. "You making me laugh," she explained.

"Oh well, some of that was due to Jane's antics." I grinned.

Lady Mary started laughing again. "Dorcas still goes on about the 'daft lummox'."

"Well, Dorcas has trained her to be a very good Lady's maid. I don't know what I would do without her."

"Yes, Dorcas said that she has trained her well."

"I have told Jane that when I have gained my strength, we will go out for tea again."

"I am sure she will like that."

"Oh, do you remember when I pawned Edwina's jewellery?" I asked.

Lady Mary nodded.

"Well, he came to call on me with a bunch of flowers. He had seen my picture in the newspapers and thought that I had been treated terribly, so he came and wanted to let me know. I gave him tea, and we had a nice chat."

"Julia!" Lady Mary said, horrified.

"Now, that is where you and I tend to differ, Ma'am," I told her, "I might be a duchess now, but I was no better; I am no better than him, so we spent a pleasant half hour chatting."

"You are a constant source of amusement, my dear." She smiled at me.

Robert came in then, "Lady Mary, how nice to see you again. How are you?"

"I was telling Julia that the house is quiet without her."

"Well, you are always welcome to our home," he said, taking her hand and kissing it.

"Did you go back to the court?" I asked my husband.

"Yes, darling. I am to take the stand tomorrow," he said, sitting beside me and taking a biscuit.

"Do you want tea, Robert?" I asked him.

"That would be nice."

I rang the bell and ordered some more tea. "Lady Mary, some more tea?"

Lady Mary stood, "No, my dear. Thank you. I have taken up enough of your time and been invited to the Theatre this evening, by your mother, Your Grace, so I must prepare."

She came over and kissed my cheek, "Rest now Julia. I have a feeling that that odious little man Penberthy might call us back."

"Oh no!" I cried.

Lady Mary left us, and Robert came over, sat down beside me, gathered me into his arms, and kissed me deeply.

"You did very well today, Julia, and you coped very well with that idiot Penberthy. He tried to make you say things that were not true."

"Why does Sir Roger want you to take the stand?"

"To clarify the condition we found you in and the trouble we had tracking you down, I think that if it hadn't been for Mrs Watson, we might not have found you when we did. I presume that it was Mrs Trevelgue who sent me on a wild goose chase across half of the country. I dread to think what might have happened then."

I shuddered.

"No, I don't want you to even think about it, and I don't want you back in that court now unless it's absolutely necessary. You have been put through enough already by those people."

"Your wish is my command, Your Grace." I smiled at him.

The Trevelgue's solicitor, Mr Penberthy, called me back to court to question me again, but his claims were ridiculous.

"Lady Rochester, you had an attraction to Mr Mark Trevelgue, didn't you, when you were living at Seaward Manor."

"Objection, Your Honour." Sir Roger stood up and said, "Mr Penberthy is putting words into Lady Rochester's mouth."

"Mr Penberthy, rephrase your question if you wish to continue with your line of questioning," the judge said.

"Lady Rochester, how did you feel about the Trevelgues?"

"I was very grateful to Mrs Trevelgue for giving me a good education. As for Mark and Richard Trevelgue, I hardly saw them, as when they came back to Seaward Manor, I stayed in my bedroom."

"Why was that?"

"Two reasons: firstly, I did not want to encroach on the family's time together, and secondly, I had heard from the house's female staff that the Trevelgue brothers would make improper advances on the females,"

"Lady Rochester, that was just hearsay from the female staff."

"I also had Richard Trevelgue try to push his unwanted attention on me. It was instigated by his sister, who had invited me into her bedroom, where, unbeknown to me, Richard Trevelgue was also. She was urging her brother to do things to me."

"Did you not find an attraction for the brothers? Did you not think that if you attracted one of the brothers, mainly Mark, the oldest brother, you could become the next Mrs Trevelgue of Seaward Manor?"

"No, never," I replied. It was a laughable notion and totally untrue.

"Mark Trevelgue has said that you made an unwanted approach to him at his sister's funeral."

"That is a lie. No, I never. I had just visited the grave of my grandfather, whose death and funeral I had missed due to Edwina Trevelgue withholding the notes that Mrs Watson had sent. I was upset. I wanted to be left alone. It was Mark Trevelgue who approached me."

"I put it to you that you made an unwanted approach to Mark Trevelgue, and to turn the tables on you, he said that you had killed his sister," Mr Penberthy persisted.

"No, not at all. Mark Trevelgue approached me and accused me of killing his sister."

"And when you argued with your husband, you went to Mark Trevelgue to try and make him have an affair with you, which you had wanted all along."

I sat up straight in my wheelchair, "That is an absolutely ridiculous statement. After Mark Trevelgue had lied about me and had me falsely imprisoned, why would I want to go to him? I love my husband, and we have never had a cross word in our time together."

"No further questions," Mr Penberthy said.

Sir Roger stood up to cross-question me.

"Lady Rochester, why do you think Mark Trevelgue accused you of killing his sister?"

"To cover up the fact that Edwina was running away with the stable boy with whom she had been having a relationship."

Mark Trevelgue jumped up and slammed his hands down. "My sister was brought up to be a lady and would never do a thing like that, unlike you, you..." Mark Trevelgue shouted.

The judge banged down his gavel before Mark could say any more. "Mr Trevelgue, you have been warned before. One more outburst from you like that, and you will be removed from this court," the judge said.

Mark sat down with a look on his face like a naughty schoolboy being reprimanded.

"How did you find out about the relationship between Edwina Trevelgue and the stable boy?"

"It was common gossip among Seaward Manor staff."

"Was there any further proof of the liaison?"

"Yes, Mrs Watson's son-in-law, Jethro, had also seen them together when he delivered Mrs Watson's note to Seaward Manor."

"How was that?"

"He gave all three notes to Edwina, who he found in the stables with the stableboy at the time."

"And do you know what happened to those notes after they were delivered to Edwina Trevelgue?"

"No. I never saw any of the notes, and it wasn't until I went into the village to visit Gramps... my grandfather, that I was even aware of their existence."

"By that time, your grandfather was dead. Do you know if the Trevelgues still employed the stableboy?"

"No, I don't believe he was. I think he was dismissed after the first time that he was caught with Edwina."

The Trevelgues solicitor stood up, "Objection, Your Honour. That is hearsay."

Sir Roger ignored Mr Penberthy and continued with his line of questioning.

"Do you know who initially found out about the liaison between Edwina Trevelgue and the stable boy?"

"No."

"No further questions, Your Honour."

Mr Penberthy stood up again. "Lady Rochester, do you know about drugs?"

"Yes, I have some knowledge about them," I answered him truthfully.

"How do you know about them?"

"Through my grandfather."

"Can you explain that?"

"As he was the district doctor, he used to talk to me about surgery and the drugs. He always said that if there could be women doctors, I would be one of them."

"Did you find it interesting?"

"Yes, I did. Also, it was a special time that I spent with him."

"So, you knew what effect they had?"

"Yes."

"Have you ever taken these drugs, Lady Rochester?" Mr Penberthy asked

"No, I have never been ill enough to need such drugs. I would never willingly take drugs."

"Did you know where the drugs were kept?"

"Yes, my grandfather kept them in a locked cabinet."

"A locked cabinet, and who kept the key for this locked cabinet?"

"My grandfather did."

"Did you know where he purchased his drugs?"

"No.

"No further questions." Mr Penberthy sat down again, and Sir Roger stood up again.

"Lady Rochester, did you know the new doctor's name, the replacement for your grandfather?"

"Yes, Doctor Meadows."

"When did you learn the new doctor's name?"

"When he was treating me after I had been rescued."

"It was Doctor Meadows that treated you after your incarceration?" Sir Roger reiterated.

"Yes."

"And you had never heard his name before that?"

"No, he hadn't arrived before I left Seaward Manor to travel to London."

"Lady Rochester, have you ever been to Truro?" Sir Roger asked me.

"No."

"So, you never called into Truro for any of these drugs and forged the new doctor's signature?

"No. Never," I replied. I was beginning to get angry at both solicitors' insinuations. Hadn't I had enough false accusations and insinuations thrown at me? Now, I was being accused of being a forger and forging the new doctor's signature.

"No further questions, Lady Rochester."

Robert wheeled me back to my seat and asked if I wanted to go home.

I told him that I would like to stay for a while. "You did so well not to lose your temper with that idiot Penberthy, darling." He whispered to me.

"The cheek of that man!" I whispered in return.

"I call Mrs Watson to the stand," said Mr Penberthy.

Mrs Watson, who looked to be dressed in her Sunday best, took the stand next. She looked across to me and smiled.

"Mrs Watson, you were the housekeeper for Doctor Trelawny, Lady Rochester's late grandfather?"

"Yes, sir, that's right."

"How long have you known Lady Rochester?" Penberthy asked Mrs W.

"I was there at her birth when her mother died."

"Lady Rochester's mother died giving birth to her?"

"Yes, sir, that's right."

"So, you have known her all of her life?"

"Yes, sir."

"You knew that her grandfather taught her about doctoring and drugs."

"Yes sir, she loved learning, did our Miss Julia."

"You mean Lady Rochester."

"Yes, sir."

"What sort of person was Lady Rochester as a child?"

"Oh, she was happy, friendly, keen to learn. She was always asking questions."

"About drugs?"

"Mainly about other things, but yes, she did ask the Doc about drugs when he was telling her about them."

"Did she have a boyfriend?"

"She was a child!" Mrs Watson said, disgusted at the insinuation.

"She was a child, then after her father died, and she'd gone up to Seaward Manor, did she say she had a boyfriend then?"

"No, she was still a child."

"What were the arrangements when she first went to Seaward Manor?"

"The Doc used to take her up daily until the cold dark nights settled in."

"Then what happened?" Penberthy asked.

"One day, Mrs Trevelgue suggested that Julia go and stay at Seaward Manor as a companion to Miss Edwina."

"How did you know this?"

"Julia told me when she came back home to collect her things, to move up to Seaward Manor, and also the doc told me,"

"Did you see her much after that?"

"The Doctor used to bring her back at times for a visit when her free time was the same as when the Doctor had free time."

"Did she ever speak of her feelings for either of the Trevelgue brothers?"

"No, never."

"Are you sure?"

"Yes, positive."

"But that doesn't mean she didn't have feelings for them?" Mr Penberthy pressed Mrs W.

Mrs Watson hesitated. Mr Penberthy asked his question again.

"No sir, but if she had done, she would have told me," Mrs Watson said.

"Would she?" Penberthy pressed her.

"Yes, she would have. She told me all of her secrets."

"Even as she got older?" Mr Penberthy urged her.

Mrs Watson didn't answer.

"Mrs Watson, did Lady Rochester tell you all her secrets when she got older?"

"I don't know."

"So, she might not have told you of any feelings for either of the Trevelgue brothers."

Mrs Watson's face looked sad, and I didn't know whether it was because I might not have told her of my secrets as I grew up or because she was being forced to admit that I might have had feelings for the Trevelgues, and she had to admit that she didn't know.

"No, I suppose not."

"No further questions."

Mr Penberthy sat down, and Sir Roger stood up.

"Mrs Watson, did Lady Rochester, when she was younger, ever mention the Trevelgue brothers to you?"

"Yes, sir, she did."

"And what did she say about them?"

"She didn't like them," Mrs Watson said, looking towards the Trevelgue brothers in the dock.

"Why was that?"

"Well, she was frightened of them."

"Why was that?"

"Well, there had been talk about Mark Trevelgue pestering the maids, and Richard Trevelgue had been sent down from Oxford for some scandal with one of the tutor's wives."

Mr Penberthy stood up, "Objection, Your Honour, that is just hearsay."

The judge looked at Sir Roger.

"Sir Roger?"

"I am trying to establish the relationship Mrs Watson had with the Duchess, Your Honour."

"Continue," the judge said.

"And Lady Rochester told you that?"

"Yes, sir, so whenever they were around, Julia stayed in her room."

"And Lady Rochester told you that as well?"

"Yes, sir."

"So, in your mind, she would never willingly be in contact with the Trevelgue brothers?"

"No, and certainly not after Mark Trevelgue had her imprisoned for murdering his sister."

"Thank you, Mrs Watson. No further questions."

Robert took me home after Mrs Watson had finished. As the solicitors had finished questioning me, I stayed home because of the stress of the lies and insinuations against me, especially by the Trevelgue brothers. Robert reported to me daily and told me about the day's proceedings.

According to Robert, Jethro was called to the stand, and Jane, even the chemist from Truro, was called. The Trevelgue's solicitor, Mr Penberthy, tried everything he could to discredit me.

401

Chapter Eighteen

The case took only just over a week. As Robert said, it was a 'cut and dried case'. However, the Trevelgue brothers tried to make out that Robert and I had argued because I had lied to him about my background, so I had run away back to Cornwall, to the only place that I felt happy in and to Mark Trevelgue, who said that I started taking the drugs after he had spurned my attention. He said that I purchased the drugs from Truro on my way back to Seaward Manor. None of it had a ring of truth, and the jury recognised that. The druggist who had supplied the drugs was asked if he recognised anyone. He said he recognised Doctor Meadows and Mark Trevelgue, who had tried to forge the Doctor's signature. I was never even acknowledged by the druggist as a person that he knew, as he said it was a man who had purchased the drugs.

The Trevelgue brothers were sentenced to thirty years, and Mrs Trevelgue was sentenced to ten years. I did feel sorry for Mrs Trevelgue, or I would have if she hadn't sent the note to me, supposedly, from Lady Mary. Also, she knew that I had been incarcerated at Seaward Manor, and she had done nothing about it. That hurt me deeply.

The newspapers had a field day reporting in great detail, but the people who came off the worst for the reports were the Trevelgues.

It must have been about a month after the trial, and I had not heard from Lady Mary. I was very concerned about her; whether she liked it or not, they were her family, albeit estranged. Robert had the carriage brought round to take me to visit Lady Mary. I took Jane with me, who spent her time with Dorcas talking, I gather, about the trial. I had managed to walk from my front door down the steps to the carriage and, with Jane's help, from the pavement to Lady Mary's door and into her drawing room. I sat down on one of the sofas, exhausted, but I had managed it. It was the first time that I had been out visiting for what seemed like years, although it was just over one year.

"Julia, my dear, you look exhausted," Lady Mary said as she fussed over me. "Lay back on these cushions and put your feet up while I order tea. I ordered the cook to make some shortbread biscuits, and I have also suggested sandwiches. We must continue to build up your strength."

It felt lovely to be back in Moldova Square, and after only a few months of living there did I begin to consider it home. I knew Lady Mary was pleased when she heard me call it such.

Lady Mary continued to fuss about me like a mother hen until a tray arrived.

When the tea, sandwiches, and cakes were brought, Lady Mary poured and then gave a brief laugh: "I remember when I used to ask you to pour so that I could make sure that you were doing it correctly. I remember even asking you when Lord Melbourne came, in the hopes that he would offer for you. Now look at you..." she said.

"A wreck," I added.

She handed me my cup of tea. "Nonsense, my dear. It is just a bit of a setback, that is all. I mean, look how far you have come. You did not have the strength to walk a few weeks ago, yet here you are in my drawing room. Considering how you were when they found you, you have come on in leaps and bounds. Be patient, my dear. You will prevail."

"Anyway, enough of me." After a welcoming sip of tea, I said, "What news or gossip do you have?"

"Believe it or not, my daughter had the audacity to write to me, laying the blame at my door. She has a nerve. It is always everyone else's fault but never hers. She hasn't changed one little bit. She is still the wilful person she ever was. Then she asked that I visit her."

"And what have you decided?"

"No, never."

"Are you sure about that, Lady Mary?" I asked her.

"How can I forgive her for what she has done, Julia? Maybe by running off with Trevelgue, I might eventually have forgiven her. After all, we cannot control who we love, as you well know, but the fact that she used you to try and get my money, then was party to your kidnapping and, near fatally, drugging you, no, that had gone too far. What had you ever done to her? Nothing," she said, answering her own question. "When she is freed from prison, if I am still alive, I might, but I only say, might, buy her a small cottage in the middle of nowhere so that she can live out the rest of her life, but even that, I am not sure of at this moment in time."

"She is still your daughter, Lady Mary."

"She is inhumane for what she put you through. Cold and heartless."

I don't think that I had ever seen Lady Mary so angry.

"Anyway, how are you progressing, Julia? I know you have managed to walk up to my front door and into my drawing room. Have they weaned you off the drugs yet?"

I nodded. Thinking back on what I had been through made me shiver, but I didn't want to upset Lady Mary any more than she was already. If Mrs Trevelgue had shown any remorse or had not blamed it on her mother, she might not have been so upset and angry. "Yes,

I have been off them for over a fortnight now. Today is my first day out; well, not being pushed around in a wheelchair."

"And you came to see me. Oh, my dear, I am so pleased you thought of me after what my family put you through."

"Lady Mary, I have always said that you can't be held responsible for what the Trevelgues did. I have been worried about you. Nobody has seen you since the end of the trial."

"Well, with the newspapers raking up the past scandal again and then this, I thought that it would be best to keep a low profile until it all blows over."

I took Lady Mary's hand in mine and squeezed it. "This is really all my fault. If you had never met me, none of this would have happened. The past would have been forgotten, and I wouldn't have caused you another scandal."

"Julia, don't ever say that. It has been my pleasure to have you here and watch you grow into the woman you are now. You taught me how to appreciate music by describing the pictures you imagined. Your coming into my life has enriched it, my dear, not destroyed it. I have never regretted that, even after the trial. You have meant the world to me."

My eyes filled with tears as I thanked her,

"So now that you are off the drugs, when can you start a family?"

"My body has to be free from the drugs for twelve months before we can even try."

"And is the duke treating you well?"

"He couldn't be more loving and attentive," I told her.

"Yes, he is a good man," she admitted. "I must admit that when he initially disappeared when Mark Trevelgue turned up with the policeman, my faith in him did wobble slightly, but when he turned up with half the population of Porth in tow, then I realised the lengths that he would go to for you, and my faith in him was restored."

"I must admit, when the policeman turned up with Mark Trevelgue, and Robert disappeared, not saying anything about where he was going. I doubted that I would ever see him again. I didn't think that I would ever be able to forgive Robert, but when he turned up like the Pied Piper and explained that he couldn't say anything to me while Mark was here, I knew that I couldn't stay angry with him for long," I confided in her. "But now that the trial is over and I am beginning to feel better slowly, I want to ride again and dance and love." I was so frustrated by my weakness and inactivity.

"My darling girl, be patient. You will do all those things again, whenever that may be, but it will happen, Julia. You must be patient. What would your Gramps have said about your impatience?"

"He would have said to be patient and let the body mend."

"He sounds like he was a very astute gentleman, Julia."

I nodded. Although my body was slowly healing, my emotions were erratic. One minute, I was fine and happy, and the next minute, I would be in floods of tears. I supposed that as I had never been seriously ill before, all of this was new to me, and I would have to be patient and listen to what others told me regarding my recovery.

We talked about Lord Melbourne and agreed that we missed him terribly. Then Lady Mary mentioned Jane. "Jane looks well in her new uniform, Julia."

"When we both left Cornwall, she was taking the same risk as I was, and because of my parentage, we are no different, yet here I am, a duchess, and she is a maid. I thought it was unfair, so I spoke with her before I married and asked her what she wanted to do. She told me that to become a lady's maid to a duchess is more than she could have ever wished because she is not as educated as I am. So, I gave her money to open a bank account and paid for her to have the new dresses. It was the least I could do, and Jane is happy with her lot. She might be classed as my lady's maid, but I look on her as my friend."

"You and my daughter could never be more different, my dear, and I am pleased about that. I might not agree with your choice of 'friends' like the pawnbroker, but I can understand Julia."

I smiled, "I can remember when I first met Mrs Trevelgue and she never looked at her servants. She would give her instructions to the air above their head and never said 'please' or 'thankyou' and I was shocked. I had always been taught to say please and thankyou as it was good manners, yet here was this great lady, (as I thought then) who never used them. I think it was then that I realised that whatever my situation was, I would always use the manners that I had been taught. I was never taught to lie either and I felt so uncomfortable doing so, firstly with Lord Melbourne, then you and I didn't like that either."

"Believe it or not, my daughter was taught good manners and not to tell lies. I have no idea when she started that, or when she thought that it was acceptable," Lady Mary told me.

Shortly after, when I felt strong enough to walk down the steps again into the carriage, Jane and I left, with me holding on tightly to her arm. It had been good to get out from the four walls of Berkley Square, however tired I felt at the end of it.

Robert and I dined together that evening, and I wanted to make a special effort, as we still had not made love yet, and I wanted the closeness to him that only making love could do. As he had said not too long ago, 'We can't make a baby yet, but when you feel fit enough, we will have fun practising." He grinned at me, with the two dimples on either side of his mouth and a cheeky look in his eyes. He still made me laugh despite everything that had happened to me.

I slowly regained my natural sense of humour, but for some time after returning to London, I had to feign light-heartedness and fun, especially after the stress of the court case. But tonight, I was feeling more like myself, so I had Jane dress my hair, how Robert liked it, in curls with the long ringlet over my shoulder. I wore the cream velvet gown I had worn the first time Robert met me. It was a little loose, but it still looked beautiful. I wore my pearl and emerald choker and matching earrings to complete the ensemble and remind my husband of our first meeting.

I slowly made my way downstairs with Jane's help and walked into the small dining room. I had told Robert to meet me there, as I suppose I wanted to make a grand entrance.

He smiled lovingly at me after Jane had left the two of us alone. "Julia, you look like you did at the musical concert. It was the first time I ever saw you, but now you are even more beautiful."

I bobbed a slight curtsey, "Why, thank you, kind sir."

He helped me to take my seat at the table. He bent and kissed my neck, "Mmm, you smell good enough to eat."

"Starter or main course, Your Grace," I asked him, flirting outrageously.

"Oh, main course."

As soon as we were both settled, I rang the crystal bell to signal the footmen to start serving.

"And how was Lady Mary today?" Robert asked as we were being served our meal.

"Mrs Trevelgue had written to her, blaming her for everything that happened, then asked Lady Mary to visit her in prison."

Robert slowly shook his head in disbelief. "Is she going to go?"

"No. She said that maybe if it had just been Mrs Trevelgue eloping, she might have eventually given in. Still, it was an emphatic no after she tried to get money from Lady Mary deceptively and how she treated me. Lady Mary did say that maybe after she has been released from prison, she might buy her a small house in the middle of nowhere, but to be quite honest, I am not sure."

"They should have thrown away the key for all of them. Anyway, did you enjoy your visit, darling? That was the first time you have been out without your chair."

"And without you, my Robert."

He rubbed his chin, "I don't know if I like this independence, Your Grace."

"I do, but I miss your arms around me when we are dancing or making love—mostly when we are making love. I want to be able to dance and ride again, Robert, but most of all, I want to feel your baby moving inside me."

"You brazen hussy, Your Grace." He grinned at me in that way that always made my legs melt, and my heart turned to butter.

I smiled at him with promise for the night to come.

After dinner, Robert took me in his arms and carried me, waltzing around the drawing room, humming a well-known waltz. "I would play it to you, but I can't waltz and play the piano simultaneously." He grinned at me, the twin dimples forming on either side of his mouth.

"Then maybe, Your Grace, you should take me upstairs and give me your total and undivided attention."

He whisked me out of the drawing room and upstairs to our bedroom, where Jane was waiting for me like the faithful friend and lady's maid she was.

"Jane, you may have the rest of the night off; I shall attend to the duchess," my husband told her.

Jane curtseyed with a knowing grin, shutting the door behind her.

"Now, where were we? Ah, I know," he said and started kissing me while he competently began undressing me, kissing each part as he removed my clothes until he lay me naked on our bed. Then he began to divest himself of his clothes swiftly and lay down next to me. Oh, how I forgot what joy and pleasure he brought to my body. When he knew I was satisfied and complete; he began our dance that was as old as time, bringing me to dizzying heights to finally burst into a million stars again.

"Oh, I have missed you, my Robert," I whispered to him as I lay in his arms, totally content.

He kissed the top of my nose, "I am always here, Julia. I will never leave you, no matter what."

I fell asleep in his arms. When I woke the next morning, I didn't know how he had done it without waking me, but Robert had left me to continue to sleep. After Jane had helped me downstairs, I went into the drawing room and asked Marshall, the butler, where Robert was. "Oh, he went out earlier, Your Grace. He didn't say where he was going. There is some post for you, Your Grace."

He carried my post in on a silver salver. It was the only piece of post for me. Sometimes, we had several invitations, but recently, they had died off. I wasn't particularly bothered, as I still didn't feel up to going out as much as I would have liked. I was waiting to be fully recovered before attending the balls again.

I didn't recognise the writing, and my brows creased together, puzzled at who it could be from. I opened it.

Lady Rochester,

You think you are so much better than us now that you have managed to catch yourself a duke, but did he tell you the whole truth about the state he found you in?

I'll wager he did not, but I thought it was only right to tell you the truth about the state he and others found you in.

Besides being drugged up and emaciated, did they tell you that your room was disgusting, a stinking mess that you had made of the room and yourself? Yes, you were filthy, unwashed and stinking of your own bodily excretions because you were so drugged up that you didn't know what you were doing. Very unladylike, Your Grace. I am surprised that your husband ever wanted to touch you again, you filthy stinking...

I couldn't read any more. My hand had gone to cover my mouth in a silent scream. How could he do that? I thought that once the court case was over, I would have nothing more to do with the Trevelgues, but they still had not finished with me yet.

I couldn't even reach for the bell that I usually rang. I just screamed, "Marshall, Marshall."

He came immediately.

"Your Grace?" he asked, practically running into the drawing room, concern etched on his face.

"Are you sure you don't know where his grace has gone?"

"I'm sorry, Your Grace. He just said he would be back later. Is there anything else that I can help you with?"

I couldn't think straight. I felt paralysed. I cringed at the thought of what I must have looked like and froze inside... Then it occurred to me: "Can you get a message to Sir Roger Ellingham to attend me at his earliest convenience, please? Tell him it's important."

"Yes, Your Grace." The butler bowed and left me.

I kept looking at the letter from Mark Trevelgue, tears streaming down my face. What had I done to him to deserve this torment and torture? Hadn't he done enough when he had me imprisoned and when he abducted me? How could one person do and say such terrible things to another person? I didn't know that Jane had come into the room until I felt her arms around me and pulling me against her so that I could bury my head in her shoulder and cry and cry. When I thought that I was all cried out, she held me away from her, "What on earth has happened, Your Grace?" I nodded to the note that I had screwed up and thrown on the side table. "Read that," I told her.

She looked at me as if I had gone mad. A servant never openly reads their employer's mail, I told her. "Go on, Jane."

She picked up the letter, read it, and then looked back at me. Her mouth formed an 'O' of shock. "Oh, Miss Julia," she said, reverting to our close friendship. "Has his grace seen this?"

"No, and Marshall doesn't know where Robert has gone," I told her.

"Oh, you poor thing. Why can't they leave you alone? You've never done anything to them. Haven't they done enough to you?" she cried. "Have you done anything about this?"

"I've asked Sir Roger Ellingham to see me as soon as possible. I didn't know what else to do without Robert here."

"Well, I will stay with you until either Sir Roger or the Duke arrives. You can't be left alone. I'm going to ring for some tea for you."

"Join me for tea, Jane, please," I practically begged her to take tea with me.

"Very well." She picked up the little bell and rang for tea and biscuits for us. When it arrived, Jane served us both and offered me a biscuit, but I couldn't eat anything; otherwise, I felt I couldn't keep it down, but I did drink the tea. It wasn't long before Marshall announced, "Sir Roger Ellingham, Your Grace,"

Sir Roger came over to me, concern etched on his face. "I came over as soon as I received your message, Your Grace. Is something wrong?"

"I—" I started to speak, but I realised that if I did, I would cry again, so I handed him the letter. "I received this this morning."

He took the letter and raised his eyes to me, asking my permission before reading. "May I?" he asked.

I nodded.

I saw the look on his face as he read the note. It was anger and disgust, but I didn't know who his feelings reflected on, Mark Trevelgue or the state that they found me in.

"Oh my God!" he exclaimed, which was very unlike him, then apologised, "Haven't they done enough to you? This continued torture that the Trevelgues keep inflicting on you is like capturing a spider and pulling its legs off one by one to continue the torture. It is sadistic."

"Can you do anything more to him? Obviously, imprisonment for thirty years is not enough."

"I shall need to consult with some colleagues, Your Grace," he said sympathetically.

"He ought to be horse-whipped," Jane said vehemently. "My Lady has always been kind and caring. They started their torture of her when Edwina was alive, and they were both still children."

Jane would never speak out normally, but obviously, there came a time when she could not hold her tongue.

At that moment, Robert returned and burst into the drawing room. Obviously, Marshall had caught him before he came into the room. He looked around and saw Jane sitting beside me, holding my hand, and Sir Roger standing with the offending letter in his hand.

"What is going on, Julia? Why is Jane here and Sir Roger?" I saw not only anger but also confusion on his face. Like me, he obviously thought that with the Trevelgues behind bars, that would be the end of their persecution of me.

Sir Roger handed Robert the letter, "I think you need to read this, Your Grace."

Once again, my tears began to fall, and Jane gathered me to her and crooned to me like I was a child.

Robert read it, and his face changed from the man I knew and loved to some predatory animal. His lips pulled away from his teeth as he snarled. "I should have killed that bastard when I had the chance! Prison is too good for him! What will you do about it, Ellingham?" he challenged our solicitor.

"If I may, I will take this letter with me and show it to the judge who presided over the trial. Can I call on you again, Your Grace, once we have conferred?"

"Yes, but if I don't get something more than just another prison sentence, I shall go over to that prison and take justice into my own hands." Robert all but roared then.

"If you do that, Your Grace, then you will be the next one in prison, and then what would Lady Julia do? She needs your love and support, Your Grace," Sir Roger said, trying to reason with Robert.

I looked at my husband, and I knew that he, at that moment, wanted to commit murder. I must admit that I would have cheered him on if I had felt stronger. I know that I would have liked to hear that Mark Trevelgue would hang; at least he could torture me no more, but luckily for him, I hadn't died. Otherwise, he would have been at the end of the hangman's noose.

Sir Roger left us shortly after that, saying he would let us know the outcome.

When we were alone, Robert scooped me up in his arms and took me to our room, where he gently deposited me on our bed. Robert told Jane that she could go, and he would take care of me. "I think you need to try and rest, darling," he said.

"Where are you going?!" I asked him.

"Just downstairs." I looked at his face and could tell that he was still in a murderous mood.

"You won't take the law into your own hands, Robert, promise me." I held on to his hand to try to make him see reason.

He sat down on the side of the bed and shook his head. "I promise you. Much against my better judgment," he said, taking my hand and kissing my palm.

"Robert," I said from the bed, "Why didn't you tell me?"

"Tell you what, darling?"

"About the state you found me in. What Mark said about me was true, wasn't it?"

"Julia, you were very, very ill. You didn't know what you were doing, darling. Your condition was down to the Trevelgues. It was their actions that had brought you to that state."

"But you picked me up and carried me in the state I was in."

"Why wouldn't I? You are my wife, and I loved... I love you. Julia, I want you to try to forget everything. You are on the road to recovery. Don't let Mark Trevelgue ruin what you have already achieved. Otherwise, he has won, and I am sure that you wouldn't want to give him that satisfaction."

I was quiet for a moment, remembering his smug look as he sat at Moldova Square and said that I wouldn't be a duchess. I remembered his smug look in the court, as if I would ever have been interested in him or his younger brother. I shook my head. Yes, he was right; if I had let Mark Trevelgue get under my skin with his words, he would have won, and I was determined that I would not let him or his family ruin my life anymore.

It turned out that Mark Trevelgue couldn't get a longer or a different sentence since it had already been passed. Sir Roger told Robert that the prison had 'taken things into its own hands', and Mark Trevelgue had been 'dealt with', which would make Mark Trevelgue or, hopefully, any of the Trevelgues think twice before even trying anything like that again.

I presume that Sir Roger had told my husband what had happened to Mark Trevelgue, which had satisfied him, but he never told me. I didn't care what was done as long as I never had any further dealings with him. Jane told me that she heard the word 'birching' regarding Mark Trevelgue, whether this was true or just speculation, I didn't know or care.

Towards the end of the season, I was allowed to ride, but as I had not been on a horse for quite some time, Robert insisted that he accompany me. Lady Mary had given me Star, as she said she did not need her now, and someone had to keep her exercised. I did not realise that Star had such a long memory, but as soon as she saw me, she snuffled my hand for an apple, which I had taken from the kitchens on my way to our stables in Berkley Square. Robert helped me onto Star's side saddle, then sat astride his own horse he called 'Thunder', which I had seen him ride over a year before in Rotten Row.

It felt so good to feel the wind in my face and the warmth of Star's sturdy body beneath me, strong and powerful. We started off slowly, just a gentle walk, and then I urged Star into a trot. Robert called after me to take it steady, with it being my first time on a horse for ages, but I just turned and laughed at him, then touched my heel to Star's side, and we shot forward in a gallop. I knew that Robert's horse was more powerful than Star, so I knew he would soon be able to catch up with me. We tore across the ground, and I laughed aloud at the joy of life that I was beginning to enjoy once more. Robert heard me laughing and laughed along with me as we raced together. I felt wonderful, and I knew that I would never go backwards. I had only forwards to go now.

After Robert had insisted that I rest that afternoon, before we had been invited to a ball at the Hiddleston's house. They had invited nearly two hundred people, but I was the guest of honour. It was to celebrate my return to society. I had had a special dress made by Madam Yvonne, who commented on my slimmer figure. "You must have a whole new wardrobe to suit your slimmer figure, Your Grace." She commented. I told her that I had gained some weight since I had been home, with Mrs Watson's nourishing soups when I was first rescued and the good, wholesome food that followed, also every woman's dream of chocolates and desserts that had been given me recently.

Lady Mary had been guilty of providing many of the boxes of chocolates. Lady Mary had obviously been invited to the ball, and Philomena invited her fiancé, Lord Davenport. Their wedding was only two months away. More than once, when we had been on our own, she had asked me what to expect on her wedding night, but I had just told her what Robert had told me on our wedding night, 'What goes on in the bedroom stays in the bedroom,' so she would have to find it out for herself.

Madam Yvonne had made me a velvet gown that fitted over my breasts in a 'V' shape and cream netting covering my shoulders. She told me that the colour was called eau de nil. I wore the emeralds and diamonds that Robert had bought me from the jeweller, the same morning I received the letter from Mark Trevelgue. Robert was going to give me the set that day. Still, after the setback Mark Trevelgue's letter caused, Robert decided to leave it until we knew what Sir Roger Ellingham had managed to get organised against Mark Trevelgue. I knew Robert had told him to leave him for two minutes with Mark Trevelgue, but Sir Roger had advised him totally against the idea.

When Robert saw me in all my evening finery, his eyes told me that the celebrations would continue once we returned home later that night.

With Robert's permission, Lord Hiddleston was the first to ask me to dance. He told me I had been sadly missed in society and hoped this was a new beginning for me. It felt wonderful to dance again. Robert asked me to dance next, and he flirted with me mercilessly.

Several other gentlemen danced with me, including Lord Waterford, who told me that the London ton had not been the same without me and welcomed me back.

I presume everyone had read the newspapers about what had happened to me, but Lady Mary, Robert, and I had all decided that the past was the past, and we must all put it behind us. Otherwise, the Trevelgues would have won.

It was a wonderful evening. Robert claimed me for several dances, teasing me about all the men who wished to dance with me again, but I knew he was pleased I was so well regarded.

After the ball, we received several invitations to concerts, balls, dinners, and, of course, Philomena's wedding at the end of the year. My life was finally getting back on track again.

In December, after we had been to several balls and musical concerts, which we usually took Lady Mary to as well, we all went to Philomena's wedding to Lord Davenport. Philomena's wedding was lavish; she looked like the typical blushing bride. Robert and I stood and watched her marry Arthur Davenport, who kept looking down at her and probably wondering how had he been so lucky to marry someone such as Philomena when once, he had restricted himself to just sitting on the sidelines at balls, for fear of injuring some young lady with his big feet? I was pleased to see them both looking so happy together. They looked like the typical happy couple. Contentment had filled out Lord Davenport a little so that he no longer looked like the gauche, gangly individual he had been when Philomena and I were first presented. It suited him. I don't know whether he had danced the waltz with Philomena yet; if he had done, she had survived the ordeal very well. Now they were man and wife, and I was so pleased for my niece by marriage. She still occasionally called me Aunt Julia, but it was always said in a jocular way.

But Edwina's marriage made me realise that, with everything that had gone on when I had been kidnapped, I had forgotten what my own wedding day was like. The Trevelgues had so much to answer for!

In May of 1851, the Queen and Prince Albert opened the Great Exhibition. It was estimated that over six million people would visit the site in Hyde Park. There were over 100,000 exhibits from all over the world. The exhibition hall had been dubbed the Crystal Palace, as it was all made of glass. At the main entrance to the exhibitions, you were greeted by a massive pink glass fountain that was twenty-seven feet high. The exhibition hall was like a great, oversized greenhouse, filled with living trees and plants, and on display were guns, lace, pottery, tapestries, and even Waterford crystal. There were exhibits of steam machinery, adding machines, printing machines, and so many different things of such a diverse variety to please all types: members of the general public, business owners, and Lords and Ladies.

I visited it several times, mainly with my husband, as once was not long enough to see all the exhibits, but I also attended with Philomena, who was now pregnant with her first child. We looked at totally different exhibits than I did with Robert. Each time we went, we looked at different things. When I was with Robert, we looked at steam engines, printing machines, and farming machinery; there was even an exhibit of a bicycle, which Robert said would soon come into fashion to enable people to get from A to B quickly and at a reasonable cost. He said that many things that would be shown at the Exhibition, would become part of our daily lives in the months and years to come. Farming implements would make the lives of farmers easier, and adding machines would make the lives of anyone who needed to use mathematics, such as accountants or bank clerks.

It was interesting to see things from all around the world. Robert and I spent a great deal of time discussing these exhibits and seeing if or how they could be used in our everyday lives. When I was with Philomena, we would look at 'fol-de-rolls', as Robert called them. Perfumes, fans, jewellery, silks from the Far East, all things to enhance a woman's beauty. The Great Exhibition was accessible financially to anyone, from the moneyed aristocracy right down to the man in the streets. There were places where people could eat, and they even had water closets for the people to use, as you could spend hours walking around the exhibition halls. At some time or another, we needed to use the toilet facilities. These amenities were being charged at one penny. Hence, the saying, 'to spend a penny' originated from. Among the exhibits, the one that gathered a lot of interest was said to be the largest diamond in the world, the Koh-i-Nohr diamond, which was eventually incorporated into the crown of the British Monarchy.

In the New Year of 1852, I received a letter from Mrs Trevelgue. Robert asked me if I would visit her as she had requested. I was in two minds about it. Part of me wanted to go because I still thought that if it hadn't been for her, I would not have received the education that I had at Seaward Manor. I wouldn't have ended up at Lady Mary's, been presented at court, or met and married Robert, but I wanted to know why she did the other things later. I needed to know. Robert wasn't very happy about my decision and let me know in no uncertain terms that he wasn't happy, but I told him that it was something that I felt I had to do. He knew me well enough by then not to argue with me once I had made up my mind, so he just nodded and told me that he would be waiting for my return. He told me to take Jane with me, but after all that had happened to me, Jane was sure to follow wherever I went, anyway.

I was a lot stronger now. Jane and I took the carriage to the women's prison and said that I was there to visit Mrs Trevelgue. Jane would not let me go anywhere alone these days.

The room they took me to see Mrs Trevelgue reminded me of the cell I had spent over two weeks in when I had been accused of killing her daughter. Now, the tables were turned. The woman that they brought out looked nothing like the woman I had grown up with. This woman looked older than her mother. Gone was her beautiful blonde hair, always so well groomed. Gone were her beautifully manicured and cared-for hands. She looked like life had beaten her. She was bowed, in a scruffy, dirty dress, and I felt I could cry for her. The other part of me was not exactly laughing, but I did get a feeling of poetic justice, which had been meted out to her.

I had taken special care with my dress. I wanted her to see that I had bounced back, no matter what had happened or what she and her sons had done.

I sat down on one side of a wooden table, and she sat the other while a large female warden stood in the corner and looked on. Jane remained out in the hallway waiting for me.

For a while, I just sat and looked at her. I did not know what to say. I had practised my speech dozens of times, but now that I was face to face with her, I had no idea what to say to this woman.

"You look better, Julia, than you did at the court hearing," Mrs Trevelgue told me.

"I am Lady Julia, as you well know," I pointed out to her, my voice did not tremble with the fear and anger that I felt inside.

"I am sorry, Your Grace, force of habit," she said.

"What did I ever do to you to warrant you or your son's actions towards me?" I asked her. I had a tight knot of anger in my stomach, but I would be damned to let her know how I felt.

"You were alive," she said. Her voice was monotone. Obviously, she still mourned her wayward daughter. Then she said something to me that was quite unexpected.

"Your father was a very handsome man. I met him several times after my husband died to discuss the mines. Your mother had been dead for some years by then," she said, looking at me to see my reaction. "I offered him complete control of all of the mines and an increase in his salary..."

"In return for what?" I asked, knowing that she never did anything without getting something from it.

Mrs Trevelgue shrugged her shoulders. "Come now, Julia. We are both women of the world now. What do you think?"

"You mean you wanted my father to marry you?" I asked. Surely, this wasn't all because my father had refused to marry her.

"Oh no, dear, I would not stoop so low as to marry him, but he was a good-looking man, and my bed had been cold and empty for so long."

I suppose that I should not have been shocked, and I could feel the anger that I had held inside bubbling up.

"Oh, my father wasn't good enough to marry, but good enough to warm your bed?" I took a deep, cleansing breath before I spoke again. "My father was better educated than either of your pathetic sons and, from what Lady Mary has said, certainly better educated than you. Until I met Lady Mary, I never realised how much alike you and Edwina were. You Trevelgue females are all the same," I said, and then it hit me. "You are nothing better than whores," I said with great satisfaction at calling her and her dead daughter that name. "No wonder my father refused your advances. He had better taste and more self-respect."

She laughed, "My dear, where did you learn such language as that, certainly not from my mother?" she said. I could tell by how her face had coloured up that I had hit the nail on the head.

"No, it was from your daughter, actually, after you had dismissed the stable boy, and she wanted to lash out at someone, and that was me. I learned never to get close enough to her so that she could slap, hit, or pinch me, so I tolerated her verbal abuse."

"I also allowed my sons to do what they did to you because you were alive," she said bluntly.

"You mean, whereas Edwina was dead?"

She nodded.

"That was no one's fault but her own. Why should I have suffered for what happened to Edwina? She made my life hell when she was alive, pinching, punching me, verbally abusing me, enticing Mark to physically abuse me, and then she kept Mrs Watson's letters from me, informing me of Gramps. Not just one letter, but all three." I knew that my voice was rising with anger, and I could imagine Lady Mary scolding me and saying, 'Ladies, do not raise their voice, Julia.'

"She was still my daughter."

"But I never did anything to her. I never did anything to you or your sons, yet between the three of you, you had me imprisoned, kidnapped, and drugged until I was at death's door."

"And look at you now." She sneered.

I took another deep breath. "At one time, I thought that I had a lot to thank you for: educating me when my father died, taking me in under your roof, feeding me, and dressing me. I even thanked you for sending me to Lady Mary, but then you...you turned on me. Was it jealousy that Lady Mary took me under her wing, and I married a duke?"

"I suppose so. Even if I had married the man I had been engaged to, he was only an earl."

"And you eloping with Mr Trevelgue caused an innocent man to take his life; the earl committed suicide because of what you did. It seems to me that for every person whose life you have touched, you have destroyed or tried to destroy. Did you really hate me so much that you wanted me dead?"

"I never expected your life to end as well as it did." Her voice continued without feeling or expression as she answered me.

"It was at your instigation that I went to Lady Mary and was to become a fraud," I said, keeping control of my temper, although I was seething inside.

"I never expected it to turn out as well as it has," she admitted. "I thought that my mother would find out who you were and turn you out on your ear," Mrs Trevelgue said.

"Then you not only misjudged me, but you misjudged your mother, who knew everything you got up to in Cornwall," I told her with great satisfaction. "Then, you turned on me because I made something of myself and married a Duke. So why did you send me to your mother? This was all your own making. Is that why you tried to murder me." I could feel my anger welling inside of me. I wanted to scream and shout and pull her rattail hair and slap her face. I had never known such anger, even at Edwina.

"I asked my mother to come and visit me, but she didn't. Did you know that?"

I smiled at her, and my heart was full of malice, "Yes, she told me. She said that if it had just been the fact that you had eloped with Mr Trevelgue, she might have finally given in. She had even been prepared to forgive you and maybe leave you her money, but after what you and your sons have done to me, there is no hope in hell that she will do it now, and whose fault is it, Mrs Trevelgue? You have no one but yourself to blame." I emphasised. "You once told me that maybe if you had been a different sort of mother to your children, they might not have turned out the way they did, but Edwina was so like her mother, even to the part of running away with the stable boy. Now here you are sitting in prison for what you did to me and for no real reason, apart from jealousy of a situation that you had instigated in the first place." I couldn't say anymore. I stood up and walked away, then I turned back to her, "Think about what I have said, Mrs Trevelgue. YOU have brought about everything that has happened to you. YOUR incarceration in here is all your own fault." Then I walked away. I heard her call my name, but I ignored it and walked away from her with my head held high. I would not let her know how my heart was banging against my ribs in fear and frustration, but most of all, I would not let her know that she had got under my skin. I would not let her or her sons win.

Jane walked back to the carriage with me, not saying a word. She could see my state—it was pent-up anger, pure and simple.

When I got home, Robert was reading the newspaper in the drawing room.

He looked up at me as I sat down and rang the bell for tea.

"Well, how did it go?" he asked me.

"When you boxed, what did you practice hitting?" I asked, not answering his question.

"Oh, as bad as that, eh?" he closed his newspaper and folded it before setting it down on one of the tables.

"I asked her why she did what she did to me, and you know what she said? 'You are alive,' as if it was my fault that Edwina was running off with the stable boy before she died! I told her like mother, like daughter. Apparently, she also tried to get my father in bed with her, but he refused. I thought she wanted him to marry her, but my father wasn't good enough to marry, just good enough to warm her bed. I told her that my father had more self-respect and was better educated than any of her family. Oh, Robert, I am not a vicious or even an angry person normally, but in that meeting, I could have willingly lashed out at her, screamed at her, even punched her!" I took a deep breath, "I did take satisfaction in calling her a whore like her daughter."

I looked at my husband and he was laughing. "Julia Beaumont, I didn't even know that you knew such words."

"I learnt from her daughter," I told him.

He laughed again at me and kissed my hand, "My little pugilist. So, do you wish you had not gone now?"

"Are you going to say, 'I told you so?'" I asked him.

"No darling, I would never do that. I think that you needed to do it."

"She was no longer the attractively dressed woman with her golden hair and beautifully manicured nails. She looked older than Lady Mary and cowed down. She was even jealous that I had managed to attract and marry a duke. I told her that she had the chance to marry an earl, thrown it all away, and eloped with a mine owner, but of course he wasn't a duke. I told her that she had no one but herself to blame. I think the visit has made me stronger because of everything that she and her sons did over a period of time. I am the one that has prevailed. I am the one to have my freedom, whereas she and her sons are in prison."

"Bravo, darling. I hope you told her so."

"I did, and then some," I said, grinning.

Neither Mrs Trevelgue nor her children had succeeded in destroying me; in fact, I was the one to come through it all victoriously.

Chapter Nineteen

Although I had my season over three years ago, now that I was back to my old self, Robert wanted to grant my wish of riding and dancing again, so we stayed in London for the season. I spent a great deal of time with Lady Mary, but she seemed to be getting frail. I think all the stress from the trial and raking up the past had unfortunately taken its toll on her. I don't think it was anything physical but emotional, and I was concerned about her. She meant the world to me. She was like the mother I never knew and the grandmother I never knew. I wanted to do something for her, to give her something to live for again. I had talked to Robert about her and hoped we could devise a solution between us. I knew of one thing that would give her something to live for, but so far, no matter how hard we tried, I had not conceived a child, and I was beginning to wonder whether the drugs given me by the Trevelgues might have sterilised me. Unknown to Robert, I had visited the doctor, who assured me that he would keep my visit strictly confidential, and secondly, he could see no reason why I couldn't conceive.

"The longer it takes for you to conceive, Lady Rochester, the stronger your body will become, and obviously, the less likely the drugs that you were given will affect the baby. In the meantime, eat healthily and get plenty of exercise."

Jane had come with me to see the doctor, and I had warned her not to tell a soul of the visit. "Yes, Your Grace," she said. After all that we had been through, I trusted Jane with my life. She was the perfect Lady's maid and the best friend I could have ever wished for, well, for me anyway. Whenever we came into the city, we would always call into one of the tea shops scattered around the city. It was our little treat.

The sight of my husband still had that heart-flipping effect on me that he had done when we had first met. How could I describe this feeling in my breast that I got every time I looked at Robert? It was obviously love, but it was also much more. I owed him my freedom and my life. Whenever I saw him walking towards me, it felt like my heart somersaulted in my breast, and I became breathless. When we danced together, I felt so light, lighter than air, as I danced in his arms. When we made love, it was not just in an effort to make a baby, but as proof of our love for one another; I felt like I was touching the heavens. Would I ever get over this absolute euphoria that I had whenever my Robert was near? I hoped not. Robert always teased me, saying that practising making a baby was fun, to which I agreed, but I longed for that moment when a life within me quickened. I am ashamed to admit that I was envious of Philomena, who was pregnant with her 'honeymoon baby'. Would I ever feel life within my body because of what the Trevelgues had done to me?

It was the season that I re-entered society after forced imprisonment, drug abuse and rehabilitation by weaning my body from the drugs. It was a wonderful time for me, all the social events of balls, concerts, dinners, riding, boating on lakes, and picnics. It seemed that it had made up for lost time, and every night, I was wrapped in the arms of the man I love, and I felt nearly complete. Robert was everything that I could wish for and everything that I wanted in my husband.

A few days before our wedding anniversary, I woke feeling nauseous, but it left me after a short time. I thought nothing of it and got up.

Jane would dress me for riding a week later, as I had intended, but then, I decided against it. "How about we go into the city, Jane, and look in the shops, then visit a tearoom?"

"I thought you wanted to go riding Your Grace?" Jane said as she returned my riding habit to the wardrobe.

"I did, but I thought of going to Madam Yvonne's for a new gown for my wedding anniversary and getting an emerald pin for the duke's cravat as an anniversary present."

"You are up to something, aren't you?" Jane said with a knowing glint in her eye.

I looked at her innocently, "I don't know what you mean?" I told her, but Jane knew me so well.

"When was the last time you bled, Your Grace?" she asked me.

"Oh, you know me, Jane, since the drugs, I have not been regular," I told her.

"That did not answer my question." She persisted.

"I think it was just after Easter," I finally admitted.

"Then do you think..."

"I dare not even think. I need to keep busy; keep occupied."

"And when were you going to tell me?" she asked.

I shrugged my shoulders.

"When are you going to see the doctor?" Jane asked me as she styled my hair.

"I have an appointment to see him at his premises this afternoon at three."

"Does the duke know?"

"No. I don't want to build up his hopes; I have missed a couple of months before."

"But that was when you still had the drugs inside your body. Over twelve months ago. Well, you are not going on your own to see the doctor. I shall go with you," she told me, brokering no argument with me.

"You are getting too clever, Jane," I teased her.

"You think you are as well, Your Grace, but I have seen that look on your face."

"What look?"

"That look tells me you have a secret," she persisted.

I gave a weary sigh. I could not keep anything from my maid and my best friend. "I woke up feeling a little nauseous a few days ago, but it soon disappeared, and I have felt well since then."

"I noticed that your breasts seemed…"

"Yes, but they also get tender when I am due to bleed," I interrupted her.

"But you know?"

"I suspect, going by what Philomena has told me." I finally gave in. "Don't you go saying a word…to anyone, Jane," I warned her. "No one must know until the doctor confirms it, and I have told the duke."

"Yes, Your Grace," she grinned at me. "Shall I order the carriage for you?"

"No, I think a nice walk will do us a world of good, and also, if we took the carriage, the coachman might talk."

It was a beautiful sunny day outside. The birds were singing for the glory of life, and the summer flowers were out in bloom, their perfume a heady scent as we made our way to the Modiste. I felt healthier than I had for a long time. Whether it was just the beautiful day or the beautiful secret I hoped that I held within me, I didn't know, but it was a joy to be alive.

When we reached Madam Yvonne's, even she commented on how well I looked. As usual, she measured me and looked surprised, "You have filled out a little since I last measured you, Your Grace."

I looked at her in shock. "It must be all the good food I am eating. The duke insists on me still eating well and building my strength."

"It is every woman's wish to be able to eat what she likes," the modiste commented with a smile.

"Lady Mary is one of the guilty parties," I told Madam Yvonne. "Whenever she comes to visit, she always brings me chocolates."

"Oh heavens," Madam Yvonne said, laughing.

We discussed styles and then moved on to materials. Madame Yvonne showed me silk in the colour of butter. "That colour would not suit many women, but with you, it brings out the colour of your eyes, Your Grace," I remembered that she always commented on my eyes. "They seem to be even a deeper shade of emerald today," she told me, "Even your skin seems to be glowing with good health. It does me good to see you looking so healthy after such a long time, Lady Julia, like the first time I set my eyes upon you in the company of Lady Mary."

I told Madam Yvonne that Robert and I were holding a dinner party on our wedding anniversary, so I would need the gown for then. She told me that with the use of the new sewing machines, operated by a treadle, which she had bought from the Great Exhibition at Crystal Palace, she could see no problem with that. "The great exhibition did a lot for British industry, even for modistes," she told me. "I don't know how we ever managed before," she said as Jane, and I were about to leave her shop.

Jane and I found a little tea shop near Harley Street, where my doctor practised. We sat in the shop and ordered tea, sandwiches, and cakes.

We arrived at the doctor's earlier than my appointment, but I was impatient to find out if I was finally pregnant. I had waited so long for this day to come.

Sir Geoffrey Armitage, our family doctor in London, came out of his office when he heard that I had arrived. He looked to be in his forties or early fifties. He was medium height, with a little excess weight around his middle. Obviously, he lived well with his success as a doctor to many of the ton. He had brown eyes, and his blond hair was peppered with white, which made him look older than his years. As his position was well known among the ton, he could afford to live and dress well.

"Lady Rochester, you are early," he stated upon seeing me.

"I'm sorry, Sir Geoffrey, am I too early?"

"No, of course not. Please come in." Then he nodded at Jane before following us into his office, shutting the door behind us.

After we were both seated and Jane stood behind my chair, he asked me, "How can I help you today, Your Grace?"

I told him my symptoms as precisely as I could.

"You suspect that you might be pregnant, Lady Julia?"

I nodded. He asked me several questions, which I answered, and then asked if he could examine me. I nodded.

He asked Jane to help me undress for his examination, and then I climbed onto his dark red leather couch.

He began prodding and poking me, then said apologetically that he needed to do an internal examination.

Once he had fully examined me, he told Jane that I could get dressed again and went to sit down at his large mahogany desk to wait for me.

Once Jane helped dress me, I went over and sat down again at his desk while Jane stood behind my chair again. My heart was racing with anticipation of his diagnosis.

He smiled at me. "Well, Your Grace, it is as you suspected, you have finally conceived." He looked at me, "Because of your past medical history of the drugs, you must be careful. I don't think it will happen, as your body has been free of the drugs for well over a year now, but there is still a possibility of a miscarriage. We are not exactly sure what the drugs might have done permanently to your body, which was why we advised you to wait to conceive. I shall be keeping a regular close check on you, and if you get any bleeding or pains in your stomach, you must send for me immediately. Exercise in moderation, no riding that beautiful horse of yours, plenty of good food, and rest as well. I shall see you in a month's time, but if you have any worries, my door is always open. Does the duke know what you have suspected?" he asked me as he stood to see us out.

"No. It is our wedding anniversary shortly. I want to tell him then."

"Well, remember what I have said, and I will see you in a month's time. From my calculations, I would say that you are already three months along with your pregnancy, Your Grace. My heartiest congratulations." He took my hand and kissed it. I thanked him and Jane and I left for the jewellers to get Robert's cravat pin. Jane couldn't stop grinning.

"Anyone would think it was you that all of this was referring to," I told her as we crossed the street to the jewellers.

"I get all of the pleasure and none of the pain," she said, grinning cheekily at me.

"So, you will be there at the birth?" I teased her.

That dampened her enthusiasm, and I laughed. "Don't worry, Jane, I don't expect you to be, and I would not expect you to be."

"But isn't that part of my duties?" she said, but her face blanched somewhat.

"Not if I say they are not," I told her.

After we had bought Robert's emerald cravat pin from the jewellers from whom Robert had bought my engagement ring, Jane and I returned home.

On the morning of our anniversary, Robert and I had breakfast together in the small dining room. I placed the little jewellery box beside his plate, and beside mine was a set of books by Homer. Robert knew I had enjoyed reading the Iliad while living with Lady Mary.

"Open your gift from me first, Robert," I told him.

He looked across the table at me and said, "Julia, I don't need any gifts from you; just that you are alive is enough for me."

"There are two gifts from me," I told him.

He had begun to open the jeweller's box with his cravat pin in. "Oh, Julia, that is beautiful. Whenever I wear it, I will always think of your eyes. Thank you, darling."

"I have another gift for you, but you won't see it for a while," I told him. I couldn't help but grin.

He looked at me in question. "I won't be able to see it for a while?" he asked me, confused.

"Am I thinking what I think I am thinking?" he said, a grin beginning to spread across his face.

"Robert, that is absolute 'gobbledy gook'." I laughed at him.

"Lady Julia, for a lady as well educated as yourself, can't you manage better English than 'gobbledy gook'?" he grinned.

"Have you guessed what your other present is?" I felt ready to burst with excitement.

"Right, no 'gobbledy gook'. Has our practising finally managed to allow you to conceive?" he asked me, taking my hand across the breakfast table and squeezing it.

I nodded, grinning from ear to ear. "Yes, the doctor has confirmed it but has told me that I need to be careful now, no horse riding or strenuous exercise."

He got up from his seat, picked me up, and swung me around. "You have made me the happiest of men." He kissed me and kissed me. "I must admit that I was beginning to wonder if all the drugs had damaged you permanently. It wouldn't have mattered to me if we never became parents, but you have made me happy, and I will ensure you are well taken care of, especially now."

"I don't want to become an invalid again, Robert. Other women have babies and don't become invalids," I told him.

"Yes, darling, but they have not nearly lost their lives through drugs."

"I feel better than I have for years," I told him.

"Even so, you are carrying a very precious cargo."

"Yes, Your Grace." I grinned.

I told him that I wanted to tell Lady Mary and also Philomena.

After breakfast, Jane and I took the carriage to Lady Mary's. When we arrived, I was surprised to see her looking so upset. All thoughts of my good news fled my mind as I knelt before her and took her hands in mine.

"Lady Mary, what on earth is wrong? Are you ill?" I asked her, greatly concerned by her demeanour.

She shook her head and handed me a letter. "Read that, Julia, please."

I read the letter from her daughter, Mrs Trevelgue, begging her to come and visit her, as she had something important to tell her mother.

"Are you going to see her this time, Ma'am?" I asked Lady Mary, sitting next to her, and handed the letter back.

Lady Mary nodded, "Would you come with me, Julia? I don't think that I can face her alone."

I told her I would go with her if she wanted.

"I have a bad feeling about this, Julia," she told me.

"Well, we will face it together. You know I will always help you in any way I can."

I couldn't tell her about my good news at that moment, so we arranged to go to the prison to see her daughter.

When I saw Mrs Trevelgue before, I thought she looked bad, but this time, she looked worse and was ill.

Mrs Trevelgue looked taken aback when she saw I was with her mother. Lady Mary had that stoic look about her, which Mrs Trevelgue had once told me about. I knew that Lady Mary was steeling herself for this meeting, and she was finding it very hard to face her daughter after ignoring her previous notes.

"I asked the duchess to accompany me before you say anything. We have no secrets."

"Ah yes, your replacement granddaughter," Mrs Trevelgue said acidly.

"And who's fault was that?" Lady Mary said accusingly.

"Yes, very well, mother," she said, sighing. "I asked you to visit me because I have something to tell you."

"Well, what is it?" Lady Mary asked.

She was very mistaken if Mrs Trevelgue expected this to be an easy meeting. Lady Mary was not going to make it easy for her daughter.

"I have not been well recently. They called the doctor to me," Mrs Trevelgue said, always looking at her mother.

"Oh?"

"Mother, can we forget the past? I have been told that I have a tumour in my stomach."

Lady Mary's face went white. "What are they doing about it?"

Mrs Trevelgue shook her head. "They can do nothing about it. Mother, I am dying!" she cried.

Even I felt sad for her. Lady Mary looked ill.

"They have told me that it is only a matter of months," Mrs Trevelgue said, pausing to see the effect on her mother. "Mother, please, can I come home and at least die in comfort? It is terrible here." Mrs Trevelgue began to cry. I had only ever seen her cry once, which was when Edwina died, and it broke my heart to see this woman who had done so much for me before her daughter's death, regardless of our last meeting.

"Will they allow that when you still have so many years of your sentence left?" Lady Mary asked, taking a handkerchief and dabbing her eyes.

"You could persuade them, Mother," Mrs Trevelgue said, pleading with Lady Mary.

I thought I should leave mother and daughter alone, so I excused myself and entered the hallway.

"Excuse me, Ma'am. Aren't you the Duchess of Rochester who was in the court case against Mrs Trevelgue? You have visited her before." It was the big female warden that I had seen with Mrs Trevelgue on my previous visit.

"Yes, that is correct. Can you tell me the name of the doctor who diagnosed Mrs Trevelgue?" I asked her.

"I'm sorry, Ma'am, what doctor?" asked the female warden in confusion.

I was confused now. "The doctor that diagnosed Mrs Trevelgue's tumour."

"A tumour? Was she diagnosed with that before the court case, Lady Rochester? Only there is no record of it in her notes when she was brought here."

"I thought that she had been diagnosed recently in here. That was why she asked her mother to come and see her."

The warden shook her head. "She has not had a doctor here, Lady Rochester."

My brows drew together, "I don't understand. She has told Lady Mary and me that she is dying."

The warden snorted, "Oh, she is coming up with that story now? She has been coming up with all sorts of excuses to get out of work here. She should have been on the stage, that one."

"Are you absolutely positive?" I asked her, my anger at Mrs Trevelgue growing even more when I thought of her lying to her elderly mother.

"Yes, Ma'am, she has been under my supervision since she arrived. You came to see her not too long ago, didn't you?"

"I did, but she never mentioned anything then, feeling unwell or anything," I agreed.

The warden shrugged, "There you go then. She is a liar. She will do or say anything to get out of her prison sentence. I've seen it all in here, Ma'am."

I was stunned.

"Could I ask you a favour?" I said once I had thought the situation through.

"If I can help, Ma'am," The female warden said obligingly.

"Could you please ask Lady Mary to attend to me out here and then tell her what you have told me?"

The warden nodded and went straight in to speak to Lady Mary. I was so angry with Mrs Trevelgue.

Lady Mary came bustling out. I could tell that she had been crying. No matter what else, Mrs Trevelgue was her daughter.

The large lady warden spoke when she had Lady Mary in front of her. "Ma'am, I understand that Mrs Trevelgue has told you that she has been diagnosed with a tumour?"

Lady Mary nodded and wiped her eyes. "How long does she have? Did the doctor say?"

I took Lady Mary's hand in mine and found that I was doing what Robert often did to me, using my thumb to gently rub the back of her hand.

The lady warden looked uncomfortable about telling this old lady the news. "Ma'am, I am afraid that you have been lied to. Your daughter has had no visit from a doctor and certainly not been diagnosed with a tumour."

Lady Mary stumbled. Luckily, I was able to get behind her before she fell. I led her over to a chair and helped her sit down.

"Are you sure? There could have been a visit while you were off duty," Lady Mary said, hoping that her daughter was not lying to her.

"No, Ma'am. All visitors are logged into a book, so it would have been logged even if she had seen someone when I was not here. Lady Rochester was the last person to visit some time ago. I am afraid your daughter is lying to you, Ma'am," said the big lady warden.

Lady Mary looked at me. The look of pure hatred that showed on her face was one I had never seen since I had met her, even when I told her that I wasn't her granddaughter.

"I am so sorry, Lady Mary," I told her.

She took a deep breath and stood up. "I think my business here is concluded, Julia. Shall we go?"

I nodded and offered her my arm. Before we left, she turned to the warden and said, "Thank you for telling me. Tell her that she will never see me again."

Lady Mary took my arm, and with her head held high, she walked out of the prison with me.

When we were in the carriage, she looked at me. "I thought I knew everything she could do, but this takes the biscuit. How could she, Julia?"

I shook my head. I wondered if she was going to use the same ploy the first time she had asked her mother to visit her.

"If I had gone back into that room, I think that I might have slapped her face. Maybe I should have done that when she was a child. What did I do to have a daughter like that? I used to think I was a good mother, but I must have done something wrong with her. Her brother, Duncan, has never given me cause for concern."

"I am so terribly sorry, Lady Mary," I said.

She patted my hand that was holding hers, "You were not to know, dear. Even if she were dying now, I wouldn't believe her. I... I... I am lost for words," she cried exasperated.

"You are not a bad mother, Lady Mary," I assured her.

"Hmm, I am not so sure."

"Your son is proof, and me," I told her.

She patted my hand again. "Thank you, my dear. I am glad that I asked you to come with me. You turned up at the right time." She thought for a while, "Why did you call on me, my dear?" she asked.

"Oh, that can wait for another day," I told her. I thought she had had enough to cope with for one day.

"No, go on, dear, why did you call on me?" She insisted.

"Well, it is good news that I wanted to tell you," I said, reluctant to say any more for the time being.

"After my day, I could do with some good news, dear."

"Well, fingers crossed, there will be another Rochester in about six months' time," I told her.

The worry that had creased her brows only moments before seemed to disappear. "A baby, at last? Oh, Julia, I am so pleased for you and the duke."

"The doctor has told me that I must take it easy, as there could be the risk of miscarriage. They don't know if the drugs might still have adverse effects, so that is why I must take it easy. No horse riding, no strenuous exercise."

"And I am sure that Robert will ensure that you abide by the doctor's instructions to the letter. I should imagine he is delighted."

"But just when he has got me back to normal, I am going to bloat up like a balloon, and he will go off me." I had tried hard not to cry, but suddenly, I could not hold the sobs back.

"Now, now, my dear," Lady Mary said, patting my hand. "It is just the baby talking. Robert would love you no matter what. All newly pregnant women get tearful during the first stages of their pregnancy. We cry for the silliest reasons, but it goes away, and then we have dreams where our babies are crying, and we forget about them. These are all sorts of strange ideas, but they are as common as morning sickness and other minor ailments. Speaking of morning sickness?"

"I felt a little nauseous a while ago but have felt really well since then."

"Oh, I am so glad, Julia. After what happened today, that is the best news I have heard."

I was going to call on Philomena after I had dropped Lady Mary off at home, but I wanted to get back to Robert and tell him the depths that Mrs Trevelgue has now stooped to.

When I got to Berkley Square, Robert was in his study, dealing with accounts. He looked up when I opened the door. "How was Lady Mary?"

"Ah well, therein lies an unbelievable story," I said as I sat down opposite him.

"Do tell. I am intrigued." my husband said, the twin dimples coming on either side of his mouth.

When I had told the story of Mrs Trevelgue and her mother, he looked astounded. "Will that woman stop at nothing to get what she wants?"

"Obviously not," I said.

"So, she doesn't know about the baby?" he asked me, resting back in his chair.

"No, I told her, and she was delighted. Afterwards, she told me everything to expect in pregnancy."

"Oh dear."

"It doesn't happen to all expectant women, does it?" I asked my husband.

"Darling, I am the last person to ask. I am just a man. My mother, Philomena, or her mother could tell you, or you could wait and see. You should be happy that you are having a baby and deal with things if and when they happen. They can't be that bad; otherwise, there would only be one child families." He laughed at my concerned face. "Go and see Philomena; she only has a couple of months before she has the baby. Go and ask her to put your mind at rest."

I leaned over and kissed him, then told him to get on with his accounts.

"Slave driver." He grinned at me.

Chapter Twenty

I went and saw Philomena to tell her my good news; she flung her arms around me and laughed, "Oh, they will grow up together, Julia. That is wonderful news," she said as she tried to get close to me to hug me, but her 'bump' prevented that. "Have you had morning sickness?" she asked me.

I shook my head, "Not really. I felt a bit nauseous, but that departed within a few minutes, and since then, I have been feeling very well. What else can I expect in my pregnancy? I have been a bit emotional, and Lady Mary said that is due to the baby, so I was just wondering what else I can expect."

Philomena eased herself down on the sofa and pulled me down with her. "Apart from being blown up like an elephant?" she sighed, "I suppose I could tell you what you told me when I asked about the wedding night..." She looked at me and grinned, "But I won't. I had morning sickness, and I got a bit tearful in the early months, but since then... I have felt fine. Was the doctor worried about you after the drugs and everything?"

I told her that he said that I should take things easy as there could be a possibility of miscarriage.

"In that case, Julia, Aunt Julia," she grinned at me, "you must do as he says. I am sure that Uncle Robert will wrap you up in cotton wool until the baby comes." She hugged me to her. "I am so pleased for you. We all worried that the drugs might have had a lasting effect on you."

I then told her what had happened between Lady Mary and her daughter. "Why that despicable woman! What decent woman would do that to her mother, who is getting on in age? Mind you, nothing should surprise me after what she did to you," Philomena said, appalled at the events.

I told her that Lady Mary said she wouldn't go and see her again, even if she was dying.

"I can't blame her," Philomena said in disgust.

"When I lived with Mrs Trevelgue, she told me that Lady Mary was hard and a harridan, but she has never been that way with me. Lady Mary has always been very kind to me."

"Maybe you were like the daughter she never had, Julia."

I then changed the subject back to babies. We spent a happy half-hour together talking about babies, husbands, families, and baby names, and then I stood up and told her that I should return to my husband, who would wonder where I was.

"I suppose after what had happened before, Uncle Robert is loath to let you out of sight for long. Now you are carrying what might be the heir to the Rochester dukedom, and he will be keeping a close eye on you."

Philomena kissed my cheek, and I left to return to Berkley Square to prepare for our wedding Anniversary celebrations.

When I got home, I asked Jane to prepare a bath for me. I lay back in the beautiful, hot, scented bathwater, thinking of Mrs Trevelgue. She was despicable for what she had tried to do to her mother, not caring that her mother was an elderly lady and how such news would affect her. I was just glad that I left when I did to speak to the female warden and found out to what lengths Mrs Trevelgue would go to get out of her prison sentence. I knew that prison was a terrible place; again, I had witnessed it, thanks to her son, but now she was on her own and good riddance.

Jane helped me out of the bath and then stood ready to wrap me in a thick, fluffy towel. I sat in front of the fire in my bedroom as she dried and brushed my hair, ready for the coming evening.

There would be a small party of about a dozen guests, including Lady Mary, Lady Virginia, Philomena's parents, and, of course, Philomena and Lord Davenport. Robert used this opportunity to tell them our good news, although Lady Mary and Philomena already knew it. It was a wonderful evening, full of happiness and love from the people we knew and cared about.

Two months later, Philomena gave birth to a little girl whom they named Daphne. She told me the next one must be a boy to carry on the family title.

"Hasn't that put you off having more children, knowing what to expect the next time?" I asked her.

Philomena smiled at me as she held her daughter in her arms, "No. As soon as they place that little baby in your arms, you forget about the pains of labour."

"I am receiving regular visits by my doctor to make sure that my pregnancy continues as normal and that I and our baby are both healthy," I told Philomena, "Robert feels the first real movements of our baby and is ecstatic. He tells me that our son is a little fighter like his father. I pointed out that it could be a daughter, and he grinned at me. 'In that case, our daughter will be a fighter like her mother.'

Philomena laughed.

"Throughout my pregnancy, Robert has been wonderful, caring, and loving. I asked him if my burgeoning waist did not put him off, but he just smiled at me adoringly and kissed my nose," I told her.

"And that is as it should be, Julia. We are providing them with the next heir to the title," she said, typically Philomena.

Lord Davenport, once the tall, gangly individual that had nearly crippled me on the dancefloor, had gained some weight and, I also think, some self-confidence since becoming a husband and a father. He stood next to his wife and baby, looking proudly on. I was so pleased for the family.

I hated to tell people, but in the months leading up to the birth, I started having dreams, well, nightmares actually. My mother had died giving birth to me, and I kept dreaming that I was subject to the same fate. I couldn't tell my husband; he had suffered enough of my ailments from the drug abuse; I couldn't subject him to my nightmares. He would think that I was losing my mind. So, the nightmares of my impending death I kept to myself, trying all the time to be the happy, carefree person they all remembered from before my debut. But my health suffered. I wasn't eating as well as I had at the start of my pregnancy, and I wasn't sleeping as well, worried that more nightmares of impending doom might plague me. Jane commented as she was dressing me one day, and Robert also mentioned that I had lost that 'glow' from the early days of my pregnancy, so I just explained it away with the pregnancy.

When I saw Sir Geoffrey for another of my check-ups, he also commented. "Lady Julia, you are looking tired. Are you eating well and taking plenty of rest?"

I nodded.

"Is there something on your mind?"

"I suppose with the birth nearer, I am thinking about my mother."

He sat behind his desk and steepled his fingers, "Your mother, Lady Julia?"

"She died giving birth to me."

"You are worried that the same might happen to you?"

I couldn't speak for fear of breaking down before him, so I just nodded.

"Lady Julia, medicine has advanced in the last twenty years. I am sure that you have nothing to worry about. Now, you are a fit and healthy young woman. I have examined you and don't foresee any problems for either you or the baby. Your pregnancy seems to be going according to the textbooks. You need have no worries, I promise you."

I left his office feeling better, but it didn't stop the nightmares.

It was only about a month before our baby was due to be born when I learnt that Lady Mary had received a letter from the prison, not from her daughter, as before, but about her daughter. She sent me a message to attend to her as soon as possible. I took our carriage to Moldova Square and entered the drawing room to find her holding the letter. She looked pale and weary.

"Lady Mary, what is wrong?" I cried as soon as I saw her.

She handed me the letter, which told her that her daughter, Mrs Joy Mary Trevelgue, was found hanging in her cell. I felt tears come to my eyes, but I knew that I needed to stay strong for her. I put my arm comfortingly around her shoulders, and she cried. I was not surprised at her grief; after all, she was still Lady Mary's daughter, and like Mrs Trevelgue was with Edwina, no mother should outlive her child.

I told her I was so sorry and that she was still Lady Mary's daughter no matter what Mrs Trevelgue had done.

The prison asked Lady Mary if she wanted the body of her daughter for burial, and Lady Mary told me that she didn't know what to do. I had never seen her uncertain. She had always been so stoic and positive about the path she should tread. That, in itself, worried me.

"Lady Mary, she was still your daughter. Now that her life is over, it is the last thing you can do for her."

Lady Mary took my hand, "I knew I could rely on you for good counsel, my dear Julia. Thank you for coming so swiftly to me when your time is so near."

"I will always be here for you, Lady Mary," I told her.

I asked her if she wanted to organise the funeral, or I offered to do it for her. She lifted her head. "I can't ask you to do that after all she and her sons have put you through."

"I still remember her and how kind she was to me when I was a child. The past is in the past. If you would like me to arrange the funeral, I will," I told her that I would do anything to help her.

The funeral was very small. It was just Lady Mary and me, Dorcas, who I imagine would have known Mrs Trevelgue as a young girl, and Jane, who refused to leave my side ever again after what the Trevelgues had done, and we didn't know if the prison would allow her sons to attend.

Robert said he couldn't go as he was still so angry at her sending ransom notes that had him running around all over the country when he could have got to me sooner. He also said that she had taken the coward's way out by committing suicide and causing more grief to her mother. Even Mrs Trevelgue's brother, the Earl of Orkney, did not attend, although he had been informed about his sister's death, but after all his sister had put their mother through, he refused to come. Obviously, Lady Mary had informed him about his sister and what she and her family had done to me.

It was a miserable day for Mrs Trevelgue's funeral. The sky was steel grey and threatening rain. Lady Mary held onto my arm as the vicar spoke. The coffin was a plain wooden box provided by the prison. Lady Mary didn't say anything about the basic coffin; she had not ordered any flowers. "She doesn't deserve any 'niceties' after what she has done." That was all she said. I looked at Lady Mary's face as her daughter was finally lowered into the ground, but her face hadn't changed throughout her daughter's funeral. She had steeled her features throughout the short ceremony as if she had decided that she would not shed another tear for her daughter.

We retired back to Lady Mary's. I was worried about her, but Lady Virginia, who had been staying with the Hiddleston's, had offered to come round and said she would keep Lady Mary company. She told me to go home to Robert and rest, as I was so near my time, although I thought I still had a month to go.

It was a good job that I left Lady Mary when I did, as my waters broke while on the short journey back to Berkley Square. I looked in shock at the puddle on the floor of the carriage. Jane took my hand for the rest of the journey, saying soothing words.

When we arrived at Berkley Square, Jane dashed into the house to tell my husband what was happening. Robert strode down the steps to the carriage. He had been concerned about me and the additional stress of the funeral but didn't expect this. He looked at me, then at the puddle on the carriage floor. Immediately, he scooped me up in his arms and carried me up the steps to our home and upstairs to our bedroom. He sent a footman for Sir Geoffrey Armitage, the doctor, and another back to Lady Mary's. Jane stripped the bed and remade it with clean sheets, helped me undress and get into a clean nightdress, then took my hair down and tied it into a plat.

Lady Mary, Lady Virginia, and Dorcas arrived, with Dorcas taking over. "If there is any blood, Jane won't be any use," Dorcas said, bustling about. Not long after them, the doctor arrived. Robert stayed by my side, holding my hand and rubbing his thumb across my knuckles to comfort me.

I could see Jane standing in the doorway, looking petrified, and I felt so sorry for her. She must have felt that she was letting me down again. I called over to her, "Jane, can you get me a pitcher of water, please, and a flannel?"

She looked at me, pleased that she could at least do something to help me. She came over and used the flannel to wipe my face free of sweat, so she felt useful to me. I thought that as long as I kept her away from 'the business end,' as Gramps called it, she would be all right.

I laboured hard for a few hours with Robert, Dorcas and the doctor encouraging me. Our son was born fit and healthy in the early morning hours. Dorcas cut the baby's cord, then cleaned him and wrapped him up to hand him to me.

Sir Geoffrey looked at me. "Lady Julia, that was a perfect birth. Considering everything you have been through, it turned out a lot better than I could have hoped, and with the help of your two maids and your husband, I was surplus to requirements. You probably would be able to manage without me next time."

Robert shook his hand and thanked him. Our son had a lusty pair of lungs on him and cried. Lady Mary and Lady Virginia came up to see their grandson (as I looked at Lady Mary as a mother to me). Dorcas patted Jane on the shoulder and said that they had worked well as a team. I think that was the biggest compliment that Jane could have ever wished for. After a while, Robert and I were left alone with our new son.

"Well, darling, we have a new future Duke of Rochester in the making, and you have made me the happiest and proudest of men. Now, we need to choose a suitable name for him, as we dared not think this far ahead before. What names would you like to give our son, Julia?"

"My father's name was Martin, and my Gramps was called Edgar, but are there any family names from your side of the family?"

"You choose this time, and I will choose the next time. I think Martin Edgar Beddoes Beaumont is a very good name for a future Duke of Rochester," he told me, then kissed me and held his son.

How could life get any better for me after being the fraud of Moldova Square?

THE END.

Acknowledgements

A special thanks to my daughters Faye and Vicky, (especially Vicky who manages to get me out of computer confusion) and my granddaughters Jules, Maddison and Brooke for their love and support during my 'creative' process.

Thanks to Mum and Dad Hall for their love and belief in my literary efforts.

Thanks to some of my old schoolfriends, from Foxford School in Coventry, the Foxyladies, who are always there to support me. Whenever I am down, they are always there to bring a smile to my face.

To my beloved constant companion and 'bed buddy,' Poppy, my beautiful beagle dog, who is always by my side.

To Sara, Paul, Audrey and all the staff that have been working on this and other books of mine and for having the faith and confidence in my literary work.

About the Author

Jill Wells-Wane has lived in the middle of England her whole life. As an only child she used to make up stories about having siblings.

Jill has been making up stories all her life, eventually having her first novel Polperro published in 2007 and her second novel St Petersburg published in 2022.

Reading and writing has become a form of pleasure and escape from everyday life for Jill.